Advance Praise

Powered by an extraordinary conceit, one man's ability to draw things into reality, Kris Faatz's *Line Magic* is more than just fantastic feats of artistry. Drawing her own rich portrait of community, one that transcends the realities of race and class and ability in post-WWII America, Faatz's storycraft and prose wield intoxicating line magic all their own--I couldn't put it down.

— JEN MICHALSKI, AUTHOR OF
ALL THIS CAN BE TRUE

Keep your hanky or box of tissues ready for this moving and heartfelt novel that will have you crying in sadness, in anger, in frustration, and, ultimately, in happiness. Faatz will cast a spell over you, weaving words and history, regaling you through Nicky True, *Line Magic*'s narrator and protagonist, of a moment in time where magic opened the minds and hearts of the people of Philadelphia. Follow the flow of *Line Magic* and open your own heart to the possibilities.

— MELISSA LLANES BROWNLEE, AUTHOR
OF *HARD SKIN* AND *BITTER OVER SWEET*

Line Magic is a novel of luminous depth and beauty, where art is both a sanctuary and a reckoning. Kris Faatz writes with exquisite tenderness, her prose composed of longing, loss, and the fragile brilliance of human connection. It's a story that lives inside you, line by line, breath by breath. Her characters are rendered with such precision and care that they *become*, carrying their histories, their regrets, and their flickering hopes with the full weight of real, complicated lives.

At its center is Nicky True, an artist whose gift is as haunting as it is extraordinary—born from sorrow, sharpened by love, and shaped by the relentless question of what art can mend. Faatz's storytelling resists easy resolutions, honoring the weight of history and the raw edges of hope.

This is a book that lingers, suffused with wonder and the shifting light of memory. Faatz writes with the soul of a poet and the precision of a master craftsman, her writing shimmers with light and shadow. *Line Magic* is both an elegy and an awakening—a meditation on creation, consequence, and the spaces between what we make, what we remember, and what we dare to believe endures.

— **APRIL BRADLEY, EDITOR AND
PUBLISHER, *RUBY***

Simply remarkable. There's not much more a reader can hope for than a uniquely original story, and Kris Faatz has done it again with *Line Magic*. This beautiful story is a fictional memoir of sorts by Nicky True—a man who can make magic with his drawings. Join Nicky as he reflects on a life of love, loss, and ultimately—and *beautifully*—finding purpose. *Line Magic* is a place where history meets fantasy, dreams become reality, and if you're open to it... you might just find a little magic for yourself, too. Brilliant.

— **CHARISSA COSTA, FOUNDER,
CHARM CITY READERS**

What if you could change the world by simply drawing it the way you wished it to be? In *Line Magic,* Nicky True shares his gift of perfecting the imperfect with the mere sketch of a pencil and, in turn, learns the value of loving people exactly as they are. This story beautifully illustrates the complicated intersection of fate and magic and why even the oldest among us still hold wishes tight against their hearts. It poignantly challenges our ideas of beauty, privilege, and friendship in ways that can never be erased.

— ELLEN WEEREN, AUTHOR AND OWNER
OF A REASON TO WRITE

Kris Faatz captured me with her very first sentence, and I was one hundred percent invested in hearing what Nicky True had to say. Immediately, I was pulled into a well-crafted story with a strong sense of place and people I cared deeply for. The way Faatz intertwines historical details from 1945, the struggles and victories of her down-to-earth characters, and a touch of magical realism make *Line Magic* a true work of art. I couldn't turn the pages fast enough.

— MANDY HAYNES, AUTHOR AND EDITOR-
IN-CHIEF OF WELL READ MAGAZINE

Line Magic

*for you who believe
that small acts reshape the world*

Also by Kris Faatz

Fourteen Stones

To Love a Stranger

Line Magic

KRIS FAATZ

HIGHLANDER
PRESS

ISBN: 978-1-956442-54-0
Ebook ISBN: 978-1-956442-55-7
Library of Congress Control Number: Applied For.

Published by Highlander Press
501 W. University Pkwy, Ste. B2
Baltimore, MD 21210

Cover design: Patricia Creedon (patriciacreedon.com)
Author photo: Laura Walker

Prologue

Picture this:

You're a kid, so little that the world is enormous. Your mom's and dad's faces float way up above you like balloons. Tabletops are too high to see, so you stretch up your fingertips to reach for their mysteries.

Everything is touch and color, color and touch. You crawl on a rug, as broad as an ocean, and feel every nub and tuft against your chubby palms. You pull yourself up on your still-wobbly feet and run your fingers along a wall. So slick and smooth! The rug is *green,* the wall is *white*: somebody tells you this, or you breathe it in, and the words fill your whole body because now you *know* white and green, and you will keep them forever.

I remember this, you see. For me it was almost a hundred years ago, but I still remember.

One day, you learn that your dinner plate is a *circle* and your napkin is a *square.* Next thing you know, there are squares and circles everywhere you look. The joy of them bubbles up in you until you laugh out loud. When you're hungry, and your mom pours you a cup of milk, and you pick it up in both hands and take a big swallow, and it slides down into you and feels so good in your stomach: shapes and colors make you feel the same.

Soon you know not just circles and squares, but triangles and ovals and diamonds. You know color-words you can chew on: *Scarlet. Peach. Daffodil.* And then, one day, somebody puts a pencil in your hand. Somebody's big strong fingers wrap around yours and guide the pencil point across a piece of paper. One line. Another. Two more. You look down at your very own square that you drew.

Your own square. Can you picture it? Can you feel what it means?

My father put that pencil in my hand and showed me how to use it, the same way he taught me all the words for the things I saw. You'll hear more about him. Not just yet.

You draw another square, this time by yourself. The pencil wiggles and you can't make the lines straight, but you try again, and you keep trying. All this time you are getting bigger, getting older. One day you draw a perfect square, a perfect triangle. Then you draw trapezoids and hexagons. You look outside a window – you can draw that too, now – and trace the individual shapes of leaves on a branch. When you hold the drawing up, it's a mirror of what you see outside.

Maybe you're thinking, *Are we still talking about a kid here? He must be pretty talented.* You're right. I was six then, what they call "precocious." But you haven't heard the best part yet.

One day you see something that doesn't look right. For now, let's say it's something simple, like an apple. (It wasn't, but I'm an old man. I'll tell my stories how I want.) It's a funny-shaped apple, lopsided maybe, as if half of it got dipped in shrink juice. You look at it and think, *That doesn't look good at all. I could draw it better.*

As you think this, you feel something shift inside you. Remember, you're still a child: you don't have the words for exactly what you feel. Later, as an adult, you might think something like, *a car getting into gear.*

You sit down with a piece of paper and your pencil and the apple on the table in front of you. You start to draw, except now you're drawing the apple the way it *should* look. Round and smooth with a perfect stem that goes straight down the middle. Your eyes move back and forth from the apple to the paper.

By the time you finish, there are *two* perfect apples. One on your paper, and one on the table.

~

Now you're probably thinking, *This old guy is senile or crazy or both*. Right? I'd think that too, if I were you. But keep listening.

The real apple, the one you changed by drawing it, doesn't stay perfect for long. Maybe an hour or so later, it slumps back into its lopsided shape. That disappoints you. (More than I can say, because it wasn't just an apple I drew that day. But that's for another time.) Still, you *did* make it perfect. Now you know you can do something extraordinary when you pick up your pencil.

You can make magic.

~

Why am I telling this? Mostly because of my daughter. Georgia – she goes by Jo – is nearly seventy now, and as determined and sure of herself as she was at age three, when she told me I was going to teach her how to draw. She doesn't need my help to do that anymore, or anybody's help, but these days she says, "Dad, you're not going to live forever."

At my age, do you think I need the reminder? But she has a point. She says I need to tell this story while I can, because I'm the only one left who remembers it all. "People should know what you did, Dad," she says. "You don't get to take it with you." She wasn't born yet when it happened, not the time she wants me to tell about. When she brings it up, her eyes give away how much she wishes she'd been here to share those days with her mother and me. Her hair is mostly silver, and maybe someday will turn as white as mine, but when I look at her, I still see the little flower who climbed into my lap and put a pencil in my hand. "Now, Daddy. Please."

Yesterday, she brought over the new laptop computer I'm using right now. (She called it an early birthday present. Early is right: it's June, and my birthday is in November.) "Now," she told me, "let's make sure it works. Just open up a new document and type a little." You can bet she wasn't only checking that she'd gotten her money's worth on a fancy machine thin enough to use for a placemat. And you can guess how much choice I had about what to do next.

Now it's early morning, barely light out. I always like to know that I'm around for another sunrise. My house is quiet, except for the creaks and taps in the old walls and floorboards, but I can hear the city waking up outside. Pretty soon, it'll be another muggy Philadelphia summer day, like so many I remember.

I'm sitting at the kitchen table where I used to draw, and where I taught Jo all those years ago. She isn't here now to watch me tap away on this keyboard, but if I know her, she'll ask me about it first thing when she visits this afternoon. "Did you try it out? How do you like it?" She doesn't need to worry too much. She got me started on this, and I've always been stubborn when I start a thing.

Now I'll take us back seventy-some years. If you're as old as I am, or anywhere near it, you might know how it feels to step into the person you used to be before time caught up with you. We old people say *It could have been yesterday.* In your mind, you go back in time, and then you look down at your age-spotted hands, or feel how your bones drag against your muscles, and for one heartbeat you know you could shed this tired body like a coat. Your real self is no age at all.

By the way, my name is Nicky True, so you know what you're about to hear is a true story. At my age, you can get away with jokes like that.

Chapter One

IN EARLY MARCH OF 1945, I got a telegram from my brother Charley. It arrived at my apartment in Los Angeles, a slip of paper light enough to blow away on a breath. It was going to unravel my life.

It was a Tuesday night. At the movie studio where I worked, we had finally wrapped our shoot for the day. Paragon Films wasn't one of the Big Eight studios, as they called themselves, but it was no coincidence that our little operation had a name almost identical to one of the great powerhouses that would keep making movies well into the next century. Our exec, Jonah Eberly, was convinced we could hit the big leagues if we poured in enough sweat. Every shoot we did left the actors and crew as wrung out as old handkerchiefs.

This particular Tuesday, we finished our work close to midnight. The clickety-whirring cameras fell silent and Sara Fontaine, our new leading lady, brushed her co-star aside to come and find me in the wings. "I'd like to ride home with you, Nick."

Her co-star was another square-jawed Clark Gable would-be; one of the many, in those days, who got their feet in any Hollywood doors they could find and kept them there good and hard. A few weeks ago, Sara had decided to ignore his handsome mug in favor of mine, which was nothing special. Her choice mystified us all.

I was never in front of the camera, not for an instant, but those four-teen-hour days still left me whipped by the time I packed up my sketch-book and pencils. "I might not be much company," I apologized. The pinprick headache I got every day prodded me between the eyes, so I took off my glasses to pinch the bridge of my nose. "I figured I'd grab a peanut butter sandwich and go to bed."

Sara stood in front of my chair, slim and vivid in the white nurse's outfit she'd worn for the sequence. Her cap gleamed against her dark hair. "Please let me come over, just for a while." Her eyes were the exact color of new leaves in spring. "I never get to see you."

We saw each other every day on set, of course, but that didn't count because she was the Next Big Thing, while my sketchbook and I were strictly behind the scenes. Sara wanted more. She had set about claiming me with the same straightforward focus she brought to owning the roles she played.

We got on the tram together. It was a shuddery ride along the fringe of Hollywood back to my place. The warm early-spring darkness smelled and tasted of summer. I had loved California's citrus sweetness since the moment I'd landed there three years earlier, fresh off the train from Pennsylvania.

I still lived in the same apartment I'd found back then. The Edwar-dian-style brick building and the nondescript side street it stood on could have come straight out of Anywhere, USA. Paragon paid me more than decently for what I did for them – I'll tell you more about that later – and by 1945, I could have afforded something better. A place in Tinseltown proper, for instance, in one of those candy-colored build-ings with walls of windows and a courtyard spiked with palm trees. I lived alone, though, and didn't much care what the surroundings looked like.

At my building, Sara and I stopped in the lobby for my mail, which I stuffed in the breast pocket of my seersucker jacket. The elevator took us up to the top floor. Sara kicked off her high heels by my door and hung her long coat on the tall iron rack. The apartment was a single room, small but bright, with a high counter that divided the narrow galley kitchen from the rest of the living space. Prints of art by some of my favorite painters hung on the walls: Peter Paul Rubens, Thomas Hart Benton, Georgia O'Keeffe.

Those prints were my only nod to what I'd once hoped to be. Sara didn't know that. In fact, no one from the studio knew they were a piece of myself that I hadn't quite managed to leave behind, the way I'd tried to leave behind everything else from my life back in the east.

Sara went to the icebox for a rummage. The lid clanked when she pulled it back. "Nick, you must be the only person in L.A. who doesn't stock booze."

"I'm sorry."

"I'm teasing." She found a bottle of ginger ale and came back to stand close to me. Drops of water gleamed on the glass and on her fingertips. "Sobriety is part of your charm."

Back in December, when Jonah had brought her on, he'd said she was going to Put Paragon on the Map. It wasn't the first time we'd heard such a thing, and she wasn't a Hedy LaMarr or a Greta Garbo, but her eyes surely had a way of catching you. Their color, and the slant of her lashes, made you want to glance at them again... and that was when you noticed the way her hair curled against the line of her neck, and the way her lips hinted at a smile, and you were caught in her spell, as quick as that. She barely needed my behind-the-scenes sketchbook.

I said, "Charm, is it? I'm glad to hear I've got some."

"You know you do." She took a sip of ginger ale and tilted her head back to look full into my face. "A gentleman, in the movie business no less, who'd rather listen than talk. That's what I first noticed about you." Her free hand reached up to take hold of my lapel. "I said to myself, he's quiet, but still waters run deep. I'm going to find out about him."

On the wall behind her, lamplight slanted across the O'Keeffe print of blue morning glories. The edges of the flowers stood out, brilliantly cobalt. I took a step back. Sara's fingers loosened on my jacket. "What is it?"

The mail in my pocket gave me as good an excuse as any. "I'm sorry." I reached for the envelopes. "I almost forgot about these." I dropped them on the kitchen counter. The telegram lay on top, thin and eggshell-colored, with my address typed in bold black ink.

Sara saw it too. "What's that?"

During the war years, those tiny slips of paper meant a lurch in the chest, a spike of hope, and a cymbal-crash of terror. They were the closest link we had to real-time news from the battlegrounds in Europe and the Pacific. They could be lifelines connecting a wife to her husband in a field hospital in England or parents to a son in a camp in the Philippines: *He's still alive. Maybe we'll make it through.* Or they could be what everyone dreaded: that final news, a shadow dark enough to choke out light for good.

I had no one sending me word from overseas. Even so, I didn't want to reach out for that telegram on the counter. I had a good idea what it was about, and I wished I could switch off the light and crawl away to hide.

My hands trembled as I ripped the envelope open. The single line of text jumped out at me like a shout.

NICKY WE NEED YOU HOME PLEASE COME SOONEST LOVE C

No stops in it, as if the sender had to force the words out in one gasp. Fog seemed to curl out of the corners of the apartment and close in around me.

"Nick," Sara said. "What's wrong?"

Still waters run deep. I didn't want her, or anyone else, to "find out" about me, but I had known this was coming. The life I'd left behind three years ago was reaching out to claim me back.

"It's from my brother, Charley." My voice sounded steadier than I'd hoped. "Our mom isn't doing well. I need to go see her."

Sara took the telegram and read the line of type at a glance. "Is your mom sick?"

My contact with my mother and brother had been thin enough on the ground, but I knew about the cough that she'd insisted for months was only "a stubborn summer cold," and I knew our family doctor had finally cajoled her, back in January, into tests that turned up masses in her lungs. She hadn't told me about that herself. I knew it from Charley, who'd written that she hadn't wanted to try surgery or any of the "ugly chemicals," as she called them, that might have done something to help. Anyone who knew her would have expected nothing else. Now my brother, sixteen years old, was trying to keep things going for himself and her both, with as much help as neighbor ladies could give. He couldn't do it much longer.

I sketched all of that out for Sara as briefly as I could. "Oh, Nick." She set her unfinished ginger ale on the kitchen counter and reached for my hand. Her fingers were chilly from the glass. "Could she still get better?"

No. I knew it, but I couldn't say it, or look it in the face. "I have to go see what's going on. Then Charley and I'll figure out what to do." If she couldn't get better, I would be the only family my brother had left.

"Okay." Sara squeezed my hand and let it go. "I won't stay now. You rest and do what you need to."

She refused my offer to see her back to her place. "A gentleman, like I said." She smiled and slipped her heels back on. "Your brother calls you Nicky?"

They had called me that all my life, back home. I had shed the old name when I'd tried to start over. "That's right."

"I think it's sweet." She leaned in to kiss me. "Good night."

THE NEXT MORNING, I WENT TO THE TELEGRAPH OFFICE first thing and sent a message back to Charley. I could have tried to call him at home, the house where he and I had been born, but the fact was that I was scared. I didn't want to hear his voice on the other end of the phone. It would drag me back faster than I had to go already.

Instead, I wrote back, FIXING THINGS HERE SEE YOU FRIDAY, and my best guess at when I hoped to arrive in Philly. Wartime security had shut down the city's airport, so I would have to see how close I could get and figure out how to make up the difference. After I sent the telegram, I went to Paragon to meet with my boss before the day's shoot began.

Jonah Eberly was one of the most ambitious men I've ever known. I've always thought it was a shame he never managed to turn Paragon into the kind of place he imagined back in those days, when it was a scrappy startup, and I was, not to sound too mysterious about it, his secret weapon.

All of us who worked for the studio dressed well. The company had an "image," you can bet, so no matter how many hours we sweated on set, all of us men arrived at work in fresh-pressed shirts and ties, and the women in skirts and blouses so crisp they rustled like autumn leaves. Jonah Eberly outdid us all. You never saw him in anything but a three-piece suit, silver-gray linen for preference, and a matching broad-brimmed fedora. Los Angeles got summer-warm even in early spring, so he sweated as much as any of us. When he took the hat off and set it on its designated corner of his wide desk, his bald bulldog head gleamed as if he'd given it a polish.

"Nick," he said when I came in. "What can I do for you?"

When I'd first arrived in Hollywood, back in the spring of 1942, he had recognized what I could offer his studio and snapped it up the way a fox snaps up a stray chick. That had been lucky for me, because I hadn't had much more than some spare clothes in a suitcase and spare change in my jeans. Now Jonah treated me like a tough cuss of an uncle who manages to unbend when a favorite nephew comes to visit.

I didn't sit down, although I did take off my own hat, a less impressive cotton fedora. "I have some family trouble, sir. I need to go back to Philadelphia for a while."

He wasn't any too glad to hear that. We were still in mid-production on one of the many red-white-and-blue pictures that hauled in the crowds during the war years. You might know the kind: they whooped up our fearless boys overseas and our true and lovely girls back home, and cast the Germans or Japanese as paper villains long on malice and short on brains. During the shoots, my job was to make sure everything looked exactly the way the producers wanted.

That was why I made good money. On paper, my title at Paragon was "production assistant," but none of the scores of production assistants in Hollywood had ever done what I did. My sketchbook and I could fix anything, from a detail on a costume to a flaw in a piece of scenery to the shape of the leading lady's face. Jonah wanted the right image in every can of magic Paragon opened up to splash on the silver screen. He used me and my magic, the real stuff that happened when I drew, to get it.

"Philadelphia?" he said. He always kept a box of fat Cuban cigars on his desk. Rumor had it that he'd trained himself out of chewing tobacco when he started up Paragon and needed a bankroll. The California hoi polloi wouldn't sign their money over to someone who chawed and spat like a country cousin. Now, he took out a cigar and sliced the end off with his bone-handled knife.

I explained about my mother and Charley. Jonah drew long and hard on the cigar, puffing smoke out into the air. He didn't need to tell me that by taking time away right now, I was leaving our cast and crew in a jam. Filming had to go ahead with or without me, which meant that halfway through the finished product, the magic would disappear.

"Okay." He tapped the cigar on his pewter ashtray. "Go on out there now and take care of things. Family's important." The haze of smoke swirled above his desk. "But listen, Nick, keep me posted on what's happening and come back as quick as you can. You know we need you."

"Yes, sir. I will."

That afternoon, during a break from shooting, I sorted out how to get back east. A combination of passenger flights and a puddle-jumper could get me as far as Trenton. From there, I'd take the train south and across the Delaware into Philly. Sara came over again in the evening to help me pack; I'd be on a red-eye out of Los Angeles as soon as we finished the next day's shoot. "Are you sure that's enough?" She sized up the little pile of clothes in my grip. "You don't know how long you'll be away, do you?"

"I can get extra clothes if I need to." I could've taken a real suitcase, but that would have made it seem like I'd be gone a long time. Whatever happened, I told myself, I wouldn't stay out there one day longer than I had to.

Friday afternoon, I stepped off the train in Philly. I'd dozed a little on the way, here and there, but my grip felt much heavier than it should have as I lugged it up the stairs into the concourse. The raw, gray weather clawed at my hands and bit into my sinuses. I fumbled to turn up the collar of my trench coat, feeling to my bones how long it had been since I'd last been back in the east. I had forgotten how winters hung on. The wind, heavy with the smells of asphalt and exhaust, pushed at me as if it wanted to shove me back onto the train. *Believe me,* I told it, *I'd go if I could.*

At this time of day, Charley would still be in class unless he'd stayed home with our mother. I decided to get a cab and go over to his school first. If he was there, I could pick him up, and we'd go back to the house together. I wasn't going to walk into that place without him.

The concourse was bustling. Voices and laughter and the noise of hurrying footsteps made a chaos of echoes. The shutters on the schedule over the ticket booth clicked and clacked, shuffling tiles to show arrivals and departures. I started toward the main doors, where the cab fleet would be lined up at the curb.

"Nicky! Hey, Nicky!"

The name cut through the noise all around and hit me like a slap. My head snapped up. For an instant, I wanted to turn and run.

Then I saw him hustling toward me, my brother Charley, in a sweater and jeans with no coat or hat or gloves. His bangs fell across his forehead. His smile landed on me like the sun coming out.

He was moving as fast as he could, you see, but he couldn't run. His left foot, in its thick shoe, was straight and normal. His right foot, stuffed into a heavy sock, was twisted in and under as if it wanted to hide. That's why he held onto a heavy wooden cane.

He couldn't run, so I did. I took off toward him across the marble floor with my grip banging against my legs. When I got to him, he let go of the cane, and I dropped my grip, and we caught hold of each other.

I hadn't seen him since I had left Philly. Back then, he'd been a still-skinny thirteen-year-old, short and scrawny for his age. From our rare phone calls since, I knew how his voice had changed, but I hadn't seen how he had shot up and bulked out, his shoulders and upper arms especially. No doubt that was from the lifetime of lugging his bad foot around. If he'd had two good feet to balance on, he would have stood taller than me now. As it was, we were eye to eye, the same gray-green eyes except that he didn't need glasses and the same thick, straight, reddish-brown hair we'd gotten from our father.

He held me tight. "It's so good to see you."

The city itself still mouthed at me as if it wanted to spit me back to California. Less than ten minutes off the train, I already ached for the place I had left, but I didn't know how I could have gone so long without seeing my little brother.

I pulled back to look at him, keeping my hands on his shoulders so he wouldn't have to reach for the cane. "You grew, kid!" My eyes smarted, and I blinked. "When'd you get so big?"

"Nicky." He laughed. "You've been gone a while."

A while. Like a handful of frames in a reel, I remembered him holding onto me the night before I got on the train. *You have to tell me all about California.* His jaw set, his throat working to swallow his tears as if I wouldn't hear them. He had tried so hard to understand why I had to leave. *Tell me where you live, and what you do, and everything, so I can pretend I'm there too.*

I had done my best to share my life with him in our letters and phone calls, but I'd never been able to tell him everything. Not, for instance, how everyone at Paragon knew me as Nick and had never heard about my family. I couldn't tell him that I wouldn't be back in Philly now if I'd had a choice. I reached down for the cane and handed it back to him. Together, we made our slow way out to the cab fleet.

Do you remember how I told you about the apples and that first time I learned what I could do with my drawing? I said it wasn't really an apple I drew that day. Now, if I tell you that I was eight years old at the time, and my little brother had just been born, perfect in every way except for that right foot: maybe then you'll know what really happened.

We got into the first cab in line. Charley gave the driver our mother's address. As we made our way out into traffic, Charley said, "Hey, don't tell Mom I cut school, okay? I was supposed to stay all day, but I had to come meet you."

He had the grin I knew so well, the little kid one that used to egg me on to prank our parents back when our father was alive. We'd be in our seats at the table, waiting for our mother to dish out dinner. Charley would lean over to me and whisper, "Make Daddy's fork look funny." I always had a pencil on me somewhere, so I'd scribble Dad's fork on my napkin, except with a curlicue handle or the tines sticking out every which way. The real fork would change then and there, right in Dad's hand if he'd already picked it up. Dad would glare at it as if he'd never seen such a trick before. "Am I raising boys or monkeys?" His Irish lilt made it sound like *byes,* and he'd hold up the fork as if it were a giant bug that had landed on his plate, and Charley would laugh and laugh until you'd have thought he would bust himself. Dad would try to frown at me, but his eyes said *Son, you are something, you know that?* Then he would start laughing too, and I'd join in, and the three of us would carry on until Mary Anna, my mother, came in with her mouth set, and told me to get my pencil back out and put that fork right.

Now, in the back seat of the cab, gladness bloomed in me to know that Charley could still grin that way. "I won't tell her you cut school," I promised. "But what classes did you miss?" Charley loved math and physics. I'd be sorry if he'd skipped out on something good.

"Just Latin. It's boring anyway." His smile faded. "Tell you the truth, Nicky, Mom might not be able to talk to you much. Lately, she's been sleeping a lot."

By now, the cab was caught up in the flow of traffic. "Sleeping?"

"Yeah. Couple of weeks ago, Dr. Sanders gave her stuff for pain. Morphine."

Doctor Sanders had brought Charley and me both into the world. When our mother's diagnosis came in, he had tried to convince her to go to Pennsylvania Hospital and let the experts there help her. "And she takes it?"

"She has to." Charley's fingers twisted together in his lap. "If she doesn't, she kind of can't stand it."

Then I had to face it. Charley's telegram had told me the same thing, but when you hear your parent is dying, you can try to stop up your ears, or tell yourself *it won't come to that, something will change, you'll see.* It's another thing entirely to feel the knowledge sink into you. All her life, our mother had shied away from medicines and "meddling." Now, she was taking the drug you took when you didn't want to feel anymore.

I looked at my brother's bent head. He was dressed the same as I remembered, his jeans a tad frayed at the hems, his blocky cable-knit sweater a bigger copy of one he'd worn three years ago. He had always been neater with his hair than I was, parting it carefully and combing it smooth. I sat there in my crisp Los Angeles threads and the trench coat that made me look like a mystery flick gumshoe and remembered how Charley and I had looked so much the same when we were boys. We hadn't had much choice: most of the time, he'd worn my hand-me-downs. He used to tag after me everywhere. I'd always kept an eye out for him and slowed down when he needed a chance to catch up.

Then you went away and left him behind. That knowledge sank into me, too. I cleared my throat. "I'm sorry, kid."

He raised his head. "You're home now. That's pretty good."

Our father's eyes had looked exactly that way when he smiled. Seeing it now, I wanted to shut my own eyes as tight as I could.

We crossed over the Schuylkill River, a stretch of fast-moving steel-gray water, and into Center City proper. Philadelphia isn't so much a single city as a web of neighborhoods. The neighborhood Charley and I had grown up in, Elmcroft in east Philly, between the Schuylkill and the Delaware, was a different world from Center City with its elegant storefronts and nineteenth-century townhouses. Elmcroft has been gentrified and upscaled since, but it was still gritty and hardscrabble in those days.

No candy-colored apartment buildings here, no palm trees or hibiscus, or fuchsia glowing with magenta blooms. I knew every one of Elmcroft's narrow streets, the shabby corner stores, the rows of squat blocky houses, and the faded awnings. Yellow ribbons, some draggled from years of service, fluttered from lampposts. Every house and shop sported an American flag. Some were full-size, hung from poles or draping from windows, and some were miniature, tied to mailbox posts or stuck into the ground next to front steps. Some houses had stars in the windows: silver for wounded soldiers, gold for those who had died.

Los Angeles had no fewer badges of the war, but they felt different to me here. In the movie business, we held onto the idea that we were helping the States to victory because our Hollywood magic kept everyone's spirits up. Here in Philadelphia, I couldn't hide behind my job. I was a kid who had tried to enlist and gotten turned down: another part of the mess I had wanted to leave behind.

The cab turned down Lawrence Street, where our parents' house stood. I held onto my grip so tight that its handle dug into my palms.

This street looked just like all the others in the neighborhood, tight and cramped, the brick houses shoulder-to-shoulder with identical tiny front yards that held only brown winter grass now. There wasn't enough room for victory gardens here. I knew every square of the side-walk. Here I had played jacks and marbles with the neighborhood kids, watched the hopscotch games with Charley, and learned to use my fists the first time a kid called my brother a gimp.

The cab pulled up at the curb in the middle of the block. Our mother's house looked just like all the others too. The same boxy build and sloping gray roof, two tiny windows on the front, three steps leading to a stoop wide enough to stand on, and a plain black front door with a brass knob and knocker. I had seen a couple of silver stars in front windows as we came down the street, as well as yellow ribbons on all the door knockers. Jake Satterfield, my old schoolmate, was in the Air Force, and our friend George Herskowitz was in the Navy. My mother's house had a yellow ribbon too, but no stars of course, since neither of her boys could serve.

Three years since I'd last been here. I stepped out of the taxi, clutching my grip. *You're Nick True, you're a production assistant in Hollywood, and you'll be back there as soon as you can.*

I paid the driver and followed Charley up the steps. Charley undid the lock and pushed the door open. In that instant, the past caught hold of me like a hand around my throat.

If Dad had been here. He wasn't, and he never would be again, but for that one instant, I imagined his footsteps coming down the hall and saw his face, his red-brown hair frosted with silver, the lines at the corners of his eyes. I saw the way those eyes would look when he realized I had come home. *Nicky, boy, what took you so long?* His hand, hard and rough from years of work, gripping mine to pull me into a hug. The warm scents of Jameson and cigarettes wrapping around me. *Get yourself in here. Take off your coat and stay awhile.*

For the space of a breath, or a lot less, it was real. If Dad had been here, everything would have been different. For a start, I wouldn't have gone to California at all.

I held the pain off with both hands and followed Charley into the house. For three years, I had done all I could to run from the past. Now it seeped out of the old walls and floorboards to meet me.

～

IN THE MASTER BEDROOM ON THE GROUND FLOOR, OUR mother lay on her side in the old bed she had shared with Dad. Her body was curled like a question mark under the faded quilt she had pieced before she got married. Her hair, still dark and curly, straggled like spilled ink over her cheek and down her neck. The old wooden crucifix hung on the wall above her head, with her black rosary beads strung around the white figure on the cross.

The room was dark and stuffy, the shades drawn firmly down over the single window. The house had always had a strong smell of camphor from the moth powder my mother kept in closets and bureaus, but now that smell blended with unwashed sheets, unwashed skin, and a sickly tang of mildew. I swallowed and tasted something sour at the back of my throat.

Charley whispered, "She usually wakes up for a little bit around dinnertime, sometimes later. I try to get her to eat."

He was leaning against the open door now, balancing between it and his cane, but the narrow chair by the bed told me where he spent most of his time when he was in this room. It was too easy to picture him sitting there by the hour, watching her slow breathing, with the dingy, musty house silent around him.

I pulled my trench coat closer around me, as if it'd been made of sheet metal instead of gabardine. The chair by the bed creaked when I sat down on it.

"Mom."

No response. I hadn't expected one. Her left hand lay on the pillow, the gold wedding band clunky-looking on her thin finger. I reached out and put my hand over hers. Her fingers were cold.

Anger unfurled in my stomach. How long had she already been here like this, holding on, not getting better, using up Charley's strength in watching over her? Back in the hall, I told my brother, "We've got to have more help here."

My voice sounded too harsh. Charley's eyes widened. "I told you, Mrs. O'Dell brings us meals, and Mrs. Franklin comes over sometimes and helps clean, and...."

It sounded like an apology. I waved it away. Yes, he'd told me about the neighbors, and I had been much too willing to believe he had all the help he needed. My brother, with his bad foot, waiting on a woman who couldn't do a thing for herself anymore.

It's not you I'm mad at; it's me. If I said it out loud, the anger would shiver into pieces, and the pain would snatch me up. "We're getting a girl or something. A maid."

Charley's mouth fell open. "Nicky, that's too much money."

"I can pay."

I headed for the phone in the kitchen. The key was to keep moving, keep doing. I'd hunt up a maid this minute. Charley followed me, his cane tapping on the worn floorboards. *Look at you,* I thought, eyeing myself from the outside. *Showing up and ordering your brother around as if you didn't run away. Acting like it's your mother's fault she got sick. You're some kind of jerk, you know that?*

The kitchen felt dingy too, with dirty plates piled in the sink and a smell of stale food heavy in the air. That smell mixed with something else, nose-burningly sharp. When I thumped the phone book on the counter, something big and dark leapt out of nowhere and landed next to the open pages.

Charley said, "Titus!"

It was a cat. A big black cat with a patch of white on its throat like a bib. It looked up at me, its yellow eyes wide and calm, and stretched its neck out to sniff my fingers. A low rumble started in its throat.

"You didn't tell me about this," I said.

"He's not really mine." Charley gave the cat a gentle push. It jumped down and landed on the floor with barely a sound. "He showed up on the porch a couple of weeks ago, and he looked so skinny I felt bad for him." He bent down and stroked the cat's back as it wound itself around his legs. "So I gave him some food."

"And a name."

"Yeah. It's Shakespeare. *Titus Andronicus.* We read it in school last year."

The cat certainly wasn't skinny anymore. It – he – also didn't look as if he planned to go anywhere else. "I guess he does kind of live here," Charley admitted. "He has a litter box and everything." That explained the ammonia smell. "Mom hasn't seen him."

And wouldn't like it if she did. She had always thought pets were too much mess and trouble. "Sounds fair," I said.

The phone sat on its old table by the icebox. I picked up the receiver, concentrating on the whir of the dial as it spun. The kitchen wallpaper had a pattern of russet apples and sage-green pears. Every single one of them seemed to have eyes that followed me. My mother and I had hung that paper together when I was in high school. We'd measured and cut, painted on the paste, and smoothed the paper onto the walls, careful to line the strips up exactly and leave no bubbles underneath. We'd been so proud of the finished job that we'd called Charley and Dad in right away, to admire it.

The first two agencies I called didn't have space for new clients, but the third told me they could send a girl on Monday morning. "She's colored," the woman on the phone said. "Will that be acceptable?"

I didn't see why it would matter. "As long as she can clean."

The woman assured me that the girl, Minna Davis, was a fine worker. We scheduled for her to come three mornings a week and I wrote down her wages, which were lower than I'd braced for. Charley still looked uneasy about it when I hung up. "Look, Nicky, you don't need to do that. I know things don't look great, but I can do more."

"Kid, you've got plenty on your plate as it is." I'd have liked to reach out and ruffle his hair, the way I used to when he was little, but he was so tall now. "Tell you what, though, let's fix this room up some now." I wouldn't stand still if I could help it.

Charley looked me up and down. "You don't want to do chores in those clothes, do you?"

I'd already taken off my coat and draped it over my old seat at the kitchen table. My shirt and slacks were a little travel-rumpled, but nothing Jonah wouldn't have approved. "What?" I said. "Why not?"

"You look like you're about to go to Mass."

My grip had a pair of jeans and a couple of T-shirts in it, but if I wanted to unpack and change, I'd have to go upstairs to my old bedroom. I rolled up my sleeves. "It's fine." After all, these were the clothes I wore to work every day.

"Okay." Charley pushed his sleeves up too and turned on the sink. The water steamed. He dumped soap flakes in, stirring up a mass of foam and filling the room with the smell of lavender. "We knew you were doing fine for yourself out there, and all," he said. He kept his eyes down, on the plate he was scrubbing with a dishrag. "You sure look like it. You never used to dress like a swell."

A swell? Something twisted in my chest. Did he think I'd changed that much?

Changed or not, I still could have moved around the kitchen blindfold. Charley and I finished the dishes and stacked them in the cabinets. I wiped down the counters and swept the floor while Charley scooped out the litter box in its corner by the back door. The cat, Titus, curled up in Charley's chair at the kitchen table and watched us both with his yellow eyes.

With both of us busy, Charley and I managed to talk. We had to get used to each other again. He told me how Dr. Sanders visited every day and sometimes stayed with our mother a while during school hours. "He said when it was time to send you that telegram. We knew you'd want to be here when..."

His voice trailed off. I was wiping the tabletop, running a damp rag back and forth over the old ridged wood. Charley was scrubbing out the empty sink with his back to me. *When she dies.*

That was real. I would be here with him for as long as our mother held on. I made my hand stop moving, made myself say to the back of my brother's head, "I'm glad you sent it."

He glanced at me over his shoulder and tried to smile. As much as he had grown up, I still saw the tiny boy who'd fought to walk in spite of his twisted foot, trying and falling and trying again. I had let him hang onto my hands for balance before he got his first little crutch, and I'd scooped him off his feet and swung him around to make him laugh.

Then you went off and left. He still needed you.

Charley emptied the dustpan into the garbage bin. I wrung the dishrag I'd used out at the sink. *He was thirteen then*, I told myself. *Old enough to handle it.*

You think so? He'd just lost Dad too.

With that, I seemed to see Dad again, standing in the corner beside the basement steps. He had his arms folded and his sleeves rolled up, the way they had been the one and only time he gave me a whipping. *What happened to you, Nicky?* No smile in those eyes now. *You went off and left, sure enough. California, the movie business, why did you do that? Why didn't you do what you planned?*

The floor seemed to tilt under my feet. *You know why, Dad. I left because you died.*

Charley turned on the lamp over the table. "Hey, it looks pretty good in here now."

If he could pretend to be cheerful, so could I. I drew a breath. "Sure does."

"You hungry? We've got leftover casserole. Broccoli and spinach. Mrs. O'Dell brought it over the other day."

My stomach did feel empty. I'd had nothing since last night, except a cup of coffee on the train. "Sounds good."

He busied himself with the oven, heating it up, sliding the pan in to warm. "Hey." The oven door clanged shut, but he stood there holding onto it as if it might decide to pop open and slide the pan back out. "Nicky, can I ask you a favor?"

He had never been shy with me before. "Of course, kid. What's up?"

"Would you draw for me?"

In his face, I saw the little boy again. *Make Daddy's fork look funny.* But that little boy had known the joke was coming, had to clamp his lips tight not to let the laugh out too soon. Now my brother looked uncertain, even scared, as if the bright thing he reached for might be snatched away.

Charley. I'm not so different, am I?

"Why, you bet I will," I said. "Did you think I'd say no?"

His face relaxed. "Maybe." Mischief tugged at the corners of his mouth. "'Cause you get paid for it these days."

Maybe so. That didn't change the fact that I could give it away whenever I wanted, and Charley had gone too long without seeing it. The two of us sat at the table, in the seats we'd used as kids. Titus watched us from the floor as I got out a pencil and paper to do the trick for its best audience.

The casserole only needed a few minutes to heat. In that time, I took a knife from the silverware drawer and drew it on the paper with a flat blade that opened into a triangle. My eyes went back and forth from the drawing to the real knife on the table, and the real blade flattened and widened until it reflected the whole bulb of the ceiling lamp. For the finishing touch, I put tines on the blade in the drawing. Right away, the knife on the table had tines too, like a miniature garden rake.

Charley picked it up and ran the "rake" along his palm. The last of his shyness melted into a grin wide enough to lift the top of his head off. "I've missed this, Nicky." For a moment, his delight made me actually glad to be home. "I've missed it a lot."

We dished up the casserole and talked about everyday things while we ate. Charley told me about physics class, his favorite, and how the last test was "so easy, I scored a hundred and four," and how the class had just started a new unit on light. "I bet you'd like it. It's about why we see colors the way we do."

His talk flowed over and around me. He felt easy with me again, exactly the way we both needed. Because, when...well, when the time came, I would take him back to California, and we'd figure out life there together.

My thoughts ran ahead before I could stop them. I'd need a bigger apartment. Charley and I would have to sell this old house. And then... well, then I'd be Charley's guardian. Responsible for him. For a while at least, until he struck out on his own, I'd be the parent he didn't have.

"Nicky." His voice brought me back to the table and the plates in front of us. "You okay?"

Managing for him and me both. The idea filled me with ice. I made myself sit up straighter, to keep from curling into a ball. "I'm fine."

"You sure? You look pretty tired."

You took care of him plenty when you were kids. You changed his diapers, for cripes' sake. And he wasn't exactly little anymore; he'd graduate from high school next year. "I'm okay," I said. "What about your math class, how's that going?"

That got him started again. I listened to him and tried to concentrate on how much he would like Los Angeles. What he would think of the colors out there, and the way the sun made even the sidewalks glitter.

You'll be all he's got. You'd better get yourself together.

"Next year," he was saying, "it looks like I'll go into Calculus II."

The highest-level math class his school had. "Oh, and you know what? Last week, my teacher said..."

He stopped. At least I was paying enough attention to see how his face changed. All the excitement drained out of it as if someone had opened a spigot.

"Said what?"

Charley shook his head. His eyes went back down to the tabletop. "Nothing much."

We'd have to do better than that. *I'd* have to do better. "Kid, you were going a mile a minute. What's up?"

He took hold of his water glass. "It's probably not something I should think about." The glass turned slowly as he rolled back and forth against his fingers. An arc of reflected light moved along the tabletop. "But my teacher said I could maybe go to college."

Back when Dad was alive, and everything was going to be different, we had all talked about college at this very table. That was so long ago that I couldn't reach it anymore. Charley, though: with the grades he got, with the way he soaked up learning as if he couldn't get enough, he deserved to have all the things I'd let go of. "You should think about it," I said. "If you want to."

He raised his eyes to mine. "You think I could go?"

A little kid on Christmas morning, seeing a Christmas tree for the first time. Afraid to blink in case it disappeared. "Sure you could," I said. "You've got the brains for it, no trouble."

A flicker of a smile moved across his face. "Maybe it would be hard, though. For me. Since I'm..."

His cane leaned against the edge of the table. He touched it, quick and light. Neither of us ever used the word *crippled*, but it hung in the air right then.

Our mother had never liked doctors or hospitals. When Charley was little, when it might have been easy or at least easier, she had refused to let anyone try to correct his foot. I took a long swallow from my own water glass before I answered. "You get around fine here. I bet we could figure it out."

This time, his smile stayed put. He reached across the table to squeeze my arm. "Did I tell you I'm glad you're home?"

I love you too, kid. Not the kind of thing we'd ever said out loud. We cleaned up the dinner dishes, and I started yawning the moment the last fork went into the silverware drawer. Charley saw it. "Go on and get some sleep," he said. "Mrs. O'Dell put sheets on your bed yesterday, so it's all ready."

"Don't you need help down here?"

He told me he was okay. "Mom usually wakes up before I go to bed, if she didn't wake up for dinner. I'll make sure she gets to the bathroom and has her medicine when she needs it."

Tomorrow night, I would stay downstairs with her. For now, he was right that I was drifting off where I sat. "Okay," I said. "If you're sure."

I had thought I was so tired I would barely notice anything about my old bedroom, beyond how the bed felt when I collapsed into it, but I was wrong. The room looked the same as it had the last time I'd seen it. I could have been six years old again, climbing up to bed in the chilly house after my mother had ordered me to put my pencil and paper away for the night, and Dad had seconded it with, "She's right, son. Growing boys need their sleep."

There was the bed with its creaky metal frame and the dip in the middle of the mattress that showed where I had slept for nearly twenty years. The wooden crucifix I had prayed to hung on the wall above my pillow. Opposite the door, there was the window with the little desk under it, where I had sat so many times to look out over the sidewalk and study the shapes of leaves and branches. Beside the bed, the dusty chrome lamp stood on the narrow bureau, next to the cloudy round mirror.

I threw my grip on the bed. I had brought a set of flannel pajamas, remembering how cold this house got at night, and I changed into them fast. Goosebumps jumped up on my arms and legs when the air hit them.

I wasn't six anymore. I wasn't twenty, either, and this wasn't that summer when the world had fallen and shattered. There in my old room, where no time had passed, the darkness rolled in from all four walls at once, and from the floor and ceiling too.

Dad.

A pair of hands seemed to catch me around the chest, squeezing so hard that my ribs ached. My heartbeat sped up to a drumroll and my legs felt as if all the bones in them had disappeared.

I folded over on the edge of the mattress and got my head between my knees. Sweat slid down my back, gluing the flannel shirt to my skin. This had all happened before, but not since the day I'd packed up and run from Philadelphia. Now the past crowded into the room.

Nicky, what happened to you? Why didn't you do what you planned?

Because you died, Dad. You died and I fell and broke and couldn't put myself back together.

I had wanted to think that summer was gone, buried the way my father's body was buried in the cemetery at Saints Peter and Paul. I'd let myself think I had, finally, managed to put myself back together. Now, as I fought to drag air into my aching lungs, I understood that I was just as broken as ever.

Chapter Two

We buried my father in the summer of 1941. I am now more than twice as old as he lived to be, but when I close my eyes, I can still call up every detail of his face.

My old hands are stiff and shaky. They navigate this keyboard well enough, although mornings are a little harder, but I work at breakfast time so I'll have progress to report to my daughter when she checks up on me later. When I pick up a pencil, I can rough out shapes and shadings. That's about all. It's not enough to make the magic work.

Jo and her children are all strong artists, Jo especially, but none of them can *put the car into gear* the way I used to. I don't know why I could, or why they can't. For now, the magic isn't around anymore. That's one thing you should know before I get back into the story.

Here's another. Back in December 1941, after Pearl Harbor, it seemed like every able-bodied man in Philly between the ages of eighteen and thirty-five got in line at the recruitment centers that sprang up all over the city like mushrooms. A handful of us Elmcroft boys planned to join up together: Jake Satterfield, Toby Dickenson, Frank Wessel, me, and a couple of others. We told each other we'd figure out a way to end up all in the same unit, the Elmcroft Squad, and we'd show Hitler and Hirohito what Philadelphia boys were made of.

My mother and Charley, my mother especially, had more than a few things to say about that plan. *Just because the other boys want to, that's no reason to jump off a bridge.* My mother, hiding her tears under a heavy coat of crossness. *Your father would never have wanted...* That was just it, though. Shipping overseas sounded like the best possible way to escape the six months' worth of days I'd spent drifting and stumbling in the dark. It would get me away from home, farther away than I'd ever been, and away from that new grave at Saints Peter and Paul.

Jake and Frank and most of the others in our group did go to war, though not all in the same unit, of course, or even the same branch of the services. Elmcroft was amazingly lucky in that all her sons came home, though none of them, except the couple of boys who didn't get farther than the home guard, escaped without scars visible or otherwise. Me, though, I never got farther than the physical exam.

The army doctor put the bell of his stethoscope against my chest. It was no different from any ordinary checkup, but with the cold touch of that steel against my skin, the room started to whirl around. I folded over where I sat on the metal table, hands on my knees, sweating so hard my wire-framed glasses slid off my nose. I still remember the clatter they made when they hit the floor. And I remember the way the doc looked at me. "I'm sorry, son. We can't use you." Of course not. You can't make a soldier out of a kid who might pass out for no reason at all.

That 4-F on my record kept me out of Europe and the Pacific. *Fits of dizziness and disorientation; no clear cause or treatment.* I wasn't about to tell anyone why I'd failed the exam – how could I admit something so weak? – but my mother wormed it out of me. "Nicky, don't tell me there's something the matter with you, are you sick?", while she hugged me so tight I almost got dizzy again. Charley didn't try to hide his joy.

But I couldn't stay in our neighborhood anymore. Mothers were saying goodbye to their sons who had been my classmates at school. That new headstone in the church cemetery dragged at me like a boulder chained to my feet. I had to find someplace where I could breathe.

When I landed on the idea of California, a desperate second best, my mother didn't forbid me to go. I wasn't heading across the ocean to get shot or gassed or blown up; I think she knew, though we never said so much in words, that trying to hold me wouldn't help anymore. She only insisted I stay in touch and get on back home if I couldn't work things out.

Later, I'll tell you more precisely how I ended up in Los Angeles, selling my magic to the movies. For now, it's enough that you know it wasn't the life I had planned on. More importantly, it wasn't what my father and I had planned on, together.

Now I need to tell you about him. His name was Desmond True.

HE WAS BORN AT THE TAIL END OF THE NINETEENTH century, in Portmarnock, up the Ireland coast from Dublin. As he used to say, he missed the First Great War by a whisker. He came over to the States on his own, as a seventeen-year-old boy. By the time the US joined the war, Desmond was working in the dye house at Phillips Textiles in Elmcroft and had met Mary Anna Halloran, the woman he would later marry. After the U-boat sank the *Lusitania*, he enlisted all right, but Armistice Day came before he had to go anywhere.

My father spent his days in the Phillips dye house, hauling fabric in and out of color vats, dipping and wringing and hanging. The dyes stained his work clothes and sank into his skin. No amount of scrubbing, even with the harshest soap, would clean the lines on his hands. The eyewatering smells of the solvents burned away at his sinuses until he could no longer smell fresh flowers or baking bread. The ache of lifting and carrying sat deep in the muscles of his shoulders and back.

Sounds bad, doesn't it? I'll tell you something, though. He loved his job.

My father loved colors. He noticed them in the simplest places: the blue shadow of a roofline on snow, the mottled beiges and grays in the concrete sidewalk. At work, he saw it as a kind of magic to take the plain spun fabric, dip it into the vats, and lift it out transformed.

I've often wondered what he might have been if his life had been different. If he hadn't grown up poor, say, or if his family had understood the things he cared about. If he hadn't had to strike out on his own and scrape the best living he could, I can guess one thing: he would have given my magic a run for its money.

Now I'll tell you about one of my first memories. My father teaching me about the things he loved.

~

It's not much more than a snapshot, to start with. A room that looks miles bigger than it ever really was. Simple things in it: a table, an armchair, a sofa, all showing signs of wear. Patterned curtains at the window. A narrow fireplace with a couple of sooty logs in it. A rug on the floor.

I can see things that are up much higher than I am, because someone is holding me. I'm in the crook of an arm, snug and safe, and I can smell something I don't have words for yet, something smoky-dark that I know means *daddy.*

We're standing close to the window. It's sunny out, but I can feel the cold coming through the window glass. A big hand touches the wall next to the window and the voice I love says, "White."

Looking back all this long time, I don't know if he had told me that before. I do know that this time, the word shapes itself in my mouth. It's big and round, and I taste it and say it back. "White."

It probably sounds more like *wye.* But the arm holding me gives me a squeeze, and I feel a kiss on the top of my head. "That's it! That's right!"

Then a finger touching the curtain, which has a pattern on it, different colors mixed together. "Green." And touching another spot: "Blue."

I can say them back too. I taste them and *know* them. They're inside me now forever.

That's one reason happiness bubbles inside me and makes me laugh. The other reason is the hands that hold me tight and swing me up high, so I can see down into the face I love, and that face is lit up and his voice is saying, "That's my smart boy!"

That was the beginning.

~

MY NEXT MEMORY IS ABOUT TWO YEARS LATER, PROBABLY fall or winter again. The sky outside the kitchen window is dark. Inside, the lamp above the table makes a pool of light.

Daddy and I are at the table. I'm sitting in his lap, his arm close around me. I lean my head on his chest and rub my cheek against the rough fabric of his work shirt. He has a piece of blank paper in front of him. His free hand holds a pencil.

The pencil moves, sliding across the paper and leaving a straight line behind. One line. Then another. Then two more.

His voice comes from above my head. "What's this I made, Nicky?"

Easy. I love shape-words. "A square."

The pencil moves again, only three lines this time. "A triangle."

Now he draws first a square, and then a triangle on top of it, and then he adds little boxes and a rectangle to the square. I laugh. "Daddy! It's a house!"

"That's right." His hand ruffles my hair.

Now I can't just watch the pencil anymore. I look up into his face. "Daddy, I want to do that."

His eyes are bright and warm, crinkling at the corners. "Do you, then?"

The pencil feels strange and wobbly in my fingers. Daddy wraps his big hand around my small one. "What'll we draw?"

"A square."

One line. Another. Two more. Daddy's hand holds the pencil steady, and the lines look clean and smooth. When we finish, he lifts my hand and the pencil away. "Look at that!" he says. "Look what you drew."

Footsteps come up behind us. "You shouldn't tell him that, Des." My mother. "You drew it for him."

The joy inside me flickers, as if a chilly breeze came in through the shut window. But Daddy says, "I helped him this time." His free hand tilts my head back to look up at him. "Next time, you'll do it all by yourself, won't you, Nicky?"

His smile tells me I can. "All by myself," I say.

~

Now we jump a few years. It's spring. I'm eight years old.

One day, Doctor Sanders comes to the house with his black bag, and the door to my parents' bedroom is shut. Dad tells me to stay upstairs in my room. People are hurrying around downstairs, and I hear my mother cry out. I do what Dad said and sit at my little desk, not moving a muscle, as if the chair has hold of me. When I can't sit that still any longer, I get a pencil and paper. I stare out the window and draw its frame, and the scraggly little tree by the sidewalk, and the angles of the houses across the street: the same shapes, over and over.

After a long while, I hear footsteps coming down the hall. My heart jumps. Dad opens my bedroom door. The lines at the corners of his eyes stand out, and his shoulders have the same tired slump they do every afternoon when he gets home from work.

He isn't smiling. "Nicky, come on and meet your little brother."

My little brother! I could have run clattering down the stairs, the way I do when it snows, but Dad's face tells me I need to be quiet. Still, my feet are too slow and I wish I could fly.

They show me the baby, wrapped in a blanket the same color as the sky outside. I can only see a tiny red face peeking out, eyes squinched shut, and hands with the littlest fingers you ever saw. My mother's face is tired too, flushed, her dark hair tangled and sticking to her neck with sweat. She tells me, "This is Charley."

The baby opens his mouth in a yawn, and I catch my breath. *My brother.* Something swells up inside me, like a balloon in my chest, and I am so happy I can only sit very still and feel the happiness sparkling all over me like sunshine.

Within the next day or two, though, I see that no one else feels the way I do. Dad says my mother and the baby are both fine, but I still can't find his smile. His face has the same look in it I've seen when his back hurts. When I go into my parents' room to see my brother, my mother lifts the bundle as if its weight drags at her. I ask if I can hold him. "Not yet," she says. "He's too little."

One afternoon, in the kitchen, I finally ask Dad. "Is something the matter with him?"

The thought scares me so much I can barely push the words out. Dad looks at me as if he's trying to decide something. He touches my face. "Come along in."

I follow him into the bedroom. My mother is sitting up in bed, holding the bundle. She looks more like herself now, her nightgown fresh and neat, her hair in a single braid over her shoulder. Dad says to her, "Moll, Nicky should know."

Her mouth sets in a line. "He's a child. He doesn't need to know."

"He will anyway, soon enough. We're not going to hide the poor boy."

The air in the room closes like a fist around me. It feels icy cold, even though the open bedroom window lets in a warm breeze. What poor boy do they mean? Hide him why?

My mother and father face one another. Neither of them speaks a word, but talk is moving back and forth in the air between them. My mother sighs, as if all the air inside her ran out all at once, and holds the bundle out to Dad. "Fine."

Inside the blanket, my brother is sleeping. I sit down next to Dad on the edge of the mattress. Dad holds the bundle in the crook of his arm and gently unwraps it. At first, I don't know what I'm supposed to see. The baby has a diaper on, nothing else. I look at his chest, moving up and down, his hands curled into fists, his little round arms and legs. Everything looks the way I think a baby should.

Dad reaches for Charley's right foot and lifts it up. I see it now. The foot is curled funny, twisted as if it's trying to burrow back into the blanket. I don't know what that means.

"What's he doing?" I whisper.

My mother clicks her tongue, a tired, impatient sound. Dad lowers the baby's foot again and wraps the blanket carefully back around him. Charley doesn't stir. "It's called a clubfoot," Dad says quietly. "It means he's not built quite right."

"Does it hurt?"

"No."

My mother says, "It will when he tries to walk. If he can."

Something snags in my throat then. Dad says, "Moll," but I'm reaching for the bundle. "Can I?" I say. "Please?"

My mother doesn't say no, this time. Dad settles the bundle in my arms and I look down into my brother's face.

It'll hurt him to walk, if he can. But he has to walk. *Don't you worry, Charley,* I tell him in my head, blinking away the stinging in my eyes. *You're going to walk, and run, and we're going to play outside, and everything.*

~

OVER THE NEXT DAYS, I HEAR MY PARENTS ARGUING. I HEAR something about *surgery*, and *risk*, and my mother says, "He's much too small now. Besides, what if it makes him worse?" I keep thinking about that twisted little foot. *It'll hurt when he tries to walk.*

Two Saturday mornings after Charley is born, I sit in the kitchen with Dad. My mother is asleep in the bedroom. Dad is cradling the baby against his chest, feeding him out of a bottle and watching the little face as Charley sucks down the milk. I think how Dad's eyes always look tired now. All of us are tired these days – Charley has a good set of lungs on him and uses them plenty – but I think how Dad used to be able to smile even after the longest days at the factory.

My eyes move to Charley's bare feet, where they peek out under his white cotton shirt. The left foot looks just right, small and pink, with tiny perfect toes. The right foot looks as if somebody took it in their hard hand and squeezed it like an orange, and now it'll never uncurl.

It's not fair. I could draw it better.

In that moment, something shifts inside me. A long time later, I'll be able to describe it: *a car getting into gear.*

I jump out of my chair. Dad says, "Did something bite you?"

"No." I gasp out that one word and run out of the kitchen. I know exactly what to do, and I've got to do it right now, there's not a second to waste. I dash upstairs to my room, snatch a pencil and a piece of paper off my desk, and tear back down again.

"Nicky!" For the first time in days, Dad looks like he's about to laugh. He pretends to scold instead. "You sound like an elephant, boy! What's gotten into you?"

Even if I knew the right words, I couldn't take time to explain. I drop into my chair, smooth the paper out in front of me, and get a good grip on the pencil. This is so important my hand is shaking. I have to slow it down to get every line right. They *do* have to be right; I know that somehow.

My eyes move from the paper to Charley's right foot. I start to draw, one line, then another. On the paper, the foot takes shape. It's the right size, all the toes in place, but now it's shaped and pointed like a foot should be. The paper is smooth and cool under my hand. The pencil scratches along as if it knows what to do on its own, even though my throat is so dry it hurts to swallow, and my heart bangs so loudly I can't hear anything else.

Finally – it doesn't take long – I finish. The paper shows a pencil drawing of a baby's healthy foot, with every line in place. I stare at what I drew, scared to look up, because all of a sudden I know this was crazy. You can't fix anything this way.

Then I hear my father gasp. "Nicky."

I raise my head. My father is cradling Charley, cupping the baby's right foot in his hand. The baby's healthy, perfectly-shaped right foot.

"Child." Dad's voice is raspy. He stares at me as if maybe I'm a creature from outer space, that's crashed through the ceiling and landed in his kitchen. "What did you do?"

I'm starting to shake again. I have to let go of the pencil; it clacks onto the table and rolls away toward the far edge. "I don't know." My eyes are swimming, but I don't take them off my brother's feet. "I don't know. I just knew it would work, so I..."

"By all that's holy."

I can't catch my breath anymore. Dad's chair scrapes against the floor as he slides it over next to mine. He puts his free arm around me and pulls me against him, so he's holding both of us, my brother and me. "Nicky, child." I hide against his shirt, pressing my face into the coarse clean fabric, because I'm shaking so much, and how can this be real, how did it work? "Hush," he says, soothing me as if I were no bigger than Charley. "That's my good boy. Hush, now."

That's the magic. The miracle. Or it would be, if it lasted.

It does last just long enough for my mother to see my brother's foot perfect. Sitting up in bed, she reaches out with both hands to cup my face. Her palms are smooth and warm and her eyes have tears glittering in them, but I've never seen her smile like that before. For that little while, I think I've fixed everything in the world.

An hour or so later, though, Charley's foot goes back to the shape it was before. When I see it, everything inside me turns to water.

After my brother is back in his crib and my mother has closed the bedroom door, Dad sits down in the living room armchair and lifts me into his lap. He doesn't care that I'm supposed to be too big for that now. "You didn't do anything wrong, son."

I've already thought I should try again. At the same time, somehow, I know it won't be any different. I did the best I could. It wasn't enough.

Dad guides my head down onto his shoulder. "Do you know something?" he says. "You've got magic in you."

I don't know how he can sound like he does, as if the sun just came up on a summer morning. His arms are holding the pieces of me together. I want to sit just like this and never have to move again.

He says, "Back home, you know, we knew about magic. We used to say you never knew where it might be floating around, waiting to catch hold of you." His hand is warm on my hair. "I always hoped I'd see some one day. I must have brought it over with me and not even known it."

Back home. I know he means back in Ireland, where he was born. Right now, I don't care if magic is real or not, if I did some or not. "It didn't do what I wanted." My voice comes out muffled against his shoulder and I know I sound like a baby.

"It's still incredible." I can hear him smiling. "I've never seen anything could touch that. And do you know what else?"

I should at least say *no, what?* like the grown-up big brother I'm supposed to be. I can only shake my head as if somebody made off with my tongue. Dad says, "Magic or not, I never saw any other boy your age who could draw like you." He kisses the top of my head. "My boy is something special."

It will still take some time before I get over the disappointment. It'll take a while longer yet before I decide that I did do magic, all right, and maybe I should find out more about how it works. For now, in spite of everything, a little flicker of pride curls inside me.

My boy is something special.

~

BY THE TIME I'M NINE AND A HALF, MY BROTHER IS STARTING to walk and talk, but my mother was right. Walking hurts him. He has trouble holding himself up, and he cries when he falls.

My parents argue a lot. Dad wants Charley to have surgery. He's told me how the doctors could open up Charley's foot to put the bones and muscles back the way they should be. My mother insists it's just as likely that would make things worse. "He has two feet now, Desmond," she says, her face tight. "If they cut him and he doesn't heal, if it gets infected, then what? What if they have to take his foot off completely?"

I don't want to think about my brother with just one foot. At the same time, when he tries to walk and can't, his crying feels like needles jabbing into my skull. I spend a lot of time in my room these days, listening to my parents through the floor and walls.

Dad says, "It would give him a chance, Moll. Don't you want that for him?"

"Not if it's a chance he'll be crippled for life."

Dad doesn't say *He already is.* I know he's thinking it, because I am too.

When I go to my room to get out of the way, more often than not I take Charley with me. He likes it when I carry him, and he likes to sit on my lap at my desk and look out the window. I've started telling him the words for colors. He likes to watch me draw, too; he doesn't know shape-words yet, but it makes him laugh to watch the pencil running along the paper.

Most of all, he loves the magic. We explore it together. I only use it at home, because like Dad says, it's not fair to make people doubt their senses. Charley and I have fun. We find out how I can bend a pencil like a candy cane without touching it, or press a face into an orange without ever picking up a knife. I learn how to link what I see in my head to the lines on the paper, and how to link those lines to what I'm drawing, so that the magic works every time. It doesn't last – everything I change goes back to the way it was in an hour or so – but Charley and I like it just the same. Charley's laughter is the best applause I could want.

Every day, when I get home from school, his face turns into one big smile. He can say my name now, and he shouts "Nicky!" and tries to pull himself up onto his feet. I drop my books and hustle over to scoop him up before he can lose his balance.

"Son," my mother says, "you've got to let him try. We don't want to spoil him." But Dad says, "It's all right, Moll. Nicky is a fine big brother."

I try to be. These days, I feel older than I used to. Nine and a half is pretty old, of course, because it means I'll be ten soon, but it's not just that. A big brother has somebody to look out for. He's got to do things right.

That's how I end up making Dad furious, for the first time in my life.

It's one Saturday afternoon at the beginning of summer, not long after school's over for the year. My mother's taken Charley and gone to Saints Peter and Paul. She does that a lot, to light candles, kneel on the hard flagstones, and pray to the big crucifix that hangs over the altar. She's sure the doctors can't fix my brother's foot, but maybe Jesus will.

Dad stretches out on the faded living room couch to read the paper. At least, he says he's reading. More often than not, he puts one of the hard round sofa cushions under his head and another under his sock-feet, smokes one cigarette down to the end and stubs it out in the ashtray, and then closes his eyes and spends the time dozing with the paper spread out on his chest.

Today, like I do on most fine Saturday afternoons, I go across the street to play marbles with three of the boys. Jake Satterfield is my good friend. We're in the same grade at school and we usually sit next to each other, because our last names are next to each other in the alphabet. Then there's George Herskowitz from up the street. To Jake and me, he's a little kid, because he's only going into third grade next year and we're going into fifth, but we like him okay. Besides, he's not the best marble player, so we have a chance to win some off him.

The other boy is Matt Jeffries. Matt goes to the Catholic school, not the public school like the rest of us. He's older and bigger, going into sixth grade in the fall.

He thinks he's the stuff, Matt does. We all know he doesn't like the nuns at his school, but he struts around in his uniform jacket to show off how nice it is, better than the plain shirts and pants public school kids wear. And he makes a big deal about how he's already ten and going to be eleven soon, but he's not much of a marble player. I'm better than him on a bad day. Today is a good day.

Jake laughs when I take my fourth shot in a row. "Nicky, you gonna give anybody else a turn?"

We're playing on the square of sidewalk right in front of Jake's house. He has the best place for marble games, because you need a good flat square without any cracks in it. Our street doesn't have many like that. The concrete is hot in the sun, so unless we're shooting, we sit on the grass at the edge of his front yard. I've been kneeling on the sidewalk long enough to wish I'd worn long pants instead of short ones, but I'm not ready to quit my streak.

"Sure," I tell Jake. "I'll give you a turn as soon as I miss."

Matt's not laughing. He's got his knees drawn up under his chin so we can all see his new lace-up sneakers. I feel him trying to stare hard enough to throw my shooter off. "Those cat's-eyes you got are pretty nice," I tell him.

They're his favorites. Cat's-eye marbles aren't cheap. He balls a fist. "If you get one..."

"If I get one, it's mine."

George gives me a thumbs-up. My clear glass shooter, winner of many games, feels heavy and solid between my fingers. I aim at a green-and-blue cat's-eye. My thumb flicks against the shooter and sends it straight and clean into the circle.

Clink! It hits Matt's marble, dead center, and rolls it outside the chalk line. I scoop the cat's-eye up. "Thanks."

Matt's face twists. He doesn't like losing, especially to us younger kids, but he doesn't have to play with us if he doesn't want to. I get ready to aim again.

Matt says, "At least I don't have a gimp for a brother."

At first it's as if I didn't hear him, or as if he was talking to somebody else. We don't use words like that at my house. Charley is still a baby.

Matt gets up. "How's he gonna walk? Is he gonna look like this?" He lifts one foot off the ground and starts hopping on the other, wheeling his arms around. "Or maybe like this." He puts both feet down and lurches back toward us, sticking his arms straight out in front of him, lolling his tongue like a dummy. "Or maybe he'll never walk. Maybe you'll have to dump him in a wheelbarrow and push him around." He laughs, loud and hard. "I bet that's it. You and your cripple brother and a wheelbarrow."

I'm not angry. My face is hot and I can hear my own breathing in my ears, and the sunlight seems to have turned faint and chilly, but I'm not angry at all. I look at Matt, standing there on his two feet, and I know exactly what to do.

Jake says, "Nicky, forget it. He's just mad 'cause he's lousy at marbles."

I'm not listening. Carefully, I pick my marbles up out of the circle, drop them in my trouser pocket, and put back the ones I already won. It's not fair to keep them if you don't finish the game. "You guys keep playing." My voice sounds light and quiet. "I've gotta go home and do something."

"Like what?" Matt says.

I don't answer. Jake says, "Nicky, hold on," and starts to get up, but I need them to stay where they are. So I say, "No, you play. I'll come back when I'm done."

Then I'm crossing the street, and going into the house, and going up the stairs to my room. I feel like a clockwork soldier, putting one foot in front of the other. Through my window, I can see them still down on the sidewalk in front of Jake's house. They're starting another game.

My window is pretty far away. For what I need to do, I need to be closer. I take a pencil and a half-sheet of paper off my desk and go down to the living room.

Dad is on the couch, dozing, like usual, with the newspaper spread out on his chest. I barely see him. I climb on the armchair, facing the window, and prop the paper up against the chair's back.

The cushion is rounded and puffy, not as good of a drawing surface as a table, and my hands are icy cold. My pencil still moves fast. My own breathing shouts in my ears, but I have never felt so still and quiet inside myself, as if the ice in my hands is filling up my whole body.

I draw Matt's foot inside its shoe. To fit on the paper, the drawing has to be a few sizes smaller than his real foot, but I've learned that doesn't matter if I concentrate right. My eyes flick back and forth, across the street to him and back down to the drawing...and the foot on the paper is all wrong. Twisted. Curled under, so the shoe leather bulges out funny.

Right away, I know it's working. From where I'm sitting I hear Matt yell. Then he's scrambling to his feet, trying to balance, jerking his bad right foot up and down. Jake and George are getting up too. I can't hear them, but I know what they're saying. *What's going on? What happened?*

It'll wear off, I know it will, but for now I want to taste Matt's fear like rolling a lemon drop over my tongue. If I could make his foot wrong forever, I am certain I'd do it. See if he called anybody gimp or cripple again.

Then someone says, "What are you doing?"

I don't know when Dad woke up or how long he's been standing behind me. His voice, as hard and cold as metal in winter, sends a shiver through my chest and all down my spine.

He snatches the drawing out of my hand. Before I can say a word, he tears the paper up, four quick rips. The noise of it rings in my head and I want to shout *No! Don't!* Because I don't know what happens if you tear up the drawing, and Dad doesn't either, and maybe it really will make Matt's foot like that forever.

It's already too late. Then, through the window, I see Matt put his foot back down on the ground. His normal foot, just like it was before.

Relief and disappointment crash together inside me. *So that's what happens.* My heart pounds and my hands tingle as if I'd grabbed a pincushion and the points went straight through into my skin. Dad wads up the torn paper. His face looks as pale and set as a skim of ice on cement, and his hair falls across his forehead like a splash of red paint. His big hand grabs the pencil out of mine. He snaps it in half and throws the two halves and the paper wad into the empty fireplace.

I'm still kneeling in the chair. He catches me by the shirt collar, dragging me up onto my feet. "You're coming with me."

I have never been scared of him before. "Dad, you don't understand." My collar digs into my neck. "Matt, he was making fun of Charley, he..."

"Quiet!"

I stumble after him into the kitchen, my shoes clumsy on the floorboards. Dad lets go of my collar and pushes me toward the table. He's rolling his sleeves up, yanking his belt out of his dungarees.

"Bend over." He's not shouting now. I want to rub my neck where my shirt chafed the skin, but I can't. Not when his eyes look so strange, like he's about to cry. "Bend over," he says. "Put your hands on the table."

I have never had a whipping. The shivering starts up again, this time in the pit of my stomach. I put my hands flat on the table and squeeze my eyes shut.

The belt swishes through the air and hits me on the seat. Once, twice, three times. I thought it would hurt, but I barely feel it, even though the *crack* of it makes me jump. Then it stops. I hear Dad's breathing.

"Sit down."

I fall into my chair. That doesn't hurt either. My face feels huge, hot and smarting as if a whole hive of bees stung it. The table's grain swims under my eyes. *You don't understand. You didn't hear Matt.*

Dad sits down close to me. His hand takes hold of my chin, gently.

"Nicky." His voice is gentle too. "Look at me."

It's so hard to raise my head that my neck creaks. Now my backside is hurting, a dull throb. I don't want to cry, but I'm going to. I feel it climbing up my throat.

"Son," Dad says. "I'm sorry. I didn't want to whip you." His hand moves to my forehead, smoothing my hair away. "But you need to understand, you can't ever do that with your drawing."

I force my mouth open. "He was making fun of Charley! He was..."

"Hush, son." I shut my mouth again, so a sob won't come out. "If you do that," Dad says, "if you change somebody like that, and they find out what you did, can you think what kind of trouble you could get into? What people might say, or do?"

You have magic in you. He'd said it himself. Who would believe what I could do?

"They would be scared of you," Dad says. "And when people are scared, they can be very dangerous." He touches my face. "I don't want anyone hurting you."

I'm hurting already. "I don't care if they do." At least now I don't feel so much like I'm going to cry. "Just so they leave Charley alone."

"Oh, Nicky." Dad smiles, but his eyes look sad. "Listen to me. If I hear about you fighting, giving a boy a seeing-to with your fists, I won't say a word against it. Sometimes you do have to teach people a lesson. You've just got to do it the right way."

I think about that. I don't look for fights, but all of us boys get into scraps now and then. I can throw a decent punch if I have to. "Dad, is Charley ever going to walk all right? Is he going to have surgery?"

Right away, I'm sorry I asked. Dad looks so tired. "Surgery, I don't think so. Your mother is set against it. I don't think it would be right to push her."

I think about how if things went wrong, the doctors might have to take Charley's whole foot off. But maybe things wouldn't go wrong. "If the doctors..."

Dad interrupts, gently. "Charley will learn to walk. He'll need help staying on his feet. When he's old enough, he'll use a crutch or a cane."

Old men use canes. I see them at Mass on Sundays, hobbling down the aisle to get communion. "Then how's he going to run around? How's he going to play games?" *I promised him he would.*

"He's not going to be the same as other boys." Dad smooths my hair again. "But he's got a good big brother to help and protect him."

If he can't run, nobody will want him on their stickball team. Nobody will pick him for tag. I think about him having to sit and watch everybody else play, and I sit up straighter in my chair, forgetting my sore backside. If he needs me to fight for him, you bet I will.

Then I think of something else. "Can I still draw?"

I'm scared he'll say no. After all, he broke my pencil and threw it away, but he says, "Of course you can." He looks surprised I would ask such a thing. "You should. You're a fine artist, Nicky."

Artist. I don't think any of us ever said that word before. If changing Matt's foot was like tasting a lemon drop, *artist* is like a hard licorice candy, my very favorite.

"But you need to keep the magic to yourself," Dad says. "Only use it when you know it's safe. Especially, you must never use it to change people. Do you see that?"

I don't like it, but I see it. "Yes."

"You'll do as I say? Promise me."

It felt so right, showing Matt how it was when you couldn't walk like everybody else, but I'm thinking a little straighter, and I realize I was pretty lucky. Matt will never know what I did to him. Dad was pretty lucky too, that ripping up the drawing turned out to be the right thing to do.

I say, "I promise."

Yes, I made him that promise. He didn't live to see me break it.

FOR A WHILE, IT'S STILL HARD TO WATCH CHARLEY TRY TO walk. By the time he's three, though, he can use a tiny crutch. Then he gets around pretty good. He can't run, and he won't be able to play hopscotch or tag or any of those games, but the other kids don't give him a hard time. Everyone knows what his brother will do to bullies, and besides, you can't not like Charley. He has a huge smile for everybody. When he's playing in the yard, he waves and shouts hello to everyone who walks past. People make a point of stopping by just to say hello back. Neighbor ladies save him a cookie or a square of cake from their baking.

Meanwhile, Dad and I have started doing something new. Once in a while, on a Saturday or Sunday afternoon when Dad's scraped some change together and my mother decides she can spare us, we go downtown to the Philadelphia Museum of Art.

This is the early 1930s, not long after the Great Crash. Men like Dad, who still have jobs, are the lucky ones. Even so, it takes no small amount of doing to save up enough pennies for such a trip. Dad rations his cigarettes tighter and wears his shoes down to their last shred of sole. When I ask if he doesn't need the museum money for himself, he says, "Some things are important."

To him and me, the great main building of the museum is another world. The marble columns lined up out front are each more than twice as tall as a man. Inside, chandeliers curve like the arms of dancers, glimmering with crystal teardrops. The floors gleam liquid-bright with polish, and red velvet draperies whisper against the walls.

As magnificent as all of that is, nothing can touch what we've come to see. The paintings. Oh, the paintings. Washes and spreads and swathes of color, bound in gilt frames so rich and gleaming you ache to touch them and feel soft gold under your fingers.

On our first visit, Dad and I tiptoe around one gallery. We're sure the exhaust from the free commuter bus is still hanging around our clothes and that our worn shoes will leave scuffs on the floor. When we get up the nerve to talk at all, we whisper. But nobody comes to scold us, and when we leave, full to the brim with color, we know we've got to brave the place again. We barely scratched the surface of what there is to see.

After a couple of visits more, the docents recognize us. They suggest galleries we might like and talk to us about the paintings and the artists who made them. Dad tells them right off the bat, with pride you could spread like butter, that his son is an artist.

One January afternoon, we stand for a long time in front of a painting by an artist named Peter Paul Rubens. By now we've learned about the Flemish School. This particular painting is a still-life of a wicker basket full of fruit, with a wine jug on one side and a smooth, heavy-looking water glass on the other. The apples are perfectly ripe, their skin a delicate pink. The dusty purple grapes look so sweet you want to pluck one off and pop it between your teeth.

Rubens died three hundred years ago, on the other side of the Atlantic Ocean. He lived in a completely different world from the one I know: a world of courtly manners, doubloons and capes, peaceful countryside. Everything in his painting, the apples and grapes and wine and all, is long gone, but I can look at that water glass and know exactly how its cool weight would feel in my hand if I picked it up. It's flat paint on a flat canvas, and it's a real thing you can touch. *That* is magic.

I get so close to the canvas that my nose would brush it if the velvet rope didn't keep me back, and I trace the lines of individual brush-strokes, trying to see how he did it. By the time Dad and I climb on the bus to go home, I think I may have figured out one little piece of it. "Dad," I say, "you know what? I think the really important stuff is what Rubens *didn't* paint."

We're in our seats now, huddled next to each other, both wrapped in our warmest coats. I'm twelve and getting taller. My head is up past Dad's shoulder. He turns away from the window to see me. "What he didn't paint? How do you mean?"

I pull my hands out of my coat pockets – I forgot my gloves today – to trace the shape of the glass in the air. "Mostly, he did the edges. Remember? The white paint?" Thin lines of white to show the glass's shape, and in a couple of places, a bigger white patch where the light would reflect off the curved surface. "He showed where the light would hit. Everything else was the background, the tablecloth and all, but that's why it looked like glass, you know? He made you believe it was there and you could see through it."

The bus chuffs away from the stop. Dad is studying me as if I'm one of the canvases. "Nicky," he says, "what would you think about college?"

The word is like a piece out of the wrong puzzle. It doesn't fit in my head, no matter how I turn it. College is for rich people.

Dad goes on, as if he's talking about what we'll eat for supper tonight. "Say to study art. There's a few colleges right here in the city, I think. I'd bet your schoolteachers could tell you about them."

At first, *study art* sounds like nonsense, as if he had said *freezing hot* or *soft as a rock.* We've had some drawing classes at school, but they're so easy I breeze through the work in ten minutes and spend the rest of the time sketching whatever I want. That doesn't count as studying. Besides, art isn't like the stuff you memorize out of textbooks. "How do you study it?"

The corners of Dad's eyes crinkle when he smiles. "Well, I never was a college man myself, so I can't say for sure. Seems to me you might learn more about the famous painters, maybe what they did and how they did it. Maybe how to do it yourself."

Then, in a rush, it's real. If I could learn how Rubens painted glass, how he made grapes you want to taste. If I could learn about things that are still just words to me, but words I want to dig into: space, perspective, vanishing point. And how to blend colors, and work not just with pencils, but with charcoals and oils and pastels. I love to use the magic I know, but there are so many more kinds to learn. Maybe I could find out not just how to make something look *right* on a piece of paper, but how to make it *alive*.

The top of my head feels as if it could lift right off. Dad is watching me. "Seems you'd like to try it."

All at once, the wave collapses. "But more school. Would we have to pay for it?" That's more than enough reason why I couldn't do it. Besides, I know my mother wouldn't like the idea. She knows my drawings are good, and she puts up with Dad and me going to the museum because it matters so much to him, but she worries I spend too much time "thinking about pictures." Boys should keep busy with practical things.

Dad's shoulder is an anchor against mine. He reaches a gloved hand over to squeeze my arm. "I bet we can sort it out," he says. "We'll put on our thinking caps."

I don't see how we'll manage. On that day, though, he and I start planning together.

Dad first raises the subject with my mother on my thirteenth birthday. The four of us are sitting in the kitchen having meat loaf, a special birthday treat. "Thirteen is a fine age," Dad says. He winks at me. I know what's coming and grip my fork tighter. "Just the right age to think about your future."

He lays the college idea out on the table. My mother's lips thin into a line.

"Go to school for art?" Her voice is brittle. "Des, we barely get by as it is. Nicky'll finish high school, which is more than you or I ever did, but then he'll have to work. Don't put ideas in his head."

I don't usually answer her back. This time I swallow and say, "He's not. It's my idea."

"Now, son." Dad isn't scolding. "You know I brought it up first."

My mother says, "I don't care who brought it up." Her knife and fork move in quick sharp angles on her plate. "Nicky, you have to be practical. You draw very well, we all know that, but soon enough you'll have to earn a living. Art school is foolish."

We have always been poor. Poorer yet, the last six or so years since the crash. Dad had enough seniority at Phillips Textiles to keep his job, but he and everyone else who wasn't laid off had to take pay cuts. I know how worry has tightened my mother's face and deepened the lines around her mouth.

"I don't mean you'll have to work to help us," she says, though I know what a difference that would make. "I mean you'll have to make your own way. That'll be a big help in itself."

Dad says, "Moll, we don't grudge him his keep."

"Of course not. He knows I don't mean that."

I do know it. I duck my head and finish my dinner, but the tangy sauce seems to have lost its savor and the meat feels like soggy pulp in my mouth.

Later, Dad takes me aside. "We'll bring her around, son."

I don't see how. My mother isn't known for changing her mind. I know it's silly and irresponsible even to want art school, but I do, now, and I can't stop wanting it. "She's right," I say. "I've got to work."

Dad tousles my hair. "Your mom is a good woman, but she doesn't know about everything. Don't give up yet."

We don't talk about college again until my first year of high school. By that time, things have gotten a little better at the textile factory. President Roosevelt is doing everything he can to dig us out of the crash. Phillips Textiles came in for some kind of government help, I don't know exactly what, but Dad's wages have crept back up a notch.

One night in the winter, during another supper, Dad says, "Moll, you've got to admit it would be a fine thing if our boys went to college. Nobody in the family did that before."

My mother cuts into her baked potato. "Nobody needed to. They got decent jobs without fancy schooling."

"Sure enough," Dad says, "but you know Nicky's an honor student. With grades like his, he could do better than work in a factory like his old man."

He loves his work, but he knows – and I know – that my mother worries about how the job tires him out, how the dye has hurt his sense of smell. She puts her fork down and sizes me up, the way she does when she's measuring with her eyes to see if I've outgrown my pants or jacket. "You do get good marks, Nicky," she says. "Maybe your dad's right, you could do some other kind of work. I still say, though, college is an extravagance."

Charley pipes up. "What's *extravagance* mean?"

He's six now, curious about everything. Dad says, "An extravagance is something big and special."

My mother adds, "Usually it costs a lot. And usually it's something you don't need."

Dad catches my eye. "Not always."

"Well," Charley says, "if Nicky gets one, can I have one too?"

That makes all of us laugh, even me. I say, "I don't know, kid. We might have to share it." He says that's fine by him. We let the talk drop.

At least, we let it drop then. I find out later that Dad keeps a quiet commentary going with my mother over the next weeks and months. One morning in the spring of my sophomore year, she sits down at the table where I'm gulping cornflakes before school.

"I think your dad may be right," she says. "If you went to college, I can see how you might get a better job."

I'm so startled I fumble the spoon. It clatters against the side of the bowl. She says, "More pay for easier work would be nothing to sneeze at. Maybe even in a nice office." My mind is catching up now. I can guess Dad's gotten her to picture me at a clean desk in a bright room, instead of working up a sweat on a factory floor. "Besides," she says, "Dad says he thinks you could try for scholarships, that your grades are good enough. Do you think that's so?"

"I'll ask my teachers." I try not to sound as staggered as I am. Is she really changing her mind? "They can tell me all about it." The teachers at my high school know that most of us kids don't plan on college, but anyone who so much as mentions the word will get pulled aside after class and roped into a pep talk for as long as he'll stand there. After all, anyone who actually does go on for a degree is a notch in the school's belt.

"Good. Then you'll ask them." My mother taps the table as if she's finished making up the week's grocery list. "But, Nicky, if you can get the money, you'll study something useful. Not art."

I swallow hard and go back to my cereal, trying to drown the icy disappointment. She still doesn't understand. She might never understand why I'd rather have a job like Dad's and draw when I can, than go to school to learn about anything else.

I complain to him when he gets home that night. He tells me to be patient awhile longer. "Son, if you're going to school with money you got for yourself, you can study what you like."

He and I have decided I should stay close to home. No travel expenses, and plus, I don't really want to move someplace else when everyone I know is here in Philly. My teachers are more than ready to help me figure things out. They know what I want to study, and they point me toward universities with good art programs: St. Joseph's, Temple, and my favorite and biggest reach, the University of Pennsylvania. I keep my grades up. Dad and I agree, too, that I won't go straight on after I graduate. I'll work for a while first and put some extra money by in case I need it.

I graduate in the summer of 1939. In the spring of 1941, things are ready. I've been working at the factory with Dad for the past year and a half. Some of my wages have gone into the family pot, but Dad's made me keep most of the money for myself. "You're helping us fine," he says. "Save up for your books and supplies and all." Because, if you can believe it – and most days, I have to pinch myself a few times – I got accepted at the University of Pennsylvania, with a scholarship to study art. No one there will know about my magic, of course, but the professors thought I "demonstrated excellent promise" in my portfolio of ordinary drawings.

The scholarship means that I don't have a choice about what I do, and neither does my mother. She's not happy about it. Every day, she wants to know what I expect to do with myself after I finish that pie-in-the-sky program.

I don't have any definite answer yet – after all, that's what I'm going to school to figure out – but her talk doesn't sting the way it might. For one thing, I've grown up some. I'm taller than she is, even a little taller than Dad, and I've started wearing glasses: round wire-frames that make me look older. My cheeks are thinner than they used to be, my jaw stronger, and the shock of hair that falls across my forehead more "debonair" than messy. Not handsome exactly, I figure, but I'll do all right for a college man.

Dad is so proud his feet hardly touch the ground. One night in May, as we walk home from work together in the warm evening, he tells me, "You're doing it, Nicky." By now, I know about the dye house fumes too. I usually have a headache by the time we punch out, and I wonder how Dad has put up with it all these years. "I'll tell you, boy," he says, "I can't wait to see what you're going to make of yourself."

He looks tired, the way he always does at the end of the day. The red-gold slants of sunlight bring out silver in his hair that didn't used to be there. When I start my new classes, I'm going to share everything I'm learning with him. He never got to study it himself, but it'll be almost as good, the two of us figuring out new kinds of magic together. His pride in me is solid rock under my feet. Whatever I end up doing with my life, I promise myself I'll make him even prouder before I'm done.

That's in May. In June, the world shatters.

～

Now I have to step back a ways. You've been hearing all this from young Nicky, the boy I was. To tell this next part, I have to remember again how old I am now, and how all of this happened a very long time ago. It has never felt like that, you see.

Dad died on June 7, 1941, the first Saturday of the month. He'd been feeling tired that morning and decided he wasn't up for our afternoon trip to the art museum. "You go ahead," he told me. I said I'd rather save the ticket money, so we could go another time when he felt better, but we had planned to see a Diego Velázquez exhibit that wasn't going to be there the following week. "Go on and see it," Dad said. "Then you can tell me about it tonight."

I went, and studied paintings that I don't remember now. Nobody else was at home. My mother and Charley were out running errands. I learned later that they got back and found Dad on the sofa with the newspaper spread across his chest, the same as always. At first, they thought he was asleep.

Dr. Sanders told us it was his heart. No warning, no pain or sickness: the easiest and quietest ending anyone could ask for. My father deserved that gift. So I would rather not tell you how I shouted after him, inside my head, *Couldn't you have said goodbye?* Or how I thought, over and over, *If I'd stayed home anyway, if I'd been here,* until a pit opened up inside me, and I looked into it and started shaking and couldn't stop.

August came, with the college year I was supposed to have started. My mother hadn't understood why I'd wanted it so much. Now she didn't understand why I turned my back on it. "Nicky, you worked for it, you earned it. Why can't you go?" I couldn't explain that I was as brittle and hollow as an empty eggshell. Everything Dad and I had dreamed of, the new faces and voices, the whirl of busyness, felt like a weight poised to crush the life out of me.

Instead, I kept my job at the factory. Everyone there had known him. The rhythms of the work let me feel as if I still had some link to him. His old workmates were kind to me, though they wanted to know, too, why I'd given up on schooling. "You ought to go ahead, Nicky. Des would've wanted it." I knew that, as clearly as I know it now.

Exactly six months after he died, the Japanese bombed Pearl Harbor. I told you how I tried to enlist and couldn't. While I packed my things for California, thinking only about getting out and finding some way to start over, I knew how Dad would have felt about me abandoning everything he and I had cared about. Sometimes I felt his eyes on me like a searchlight so hot and bright it burned. Other times, I knew he was nowhere. I couldn't tell you which was worse.

I ran from it all, and from the dark inside myself, as far and as fast as I could, and I stayed away until Charley's telegram pulled me back home.

Chapter Three

THAT FIRST NIGHT back in my old bed, I barely pretended to sleep. Every tap and creak of the old house settling sounded like knuckles rapping on the walls. The mattress dipped so deeply in the middle that I felt trapped at the bottom of a trough. I thought about Jonah Eberly, how I'd call him on Monday and where I'd say things stood. I thought about how I'd have to run downtown for some spare jeans and a shirt or two, I hadn't packed enough clothes after all, and I thought about Sara, her bright green eyes and her smile, and how she'd say "I told you so" when she heard she'd been right. I thought, over and over, *I don't live here anymore, this is just for now, I'm a production assistant in Hollywood.*

I dozed off some time after midnight and woke up to a misty gray dawn. The window over my desk was fogged with tiny raindrops. I dressed as quietly as I could, the same slacks as the day before and a fresh button-down shirt, and crept out to the bathroom. It was Saturday, so Charley didn't have to get up for school. I wouldn't roust him if I could help it.

My face in the spotty mirror didn't look any too great, between the dark circles under my eyes and the five o'clock shadow that stubbled my face all the way down to my neck. I'd have liked a shower and shave, but

Charley's room was on the other side of the wall, and the water rushing through the pipes made a noise like a gale. I tiptoed downstairs. Every floorboard seemed to squeak underfoot.

In the dim kitchen, Titus the cat jumped down from Charley's chair and padded over to me. I bent down to rub his ears. "Hey, pal."

The master bedroom door stood open like the mouth of a cave. Charley wouldn't have closed it overnight, in case our mother needed something and called out. *And how'd he hustle down here to take care of her? You let him deal with all this alone.*

I straightened up. I was here now; I could look in on her. I made myself walk over.

In the faint light that edged around the closed blinds, she lay on her back, still sleeping. Her face looked fragile but quiet. The sheet rose and fell with her shallow breathing. While I stood in the doorway, watching her, her eyes opened. They looked so large and dark, the movement so sudden, that it was as if a doll's eyes had opened, or a statue's.

"Charley?"

Her voice sounded creaky and thin. I couldn't tell if she knew someone was there or if she was calling him (*and how would he hear her if she was?*), but I swallowed and took a step into the room. My sockfeet made almost no noise against the floorboards.

"Charley?"

My own voice didn't want to come out. "Mom, I'm here."

She turned her head. Her skin was pulled tight across her cheekbones, the shadows under her eyes deep bluish-purple. When she saw me, she started, and tried to push herself up in the bed.

"It's me," I said. "It's Nicky."

She leaned back against the pillow. "Nicky."

The sun had gotten higher. The brighter light brought out the tangles in her hair and the wrinkles in her faded nightdress. I stood behind the straight-backed wooden chair, keeping it between me and the bed. "What do you need?" I asked her. "What can I get you?"

Her thin hand moved, motioning me closer. "Sit down."

I edged into the chair. She reached out for my hand. Her fingers were cold and clammy but still strong. "Turn on the light," she said, "will you?"

I fumbled for the switch on the lamp on her bedside table. The warm light through the yellow shade brought a little color to her face. Her mouth was set in the tight line I knew well, but her eyes looked as if they wanted to swallow me.

"It's been so long," she said.

I know. I'm sorry. My throat felt so tight I didn't trust myself to get words out. In Los Angeles, Nick True would still be asleep right now, trying to catch up on rest after the long week. He'd get up late and probably go out for some breakfast and a decent cup of coffee. Later, he'd go for a walk, maybe to Echo Park, and then no doubt he and Sara would meet up for dinner. *That's who I am, I'm a production assistant in Hollywood...*

"When did you get in?" my mother said.

I cleared my throat. "Yesterday afternoon. Charley told you I was coming, didn't he?"

She shook her head, an impatient movement. "Of course he did. It's this medicine I take, I forget things." She caught her breath and touched her chest with her free hand. Her eyes closed briefly, but not before I saw the flash of pain.

"Do you need some medicine now?" I asked.

"I don't like that stuff. It makes me too tired." Her hand gripped mine harder. "How long are you staying?"

"As long as I can help out."

Her eyes rested on my face. She had to know what was happening to her; she had never been one to shy away from hard facts. I wanted to tell her I was sorry. I wanted to tell her that if she was scared for Charley, I would do my best for him and make sure he was okay. When she spoke, she only said, "You look all right. A little tired yourself."

"I guess I am."

"They keep you busy out there." I could feel how much effort it cost her to talk, and how determined she was to do it. "In California."

I tried to smile. "They sure do."

Over the time I'd been gone, I had always said I was so caught up in work, it was tough to find time for a cross-country visit home. My mother and Charley had accepted it, though she'd nudged me more, telling me in her letters how my brother missed me and how much he was growing up. Charley had understood more than she did about the real reason I didn't come back. He knew I still couldn't face what was gone.

Now she said, "I hope I've told you." Her hand came back to her chest. "The money you send back, you don't have to do that. But thank you."

Every month since I'd started working at Paragon, I'd sent home a cut of my wages. Every time, she'd written back pretty much exactly what she'd just said. "You're welcome, Mom." Whether she admitted it or not, she and Charley did need the money. Dad's savings stretched as far as they could, but it wasn't quite enough.

"Your dad would be glad to know you've been helping."

No. He wouldn't. Dad would never have wanted me leaving in the first place, much less selling the magic and breaking the promise I'd made him. That truth shouted in my head. In the next instant, it called something out of the dark to eat me alive.

If it's never happened to you, you might not understand. Imagine that you're sitting in your house, in a room you could navigate with your eyes shut. You feel your chair under you and the floor against the soles of your feet. You feel the air around you and the textures of your clothes against your body. All of these things are real.

Now imagine that suddenly, they're not.

Imagine that your mind tells you, *Maybe you're not sitting here at all.* It tells you that this all might be a dream, or a hallucination. Maybe you don't know what's real and what isn't. The idea unsheathes hooks that sink into your bones.

It sounds nonsensical, of course, but when it comes out of nowhere and swallows you, trust me: you believe it. Next thing you know, you feel cut loose from yourself, floating and weightless. The light in the room you're in is wrong, so bright it hurts your eyes. Everything looks distorted, as if you're trying to see through the bottom of a heavy glass. The air shimmers with a strange haze.

That's what happened to me in that moment, sitting in the chair beside my mother's bed. Not for the first time. I'd gone through a couple of rounds of it three years ago, before I'd left home: once at Phillips, in the middle of an ordinary workday, and once at church, during a Sunday Mass. My mother and Charley knew why I'd failed the army physical. I'd never told them about this.

Now fear shuddered through my chest. I started to shake, first in the pit of my stomach, but soon the tremors would spread into my legs and arms and down into my fingers and toes. My mother was holding my hand. She would be able to feel it. I couldn't let that happen.

"Hey, Mom." Charley's voice, behind me. "How are you doing today?"

My mother let go of my hand. "Just the same," she said. "Tired. Sore."

A gasp of relief filled me. She'd let go. Charley said, "Lemme sit, Nicky. I put some cereal out. Go on and eat."

I stood up so fast I had to catch the chair before it went over backwards. My mother said, "You don't one or the other of you have to stare at me all the time."

"We have to make sure you don't get bored." Charley had always known how to talk to her. His voice, teasing and kind, sounded like Dad's.

He'd set a bowl of cornflakes and the jug of milk on the kitchen counter. My hands shook pouring the milk and some splashed on the floor. Titus lapped it up. *Not this,* I said to the dark inside myself. *Not now.*

~

OUR MOTHER TOOK HER MEDICATION MIDMORNING AND went back to sleep. I made Charley take a break from sitting with her and go do his homework, which, believe it or not, counted as fun to him. He'd carried a lot more weight than his share.

After what had happened earlier, I felt raw and queasy. Sitting still was out of the question. Real housecleaning would start on Monday, with the maid's help, but meanwhile, I decided to do something about the dust that made a gritty film on my mother's bureau and the bedframe. I got a damp rag and started work, moving as quietly around the room as I could.

A knock at the front door interrupted me. Through the half-open window blinds, I saw Adelaide O'Dell, our longtime neighbor from a couple of doors down, standing on the front stoop. She had a covered dish in her hands, wrapped in a red-and-white checkered towel.

Not now. Please.

When Charley and I were little, Mrs. O'Dell had been grandmother to all of the neighborhood's children. She had known about our friendships and fights, and what grades we got in school, and our wildest daydreams about what we'd do someday. She had admired my drawings any number of times, though like the rest of the neighborhood, she'd never known about the magic, and she had given her cautious approval when I'd told her I was going to college. She hadn't had the chance to sign off on California. I had been halfway across the country before the neighborhood knew I was gone.

Now, feeling as fragile as a broken mug patched up with mucilage, I didn't know how to face this woman who had known me since the day I was born. I wanted to duck into my mother's closet or curl up under the bed. But I couldn't pretend I hadn't heard the knock, and I shouldn't make Charley do an extra trip downstairs.

Mrs. O'Dell's tight-curled gray hair and wire-rimmed glasses looked exactly the way they had fifteen years ago, when I was one of a pack of kids playing Capture the Flag through any yards that would have us. Her faded but perfectly clean apricot-colored housedress could have been the same one she'd worn back then. Now she looked up at me with the kind of look you might give a puppy who just turned your favorite slippers into a pile of cotton stuffing. *Look at you. You're some kind of trouble, but you make me smile.*

"Mrs. O'Dell." I hung a smile on my face. "It's great to see you."

"Nicky True. Here, take this." She set the dish she was carrying in my hands so she could take hold of my arm. "Child, it's about time you came home."

She propelled me inside in front of her. It could have been her house, not my mother's, and I could have been six years old again, showing up on her doorstep with a skinned knee or a cut finger. She nudged me into the living room. "I can only stay a minute right now, but you wait here 'til I go check in on your mother. Then I need a good look at you."

The towel in my hands was rough from many washings and starting to fray at the corners. Through it, the dish felt solid and warm. I realized I was smiling.

Mrs. O'Dell came back after only a minute or two. "Oh, Mary Anna." She dabbed at her eyes with the corner of a plain pocket handkerchief. "It doesn't seem right at all. You have to trust that the Lord knows best, but sometimes, I'll tell you, I wonder."

She came to stand next to me at the living room window. Outside, the sky was that robin's-egg color that promised spring around the corner, and the sun spilled between the houses and made bands of light on the sidewalk. Our yard, with its brown winter grass, still looked faded and bleak. Three houses down, Mrs. Franklin was bringing a load of sheets in off the clothesline. They billowed in the breeze, wrapping around her as she wrangled the clothespins.

Mrs. O'Dell said, "She's so much younger than me, your mother, and you two boys still young too. I haven't had even a husband to look after in thirty years."

She had been one of the first people to welcome my mother and father to the neighborhood when they moved in all those years ago. She'd been a widow then already. Whenever any of us kids asked her why she didn't get married again and have kids of her own, she'd said, "You all keep me plenty busy. Don't you worry about that."

I said, "Don't talk like that, Mrs. O'Dell. You're no age at all."

Her mouth twitched up at the corners. She took off her glasses, wiped them on the edge of her sleeve, and set them back on her nose. "Nicky True, I don't believe you've changed a bit." She patted my hand. "Now, that's some meat loaf and mashed potatoes I brought you boys. It should last you a couple of nights."

"Thank you." I set the dish down on the coffee table. "And thank you for everything. Charley says you've helped a lot."

"Just a little bit, now and then." She looked me up and down, no doubt to see how much I really had changed. I must have, I thought; the kid she'd known would've been standing here in jeans and a T-shirt, not slacks and a button-down. Surely Paragon hung around me even on the far side of the country. "My goodness, child," she said. "To think of you being out there in California making movies."

She hadn't signed off on my going, but she and the rest of the neighborhood had found out about it before I'd arrived in Los Angeles. Once I became a *production assistant*, Charley reported that everybody wanted to know what it was I did, and what it was like in Hollywood, and whether I knew honest-to-goodness movie stars. He and my mother passed along as much of my news as they could. They didn't tell anyone exactly what my job involved, or exactly why I was so good at it. That was a secret between the three of us and Paragon.

Now Mrs. O'Dell said, "To think of you being out there making movies," and I said, "Yes, ma'am," and she said, "You were always so good at drawing, and come to find you can make a good living by it. We were all sorry when you left, Nicky; well, of course you know that. But I can see you wouldn't have had the same kinds of chances here, like you do out there."

What she didn't know, what no one but Charley and my mother knew, was that I hadn't gone to California with any idea of working for the movies at all. That had come later. But I said, "No, ma'am, you're right. It's not the same here."

"And you really know movie stars?"

The glitter of it had caught her. "Not the really big stars." Those actors and actresses were as famous as they were exactly because they didn't need me and my sketchbook. "But plenty of actors, yes."

She smiled as if I might have become a screen sensation myself. "My word. You've done us proud, that's all I can say about that."

The floor seemed to shiver under my feet. *Proud?*

She held out her arms the way she used to when I was little. "Now, you come here, child."

Once upon a time, she'd had to bend down to hug me. Now I stood so much taller that I was the one leaning over, but her arms felt as strong as they had all those years ago. Her curls brushed my cheek, and I caught a so-familiar whiff of the lavender sachets she always used in her laundry.

"My only quarrel with you, Nicky, is you stayed away too long." She held me tight. "You've got to come back and visit more, you hear?"

If she'd thought things through, she had to guess that I would take Charley back to California with me when the time came. Would we come back to visit the old neighborhood at all? With nothing to hold us here, it was hard to imagine.

I couldn't say so. Not then. "Yes, ma'am."

After she left, the house felt oddly empty. I put the dish in the icebox to heat up for supper. One way or another, I told myself, Charley and I would find a way through all this. We would manage. Then California, and the sunshine, and my job would be waiting, and I would be safe again.

Chapter Four

One way or another, Charley and I made it through Sunday. Father Hagerty, the young priest from Saints Peter and Paul, came to see my mother. He hadn't been at the church when I'd left. Doctor Sanders came by, and Mrs. O'Dell and a few other neighborhood ladies visited for a while. Charley and I put some more covered dishes in the icebox. I moved extra chairs into the bedroom and fielded questions as best I could: yes, I got back home on Friday; yes, California was fine and my job was going well; yes, it'd been a long time, it was good to see everyone. My mother had refused her morning medication so she could stay awake. She made short answers to everything everyone said to her, trying to hide pain, but I saw how she reached out for every hand.

Monday morning, the sunshine we'd had over the weekend gave out again. The air in the house felt shivery and raw. I went downstairs early, wishing I'd thought to put a sweater in my grip. Our mother was still asleep. The gray morning light in the kitchen could have been filtered through ice; it made the room seem colder than it was.

By the time Charley came down, dressed for school in jeans and a heavy sweater, I'd stirred up a batch of eggs. Since Pearl Harbor, fresh eggs had all pretty much gone to the troops in the training camps, along with fresh milk and cream, and a lot of the meat and vegetables from local farms. Every family had ration cards, carefully stocked and counted for ordinary grocery trips and those times when you needed something extra. For those of us who'd gone through the Depression years, rationing was nothing new: meat, eggs, cream, sugar, and plenty of other onetime staples were all luxuries we knew how to do without.

Powdered eggs had nothing on the real kind. You mixed the yellow powder with water to get a blobby soup that smelled of sulfur. You could never quite get all the lumps out, however much you whipped at them with a fork, but when you cooked them up, they'd line your stomach well enough.

Charley sized up the stovetop, where the eggs sizzled in the skillet and coffee simmered in our mother's old enamel-coated saucepan. "What are you doing?" he asked.

"What's it look like?" I gave the eggs another stir. Titus sat at my feet, watching the spatula hopefully. "This is almost ready. Go on and sit down."

He slid into his chair. "You really did learn how to cook."

"How do you think I kept myself alive all this time?" In truth, I only knew the bare basics. My wages at Paragon meant I could afford to eat what other people cooked, and some restaurants still managed to stock most of what their customers wanted. Nick True had lived decently high on the hog. Another adjustment, for now.

I dished up the eggs with some toast out of the oven, and set the plate and a mug of coffee in front of my brother. "Eat up."

"You know, you don't have to do this." He started in on the eggs. "I like cornflakes fine."

I filled another plate and sat down across from him. "Don't get too used to it. I'll only spoil you a little."

I'd meant it as a joke, but we both knew how soon I would be the only one to spoil him or not. He lowered his eyes to his plate. "Okay. This is good, Nicky. Thanks."

Again, I wished I could reach over and ruffle his hair, but he'd combed it nice and neat. "Of course, kid."

The maid arrived at nine o'clock, after Charley had left for school. For some reason I'd pictured an older woman, something like Mrs.

O'Dell, brisk and efficient with strong hands. The woman waiting on the porch was young, somewhere between Charley's age and mine.

She wore a plain navy-blue dress, a white apron, and a white cloth wrapped around her hair. Her dark, smooth hands and face stood out against the white fabric. Her eyes had no smile in them. "Mr. True? I'm Minna."

Paragon had two colored men on staff. John Decker and Bert Williamson were both older than most of the rest of us, with salt-and-pepper hair and work-rounded shoulders. The two of them were always in the shadows, scrubbing the bathrooms and sweeping the halls, cleaning up the set after the rest of us had quit for the day. The movie crews sent them hustling on errands the way you'd tell a neighbor kid to run and get you a newspaper. "Bert, get me a cigarette." "John, take these shoes for a polish." "Hurry up, boy, I don't have all day."

I'd never seen them as more than shapes moving in the background. Now I realized I had no idea how to talk to this colored "hired girl."

"Good morning, Minna." I hoped I didn't sound nervous. It didn't help that the boy who'd grown up in this house had never imagined having a maid. "Please come in."

The heavy wooden bucket at her feet held a long-handled mop, a stack of neatly-folded rags, and a couple of bottles of cleanser. She hoisted it up with both hands on the handle. She was built small, but strong, like some of the dance-trained actors I knew. When I shut the door behind her, her eyes went quickly from it to me and back again, as if being closed in made her uneasy.

"Where do you want me to start, sir?"

In the narrow hallway, she managed to keep several feet of space between us. I wondered if my height seemed like a threat, or if maybe she was used to dealing with "the woman of the house" and it felt wrong to have a man come to the door. I'd have liked to say something reassuring, but before I could think what, my mother called out from the bedroom.

"Nicky? Charley?"

I hadn't told her about hiring a maid. It had seemed easier not to, knowing she wouldn't like having a stranger in the house, but we had to deal with it now.

"My mother," I told Minna. "Could you wait out here for a minute?"

She stood outside the bedroom while I went in. My mother had propped herself up against the pillows. "Charley's gone to school?"

You've heard the phrase *keeping body and soul together.* My mother was doing exactly that. Worn and fragile as she was, you could feel her holding on with both hands, as tight as she could, anchoring her soul to her body.

I told her yes, Charley had headed out. She said, "Were you cooking something?"

"Eggs and toast." I knew she probably wasn't hungry, but I tried, "Would you like some?"

"No, I don't feel like eating." She held up a hand as if I'd started to say something else. "I don't want that medicine yet either."

I braced myself. Minna was waiting, and we needed to get this over with. I told my mother that if she could stay awake a little while, there was something we should do, and I went to the door and motioned Minna in.

My mother's mouth set hard. "What is this?"

It was trouble, sure enough. "Her name is Minna Davis. I've hired her to help out some." To Minna, I said, "This is my mother, Mrs. True."

Minna nodded, expressionless. "Good morning, ma'am."

My mother's eyes raked me. Never mind the years I had spent away; with that look I was a little boy facing a scolding. She said, "What do you think you're up to?"

I took a breath. "The house needs a good clean. This room especially. You'd be more comfortable."

My mother pushed herself up straighter against the bed's headboard. "You brought in a *negro* to clean?" She didn't bother looking at Minna, as if Minna couldn't hear any more than the bedside chair could. "Nicky, that girl is liable to do anything. Steal from us."

Irritation coiled up my spine. My mother didn't know anything about colored maids either, and what did we have worth stealing, anyway? But the pain-etched lines stood out around her mouth, and I could see how hard she had to fight for enough air to scold with.

"Mom, please." It came out gently. "She's just going to fix things up."

She held my eyes. The lift of her chin still said *How can you be so foolish?*, but she was wearing out. She slumped back against the pillow. "Have it your way."

We had to work quickly, while she was alert. The first thing was to get her out of bed, so we could change the sheets. "Can you get up for a minute?" I asked.

"You don't need to speak to me like a child."

Only a couple of days ago, she had been able to get up on her own. Now she held tight to my hand while I helped her into the chair. Minna pulled the sheets off the bed. "Sir, if you'll tell me where the clean sheets are, I'll put them on and get these washed."

My mother hadn't let go of my hand after I'd set her down. She raised her head. "Keep that girl out of my linen closet."

Minna's face stayed as impassive as if she really couldn't hear us. My own face felt warm, but my mother sat quiet while I told Minna where the linen was upstairs and where the washer was in the basement. "It's pretty old," I said, remembering the stubborn wringer.

"She'd better not break it," my mother said.

Minna spoke directly to me. "I'll take care of it, sir." She carried the pile of sheets out.

I asked my mother if she wanted to try a bath. She raised her head again. "How am I going to do that?"

The half-bath off the kitchen had only a sink and toilet. The full bath with the tub was upstairs, between Charley's room and mine. I said, "We can get you upstairs."

Whatever energy she had seemed to gather itself in her eyes. "You can see for yourself I can't get around."

Yes, I saw it. I didn't want her to see how it hurt. "You're pretty light." I had helped move scenery plenty of times at Paragon. Those flats weighed a lot more than she did. "I'll carry you."

To my shock, she smiled. "Piggyback, I guess."

That was a picture. I almost laughed. When was the last time she and I had laughed together? "No," I said. "Like this."

I got one arm around her and the other under her knees, ready to lift. It would have worked, but when we were eye to eye, she put her hand on my chest. "No."

"I won't drop you."

"I know that." Her palm pressed against my shirt. It felt, strangely, as if she wasn't pushing me away so much as trying to link herself to me. "I said no."

The words were clipped and hard, but her eyes, so wide in her thin face, were too bright. She knew exactly what this meant. We both did. She couldn't do something as simple as go upstairs and take a bath on her own. She would never do that again.

"Get me a kitchen towel and a clean nightdress," she said. "Then help me to the bathroom down here."

I did as she said. She walked to the bathroom as best she could, leaning on my arm. I leaned against the kitchen counter and listened to the sound of running water coming from the bathroom sink, and the rasping and rumbling downstairs in the basement as the old washer ground itself into life. The clean pillowy smell of laundry detergent wafted into the room.

Minna came back through, carrying an armful of clean sheets from the linen closet. I remembered my mother spitting the word *negro* as if it tasted bad. "Minna," I said, "hold on a second."

She stopped about an arm's length from me. Her face still had no expression in it that I could read, but she backed away, toward the table, holding the sheets in front of her like a shield.

I won't do anything to you, if that's what you're thinking. I'd never had anyone scared of me before. Between that and my mother's attitude, I couldn't help wondering if bringing a maid in had been such a good idea after all.

"I just wanted to apologize," I told her. "For what my mother said in there. It was rude, and I'm sorry."

Her expression changed. Her eyes widened with surprise that vanished in the next moment. "It didn't bother me, sir."

It must have. It would have bothered anyone. "My mother's very sick," I explained. The bathroom sink had stopped, so I went on more quietly, telling Minna what was wrong. I couldn't bring myself to say, *She doesn't have much time left.*

Minna heard me out. When I finished, she said, "You can't mind what sick people say."

That handful of words seemed to come straight out of her gut. She wasn't talking about my mother: I knew that as clearly as if she'd said so. The simple sentence held a weight of pain I didn't understand.

"I'll get the bed ready, sir." She hurried out of the kitchen.

By the time my mother finished in the bathroom, Minna had made the bed and started dusting the bureau. My mother could barely hold herself up long enough for me to help her get under the covers. "Don't touch my things," she told Minna.

"As you say, ma'am." Minna turned to me. "Sir, should I start on another room?"

I asked her to work on the living room. She picked up the heavy, clanking bucket and went out, and my mother lay back against the pillow. "I still don't know why you brought her here."

She wouldn't let go an inch, not while she had fingers to hang on with. "Do you want your medicine now?" I asked.

"I guess I have to. Get me some water, please."

In the minute it took to bring the glass back, I thought she might already have fallen asleep, but she turned her head when she heard me. Her hand trembled as she tipped a pill out of the brown glass bottle. "Stay here for a minute."

The bedside chair felt hard and chilly. She closed her eyes. "I've been thinking," she said, "about your dad. I wonder if I'll see him again."

That pair of hands wrapped around my ribs. "I hope so."

"I've missed him. So much." She didn't open her eyes, but a smile lifted the corners of her mouth. "Do you know what I keep thinking about?" I couldn't say a word, but she didn't need me to. "The way he talked."

In spite of all his years in America, Dad had never lost what he'd called "his Irish." When we were little, first I and then Charley had begged for his stories about the place where he'd been born, all the way on the other side of the ocean, and the little rundown house on the narrow street where he'd grown up, and Portmarnock harbor with all its blues and greens.

My mother said, "That was the first thing I ever noticed about him."

She was close to drowsing now. The words came slow and quiet. "In church one Sunday. I heard him talking."

I knew that story too. How, before the start of Mass, my mother had been sitting with her parents at S.S. Peter and Paul and had picked out Dad's voice a couple of pews behind. She'd made up her mind then and there to find out who he was.

She opened her eyes to see me. "He always doted on you."

I saw his face, his eyes, that afternoon when we'd walked back from the factory together. *You're doing it, Nicky. I can't wait to see what you'll make of yourself.*

My mother said, "He was so proud of you."

Then I was lost. I remembered his voice as well as she did, every tone and cadence of it, and I heard it in my head again, louder and clearer than ever. *What happened to you, Nicky? Going off like that, leaving your mother and brother alone...*

My heart clamored against my ribs. The dim light in the room, nothing more than the gray daylight filtering through the blinds, felt so hot and bright I wanted to hide my eyes. I didn't dare, any more than I could duck my head or gasp for air the way my lungs begged me to. Not with my mother watching me.

If it hadn't been for the morphine, she surely would have noticed something. As it was, her eyes drifted closed again. "I guess I'll sleep some more." She was half dozing already. "You don't need to stay."

I struggled to my feet. The floor seemed to pitch, but I made it to the door and pushed myself through into the kitchen at the same time that Minna came up from the basement. "Mr. True, should I..."

Her voice cut off. My heartbeat thudded in my head and the bones in my legs had turned to soup. I stumbled to the counter and leaned against it, palms flat on the cool Formica, head down. *Please stop this. Please...*

A hand closed around my forearm. "Sir," Minna said. "You should sit down."

The steady grip cleared my head a fraction. She helped me over to the table, not letting go until I was safely in a chair, head in my hands. "I'm sorry," I said. One deep breath, then another. Minna stood beside my chair, not saying a word.

After a minute or two, I could lift my head enough to see her. "Thank you."

Her quietness – I couldn't help thinking of it like a mask – had shifted again. She was intent, studying me as if something she saw looked familiar, and she wanted to understand it. "Are you all right, sir?"

"I'm fine," I said. "I just need a minute."

"Do you want me to hang the sheets up outside?"

The clothesline was out front, with pins waiting. "Yes, please."

She got on with the laundry. When her shift ended, at just past noon, my hands held steady to count out her wages. "Thank you, sir." She put the money in her skirt pocket and hoisted her bucket, but hesitated in the hallway. "Forgive the impertinence. May I ask you something?"

I told her yes, but I wasn't ready for the question. "Were you a soldier?"

It felt like a blow to the face. "No," I said. "I was 4-F." *Why do you want to know?*

"My husband was in France. He's home now, discharged, but he's sick too."

What did that mean? I remembered what she'd said earlier: *You can't mind what sick people say.* She shifted her grip on the bucket. "I'll see you on Wednesday, Mr. True."

"See you Wednesday. Thank you."

She walked down to the end of the street to catch the bus to her next job. The mop handle banged against her shoulder. Watching her, I found myself thinking she carried a much heavier load that I couldn't see.

WHEN CHARLEY GOT HOME, HE WANTED TO HEAR HOW things went with the maid. "What's she like? She do a good job?"

School was solid ground under his feet. With me here, he could set down some of his own load of worry. Over more of Mrs. O'Dell's meatloaf, I told him how much Minna had gotten done in just one morning, and we talked about his day and the history essay he had to dig into tonight. I didn't mention my dizzy fit. We cleaned up the dishes and he and Titus went upstairs to work.

Our mother had woken up enough to say hello when Charley got home, but now she lay sleeping again, that too-heavy, too-silent sleep. The clock above the stove ticked off the seconds like drops of water falling into a well.

Back in Los Angeles, the early spring evening would be breezy and clear, with a tang of salt from the coast. If, by some miracle, we had wrapped the day's shoot early enough, Sara and I would have taken the tram out to Echo Park. The city's light haze hid the stars, but the air smelled fresh and clear, and the water looked like charcoal glass with long arrows of lamplight along its surface.

Sara. I remembered one evening not long ago, when she and I had stood by the water and listened to the fountain splashing in the distance. She'd put her arm through mine and leaned her head against my coat sleeve. In the dark, her face had looked as smooth and pale as a lily's petals. The breeze had tugged a wisp of her hair across her cheek.

I'd last seen her only four days ago. Why was it so hard to conjure up her voice?

It was too cold here in Philly to go out for a walk. Early spring evenings usually came with mist that sank into your clothes and clung to your skin, and besides, with Charley busy upstairs, I shouldn't leave our mother alone. Casting around the tidy kitchen for something to do, I came on the pad and pencil by the phone.

Make Daddy's fork look funny...

For the past three years, my magic had been a reliable workhorse on one movie set after another. It had let us shoot countless flawless squares of film. Now I sat down at the table and let my drawing hand do whatever it wanted.

Charley's chair stood across from mine. One line, then another: the pencil danced across the paper and the straight back of Charley's chair bowed outward like the side of a barrel. A few more lines, and the back sprouted a jagged edge along the top as if a shark had chewed on it.

It was hideous. I almost burst out laughing, and then I thought of what my mother would have said if she saw it. *Mother Mary pray for us. Nicholas, you fix that, this instant!*

She couldn't come into the kitchen and give me that scolding. I crumpled up the drawing and tossed it out. It only took a minute or two to redraw the chair and let it slide back into its right shape.

I don't think I told you this before. When I changed something alive, a face or a plant or a dog's tail, I could undo the changes quickly by tearing up the drawing, the way Dad did when I drew Matt Jeffries's foot. When I changed an object, on the other hand, tearing up the drawing wouldn't undo a single line. I'd have to redo it or wait for the magic to wear off. I never knew why that was.

Dad wouldn't have scolded me for remodeling the chair. I could almost hear him laughing. The ceiling lamp above the table cast a circle of yellow light down onto the wood. So many evenings, Dad had sat here for a cigarette. I remembered exactly the way the lamplight had caught his favorite ashtray, the one made of blue glass, and the way the smoke had curled into the air.

The kitchen began to seem huge and empty, the house around me much too still. I shook myself. *What are you, five years old?* I wasn't exactly alone here, with my mother in the next room and Charley in his. I wandered out into the hallway and then up the stairs. Maybe I would think of something I needed out of my grip.

Charley's bedroom door was shut. As I walked past it, a faint sound brought me up short.

My brother had never been a crier since he was a baby struggling to walk. He had learned early on how tough life could be. As quietly as I could, I moved closer to the door and leaned in to listen.

The sound came again, and now I heard it clearly. A sob.

He wanted to be left alone. The closed door made that clear. Even so, I thought of him sitting there alone, and I lifted my hand to tap a knuckle on the wood.

"Charley? You okay?"

No answer. The door was closed but not latched. I pushed it open just enough to see in.

He had turned off the lamp. In the dim light that came in through the window, I could see schoolbooks open on the desk and Titus curled up on the pillow. Charley sat on the far side of the bed. He was so still he could have been sculpted there, his elbows on his knees, his fingers forming a cage to shield his face.

I took a step into the room. "Charley?"

He shook his head, telling me to go away. Part of me, the part that hadn't wanted to come home for three years, was willing to obey, but my feet wouldn't quite do it. My little brother was hurting.

I edged onto the mattress next to him. "Hey." I put my hand on his shoulder – when did his shoulders get so broad? – and braced myself to get shrugged off. "What's going on?"

He didn't push me away. For a long moment, he didn't move a muscle. Then, as abruptly as if something had snapped inside him, he let his guard down and reached out for me. His arms wrapped around me, holding on.

Our mother had been his only parent, his only real family, since Dad's death. He had never said a word to me about the fear and pain he felt as we watched her fade away from us. He didn't say a word now, or let out any more tears, but I felt him shivering as if the window had been open to let in a knife of winter wind.

I held him. "I've got you, kid. I'm here."

He pressed his face against my shoulder. We sat there, just like that, until he let go and wiped his eyes on his sleeve. "I knew she wasn't going to get better."

So much ache in that quiet handful of words. I wanted to give him something to hold onto, the way he used to hold onto my hands for balance. "Charley," I said, "listen, we're going to stick together. We're going to get through this." *I will take care of you.*

He nodded, the smallest motion. "I didn't want to think about…" His voice snagged in his throat and he coughed. "About how it was going to be, after."

When he was little, I'd been able to catch him so he wouldn't fall. Now he looked so fragile, his face pale and tired in the thin light. "I know what you mean," I said. Of course it was a huge change for him to think about: not only the reality of losing our mother, but the idea of moving across the country with me, setting up housekeeping in Hollywood.

Maybe, I thought, it would help if he could start to picture that different life. "We'll get everything figured out," I said. "My place is a little small, but there's plenty of room for you and Titus." It would be a tight squeeze. We could fit in a second bed if we pushed the couch against the wall, and we could split the closet down the middle, but we'd have to find something else before long. "Then in the summer, maybe, we'll look around for a bigger place we both like." If he wanted, we could afford to live in one of the upscale buildings with a courtyard and walls of windows. "We'll find something just right."

He was shaking his head. I saw he'd closed his eyes. "What is it?"

No answer, except to slump a little, as if he wanted to curl in on himself. I put my arm around his shoulders again and tried to look into his face. "Charley. What's going on?"

He raised his head. His eyes looked like a little boy's, caught in a bad dream. "I think I'd be in your way."

For all that I could wrap my head around that, he might have been speaking a different language. "What do you mean?"

"Nicky, I..." He looked up at the ceiling, as if the explanation he needed might be hidden in the paint. "I know how things are here. I know everybody, and how to get around, and stuff. Los Angeles sounds pretty nice, but..."

Then I understood, or thought I did. He had an idea about the city where I lived, but that didn't mean he could imagine it as a home. A lot of ordinary, everyday things could be harder for him than for most people. Navigating city streets. Catching a bus. Shopping for groceries. He would need time to get used to it, and he knew how busy my job kept me.

"Kid, listen. I've missed you a lot. It'll be great having you there with me." I made it as firm as I could. I hadn't forgotten the reality of things, how the Nicky he knew wasn't Nick True, how the Paragon crew had barely known I had a brother until a week ago, how that word *guardian* still pinched at me like a too-tight pair of shoes. For now, I ignored it as best I could. "Sure, I'm at work a lot," I said, "but it'll be summer soon, and then I'll have plenty of time." Things calmed down at the studio in July and August. Even Jonah took a vacation. "We'll check out the city together. I'll show you all around." I gave him a little shake. "You won't be in my way for a minute. Don't you think that."

It didn't seem to help. Charley twisted a corner of his bedsheet between his forefinger and thumb. So quietly I could barely hear it, he said, "But this is all I've got."

What did he mean, *this*? I wanted to say, *You've got me, don't you?* I hadn't been much good up to now, we both knew that, but I would do better. If he was afraid I'd get him out to California and abandon him, he didn't remember what his brother was like.

That thought went through my head and stopped me cold. *What his brother was like.*

Finally, I understood. Really understood. I had left him once. Maybe he wasn't sure, anymore, what his brother was like. Our old house here was home, the only one he had ever known, and I was planning to cut him loose from the last anchor he had.

As if he heard me thinking, he raised his head again and looked me in the eye. "I'm sorry, Nicky." His voice was quiet but clear. "I don't want to move to California."

Well.

All the things I could have said lined up in my head, ready for a chance to march out of my mouth. *That's where my home is now. That's where my job is.* After all, he didn't have much choice, and he certainly knew it. *It won't be so bad. Give it time, you'll get used to it.* I was going to be his only family. Until he had a way to look after himself, he had to take the life I could give him.

It's funny how fast your thoughts can run. In less time than it takes to tell, I thought about my contract with Paragon, the long days of filming, the many projects I'd helped bring to the screen and the many more where my magic was slated to be a key ingredient. I thought about Jonah Eberly champing on his cigar and waiting for me to let him know when I would be back. I thought about my apartment, and Sara's hand on my lapel, and her smile and the softness of her hair against her neck. And I thought about how, three days ago, I had sat in the cab while it pulled up in front of my parents' house, and promised myself that I wouldn't be here long. I didn't belong in this place anymore.

Then I thought of my mother's face against the pillow and what she had said to me only this morning.

Your dad was so proud of you.

"Okay," I said to Charley. "We don't have to go."

His mouth fell open. I still had my arm around his shoulders, but he pulled away as if I had suddenly sprouted tentacles. "What?"

"We don't have to move," I said. "We can stay here."

"Nicky." He shook his head, incredulous. "That's nuts. I know I have to go out there with you. Just because I don't want to, that doesn't mean..."

If I thought about it too much, I would lose my nerve. I interrupted him. "We've got to figure things out together. Sounds to me like it'd be better for you to stay here, so I vote that's what we do."

He still looked so baffled that I might have laughed, if I hadn't felt so cold all over at the thought of what I was letting go. "But," he said, "what about your job and all?"

Yes, the job. I could just hear what Jonah would say about me not coming back at all. And there was Sara, too. And however bad all of that would be, nothing came close to the worst thing I'd lose. I had been safe out there.

He was so proud of you...

I shook myself. "I'll figure out the job," I said. "I'll find something else."

Now Charley started to smile. It looked uncertain, but it was a smile. "We don't have movies out here. Not like in Hollywood, anyway."

"It doesn't have to be movies."

I hadn't planned to sell my magic that way in the first place. Like a film spool unrolling, I remembered the long train ride west. I had pointed myself away from home and figured I'd find work in a shipyard or munitions plant somewhere on the coast. Then, one day, I overheard two girls in the dining car. "I've got to see Hollywood," one of them told the other. "I bet it's the prettiest place in the world. In the movies, you know, everything looks so perfect."

Perfect. That word settled down into me like a stone settling to the bottom of a pool. For the rest of the trip, as we shuddered and jarred our way to the Pacific coast, I considered, for the first time in my life, what someone might give me in exchange for the magic. Dad would never have wanted such a thing. In the train, I felt cut as loose as a balloon from him and home and everything I had always been.

Now, because it was easier than thinking about coming back to this old house for good, I thought about how Hollywood wouldn't be the only place that put a decent price on "perfect." "I can find something else," I told Charley. "Somebody'll have a use for me."

"Nicky, be sure about this." He wasn't smiling now. "Because it's a huge thing to ask. I don't want you feeling stuck here, thinking what a drag you have for a brother."

"Never." It came straight out of my gut. "Not in a thousand years, kid."

The relief that lit his face was the best thanks I could have asked for. For the first time since I'd been back, it felt right to reach out and tousle his hair the way I used to.

Later, when I made myself turn in for a few hours, I thought about where I would try selling the magic next. That had worked fine at Paragon, and Philadelphia had one obvious buyer candidate: newspapers.

The city boasted plenty. Weeklies, dailies, morning and evening locals. If you leafed through any of them, you'd find no shortage of eager sellers of everything from cigarettes to cough syrup, fountain pens to Packards. Merchants ran the biggest spreads they could afford, with the brightest colors they could splash on the page. Every one of them would want as close to a perfect image as they could get.

That was my answer. As soon as I could make it happen, my magic would go to work for the ads.

Chapter Five

TODAY, I'm putting in my time on this laptop a little later than usual. My grandson Matthew, his wife Kathryn, and their daughter Hazel stopped by this morning to visit. Matthew told me they were going up to the Jersey shore this afternoon. "But Hallie wanted to see you first, Granddad. Right, Hal?"

One thing about getting older: you never outgrow wishing. At my age, you can't help looking out at the world and thinking about how you likely won't be around in it much longer, and there's precious little you can do about the way it is. You wish for big things: for instance, to be able to fix things up more before you go, and to know the ones you leave behind will be all right. And you wish for small things, too: that you could scoop up your little great-granddaughter, the way you used to do with your grandkids.

Hallie gave me her trademark biggest hug and unzipped her purple backpack. She always brings over her sketching paper and pencils. "Grandpa Nicky, let's draw."

She and I play the game Dad taught me so many years ago. The rules are simple. Hallie draws a shape and I copy it, and then I draw one for her, and so on back and forth. She's convinced my drawing hand is just rusty, and that if we practice enough, I'll get as good as I used to be.

Today she drew a bird for me. Not simple shapes joined together, oval and circle and trapezoid and triangles, the way we used to do, but a real bird with a narrow head, a bright eye, and wings you'd think would spread right there on the paper. You should see her when she draws. She loves to be in motion, her curls are always tousled and tangled, and she puts so many different colors together in her outfits that she looks like a little kaleidoscope. But when she draws, nothing moves except her eyes and her drawing hand. You never saw such an intent look on such a small face.

"That is one lovely bird," I said, when she finished. The things she notices, and the way her eyes and hands work together to capture them on paper, remind me of how it was for me. I wonder if she might be able to *put the car into gear* someday. I wonder if I might be around to see it.

She turned her bright face up to me. "Now you draw it."

Mine didn't look nearly as good. It's been a long time since my drawing hand did exactly what I told it. "That's okay, Grandpa Nicky," she said. "We'll keep practicing. But you know what?"

"What's that?"

"When I grow up, I'm going to be an artist, just like you and Grandma. And you know what else?"

"What, sweetheart?"

"I'm going to have my pictures in a gallery, like Grandma does." Jo started exhibiting her work as soon as she finished school and has never stopped since. "When I do," Hallie told me, "you'll come and see them, right?"

"Why, you bet I will." That's another thing to wish for. To know I have another fifteen years in me, so I can see how she'll light up the world.

⁓

AFTER THE NIGHT WHEN CHARLEY AND I DECIDED TO STAY IN Philly, our mother held on for almost two more weeks. For as long as she could, she clenched her fists at death.

The house filled up at the end. Charley stayed home from school and he and I sat with our mother around the clock. Neighbor ladies went in and out. The doctor checked in every day. So did Father Hagerty from S.S. Peter and Paul.

Our mother died on the last Sunday in March, late in the afternoon. Charley and the priest and I were with her. By then, it had been two days since she'd last opened her eyes. Father Hagerty administered the last rites and draped my mother's black rosary beads around her folded hands.

I remember the stillness. While the house seemed fuller than ever, with neighbors and friends and sympathy and funeral arrangements, Charley and I had an invisible shield around us that kept the noise out. We could have been standing together at the bottom of a well.

That night, after our mother's body had gone to be prepared for burial and the house had emptied again, Charley and I sat side by side on my bed. The lights were off so that the dark wrapped around us like a blanket. Charley said, "I guess we're orphans now."

He hadn't cried again, not that I knew of, since that night two weeks earlier. Now his voice sounded quiet and matter-of-fact. "I guess we are," I said.

In one of the last times we'd been able to talk with her, our mother had approved the arrangement that made me Charley's legal guardian. We told her, too, that we would stay in Philly instead of going back west. We'd sat side by side next to the bed, with Charley holding our mother's hand. Her eyes stayed fixed on me, as if blinking would snap the thread that held her to us. "I'll be able to find another job," I'd told her. "I'll make sure we're okay, Mom." I had wished I could see inside her head, to know how to make it easier for her to let go.

Now I said to Charley, "We're not on our own, though, if our icebox is any proof." Mrs. O'Dell, Mrs. Franklin, and the other neighborhood ladies had brought over so many casseroles and pies and roasts that the icebox lid would barely close on it all.

Charley smiled at that. His shoulder rested against mine. "I'm not glad she's gone, but..." His left foot traced a line between two of the floorboards. "You know, I'm glad it's over."

I knew exactly what he meant. "Me too, kid."

We held the funeral mass on Wednesday and laid our mother in the cemetery plot next to Dad. I had never found it easy to believe in heaven, despite everything the church told us from Sunday school on, but that cool gray morning, as Charley and I leaned on each other beside the new grave, I hoped our mother had found Dad again, as she'd wanted to. I hoped the two of them were together somewhere, catching up on all the time since they'd last seen each other.

Then, with the mass over, it was time for me to keep my promise to Charley. We were going to stay in the place where he belonged.

I didn't like it. I hadn't liked it from the minute I made that promise. A big part of me wanted nothing more than to stuff my things in my grip and split town as fast as I could, but I was a *guardian* now, like it or not, and I'd run away once before. I could for damn sure do better this time. Sometimes boneheaded stubbornness can do the work of good intentions.

The first things had to get cleaned up first. I'd spoken with Jonah Eberly during my first week in Philly, when I'd still planned to go back west. Now I had to tell him the real situation. I called him on Thursday, the day after the funeral.

"Leaving Paragon? What the hell are you talking about, Nick?" At first, he sounded more disbelieving than angry. "You are under contract until June of next year at the earliest." He sounded like he was gnawing on something; his cigar, no doubt. "I don't have to remind you that the studio has the option to renew, which of course we will want."

The kitchen counter felt smooth and solid behind me. "Yes, sir. I'm sorry." I wouldn't tell him I wished things could be different. They couldn't. "I have my brother to take care of now."

"Your brother?" He'd probably forgotten I had one. "So bring him out here with you."

"That won't work. It's better for him here."

"What's the matter with him, is he sick?" Now he was angry. He didn't give me time to answer. "Nick, California's the best place in the country. It'll be better for him here. You take care of what you have to do, and then the both of you come back here."

"I can't do that, sir. I have to respect what my brother needs."

"He's as stubborn as you, is that what I'm hearing?" Jonah gave his desk what sounded like a ringing smack with the flat of his hand.

"Listen to me. You have obligations. You're not going to leave us high and dry."

That was all very well to say. The fact was, though, I had already left them in the middle of a shoot, and they had found a way to manage without me. "Sir," I said, "I have a lot of obligations. You understand that I can't be in two places at once."

I heard a sharp exhalation. "Look. I know you just lost your mother and it's a tough time. Take a while to think about it, but not too long, because..."

"No, sir." My hand tightened around the receiver. "There's nothing to think about. My brother and I will stay in Philly."

Silence. Then, after another champ on the cigar, "I don't like to say this. But you know if you break your contract, we can cause a lot of trouble for you."

The temperature in the kitchen took a dive. I had known this might come up, because it was the best weapon Jonah had. He didn't only mean legal trouble because of the shoots I was supposed to do. He meant my non-disclosure agreement with Paragon.

When I had first signed my contract, I'd insisted on it. Neither I, nor any of the actors I worked with, nor any of the crew, nor Jonah himself: none of us could discuss my magic outside work. Anyone who did risked losing their job in a time when no one could afford that. I was selling the magic, fair enough, but if I could help it, every Tom, Dick, and Harry on the street wouldn't find out what my drawing could do.

Some of the actors had wanted to know why I kept myself so small. "You could be famous. Why don't you tell the world about this?" It didn't matter that the magic wore off. For those sixty minutes, they had the eyes they wanted, the perfect jawline and nose, the hair that fell just so. "Everybody would want this. You could be richer than your wildest dreams."

I only cared about money up to a point. The magic was mine. And though I had broken my promise to Dad so thoroughly that no one would ever be able to sweep up the pieces, I had never forgotten what he'd said. The magic could scare people too. *When they're scared, they can be very dangerous.*

Now Jonah was reminding me that if I walked out on my contract, our non-disclosure agreement didn't have to hold up either. The studio could spill my secret into as many ears as they wanted. That fact set a knifepoint against my chest, but I had worked out an answer to it before I picked up the phone.

"Non-disclosure can work both ways, sir." Charley came into the kitchen, heading for the icebox. "You do what you have to, and I'll do what I have to."

Charley stopped in the middle of the room. His eyes asked me what was going on. I held up my free hand and mouthed *it's okay.*

He came over to stand next to me. On the other end of the phone, I could hear Jonah breathing again. He said, "Listen, this doesn't need to get bad."

He was thinking about secrets too, as I'd hoped he would. For instance, what might happen if people found out about this one piece of Hollywood magic. If I chose to talk, perhaps to a newspaper, about exactly what I had done for Paragon. Jonah was thinking, in particular, of what his backers and money men might say – everyone who had invested in Paragon's schemes and promises – if the secret came out *after* I had slipped through the studio's fingers.

"I agree," I said. "Nothing will get bad, if we can just call it quits."

That wasn't what he wanted to hear. "Damn it, Nick." Another pause. Charley leaned in close, trying to listen. "What's out there in Philly for you? What are you going to do?"

My plans weren't his business. "I'll figure something out."

In the end, Jonah backed down. One of us had to. He agreed, in a tone that said the cigar was reduced to a pulp, to draw a line through the rest of my contract. "We won't go public about what you did here if you don't. Gentlemen's agreement." That meant no reference from him for another job, but that wouldn't matter once I had made my point to the right possible employer. "And listen, Nick, if you do decide to come back here someday, we could probably find a use for you."

I bet. "Thank you, sir."

The line clicked and went silent. I felt all right, only a little sweaty, but my hands shook so much I had trouble balancing the receiver back on the hook. Charley saw it. "Are you okay?"

"I'm fine. My boss tried to scare me, is all." I told him what Jonah had said. "It's okay now. I'm through with the movies."

Charley leaned against the counter and ran the tip of his cane along the join line between two pieces of linoleum tile. Up and down, up and down. "Nicky, do you have to do the ad thing?" He knew I'd already started searching out firms to apply to. "Would you rather some other kind of work?"

I couldn't think of any better option. "Like what?"

"I don't know. Something that didn't use the magic."

For one heartbeat, I saw it. An ordinary job, like the one I'd had at the textile factory, where I could go to work and draw pay and come home, and my drawing could stay hidden like a tiny treasure in a jewelry box.

But there was that word *guardian.* With Charley's future to think about, I needed a good living, didn't I? "I just want to know we're okay," I said. "The magic's the best way I've got."

"I don't want you thinking you're stuck."

"Kid, if this is going to be about you getting in my way..."

"It's not." He saw my expression and smiled for the first time since he'd come into the room. "Honest. But maybe we don't need that much money. I was thinking, with just the two of us, do we still need Minna?"

I'd been thinking about that too. Technically, I guessed, we could manage without her, but she had made all the difference in the past few weeks. Charley and I would barely have had the sense to feed ourselves if she hadn't made a point of heating up some of the dishes from the icebox. We had come to rely on her. It was hard to imagine doing without her help as we figured out this new shape of things.

I said, "I think it'll be better if she stays. When I'm working again, and you're in school, we might need the extra hand."

"Okay." He looked me up and down, the same way he had the night I'd come home. Now he seemed to be sizing up my T-shirt and the jeans I'd bought downtown. "Just, you know, don't work too hard."

That made me smile. "Are you thinking I will?"

"You seem good right now. Don't change it."

I knew what he meant. My Paragon three-piece hung in my closet upstairs and I didn't look like a California swell anymore. Charley had his brother back. If he could help it, I wouldn't get lost again.

~

I HAD TO GO OUT TO LOS ANGELES ONE MORE TIME, TO empty out my apartment. I left on the Sunday after I quit at Paragon. The out-and-back travel was anything but cheap, but it had to happen fast.

Charley insisted he'd be fine on his own. Mrs. O'Dell and I between us convinced him anyway to camp out at her place until I got back. Neither of us wanted to think of him alone in the empty house. "It's just for two nights, kid," I told him on Sunday morning, when the cab pulled up to take me to the airport. "I'll be back before you know it." He lifted his chin and told me to have a good trip. We both knew why he was scared.

My apartment had come furnished, which made packing up easier. I stuffed as many clothes as I could into my suitcase for the flight back and boxed the rest to be shipped. The artwork, the Rubens and O'Keeffe and Benton prints, came down from the walls last. They were like memories of a loved face, my last link to dreams I was no closer to reclaiming. I wrapped each frame in a pillowcase and closed the box lid gently.

I had told Sara when I would be in town, so between her and Jonah, everyone at the studio knew I was leaving. Most of them turned up on Monday night to say goodbye. By then, my apartment looked exactly the same as it had when I had moved in. I'd slept on a bare mattress that first night because I hadn't brought any sheets. Now I had packed up the ones I'd used, so it would be bare for the last night too.

Sara stayed until everyone else left. After the door closed behind the last couple of crew folks, she slipped her arms around me and looked up into my face. "Nick, don't be a stranger, okay?" She tried to smile, but her eyes looked too bright. "You know where I live. Send me a letter now and then, tell me what you're up to. Who knows, maybe someday…"

Maybe someday, we would end up in the same place again. She and I both knew how unlikely that was. She deserved someone better than me, someone who had more to give than secrets and shadows, but when the door shut between us for the last time, I sat down on my bare mattress and hid my face in my hands.

Next day, Tuesday, I made it back to Philly in time for dinner. The cab dropped me off in front of Mrs. O'Dell's house. I'd barely wrestled my suitcase out of the trunk when her front door swung open and Charley hustled down the steps to catch me in a one-armed hug.

I held him tight. "Don't worry, kid. I'm back for good."

The important thing was to keep busy. As long as I did that, I couldn't think too hard about anything. Wednesday was my day to hunt for a new job. On Wednesday morning, I had my list of likely ad agencies ready, and I was gearing up to start phone calls when Minna arrived for her shift.

She and I usually traded good-mornings in the hall before she got to work. Today she gave me a nod at the door, brushed past with her head down, and went straight upstairs without a word. I heard the bathtub faucet running, and then the sound of a mop clacking against the wall as she started scrubbing the floor.

She had been a big help to Charley and me, but I had never thought of her as more than useful background, someone we could always count on to do exactly what we needed. I had been so caught up with everything else that I'd barely thought of her at all. Now I found myself wondering about her life. From the little I'd seen, I could guess she didn't have an easy time of anything.

She had done her shifts as usual when the house was full of neighbors. Now, as if the pictures had been waiting in the back of my mind for the right moment, I remembered the way some of those neighbors had eyed her, as if she might empty the silverware drawer into her bucket when no one was looking. Others had steered clear of her as if she was contagious or might bite. She'd kept her head down and worked hard, no matter what...and I remembered how, at Paragon, John Decker and Bert Williamson had run errands without a word of complaint, even when the people demanding coffee or cigarettes or a newspaper had groused at them for "laziness," or in spite of their work-lined faces and silvering hair, called them "boys."

I had never thought about what that must feel like. If anybody called Minna lazy in front of me or Charley, they'd wish they hadn't, but I wondered if someone had said or done something today that had gotten past the shield she kept up against the world. Some other employer's dissatisfaction or insults; some extra weight added to an endless round of work.

The thought of *work* pulled me back to the task at hand. I had to get down to this job business. I sat at the kitchen table with the list I'd made of possible ad agencies and pored over my notes on each one. Some were big guns, longtime Philadelphia institutions. Others were younger and smaller, likely to be hungry for a leg up in the business. I worked out the script I would use on the phone and tried to decide which number to call first.

Minna came downstairs again. "Sir, the bathroom and upstairs hallway are done. Do you want me to do the bedrooms today?"

Something was definitely wrong. I was used to the quiet mask she wore at work. Today, she seemed not just quiet but shut down, as if something had gone dark inside her.

"Are you okay?"

The question came out before I thought. She shook her head, the smallest motion, as if she didn't want to.

I remembered her hand on my arm, the way she'd guided me to the table when I had been sick. "I don't mean to pry," I said, "but is there some way I can help?"

She lifted her chin. "I don't think so, sir. Unless you know a way Timothy could get a job."

"Timothy?"

"My husband."

She had never mentioned his name before. "What kind of job does he want?"

She looked past me, over my head, as if she was talking to the clock above the stove. "Before the war, he worked at Reading Parts and Supply." Reading was an auto manufacture plant not far from Phillips Textiles. In its industrial heyday before the Depression, Philadelphia had been home to any number of small busy plants like that. Minna said, "Now his boss says they can't hire him back. They're moving out of the city, to Bala Cynwyd." That was one of the blue-blood suburbs. "Timothy and I could never manage to live out there. We'd never afford it, and besides, it's not for people like us."

People like us. I didn't know much, but I could guess what she meant. Her skin stood out in a roomful of Lawrence Street people, and we eyed her sideways, poor as we were, used as we were to pinching and scraping. Surely, we shouldn't have figured we were so much better than anyone. How much worse would it be for her in a place where people had money to flash around, and fancy pedestals to sit on and look down at everybody else?

"He has trouble, too. Dizzy spells." She kept talking now as if she couldn't stop. "That time you had one, he gets the same way. Sir," she added, as if just remembering what she was supposed to call me.

Dizzy spells like mine. She had carried this load long enough for its weight to dig into her bones. "He can't sleep much either," she said. "He has dreams. Some nights, he can't come to bed at all."

During her first week of cleaning the house, she had told me that her husband had served in France, that he'd taken a bullet through the right thigh and been sent home with an honorable discharge. "He wants to work," Minna said. "He hates sitting home all the time, but he can't find another job. No one seems to want him."

I thought about spending hours on end trapped between four walls, with only nightmares for company. I didn't know what Timothy looked like, I couldn't picture his face, but Minna's was right here, and I knew how she scrubbed and dusted other people's houses, took out their garbage and washed their dirty clothes. I knew, because I had seen it, how those people could look at her and speak to her. Accusing her of wanting to steal from them. Throwing her first name around while she called them *sir* and *ma'am.*

"Minna, could you call me Nicky?"

The words were out of my mouth and hanging in the air before I realized I had thought them. Her quiet mask slipped back into place as smoothly as if it had been there all the time. "No, sir. I couldn't do that. Should I clean the bedrooms now?"

If you spilled ink on a half-finished sketch, you could start a new drawing and make it decent, but you wouldn't forget your clumsiness. "Yes," I said. "Thank you."

She went upstairs and I went back to my list. This afternoon, I told myself, I'd better land a chance at a job.

~

I CALLED SEVEN AGENCIES TOTAL. WITH EACH, I TOLD THE secretary who answered the phone that I was a transplant from California, where I'd worked in the movie business, and I had an unusual skill that allowed me to guarantee the finest quality ad visuals available. I offered to come in at the management's convenience and demonstrate.

The script – at least the part about my skill – was almost the same one I'd used on film companies when I arrived in Los Angeles. Now, of course, I had the bonus of being able to say I'd worked for Paragon. It should have been easier, this second time around, to work out how to sell my magic for a decent wage. It wasn't. Not when I could picture Dad leaning against the kitchen counter, listening to every word of every call. *Nicky, boy, what do you think you're doing?*

Still, four places scheduled me for interviews right away. The first was a firm called Allen and Allen, on Market Street in Center City.

The next morning, Thursday, after Charley left for school, I got the three-piece back out of my closet and dressed as if I'd been headed to the studio. The cab took me down Girard Avenue, which cut west toward the Schuylkill River. Dad and I had ridden the same route to the museum. The bus had gone around the same corners, brakes clashing, metal body jolting and shuddering. I could almost smell the vinyl seats and the cloud of cigarette smoke and exhaust.

He was so proud of you.

The searchlight I had felt before, so hot and bright it burned, seemed to bore through the cab's windows and flood over me. *Ads, Nicky? Selling yourself again to the highest bidder? You don't learn, do you.*

He had never spoken to me that way in life. I almost answered him out loud. *Look, Dad, I have to take care of Charley now. Don't you understand?*

The cab pulled up at the intersection with Market Street, at the edge of Center City's big business district. The searchlight snapped off, and ordinary sunlight slanted through the window and across my lap. The back of my neck was damp with sweat. My hand shook as I reached my handkerchief back to dry it.

The driver let me off in front of a tall concrete-and-glass building in the middle of a crowded block. A stream of here-and-gone faces, men in business suits and hats and women in long bright coats, moved past me along the sidewalk. I went in through a revolving door and an attendant at a desk in the lobby pointed me up to the fourth floor.

Allen and Allen had a spread of rooms on the east side of the building. The offices must have been recently remodeled; the smells of new carpet and fresh paint hung sharp in the air. At the main desk, a young redheaded secretary in a frilly white blouse smiled as if my arrival was the highlight of her day. "Good morning, Mr. True. Mr. Allen and Mr. Allen are waiting for you in the boardroom."

The two Allens were brothers, both in their late thirties, with dark hair and toothpaste-ad smiles. Stephen, the older, was tall and rangy, Mark shorter and solid. In the boardroom, which had the same new-paint smell, the young secretary brought us coffee and backed out the door, closing it as gently as if she'd put a baby to bed.

"So, Mr. True." Stephen Allen motioned me to a seat at the near end of the big oval table, which gleamed as if it had been varnished the day before. He and his brother sat down across from me. "That was quite a pitch you gave us." Mark Allen wore a full three-piece, like me, but Stephen hadn't bothered with a jacket or vest. His Kelly-green suspenders stood out against his white shirt. "Finest available ad visuals," he said. "You guarantee it?"

"Yes, sir."

Face to face, I noticed more differences between the brothers. Stephen Allen had bright hazel eyes and the kind of face that looked consciously open, as if he wanted the world to know what an honest, friendly fellow he was. Mark's eyes tended more toward the brown, and he didn't smile nearly as often. If Stephen was the mouth of the operation, Mark was its eyes and ears, quiet and watchful.

Stephen said, "No need to call me sir." The smile again. "Stephen, please."

I thought of telling him to call me Nick. That wouldn't protect me, not here in the city where I'd grown up, and it wouldn't change what I was about to do. "Then I'm Nicky."

"Good. As you may know, Nicky, my brother and I started this firm only a few years ago, but we're making a decent name for ourselves." That was why they'd seemed worth trying. Stephen steepled his fingers on the tabletop and a gold wedding band caught the light. "We're always looking for an edge in the business," he said.

Mark Allen spoke up, for the first time since we'd come into the boardroom. "We should tell you, we do have two excellent artists on staff. We aren't actively seeking new employees." I felt sure he'd had this conversation with Stephen before I'd arrived. "If you do offer something out of the ordinary, we'll be glad to see it, but we can't promise to bring you on."

"Certainly." My voice stayed level, but my pulse was speeding up too much. I had my sketchbook in my lap. I gripped it in both hands so that the hard edges dug into my palms.

Stephen leaned back in his chair as if he was in a movie theater, getting ready for the main feature to begin. "Please show us."

This was it. I set my sketchbook on the table and tried to imagine that I was back in my usual chair at the studio, waiting in the wings to add the next dose of magic to the scene in progress. Working with people who knew me and were used to what I could do. "Before I start," I said, "I'd like to ask one favor. I'd like your word that what I show you will stay in this room. Whether you choose to hire me or not, you won't discuss it with anyone."

I'd asked the same of Jonah Eberly when we'd first met. Stephen looked surprised. Mark eyed me intently, as if trying to decide what I was up to.

"Sounds mysterious," Stephen said. "But yes, that's fair. You have our word."

"Thank you." I opened the sketchbook. "Please choose something in this room for me to draw."

When I'd interviewed with Jonah, I'd still been riding on that weightless cut-loose feeling from the train trip. Now, in this room, in this city, the past coiled around me like vines. *Nicky, what are you doing?*

Stephen said, "How about my coffee cup?"

It was a plain white paper cup, the kind you could buy a hundred of for a dollar. I told him it would work fine. "Now tell me how you'd like it to look different."

"Different?"

"Yes. Have me change it somehow."

Stephen shrugged. "I don't know. Give it a handle?"

I picked up my pencil. It held steady between my fingers. Mark said, "Hold on. You're just going to draw his cup, except with a handle?"

"I'll show you."

The pencil glided over the paper. One line, then another. My eyes went back and forth from the drawing to the subject. Now I began to add what wasn't there, bringing the side of the cup out in a smooth arc, adding an inner line. Back and forth from the page to the cup, a few more lines, and now the real cup stood there, slightly shorter than it had been, because some of the paper formed a half-oval handle wide enough to fit one finger through.

I put my pencil down. My heart raced and I tasted metal when I swallowed. Even with my eyes on the paper, I felt the brothers' stares lancing across the table.

"What the *hell*?"

Mark again. "That's not real, is it?" he demanded. "It can't be."

I couldn't sit here staring down like a kid waiting for a grade on an exam. I made myself raise my head.

Stephen picked up the cup. His index finger trembled slightly as he slid it through the new handle. That steadied me a little. "Feels real," he said. He sounded as if he had just woken up, as if he was trying to decide what was a dream and what was fact. "Is it?" he asked me. "You didn't switch it for another one somehow?"

In spite of everything, I almost smiled. How could I have switched the cup when I was sitting on the other side of the table?

Mark jumped in. "He must've switched it. It's got to be an illusion." He leaned forward, his jaw tight. "Tell us the trick."

People will be scared of you.

I set my pencil down. It clicked against the table. At the very least, I had to make them understand that what I did had no danger in it. I took as deep of a breath as I could. The air felt as thick as syrup.

"It isn't a trick." Both brothers leaned forward, listening as if I had been a newscaster delivering the latest updates from Germany and the Pacific. "This happens when I draw, if I want it to. The changes will wear off in an hour or so and the cup will be the way it was." I thought of the day Jonah had first seen my magic. I had stretched one of his cigars out thin and tied it into a bow. One instant of shocked silence, before his delighted shout of laughter shattered it. Now I gave the Allen brothers a version of the pitch Jonah had barely needed to hear before he offered me a job. "I can change anything, however you'd like." I explained how, in an ad shoot, I could make the subjects look exactly the way the client wanted. "Your photographers will get perfect pictures."

Stephen picked the cup up again. He turned it around, looking at it from every angle. "You did this kind of thing in Hollywood? For the movies?"

"Yes." I laid out briefly how Paragon had used the magic. "Even the actors," I finished. "I could make them look exactly right on camera."

Mark cut in again. "You're saying you can change a person? That's not possible."

I didn't raise my voice or let my own politeness slip. "I give you my word, it's real."

"So you could change me somehow?"

"Yes."

"Prove it." He sat back in his chair as if he had flung a gauntlet down on the table.

Stephen set the cup down. "Mark, you can see what he just did here."

"That cup could be a trick somehow. If he changes me, we'll know it's not. He couldn't fake that."

Stephen turned to me. "Could you do something about his nose? That snub one he's got, he's never liked it much."

He turned up the smile again, making a joke, but his left hand patted the tabletop restlessly. I said, "Sure, if Mark would like me to."

Mark said, "No, you can't."

He didn't mean I shouldn't. He meant that nobody could do it, certainly not me, an average Joe off the street with an ordinary sketchbook. Part of me wanted to pick up that sketchbook and get out. Mark was afraid of me, and Stephen didn't seem much better. This was worse than anything I had braced for.

That was one part of me. The rest knew I had to see this through, because – I felt it down to the soles of my feet – I couldn't do another interview if I didn't have to.

I told Mark I could do what Stephen asked. "It'll only take a minute or so. Then I can tear up the drawing, and you'll go back to the way you were."

"Fine." He folded his arms, gripping disbelief like a shield, and looked straight ahead at the far wall. "Show us."

I turned to a fresh page in the sketchbook. Mark's nose looked stubby, all right, but it wouldn't take long to draw it straight, aquiline, the shape that suited a leading man. Stephen's eyes followed my pencil. Mark didn't relax his posture or look at me.

I set the last line in place. His face changed, exactly as I knew it would. Stephen's mouth opened in shock. "Mark. He did it."

Mark's fingers moved over his nose, tracing its new shape. Stephen said, "It looks much better." He laughed, but it sounded shaky. "Nicky, you said it'll wear off?"

I set the pencil down. "That, or I can tear up the drawing now and it'll go back."

"Oh, no, don't do that. Too bad he can't keep it like this for good."

Mark lowered his hand. "Why didn't I feel it happen?"

His mouth barely moved, as if he thought his face might crack into pieces. "I don't know," I said. "The magic doesn't change what's there, it just moves it around. Like shaping a piece of clay." Mark still didn't look at me. I didn't know if he was taking in anything I said, but I went on, "I've thought maybe, because it happens so fast, it tricks your face into thinking it was like that all the time."

"And you can't tell us why it works?"

"I can't. I'm sorry. It's just a thing that happens."

Stephen seemed to pull himself together. "Have you always been able to do it?"

"Since I was a kid. I was always pretty good at drawing."

"Pretty good?" Stephen shook his head. For a slow handful of seconds, we all sat quiet. I didn't dare reach for my own coffee cup; the Allens would have seen my hand shaking like delirium tremens.

Stephen broke the silence. "Right." He turned to his brother. "You can see what we have to do here."

He was sold. Relief washed over me as if someone had opened a warm faucet over my head. Mark said, tight-lipped, "I don't know about that."

Stephen picked up the changed coffee cup. "Mark, what else do you need? This guy just did some kind of fairy-godmother trick on your face. We'll never have a chance like this again."

"I don't like it." Mark didn't relax a muscle. He sat rigid in his chair and talked straight to his brother as if they had been alone. "Magic isn't real."

The Allens were much tougher nuts to crack than Jonah Eberly had been. I hadn't expected that.

It made sense when you thought about it. My magic had gone down easier in Hollywood because the film industry itself ran on doing the impossible. In the 1940s, moving pictures were still a revelation. We were used to radio, which gave us sounds that let us make our own pictures in our minds. But to have the picture itself too, to feel as if we had entered the beautiful world on the screen and sat down with its larger-than-life people, to shed our humdrum lives and take a leap into a glittering place where everything was possible: that, now, that was a dream.

The advertising world was very different. Ads use illusion too, but to push the sell. Ad men have cynicism baked into the bone. Mark had run up against my magic, the real stuff, and it worked on him like sand in a gas tank.

I didn't know what might happen next, so I did the only thing I could think of. "Mark," I said, "all I can tell you is, there's no trick here." I managed to pick up the sketchbook and get a grip on the page

I'd just drawn on. "I'll be glad if you can give me a job. If you can't, I understand." Then I tore out the sketch and ripped it up.

Both of Mark's hands flew to his face as if he thought I might have taken his nose clean off. Stephen's eyes registered pure shock. Then he burst out laughing. "Damn! That's a shame. You looked better the other way."

Mark's fingers confirmed that his face was back in its old shape. His shoulders sagged with relief.

I pressed whatever advantage I had. "You see, it's easy to undo. It would also be easy to do again, if you wanted. I give you my word that I don't make changes unless someone wants them."

Stephen didn't need to hear anything else. "Mark, we can't let him walk out of here. He'll get another job before the day's over." If, of course, I could stand to try again somewhere else.

Mark held out a hand. "Show me that sketchbook, will you?"

I passed it over, and my pencil too. He rifled through the pages. The rest were blank, nothing but ordinary paper with a spine of brown tape. He turned the pencil around and around between his fingers. Nothing unusual to see; nothing to give him the explanations he wanted.

"If we pass this up," Stephen said, "we won't get another chance. Do you want him working for our competition?"

That sank in. Mark's face tightened again. He passed the sketchbook and pencil back to me.

"If we hire you," he said, "you will sign in your contract that you don't do this...trick...unless it's by specific instruction. You won't go around the city displaying this stuff. Understood?"

He didn't want Allen and Allen's name linked publicly with my "trick." Luckily for him, I wanted privacy as much as he did. "I would be working for you," I said. I told him I would follow the firm's directions and no one else's. "On my end, I'd need a guarantee too." I couldn't let either of the Allens forget the promise they'd given me a few minutes earlier. "I would need to know," I said, "that neither you, nor anyone in this agency, nor any of your clients I'd work for, would discuss my drawing with anyone else. Non-disclosure all around."

Mark or no Mark, Stephen was determined to close the deal. "Absolutely," he said. "You'd be a contractor for us. The clients you'd work with would all be required to sign confidentiality." That wouldn't stop anyone spilling the beans if they really wanted to, but good legalese had always worked at Paragon. "Now, Nicky." The smile again. "Brass tacks. I get a feeling you can name your price, and I don't want you getting a better offer from one of our competitors. So what's it going to be?"

His brother threw in the towel, with one more warning. "Be careful. No point hiring him if he's going to bankrupt us."

"Bankrupt?" Stephen held up the changed coffee cup as if it already had the first load of cash in it. "For this, our clients'll pay anything. Nicky, go ahead and write your check."

I had thought this all through yesterday, and a good thing too, because I'd never have managed to do it on the spot. Philly was less expensive to live in than Los Angeles, but I had promised Charley college. I laid out the offer I'd come up with: a guaranteed minimum number of jobs per pay cycle and a specific rate per job, which I high-balled a little for the hell of it. Give them room to haggle. Overall, it would work out to slightly more than I'd made in California, a better-than-decent living.

Stephen didn't want to haggle. "Done." His fingers gripped mine in another handshake and he grinned like the cat who'd swallowed not just the canary, but the canary's wife and kids and all its brothers- and sisters-in-law. "Welcome to Allen and Allen."

Mark shook hands again too, with much less warmth. His expression said he'd be keeping a close eye on me. Stephen said, "Tell you what, Nicky. If you've got a few more minutes, let's nail everything down right now."

It didn't take long to hammer out the wording for a contract. The young secretary, Barbara, typed it up in duplicate, and Stephen and Mark and I all signed. I would start my job the coming Monday.

"Looking forward to it." Stephen clapped me on the shoulder at the door. "This will be a great partnership."

In the afternoon, when Charley got home from school, I pulled out my copy of the contract to show him. "All set, kid."

He read it carefully. "Are you okay with this?"

"Of course. They gave me everything I asked for."

"That's not what I mean, Nicky."

I knew that, and I knew what he meant. After I left Allen and Allen's offices, I had hailed a cab and gotten out of Center City as fast as I could. I'd hustled into the house, changed out of the interview suit, and scrubbed myself down in the shower as if I could flush the job down the drain with the sweat and soapsuds.

The magic was what I had, to build us a decent life. "It'll be fine," I told Charley. "It's a good firm."

He didn't need to tell me that he didn't feel much better about it than I did. *You can do this,* I told myself. *You have to.*

Chapter Six

Minna came for her Friday shift the day after I signed my contract. I didn't like telling her I'd found a job twenty-four hours after I started looking, now that I knew how much her husband needed and wanted work, but she had to know I wouldn't be home next time she came to clean. "I start Monday," I said.

Her mouth set, the smallest fraction. "Then you'll need me to change my schedule, sir?"

I hadn't thought that at all. "No, what I thought was, I'll give you a key." I told her I'd leave her wages in the kitchen before I went to work. "So you can let yourself in, and take your pay before you go."

"You'll give me a key to your house?" Her voice was as polite as ever, but that didn't hide the current of disbelief. "And leave the money for me to take when I finish?"

"Sure. Is that a problem?"

"No, sir. Not for me." She stood very straight, her body poised as gracefully as a dancer's. "It's just that my other employers wouldn't want me in their houses unsupervised. Also, if you'll forgive me saying so, your neighbors might not like it."

As soon as she said it, I saw it. Mrs. Parker or Mrs. Franklin, or even Mrs. O'Dell, who ought to know better, twitching a front curtain aside for an eyeball's-width view down the street. Scrutinizing Minna's every move as she lugged her bucket up to our stoop and let herself in. Examining her again when she left, to see if she was carting off something she shouldn't.

And those other employers, the ones who wanted to stand over her and watch her scrub. Anger threaded up my spine. "I'll take care of the neighbors," I said. "And whether anybody's here or not, I know you'll do excellent work."

She smiled. It didn't exactly look happy. "Pardon me, sir. You're a little different from most people."

More than she knew. We agreed to keep her shifts at the same times, as long as she didn't run into any problems with being in the house alone. When she left that afternoon, she took the spare key with her.

I walked down to Mrs. O'Dell's house. Anything that reached her would soon reach the rest of the street. "Nicky, child." She beamed as if it was my first day back home, all over again. "Come on in."

You didn't "stop by Mrs. O'Dell's for a minute" unless she was in the middle of laundry day or about to leave on some essential errand. Any other time, she would park you in a chair, put the teakettle on, and work around you, if need be, while the two of you talked.

Her kitchen was a mirror of my mother's, with the same stove and icebox and sink. The only difference was the blue-and-green striped wallpaper. "I'm glad you came by." She bustled around, filling the kettle and lighting the gas. Today's housedress was the color of dandelions. "I've been wanting to talk to you. Thank goodness you boys aren't going all the way back out there to California." The neighborhood had known Charley's and my plans before our mother's funeral mass was over. Mrs. O'Dell set the kettle on the burner to heat and sat down facing me. Her eyes were the same warm brown as ever, maybe with a few more wrinkles at the corners. "But now," she said, "it must be hard, giving up your movie job and all. Do you know what you're going to do instead?"

"Actually, I've got another job lined up." That impressed her. I told her about Allen and Allen, holding back, of course, what exactly I'd be doing for them. "Good for you!" she said. "Finding a new place just like that. I had no idea a person could get such good work drawing pictures. You must be even better than we thought."

I'd always carried my secret around the neighborhood, but now I wondered if I'd have a harder time hiding it when Allen and Allen were paying me to take it all over the city. Non-disclosure had better not let me down. The kettle whistled and Mrs. O'Dell stood up. "I know you liked it out there in Los Angeles." She filled two teacups, talking over her shoulder. "It always did sound nice, from what Mary Anna told us." The tea was dark and strong, with stray leaves floating in it. "But," she said, taking her chair again, "this is home. This is where you and Charley belong."

Belong? The kitchen walls seemed to want to squeeze together. Like all the Lawrence Street kids, I'd had countless glasses of milk at this table, usually with a gingersnap or so. In those days, the counters had been much taller, the distance from the sink to the table much wider. When had everything shrunk down?

I sipped at the tea and managed something about how it made good sense to stay here, when Charley and I had a fine house to live in, and he had his school and all. She smiled, the kind of smile I remembered from the times when I'd brought over a favorite picture to show her. "We all know it's easier for him here." She reached over to squeeze my hand. "You always were a good boy."

No. Not always. "Speaking of my job," I said quickly, "I wanted to tell you something else." I explained how I'd be out of the house on weekdays. "You remember Minna," I said.

"The colored girl."

Her tone said more than enough. I got a grip on my temper. "Yes," I said. "She's been a big help to Charley and me. She's going to keep taking care of the house now when I'm at work."

"Going to…" Mrs. O'Dell set her teacup down. "You mean she's going to be in the house when you're not there?"

"Yes, ma'am. I wanted you to know it's all right, in case anybody sees her there."

"Nicky, child." Now Mrs. O'Dell looked as if I had spiked a fever right there in front of her. "Giving her a key, now, that's not sensible. People like that, you don't know what they're liable to do."

She's liable to do anything. Steal from us. Mrs. O'Dell had been kind to me all my life. I held onto my temper with both hands, as tight as I could, as she went on, "If you need help keeping the house up, why, you only need to ask."

"Yes, ma'am," I said. "I appreciate that, but you've done so much already." Mrs. O'Dell opened her mouth again, but I went straight on, "Minna's an excellent worker. Charley and I trust her."

She thought I had lost my senses. Still, though she called me child, I was the man of the family now, and my brother and our parents' house were my responsibility. She let it go, but I knew she and everyone else within sight distance of our house would have an eye trained on our stoop on Monday morning.

That didn't help my mood when I reported to Allen and Allen for my first day on the job. I'd left a note for Minna along with the wages, giving her the office's phone number. If she ran into any trouble, I wanted her to be able to get hold of me.

That call didn't come. Instead, Stephen Allen had a prospective client for my new roster. Carol Willis, or Miss Carol, as Stephen called her, owned La Belle Epoque, an upscale dress shop farther south on Market Street. Stephen ushered me into the boardroom to meet her. "Miss Carol is one of Allen and Allen's best clients."

I was supposed to be ready to jump in and make a good slice of money for my new bosses, not to mention myself. Miss Carol, a strait-laced woman with ginger hair pulled back into a smooth bun, seemed ready to be impressed. "Mr. True, I'm eager to see your innovation." She shook hands as firmly as a man would have. No rings, I noticed, but her nails were perfectly manicured. "Allen and Allen has always done excellent work for me. Stephen assures me you can offer something extraordinary."

I could. As I opened my sketchbook, though, and prepared to show her, an unwelcome thought hovered at the edge of my brain.

At Paragon, we had often lived a couple of steps outside the world. We trafficked in magic every day and escaped, during our shoots, from the reality of news bulletins, of bombs falling in England and France, of American ships going down in fire in the Pacific. At the same time, we'd worn ourselves out during the long days in the knowledge that our finished product would give moviegoers a chance to breathe. Along with us, they would step into a world where the good men always won and the lovers always made it back home. That break from terror and heartache would give them the strength to get up and try again tomorrow. We were nowhere near the front, I hadn't even made it to a training camp, but in our own way, we were helping to win the war.

Now I was going to help sell silks and velvets to women who probably had enough ration cards to buy anything they wanted for their tables. Not the same at all, was it.

Fortunately, my drawing hand didn't need my brain's help to get to work. When Miss Carol's fountain pen changed shape, winding itself into a neat coil on the brightly varnished table, she didn't swear the way Mark Allen had. The only sound I heard was a faint intake of breath. She picked up the reshaped pen and held it on the flat of her palm.

Stephen gave me a cat-in-the-dairy grin and assured her it was no trick. "Nicky's ability is nothing short of magic."

"I can see that." If what she saw frightened her, she made no sign. She tipped the pen down onto the tabletop. A coffee cup would have stood on it. "I can also see why you want to keep this meeting private."

Briefly, in the same matter-of-fact way, she told me how she hoped I could help her. She used models for the ads she placed in city papers, and recently had hired an exceptional new girl, but she'd run into a problem. "The new model's name is Louisa Murray. She herself is precisely what I need. The difficulty is her sister."

It turned out that this Louisa Murray had agreed to model for La Belle Epoque on the condition that Miss Carol also used her sister Justine. I knew Louisa must be something, all right. Most models didn't get to set any such condition. "Justine Murray is a very pleasant young lady," Miss Carol said. Her face stayed carefully blank of expression. "In other essential ways, however, she is not suited to the work."

She described the shoot she wanted Louisa to do soon. It would go in the Philadelphia *Record,* which hit pretty much every doorstep in the city. "You can appreciate, Mr. True, that the photos must be up to my store's standards." If Justine was going to appear in the shoot with her sister, she would need "assistance." "I can put her in dresses that compliment her figure, but her lines would need improvement. Her arms and waist and so on. Likewise her face. She is not unattractive, but she is certainly not exceptional."

Stephen stepped in quickly. "I'm sure Nicky can do all that. He used to work with movie stars in Hollywood. This is the same kind of thing, isn't it, Nicky?"

Movie stars. He'd probably been waiting to toss that out. The glitter caught Miss Carol, though she showed it with nothing more than a tilt of an eyebrow.

"Yes, ma'am," I said. The magic could do whatever she wanted. At the same time, I had never done such wholesale change on a person before. This girl Justine sounded like she had no real business modeling.

"I'd like to meet Miss Murray," I said. It wasn't my job to argue, especially with Stephen sitting there like an angler who just felt a strike on the line. "Then I can give you particulars about what I'd do." Miss Carol told me we would set up a meeting the coming Saturday morning, at La Belle Epoque. Stephen showed her out of the boardroom, beaming as if the extra slice of commission was pie he could already taste.

That afternoon, I got home to find Charley already back from school. He called out a greeting from upstairs. "Hey, Nicky!"

"Hey, kid." I hung my coat up on the rack by the door "How's tricks?"

"Not bad." By the time I got my foot on the bottom step, he and Titus were already coming down to meet me. "You stay put," Charley said. As he worked his way down, one slow step at a time, I thought about what he'd say if I told him to save himself the trip and let me come up to his room instead. Then I thought about how my mother hadn't let me carry her up for a bath that one last time. We Trues came by our stubbornness honestly.

Supper was bacon-and-rice casserole from Mrs. Franklin. Our icebox supply was finally running out. Charley and I talked about his day at school, and the physics class's new unit on sound, and how we'd have to start cooking as best we could manage. We tried to imagine how many ways you could fix tuna and scrambled eggs. Then Charley put his fork down. "Tell me straight, Nicky. Is your job okay?"

I told him it was fine. "And listen," I said, switching gears, "think about if you'd like to do something this weekend." Stephen had said I could take Friday off, since I'd be meeting the Murray girls on Saturday, but that certainly wouldn't take all day. Plus there was Sunday after Mass. "We could go to a flick or something, if you want," I said. For too long, during his weeks and months of caring for our mother, he hadn't been able to take a break for himself.

"I'll think about it," he said. He nudged a grain of rice with his fork. "Hey, you know, you never unpacked most of your California stuff."

My boxes from Los Angeles had gone straight into the basement, after Charley had helped me sort through them for the rest of my clothes. "I don't need most of that," I said. "I'll deal with it some other time."

"But I liked your pictures." He raised his head. "You should hang them up."

The O'Keeffe and Rubens and Benton prints. For a split second, I thought about where I could put them, where those colors would belong on these walls. Then the *no* filled me, loud and clear as an air raid siren.

In this house, I couldn't have the memories of what I'd once hoped for staring down at me. "I'll think about that," I said. "Sounds like you and I both need to do some thinking."

Charley was always older than the calendar said. He thought into things, maybe because he could never rush into them on his feet, and he watched and listened and understood. I should have remembered that he understood me.

He smiled, a half-smile that lifted his mouth at one corner. "Fair enough."

〜

I MADE IT THROUGH THE REST OF THAT FIRST WORKWEEK. Stephen was plenty quick off the mark in bringing me prospective clients. I'd have no problem meeting the "guaranteed number of jobs" part of my contract, and if I didn't care much for the work itself, I knew I'd better hold my nose and be grateful.

Friday morning, I fixed Charley a hot breakfast again. It felt good to set the full plate in front of him and have him tease me about spoiling him, when his grin said he didn't mind it a bit. Once he'd gone to catch the bus, I got out our ration cards and parsed a grocery list. The A&P we'd always gone to was only a few blocks away.

From the kitchen, I heard Minna's key turn in the lock, so I went out into the hall to say good morning. She hefted her bucket inside, lifting it carefully to keep the mop handle from knocking against the window. Then she saw me. She froze, with such a scared look on her face that I thought she figured me for a burglar.

"It's okay," I said. "It's just me." Then I saw the man behind her. He was about my height, slim-built, his skin a shade lighter than Minna's. He wore a plain button-down shirt, jeans with threadbare patches at the knees, and a pair of old hunting-type boots that looked as if they held together out of sheer force of habit.

"Mr. True." Minna set the bucket down on the hall carpet. Her hands twisted together in her apron. "I'm so sorry. I didn't think you'd be home."

The man had stopped in the doorway. "Never mind," he said to Minna. "I'll sit out here."

Confused, I looked from him to her. "I'm so sorry," she repeated. I had never seen her face so open and unprotected. "Sir, this is my husband, Timothy."

Timothy. Who couldn't find work; who had dizzy spells like mine. Minna hurried on, "Mr. True, I promise you, I haven't brought him here with me before. It's just that today, he isn't...that is, he..."

Timothy said, "You don't have to tell him, Minna."

The words were hard, rough-edged. His eyes met mine and shifted away. In that one glance, I saw raw heat in his face, as if he hated me and the house and everything in it.

His boots weren't the only thing about him that looked like a few hundred miles of hard road. His dark skin, stretched tight across his cheekbones, had an ashy, fragile look. Heavy lines etched the corners of his mouth. "Mr. Davis," I said, "your wife does excellent work here. You're welcome to come in and make yourself comfortable."

By the rules of the times we lived in, a man like me didn't call one like him "mister." He looked to Minna. Her hands still gripped each other tight, but she said, "I told you, he's not like most people."

He stepped inside. Now she relaxed enough to close the door behind him. He said, "Thank you, Mr. True." Some of the heat had ebbed away. "My wife was going to tell you, some days I have a hard time."

I could guess what it cost him to admit that. "I know what you mean, sir. I have bad days too."

If "mister" had reached him, "sir" threw him. Not so long ago, I'd have wondered what kind of life a person must have had, if common politeness came as a shock.

I wasn't supposed to call him sir, or offer hospitality, or sit down with him at a table like equals. Those things all happened anyway. In the kitchen, I brewed fresh coffee in my mother's porcelain-lined saucepan. The rich smell filled the room. When Timothy Davis wrapped his hands around his mug, I saw his lean fingers trembling.

I didn't know what he had gone through in France. I could try to imagine the trenches, claustrophobic, muddy, shoulder-to-shoulder; I could try to hear the rattle of enemy fire, smell the powder and smoke, feel the gut-numbing certainty of waiting death. But I had gotten no closer to the reality of it than our carefully staged film shoots. I had no idea what Timothy had survived, but I would have bet my last dollar that the same pair of invisible hands I knew had wrapped around his chest. He had felt his pulse hammering in his temples, felt the floor pitch under him when he tried to take a step, fought for air while the room around him wheeled like a nightmare carnival ride.

Minna turned on the sink to fill her bucket. "Mr. True, this is very kind of you."

"Mrs. Davis," I heard myself say, "if you can't use my first name, I won't use yours."

She turned off the sink. Her face was absolutely quiet. "My employers don't address me that way, sir."

"Yes, ma'am, I understand. But I would prefer it."

A drop of water fell from the faucet into the bucket, splashing loudly into the silence. Then a smile dawned in her eyes and mouth together, and she laughed, a warm and free sound like a bird taking flight. I had never heard her laugh before.

"I believe you," she said. She and her husband traded another glance. "All right. Nicky, then."

While Minna worked, Timothy Davis and I sat and talked. I told him how I had tried to enlist and why I had been classed 4-F. "I went for my physical and damn near passed out, for no reason at all." I followed that up with the other thing the neighborhood didn't know. "Everybody thought I failed because of my glasses. I didn't tell them I never got the vision test."

Timothy had relaxed a fraction, sitting back in his chair. He was cautious about looking me in the face, in a way that made me think of a prisoner, maybe, too used to being struck or whipped for mistakes real or imagined. At the same time, I knew from that first meeting how proud he was. His sickness weighed enough to bend him double, but he kept his back as straight as he could.

He asked, "Do you still get sick like that?"

"I do. Off and on." That, too, was more than Charley knew.

A light went on behind his eyes. I knew why, because I was thinking the same thing. *I'm not the only one.* He said, "Do the doctors know what's wrong with you?"

"Not a clue. At least, they didn't, back when it started. I haven't asked about it since."

That was what we talked about while Minna worked. The things our bodies did, that we couldn't understand or control, that no one else seemed able to explain. How sick we could feel, for no reason, and how we tried to hide it from the people around us. That day, he didn't tell me anything about France. I didn't tell him about my own worst times. We stayed on the surface of ourselves, but it was enough.

I found out later that we both felt the same way afterward. As if we had been floating out on dark water and drifted against something to hold onto.

Chapter Seven

Yesterday morning, I took a cab down to the market. My daughter doesn't always like me going places alone, especially when they're liable to be crowded, but the air was clear and cool and the sky was irresistibly blue. When you luck into a beautiful summer day here in the city, you don't waste it. Besides, I always wear the "smart watch" she gave me – it must be smarter than I am, if it knows what to do if I take a fall – and I never had any car keys for her to hide.

Market Street is one of Philly's business hubs, but what gave it its name, back in the oldest of olden days, was the market itself. The city has changed quite a bit over the many years I've known it, but the market is still very much what I remember.

The bustle. The scents. The colors. If you want to feel caught up in the sweep of the world, there's no better place to go. You don't have to shop at all, although, believe you me, when you get a whiff of some of those food stalls, your billfold will be out and your money in your hand before you know what you're doing. If you don't have any money, or if you've got ironclad self-control, it's enough to walk the aisles. You can admire the shapes and textures of loaves of bread, the sheen of fresh fish on ice, the sudden rainbow of a vegetable stall.

Yesterday, while I was making my careful way along – I use a cane these days, but I still stand pretty straight for such an old cuss – someone tapped my shoulder. "Mr. True?"

At first, I saw nothing familiar about the two men behind me. The taller one, who had said my name, was black, dressed in dark blue jeans and a tangerine-orange linen shirt. He wore glasses with round black frames. The other man was white, shorter, with feathery blond hair, his clothes similarly casual but sharp. They were both in early middle age, though most people look young to me now.

The man who had spoken said, "It *is* you. You don't remember me."

In point of fact, I didn't, though I never like to admit that. He said, "I'm Adrian Taylor. You had me in class way back when."

Memory caught up at last. "Adrian!" He had been in the last class of students I'd taught before I retired, over twenty years ago now. "Of course I remember you, son. How are you?"

We shook hands. He introduced the blond man, his husband James. To him, Adrian said, "This man is the reason I went to art school."

When I'd last seen him, Adrian had been a high schooler in the program I ran. He'd had an easy, fluid drawing style, but more than that, each new technique and challenge had lit a flare in him. It came as no surprise to learn that he was now a professional illustrator living in New York. He and James had come down to visit family for the weekend.

"I can't believe we ran into you," he said. "I'd have known you anywhere. But I have to ask, Mr. True. You told us, back when, that you were retiring because you were 'getting up there.'" At the time, I hadn't been too far shy of eighty, which did count as "up there." What I hadn't told my students was that after decades of work, my drawing hand had let me know it couldn't do the job anymore. Adrian said, "So these days, you must be...how do I say this?"

I kept a straight face. "Old?"

He laughed. "Well, yeah."

"I'll admit it. Don't ask how old, though. I tend to lose count."

The three of us took a turn through the market together. Sometimes, quite a bit more often than I like to admit, I miss the skill I had, the easy flow of putting pencil to paper. Those two young men gave me a great gift. Talking with them, I shed a few years.

This morning I'll go back to Market Street again, but this time only in my mind. Back to the day when I met the person who was going to change everything.

~

The day after I met Timothy Davis, I went back down to Market Street. It was time to see what I could do for Miss Carol and her new model.

Even bright and early on a Saturday, the market itself was crowded. The war years meant thinner times in those aisles. Far less to choose from than usual at the butchers' and poulterers' stalls, a scarce selection of milk, less cheese, and no eggs at all. Dry goods did better: canned and dried beans, milk and egg powders, coffee, sacks of flour and rice. For those with enough to spend, there were still jams and jellies, and bakers with fresh loaves, and smoked meats, plus ready-made sandwiches and an assortment of sweets. There was fish, too, and today, enough fresh fruits and veggies to gather a crowd of housewives wanting that taste of spring. On this beautiful April morning, they stood shoulder to shoulder at the stalls, drinking in the chance to swap news and a taste of laughter. Some of their spring dresses might have shown some fading and wear, but the colors mingled like a garden in bloom.

Miss Carol, straight and proper in a forest-green dress with no frills whatsoever, stood waiting for me under La Belle Epoque's lavender awning. "Mr. True. Thank you for coming."

The shop window made me think I might have taken a wrong turn somewhere and ended up back in Los Angeles. A glittering silver evening gown revealed the bare shoulders and back of one faceless mannequin. Another wore a high-waisted confection made of chiffon, with ruffles and flounces like whipped cream. These dresses belonged on a set's costume rack. None of the women I'd just seen at the market would wear them.

Miss Carol ushered me through the main showroom. Here, a few more mannequins, ghostly in the store's dim after-hours lighting, showed off equally improbable costumes, but most of the space was given over to bolts of cloth. Brilliant reds faded to soft petal-pinks; powder-blues gave way to cornflower and midnight. "My ladies often come in with a dream," Miss Carol told me. "I help them make it a reality."

I could just about imagine how much it cost to have a dream tailor-made out of silk or velvet. At the back of the showroom, Miss Carol opened a door that gave into a little office. Inside, there was a broad wooden desk that looked too big for the room, a mirror on the far wall, and two chairs with chestnut-colored upholstery.

A girl stood up from the nearest chair. "You must be Mr. True. I'm Louisa Murray."

I saw at once why Miss Carol wanted her. Anyone would have. She was dazzling, slim and elegant in a plain navy-blue pencil skirt and white blouse. She had a leading lady's heart-shaped face and cornsilk hair that fell past her shoulders in the sleek curls we called victory rolls. Her eyes, too, were that particular shade of blue that conjured up glass and deep water. Jonah Eberly would have signed her up for a screen test on the spot.

She held out her hand like a society hostess. "A pleasure to meet you." She stood just enough shorter than me to tilt her head up with maximum charm. "May I introduce my sister Justine?"

"I'd be delighted."

Justine. That was the first time I saw her.

Now, I won't tell you it was love at first sight. This was the girl I was here to help, and so I looked at her with an eye to what I needed to change. She was no model. That much was clear. She was shorter than her sister, small-built and round-faced, with dark eyes and soft brown hair, nicely styled and pretty enough but nothing special. She had chosen her clothes in imitation of her sister, but the close-fitted skirt and blouse didn't suit her the way they did Louisa.

Jonah Eberly would have looked right past her. Miss Carol certainly couldn't use her in ads, not as she stood right now, but there was something about her face. Something I could have looked at again and again.

"Mr. True." Her smile had just a hint of shyness in it. We shook hands. "I'm so glad to meet you," she said. "I've heard wonderful things about your drawing."

When she smiled, I had the oddest feeling. Have you ever met someone and felt, somehow, as if you must have known them a long time ago? As if, maybe, you had been best friends when you were tiny, and now you'd found each other again. I had never seen the Murray girls in my life. They came from an entirely different world than the one I'd grown up in, but when Justine said, "I'm so glad to meet you" and smiled that way, I felt a twist deep in my gut. For once, it had nothing to do with another dizzy spell coming on.

Miss Carol said, "Before Mr. True can begin his demonstration, he will need each of you to sign an agreement."

That brought me back to earth. I handed each sister a copy of the non-disclosure letter Stephen Allen had drawn up, which stated that any breach of confidentiality about me or what I did would result in "litigation not limited to damages involved" by Allen and Allen. Louisa read it and raised a perfect eyebrow. "Doesn't this sound serious!"

Miss Carol assured her it was. "If you would like Mr. True to proceed, please sign." She handed Louisa a fountain pen from her desk.

"Why, certainly. Let's see what this is all about." Louisa smoothed the paper out the desk and signed with a flourish.

Justine set her copy on the desk too, but when her sister handed her the pen, she hesitated. Her face made me think of a little girl standing on the end of a too-high diving board, bracing herself to plunge into chilly water below.

I struck in. "Miss Murray, please don't be concerned. If you don't like what I show you, we'll forget about it."

I had no business saying it. Miss Carol had to have Louisa. For that, she had to have Justine, and for that, Justine needed my magic. Otherwise, Allen and Allen could say goodbye to the hefty extra commission from La Belle Epoque. And if I lost this first big client, I might say goodbye to my job too.

But I wouldn't have Justine scared of me. Not for this commission or any other.

She raised her eyes to mine. "Could you tell me something about what you're going to do?" Her voice was quiet, with just a touch of throatiness. "Why does it have to be such a secret?"

Louisa said, "Jussie, it says right here, you have to sign first."

I ignored that. "What I'm going to do is pretty unusual." I talked directly to Justine, to the dark quiet eyes studying me. "Sometimes people gossip, and that can get around. I prefer if it doesn't."

I didn't say *please trust me* out loud, but she seemed to hear it. She gave a tiny smile and bent to sign the paper in a neat careful hand.

"Excellent." Miss Carol collected the contracts and passed them back to me. "Please go ahead, Mr. True."

I had planned this out. The Murray girls needed to know about the magic first, then what it could do for them. I took the straight-backed chair behind Miss Carol's desk and talked to Justine as if we had been alone. When I told her I could change any object in the room, however she wanted, her surprised laughter thanked me for the joke. "But that's not possible."

I couldn't help smiling too. "I'll show you how it works, miss. Pick something and tell me how to change it."

She still didn't believe me, but she played along. The little mirror on the far wall was square-shaped. "Could you make it round?"

"Certainly."

Nothing easier than changing one simple shape into another. She followed my drawing hand, one line at a time. I could feel her laughter bubbling just under the surface. Then her sister gasped.

"Jussie! Look!"

Justine did. At the sight of the round mirror, her laughter vanished as completely as a candle's flame when you blow it out.

Miss Carol unbent enough for a touch of smugness. "Now you see, ladies, why you must not discuss this outside this room."

Louisa demanded, "Is that *magic*?" She leaned forward in her chair as if she wanted to catch hold of me. I didn't answer her. Justine was still staring at the mirror, lips parted. When she pressed them together and turned back to me, her fear wrapped cold claws around my chest.

"I don't understand."

Her voice trembled so slightly, a leaf catching a breeze. I heard myself say, "My dad always called it magic."

I hadn't meant to bring him into this room. Her eyes stayed on me, and I went on, "He was from Ireland." I told her how Dad had talked about the magic back in his homeland. "He said he must have brought some with him by accident, when he came to America." I could feel his arms around me again, holding me that night after Charley's foot went back to the wrong shape. *My boy is something special.* "I can do regular drawing too," I said, "but when I want to, I can do this."

Louisa barged in. "Mr. True, this is amazing! Can you do it with anything? Can you teach other people to do it?"

That let me smile. "If I could do that, Miss Louisa, I'd probably be out of a job."

Justine said, "But now...will the mirror stay like that?"

"No, miss. In a little while, it'll go back to the way it was, or I can undo it right now."

She wanted to see that. It only took a couple of seconds to redraw the mirror. When it went back to its old shape, she let out her breath.

Now I had to explain how the magic could change people. I told the girls what I had done for Paragon, to make our shoots perfect. Louisa was fascinated. "This is simply incredible!" She leaned both elbows on the desk, too eager for elegance. "Could you change me right now? Somehow?"

"What would you like me to do?"

She wanted me to make her hair brown, like Justine's. Colors were trickier than shapes, but I could do it, if I used the right pencil shading and had the intent clear in my head. Someone else might have had a hard time keeping his drawing hand steady, with those movie-star eyes following his every move, but the only eyes I cared about were the quiet brown ones across from me.

I drew Louisa's face, framed by her hair, exactly as I saw it. Next I added a soft layer of what looked like gray shading on the page. When Louisa's hair darkened to exactly her sister's shade of brown, I bit down on my satisfaction. *Not bad, boy.*

Justine's mouth fell open. "Lou. Oh, my goodness."

Louisa hopped up out of the chair and swept over to the mirror. "Gracious!" She primped her hair, patting the curls to make sure they were real. "This is amazing! And much easier than a dye job, I must say."

Justine laughed. It sounded only a little shaky. "You look better blonde."

"Oh, I don't know. Brown's nice too."

I said, "Now, Miss Louisa, I need to undo it again, so you can see how easy that is." She turned around with a faint pout, but gave me a wink, playing it up for Justine's benefit. I tore the page out of the sketchbook and ripped it up. Her hair instantly lightened to its perfect cornsilk.

She agreed the whole business couldn't be easier. "Jussie," she said, "go on and give it a try. You can see it's no trouble."

Justine's hands closed around each other in her lap. "Mr. True, you're sure you can undo it?"

"In a second. All I have to do is tear up the drawing."

"All right." Justine swallowed. "Lou, what should he change?"

Louisa tilted her head, considering. "Well, you've always wanted a different chin."

"Could you do that, Mr. True?" Justine tried to sound easy, but her fingers stayed tightly twined together. "My chin is a little too round, you know."

I didn't know, as a matter of fact, but I was here to do a job. "Anything you like."

In the early days of cameras, a photo subject had to sit motionless, sometimes with a rod up the back of their coat or dress, or even a clamp to hold their head still, because the slightest motion during the film's long exposure would blur the picture. Justine sat that still now, while I drew her face.

The drawings always had to be right, as close in detail as I could make them. This time, the need for perfection had nothing to do with the way my pencil wanted to take its time over the curve of her cheek and the line of her nose. Some critics might have called her chin a little too round for classic beauty. I redrew it, lengthening it, bringing it down to a leading-lady-style soft point.

Louisa said, "Now *that's* more like it."

Justine felt the new shape with her fingertips. She bit her lip. "Why didn't I feel anything?"

I hadn't been able to explain that to Mark Allen either. I hadn't felt nearly as sorry about it as I did now. "I'm not sure," I said. "I would tell you if I could." I did tell her my theory about how the magic "tricked" her face to think it had always been that way.

She stood up, holding herself carefully, and went to the mirror.

When she saw her reflection, she didn't exclaim or preen. In fact, she didn't make a sound. She took in the new shape of her face, running a fingertip over the line of her chin and back again.

From where I sat, I could see her reflection. A glow of delight mounted in her eyes and touched her lips with a smile.

She turned around. "You're right, Lou. This is so much better."

Even so, she asked me to tear up the drawing. "I just need to know I'll change back." I did as she asked. When she ran her fingers over her ordinary face, the last trace of fear left her.

I explained how I could do more yet. I could have done it right then, with the drawing in front of me, adjusting her face by degrees until the mirror showed her what she thought was perfect. I described how, if Justine wanted, we could adjust the lines of her neck and arms, and even fine-tune the shape of her waist; nothing drastic, only enough to set off her figure to suit the dresses she would model.

Miss Carol seemed to be making a checklist in her head. When I finished, she gave a nod that said the total had worked out to her satisfaction. Justine looked as if she was watching a sunrise. "You could do that, Mr. True?"

I told her it would be no trouble at all, though that wasn't quite right. It would still be one of the most thorough jobs of this kind I'd ever done. And, when I finished, would Justine still be herself?

She looked so glad that I couldn't have said a word against the plan, even if I'd had the right. Miss Carol said, "All of this will work very well. Girls, we'll set up your first photoshoot, the two of you together. Mr. True, we can coordinate that with you now?"

"Yes, ma'am."

We set it up for the following Saturday. Miss Carol had a regular photographer she'd bring in. Stephen Allen, I knew, would be delighted, especially when Miss Carol paid him that sizeable extra slice. He'd probably give me another Friday off.

Justine and Louisa were going to stay in the shop now to "discuss attire" with Miss Carol. Before I left, Justine took my hand between both of hers.

"Thank you." When she looked up at me, I remembered Sara on that last evening in Los Angeles. *Don't be a stranger.* Sara had been lovely, more so than I'd ever deserved, but somehow her face couldn't compare to the one in front of me now. Justine said, "This means so much to me. I can't tell you."

She didn't need to. I wondered why it did mean so much; if the modeling was a dream she'd held close since childhood, or if she wanted to know what it was like to be the beautiful one, the way her sister no doubt had always been. I looked down into her face – her ordinary face – and tried to be glad I could give her what she wanted.

"You're very welcome, Miss Justine. See you again next week."

CONSIDERING THAT I'D BEEN OUT FOR A COUPLE OF HOURS all told, I hadn't needed to take yesterday off work at all, but the Allens wouldn't hear that from me. Charley had still been asleep when I'd left the house. I got back to find him up and making himself busy in the kitchen. "Brunch," he announced.

"You're going to cook for me?"

"You bet. You won't be the only one working around here."

By the time I changed out of what I already thought of as the ad-man suit and into a T-shirt and jeans, he'd dished up more scrambled powdered eggs and some fresh cornmeal muffins. "Didn't know I could bake, did you?" he said. "Mrs. O'Dell showed me how."

"Nice work." I spread oleo on one. "One thing we know, we won't starve."

"As long as you can pay for groceries."

Titus hopped up onto the table and made himself comfortable in the empty place that had been our mother's. It was a bad habit, but Charley and I didn't correct him. We each pretended not to notice when the other slipped him a bite of egg, and we talked about Miss Carol and the Murray girls. "Louisa Murray doesn't need the magic," I said. I polished off my first muffin and took another. "Justine, well, Miss Carol's right. She's not model material."

She wasn't...but when I remembered the warmth of her hands around mine, the kitchen seemed to slide out of focus. My eyes wandered to the window. On the house behind ours, I noticed, one of the top-floor window shutters had started to sag.

"Are you done with that knife?"

I'd forgotten I had it in my hand. "Yes. Sorry."

Charley cut a muffin in half, slathered oleo on both halves, and stuck them back together. "You know, I think you liked one of those girls." He could have been mentioning that we were due for some rain. "Justine, I bet."

My stomach gave a hop, as if my chair had tilted sideways. "Liked her?" It was a nutty idea, of course. "I only met her for five minutes."

"An hour or so, actually." His bangs fell across his forehead the same way mine did. Under them, his eyes looked very green, lit up with mischief. "Am I wrong?"

When had he gotten so nosy? The fact was, I had never really fallen for a girl before. In California, I hadn't wanted anyone to get that close to me. Justine was different. I knew that already, as surely as I knew the grain of the tabletop under my hands, but with the heat crawling past my shirt collar and up the back of my neck, I said, "Yes, kid. You're wrong."

"So you say." Charley set his fork down. "But listen, let's talk about something else. You said I should think about what I wanted to do this weekend." I had just enough time to be glad about the change of subject before I wondered why he looked so serious, all of a sudden. "I'd like to go to the art museum."

The air seemed to turn heavy all at once, as if a thunderstorm had blown in and we were waiting for the first drops of rain to splash on the roof.

Not the museum. I couldn't do that. I couldn't ride up the long curve of the driveway, much less walk between the columns, those massive sentinels, and pull open the doors to step into the huge echoing lobby. I didn't even dare imagine it, because my heart began to tap too fast against my ribs. *No. No. No...*

I played for time. My fork didn't want to hold steady between my fingers, so I set it down on the edge of the plate. "The museum? You didn't like that so much when we were kids."

Charley had never gotten as excited about art as I did, but that was only one piece of it. The real trouble, for him, was his wheelchair. He never used it if he could help it, even around the neighborhood; it lived down in our basement, out of sight, except for the rare times when he couldn't make do any other way. A museum trip would be one of those times. It would take more walking and standing than his bad foot could handle, even with help from his cane.

He knew all that as well as I did. "I didn't used to like it," he said. "But you haven't been there in a long time, and I was thinking, I'd like to see it with you."

My chest felt as if someone had wrapped a belt around it. Charley went on, "Because the other thing is, your pictures from California." The prints I'd boxed up and stowed down in the basement with the other things we didn't want to see. "It doesn't seem right," Charley said, "keeping them down there." His smile seemed to reach straight into my head and shine a flashlight on the tangled mess in there. "You should take them out and hang them up. Because you always loved art, Nicky. You and Dad."

Damn it, Charley! I wanted to say it, but I couldn't, because now my pulse took off, pounding like running footsteps in my ears. The air felt as thick and impossible to breathe as glue. I pushed my chair back, braced my elbows on my knees, and rested my head on my forearms. *I'm so sorry, kid. You shouldn't have to see this.*

Charley's chair scraped against the floor. His arm caught me around the shoulders. "Nicky!"

I couldn't say a word. Charley held onto me, his arm so tight it hurt, his forehead against my hair. Seconds ticked past. The room whirled around me, nauseatingly fast at first, but finally, gradually, slowing down, like a merry-go-round running out of steam.

I found I could breathe and raise my head. Charley let go and moved back just enough to see me. He looked about as sick as I felt. "Shit, Nicky. Are you okay?"

My glasses had slid all the way down my nose. I took them off, wiped them, and propped them back in place. "Yeah. I'm fine." Now I could at least say it out loud: "I'm sorry."

"*You're* sorry? Cripes." He peered into my face as if something there would tell him whether I was about to collapse or not. "That's what used to happen to you before, isn't it. When you used to get sick."

"Yeah." I drew in another long breath. The air felt cool and clear, filling my chest. "It didn't happen for a long time."

"When did it start again?"

"That first night I came home."

"That first night? And it's been happening since?" Charley's jaw set. "Why the hell didn't you tell me?"

"It's nothing to worry about. I promise." He didn't need to wear himself out with another sick person. "Now, look, we should eat this good food before it's all cold."

He planted his elbow on the table. "Do you need a doctor?"

Absolutely not. "I'm fine. Listen, let me think about the museum. Maybe not today, but you're right. We should go sometime." I couldn't be scared of the damn place. That made no sense at all.

"Nicky, I swear, if you change the subject again..."

"The subject?" I picked up my fork. It didn't wobble in my hand. "Kid, if you don't eat your food, I'll get a pencil and paper and change a lot more than the subject."

That got him. He tried not to smile, but I saw it. I peered at him over the tops of my glasses, my best mock-schoolteacher glare, and he couldn't keep a straight face anymore. "Are you threatening me? My own brother?"

"Get me that pencil and paper and we'll both find out."

He burst out laughing. "Nicky, you're something else, you know that?"

"Sounds about right."

We went back to the food. He ate slowly, keeping one eye on me. The scrambled eggs felt rubbery against my teeth and my heart still clattered against my ribs.

In another week, I would see Justine again. That was something to hold onto.

Chapter Eight

CHARLEY and I didn't go to the museum that weekend. Saturday afternoon, we went to a ball game at his school, watching from the benches with some of his buddies. It was good to meet them and see how they treated him just like one of themselves, apart from needing a little extra time to get places. It felt all right, too, when Charley introduced me as "my big brother, he's in charge of things now."

As I had figured, Stephen Allen gave me the next Friday off too. On Wednesday, I left a note for Minna with her wages to tell her when I'd be home. She left one back, on the flip side of the paper. *Timothy liked talking to you. He might come with me again. I hope it's all right.*

I didn't have her phone number or address, so couldn't tell her I would be glad to see him. As it turned out, though, no one went anywhere on Friday. On Thursday afternoon, the world shut down.

April 12, 1945. The death of our president, Franklin Delano Roosevelt.

You who are reading this, all these years later: you are used to one- or two-term presidents who make greater or smaller marks in office. I had been in grade school when Roosevelt was elected for the first time, and Charley hadn't been much more than a baby, but the place he held in our hearts had to do with more than his thirteen years of leadership. He took office in 1932, two years into the Great Depression. I remember those years very well.

Imagine struggling, hour by hour, day by day, to scrape together money: not a stack of dollars for a mortgage or car payment, nothing so costly, but only a couple of dimes or a few nickels at a time. Imagine stretching those coins as far as you can, to put some bread or potatoes on the table every night, and to buy enough powdered milk for your kids to drink so they won't hollow out with hunger. Imagine that the elbows of your shirts and the knees of your trousers get thinner all the time, and you slip cardboard into your shoes when the soles wear out, and every day, another factory closes or another plant shuts down. You're balancing on a thread above a pit so deep it goes right through the center of the earth. It's only a matter of time before that thread breaks.

You start to think how easy it would be to quit trying. Then, one day, something happens.

For so many of us, it was a voice on the radio. Roosevelt began that. He talked straight to us, the people who had never been to Washington D.C. and never thought of going, the people to whom top hats and fast cars and full wallets were no more real than Santa Claus. Our President came into our homes and told us he knew what we were going through, and he was going to make sure it got better. We believed him. If you had heard him, you'd have believed him too.

My family was lucky. Phillips Textiles stayed open and Dad held onto his job, though he had to accept pay cuts that meant a lot of meals of bread and oleo, and made my growth spurt, coming as it did in the middle of those years, a source of despair for all of us. Even so, Dad kept his head up with genuine True stubbornness. One day, he said, things would all turn out all right. Especially if that man Roosevelt stayed in charge.

Then the war came. Here in the States, we never had German bombs falling on our cities. After Pearl Harbor, we drove the Japanese into the Pacific, where we would spend the next four years sending countless boys to die in brutal scraps over islands that you had to use a magnifying glass to see on a map. The Axis never got a toehold in our country. Even so, we woke up every day knowing that *this* day, things might change. Hitler might reach out a long arm. Hirohito might sprout wings strong enough to carry him back to our mainland.

For most of the war, up until the spring of 1945, I had been in California, perched right on the edge of that Pacific. People out there were scared. In San Francisco, shipyard guys and dock workers hit the liquor and went out looking for revenge on any "yellow" face they could find. We all heard about the things that happened in Chinatown. The Chinese and Japanese fought on opposite sides in the war, but those distinctions were lost in the fires. And we all heard, much later, about what our government had done with Japanese immigrants who had lived in our country for decades, and with their children, too, who'd been born here. We were scared, as I said. That doesn't turn wrong into right.

But as for me...all through those years, until the spring of 1945, I'd been running from the shadows I had brought west with me. Trying to leave my grief behind. Now, back in Philadelphia, with the news of our president's death coming over the radio, there was nowhere left to run.

Roosevelt had guided us through the long years of war. In April of 1945, it finally looked as if Hitler was about to roll over, and Hirohito might not be feeling quite so brash either. We were starting to dare to believe in that *one more big push and it's over* talk we'd been listening to for the past four years. Right then, when we needed our Chief to see us through, when we were certain only he could get us to the other side, he was gone.

That Thursday night, the night of April 12, Charley and I sat in the dark kitchen and listened to the radio. We barely said a word, except when Charley pointed out, "So Truman's president now." Truman was nothing more to us than a cutout who had sat in Roosevelt's shadow for the past dozen-plus years. We had to hope he'd learned something there.

I know what we both felt, Charley and I, even though we didn't say it out loud. Losing Roosevelt seemed to orphan us all over again. All over the country, in farmhouses and tenements and city apartments and mansions, in shipyards and munitions plants and factories, the same radio broadcasts played, to people who felt as unmoored as we did.

~

THE COUNTRY STAYED IN MOURNING THROUGH THAT weekend, the second in April. Roosevelt's funeral train made its way up from Georgia to Washington D.C. After the procession and funeral service at the Capitol, the president's body went on north to New York, where he was buried at his family's home.

Harry Truman had already been sworn in and had jumped into talks with the Allied leaders. Up and down our street, neighbors gathered to grieve for Roosevelt, whisper doubts about his replacement, and speculate on how much of a difference this might make in the length of the war. On Monday – no good letting the moss grow, people agreed, our Chief wouldn't have wanted that – we got back into our lives.

The La Belle Epoque photoshoot had been rescheduled to the coming Saturday. The days at Allen and Allen stretched out long, in between. Each one of them felt like a sideways shift into another world, where real fears – like whether our new President could manage the job, and how many more of our troops wouldn't make it home, and how far ration cards would stretch this week – real fears like those could never come inside, but only rap on the doors and toss gravel at the windows. Inside the firm's offices, we put together ads that imagined life as clean and sparkling and savory.

I told myself I'd better get used to it. Still, I was plenty glad when Stephen gave me Friday off again, to make up for the photoshoot. Even better, Minna and Timothy came to the house that morning together. In the moment of empty air after Minna told me good morning, I heard *Mr. True.* When she made it "Nicky" instead, the change in her look felt like the sun sneaking out from behind a cloud.

Timothy and I had coffee again. I said before that Timothy was about my age; it turned out he was almost exactly a year older. His quietness, and the way he drew back into himself, made me think of a strong, steady tree, firmly rooted but worn down in weather he couldn't get out of.

At first, he kept his eyes down on the kitchen table so steadily that I wondered if we would say anything at all. Finally I told him how Charley had brought up the museum, the week before, and what had happened afterward. Thinking about it made my heart speed up again.

Timothy saw it. "You're feeling sick right now."

To anyone else, even Charley, I might not have admitted it. "You bet."

With one fingertip, he traced quarter-sized circles on the wood grain, one on top of another. "Minna wants me to tell her about France. What it was like over there." The motion of his hand was quick and smooth, but I couldn't help noticing how, each time his finger paused at the top of the loop, it trembled slightly. "I can't do it," he said. "I think about the least thing, say the damn salt crackers we used to get at mess. And then..."

His voice trailed off. I finished, "You get sick."

"You bet." He smiled, a thin light through shadow.

He told me a little about his time in the hospital in France, after the bullet went through his leg. "We were in these big wards. Fresh sheets, fresh pajamas, soap and water, you can't believe how it felt to be so clean." The men on his ward had seemed willing, even eager, to talk about where they'd been and what they'd seen. "The nurses came around. Pretty girls, you know. Some of these guys would talk them up." He picked up his mug, holding it steady in tense fingers. "I'll tell you something, I never saw another guy get green around the gills when he talked about it." He took a swallow of coffee. "Guys don't faint, Nicky."

The first time he'd used my name. "I know," I said. "But we do, you and me. Or we get damn close."

"Yeah."

We sat quiet while the clock over the stove ticked off seconds. I couldn't help thinking how much more right Timothy had to his sickness than I did. He had spent months on the knife edge between life and death before his wound plucked him away from the battlefield. I'd sat with my pencil in the wings of a film shoot, far out of reach of any real danger, and drawn pictures.

Timothy broke the silence. "You know, Minna likes you. She doesn't have to watch her back with you." By now, I knew more than I would have liked about why she'd have been scared, arriving at my parents' house to find she was effectively alone with a white man whose sick mother could barely get out of bed. More than once, I'd wished for five minutes alone with some of these people who thought they had the right to reach out and snatch whatever they saw. "But," Timothy said.

He stopped. His eyes went back down to the tabletop, as if I had been a prison guard standing over him with a billy club, waiting for him to breathe wrong.

"Timothy," I said, "whatever's on your mind, I wish you'd spill it."

I don't know why he did. He still didn't know me at all, had no real reason to trust me, except that we had trusted each other with something no one else understood.

"She's my wife." He said it to the wood. "I never wanted her doing work like this. Scrubbing floors and hauling garbage to keep us fed."

"I understand."

He raised his head. "Do you?" His eyes challenged me. "You don't figure I'm lazy, I'm fine with sending her out so I can put my feet up and sleep all day?"

"Of course not."

"That makes you the strangest damn white man I ever met."

That was more accurate than he knew, just as it had been when Minna said I wasn't like most people, but the words were the skim on a world of wrong. "My brother and I are lucky to have Minna's help," I said. "Any time she finds something better, and she doesn't want to keep coming here, we'll miss her, but we'll be glad for her too."

Timothy exhaled. "She's got to take the work she can get. If I could pull my weight, it might be different." Tired, he let his shoulders slump. "She says you work for an ad company. You draw?"

By the rules of our time, even a direct question like that could have brought trouble down on him, if he'd asked it of the wrong person. "Yeah," I said.

"I used to draw too. Did a lot of it over there."

In France. "Yeah?" I didn't want to push him to talk about anything to do with the war, but I couldn't help asking, "What kind of drawing?"

He didn't answer at first. Only later, I realized that he was trying to decide whether he and this strange white man, his wife's boss, really could stand eye to eye as equals.

"Make you a deal," he said. "I'll tell you about that if you tell me about the art museum. What it's like inside."

He knew I didn't want to talk about it any more than he wanted to lay out his memories of France. "You've never been?" I said.

"No. Always wished I could, but they don't want me there."

Dad and I had once thought they wouldn't want us there either. We had been wrong, but I knew Timothy wasn't. Philadelphia had no "Whites Only" signs you could see.

I accepted his deal. At first, I planned to sketch out the museum as briefly as I could. I talked about some of the galleries Dad and I had liked the best: the Flemish masters, a special exhibit of Impressionist painters, and the gallery of modern art. Then I found myself telling Timothy more than I'd meant to, how Dad had pinched pennies to make sure we had admission money, how we had always taken the free bus and gotten to the museum as close to its opening time as we could, and how we'd milked every moment before we had to catch the bus back home, the way you'd tilt the last drops of soda from a can. I told him about single canvases that had mesmerized us, especially the Rubens still-life that captured glass as edges of light. I even told him how Dad and I had talked about that particular canvas during the ride back home, and how Dad had brought up the idea of college.

I had never told anyone so much about those visits, not even Charley. Timothy didn't interrupt or ask any questions. "I never did go to school, though," I finished. "And I haven't been back to the museum in a long time."

"Where's your dad now?"

"He died a few years ago." I had to spit out the words the way you would spit out a fish bone in your tuna salad. "Heart attack."

"Sounds like you were close."

My chair seemed to tilt under me. *Not again, damn it.* I closed my eyes, as if that would help. "Yeah," I said. "We were."

His matter-of-fact voice cut through the haze like a breeze through fog. "That's why you get sick, isn't it. Because he died."

I managed to open my eyes. "After he..." I swallowed. "That's when it started. After." The dizzy fits had started months after Dad's funeral, but none of it made any sense; why should the timing? "It's been almost four years." I wanted to shout that part, but I was lucky it didn't come out as a sob. "When do I get over it?"

"Maybe you don't."

"The hell with that. I can't be like this for the rest of my life."

"Neither can I. We're both stuck with it."

The hell with that. I wanted to say it again. I wanted to tell him at least he had good reason to be sick; I still couldn't forgive myself for my own weakness. Instead, because I had to know how much he really did understand, I said, "Tell me something. You ever get that feeling, all of a sudden, where you don't know what's real?"

My worst thing. My nightmare, which not even Charley or my mother had any idea about. Timothy didn't answer right away. I had time to think, *Of course he doesn't know about that, you idiot, you're the only one who's that messed up.*

Then he smiled. "Do I get that feeling? Shit, yes."

Next thing I knew, I burst out laughing. Because he knew what it was like; because I wasn't the only one; because he'd thrown that *shit, yes* down the way you'd toss a losing hand at cards. For a moment, he stared at me in surprise, and then he joined in. We sat there together and laughed our heads off at something that wasn't funny at all. We laughed and laughed until it felt like a knife in the ribs.

Minna came in when we were trying to pull ourselves together. I'd taken off my glasses to wipe tears away. She stopped in the doorway and folded her arms. "Sounds like a playground in here. What's gotten into you two?"

"Nothing." Timothy cleared his throat. "We were just talking."

"I'll say." She sized him up. I couldn't help seeing how he looked right then: as if a fifty-pound weight had lifted off his shoulders. She said, "Don't let me interrupt. I just need to clean the bathroom down here and then I'm done."

After she had gone through the kitchen, Timothy said, "We're both crazy, aren't we."

"Seems like." I wished Charley had been home. He would have to meet Timothy sometime. "You said you'd tell me about your drawing," I reminded him.

"I did say that." In this moment, the prisoner and guard were gone. We were two people balancing on a wobbly plank over a river, holding it steady between us.

By the time Minna finished cleaning, Timothy had told me about how he started to draw when he was five, studying the funny pages in the paper, and how once he got to school, he'd racked up a few detentions for drawing the teachers. "I used to give them cartoon-faces, make the other kids laugh." He told me how the drawing changed once he got overseas. "The guys in my unit, I wanted to do more than just draw what they looked like. Because you never knew what was going to happen, but if I got a guy down on paper, then..."

I saw him there, huddled in camp, with no man's land between himself and the enemy. I saw him taking up a piece of paper and a pencil to sketch a friend's face, to capture more than the shape of the eyes and the line of the jaw. Not knowing what tomorrow would bring. "I used to draw Minna too," he said. "I had her photo with me, but I used to draw her every night before I went to sleep. To make sure I'd never forget."

"Listen to him. Making it sound as if he could've forgotten his own wife."

Minna had finished the bathroom and come back to stand in the doorway. "His own wife," she said, "that he'd just married before he left."

Timothy said, "That's what I'm saying. I wasn't going to lose you."

Just then, they could have been alone together. It was all too easy to see what it had cost them both when he'd gone overseas. What it still cost them now, because the man who had come home wasn't the same one who'd left.

I'm not sure why I crashed in. "Timothy, could I see your drawings sometime?"

"Oh, no." It was as flat and final as a door closing. We might never have traded a single word before, much less laughed together. "You wouldn't want to." He swallowed the dregs of his coffee. "Besides, I don't do that anymore."

Minna hadn't moved from the doorway. "You could," she told him. To me, she said, "You should've seen him. When he'd draw, his hand moved so fast, you could hardly see the pencil. Next thing you knew, there was this picture." Her smile called up the old delight. "Whoever he drew, it would be just perfect. I laughed so much."

I heard Charley's voice in my head. *You loved art, Nicky. You and Dad.*

"I told you, I don't do that anymore." Timothy pushed his chair back. "You finished here?" he asked her.

She was. She gathered her supplies and I put the cups in the sink. When Timothy handed me his, I noticed his hands trembling again.

Maybe that was why he didn't draw: because he couldn't trust his hands to do what he needed. Or maybe, after he had lost someone, and had nothing left of them but pencil lines on a scrap of paper, he couldn't see the point anymore.

At the door, I told Minna I'd keep her posted about the next time I had a Friday off. I wanted to say that if I didn't have one soon, I still hoped to see her and Timothy again. The words stayed in my head because I didn't know how to put them together.

Chapter Nine

T HE NEXT DAY, the Murray girls had their photoshoot. I got to the shop early to go through the non-disclosure rigmarole with the photographer, George Hanley, whose short wiry build said he might have jock-eyed racehorses in another life. Justine and Louisa were already back in Miss Carol's office getting ready. They appeared in the showroom at nine on the dot.

Both wore what Miss Carol called "summer creations." Louisa's deep-blue dress had a high collar, short sleeves, and a bow at the throat. Justine wore a sunshine-yellow sundress with cap sleeves, a deep V-neck, and a narrow black belt cinched around the waist. Where her sister carried herself as if she was going to drink tea with the Queen, Justine stopped in front of the photographer's screen and gave a twirl, so the yellow skirt flared out like a flower.

"I'm sorry." She laughed at herself. "I'm not being very professional, am I?"

I would have liked to do nothing but take in her smile and notice how it brightened every shade of color in the showroom, so that even the mannequins should have wanted to smile back. But I had a job to do.

In point of fact, the sundress didn't suit her as well as it needed to.

Three-quarter sleeves would have looked better on her than cap. The color was good, but her hair wasn't quite dark enough against it, and she didn't have the swan neck you wanted if you were going to show it off so much. The belt was designed to set off a stylized hourglass waist, the kind a man could span with his hands; Justine was slim, but not many women would have been slim enough. And her face, yes, wasn't a model's face. That seemed even more obvious against the fancy dress and the white backdrop screen. It was too round, her nose too small and a little crooked, her smile not quite even.

It was my job to size her up for flaws and see what to do about them. I didn't like it, though, any more than I liked the showroom itself, or the Hollywood-costume-rack dresses in the display window. And I liked it even less when Justine came over to my chair, and I set the sketchbook on the floor and stood up, and she took hold of my hand again between both of hers.

"Mr. True, thank you. I wouldn't be doing this without you."

Why should you have to do it at all? I didn't say it. Another girl might have seemed silly and self-centered, caught up with her pretty face and pretty clothes, but Justine didn't. Though I didn't know why, this morning mattered to her, the way roots matter to a rose.

I managed something about how I was glad to help out and how she and her sister both looked lovely. My tongue didn't tie itself in knots, and my neck didn't flush all the way up to my forehead, but to this day I don't know why not.

We got started. I'll skip over Hanley's reaction when he saw why he'd had to sign a confidentiality agreement. I made the changes Miss Carol and Justine and I had agreed to the week before, fine-tuning them to suit Justine's yellow dress. One line after another, arms and face and neck and waist, Justine's shape adjusted itself until she looked as born to model upscale women's fashion as her sister had been.

Miss Carol had seen the magic before, but she didn't look much less impressed than Hanley. "My word." The crispness had gone out of her voice. "Justine, you look extraordinary."

Justine couldn't see the changes herself without a mirror. "May I look?"

A full-length mirror stood partway across the room, next to a display of fabrics in burgundies and chocolates. Justine hurried over to it. When she saw her reflection, she stopped as if she had run into a wall.

"Oh." The word fell into the room like a raindrop into a pool. "Oh. Goodness."

Hanley was muttering something about "different girl" and "that's not possible." Miss Carol came over to my chair and squeezed my shoulder. "Simply excellent, Mr. True. Couldn't be better."

Justine stood in front of the mirror, looking her reflection in the eye. Slowly, she lifted one hand and traced her forehead and nose, the new line of her chin, and her cheeks, one at a time, which I had drawn a shade thinner to give her face more definition. Her hair fell in the same soft curls as Louisa's, but I had darkened it enough to stand out like velvet against the fabric of the dress. She took one curl between her thumb and forefinger and rubbed it softly. Then her hand went to her neck and traced its new line, and then to her upper arms, and finally down to her waist. She set both hands there, lightly, testing how near her right and left fingertips came to each other, and turned sideways to look at her reflection over her shoulder.

She was a work of art. As perfect as a doll.

The four of us, Miss Carol and Louisa and Hanley and I, watched in silence while Justine took in this new version of herself. Standing in front of the mirror, she didn't smile once.

When she came back to us, though, she was smiling, a perfect leading-lady smile. No twirling or hurrying now; she had adopted Louisa's walk the same way she had put on her sister's style of beauty.

"Mr. True," she said, "I can't thank you enough. It's exactly what I hoped for."

I told her she was very welcome and she looked beautiful. I couldn't let her see how I already felt like a burned-down cigarette, or how I would have liked to pick up my sketchbook and pencil and tell Miss Carol I had done what she wanted and was knocking off now.

The job wasn't over. Not by a long shot. Justine and Louisa would each model a few different outfits and would need "adjustments" each time. I would also need to touch up the original changes as they wore off. Under Miss Carol's eye, Hanley shook off his astonishment and got to work. The girls, bright and shiny as porcelain, moved into different poses for the camera, smiling at each other, pretending to walk arm in arm, pretending to stand chatting like society ladies.

Watching them, I got to thinking about my name, maybe because Justine had said it. "True."

It's an odd name, when you do think about it. I never met anyone outside our family who had it, though Dad had said the Trues went back hundreds of years in Ireland. He said the name had likely once been spelled "Trewe," or some such, until someone changed it along the line so people would know how to say it.

As much as I had ever thought about it before, I'd thought of it as *true up*, where you straighten things out. That was what I did with my sketchbook. Now I began to wonder if it could mean something very different.

After a series of photos in the blue and yellow dresses, Louisa and Justine changed outfits. They modeled evening gowns, lightweight coats, and "casual wear for the home," as Miss Carol described it, which made me wonder what kind of home you had if you needed to dress up in bows and ruffles to eat your morning cornflakes. I retouched Justine as often as she needed it. For every wardrobe change, I did the "adjustments" Miss Carol and the girls asked for. Even Louisa wanted a taste of the magic, as little of a difference as it made to her.

Hanley had started by taking black and white photos, but Miss Carol asked him soon enough to switch to color. "The expense will be worth it." She was going to do a bigger spread than she had originally planned on. I wondered if any of her other models had met Justine as she really was, or would recognize her from this shoot. They would probably think Miss Carol had found another new girl, a rival to all of them.

We finished a little before noon. Miss Carol was delighted. "Excellent work, girls. I know we'll be pleased with the results here." She and Hanley launched into talk about when she could expect proofs and when she wanted to format the ads for release. Justine wandered back to the mirror. Louisa came up to me.

"Mr. True, are you going to tear up the drawings now?"

Of course I needed to. At Allen and Allen, we'd adopted the same cover story Paragon had used, letting people think I had unusual skill at retouching photos or film, and I used that skill at the shoots to make their subjects look as good as they did. I had to undo the changes I'd made before anyone could find out the truth.

Justine, at the mirror, had overheard her sister. "Oh, no, Lou. I'd like to stay like this, just a little longer."

"Jussie," Louisa said patiently, "I'm sure Mr. True has other things to do today."

Justine lifted her chin. "I can tear up the drawings myself. Mr. True can leave whenever he needs to."

That wouldn't work. I had to know for myself, before I left the store, that neither girl showed any trace of the magic. Justine turned to me. "Mr. True, may I have the drawings? Please?"

I don't know how I did it, when I saw how much it mattered to her. "I'm sorry, Miss Justine. I can't do that." I took the last drawings out of the sketchbook, the ones that had all the final touches I'd made to her and Louisa both, and tore them up.

The change barely affected Louisa, apart from a slight reshaping around her mouth and nose. She shook hands with me. "Thank you, Mr. True. Jussie and I both appreciate it so much. I'm sure we'll see you again soon."

Miss Carol drew her aside to say something about a next shoot – "to follow up on today, we won't want to wait too long" – and the two of them moved off toward the office. Hanley was packing his gear. Justine hadn't moved from her place in front of the mirror. I set my sketchbook and pencil carefully down on my chair and walked over to her.

She was facing her reflection, the same one she had seen every day of her life until today. Though she had her back to me, I could still feel her sadness, as if some priceless thing had slipped out of her hands and smashed on the floor.

She had to see me in the mirror, but she didn't look around until I put my hand on her arm. "Miss Justine."

Then she put a smile on. A fake smile, yes, but her real face. The one that made me want to look at her again and again.

"Don't mind me, Mr. True. I just wasn't used to being so pretty."

You're exactly what you need to be. Don't ever think you're not. I wanted to say it, but what came out instead was, "Would you like to take a walk with me?"

I had asked Sara the same thing, more than once. Somehow, the question sounded idiotic now, the instant it hung in the air where I couldn't reel it back in. Here there was no Echo Park, no lake glimmering like silk or fountain splashing in the dark. There were only the ordinary Philadelphia streets and crowds and car exhaust.

Justine looked surprised, as well she might. "A walk? Do you mean right now?"

My neck felt warm under my jacket. "If you have time," I said. "But if you can't, or if you'd rather not..." With an effort, I shut myself up. For all I knew, she already had someone in her life, maybe a jealous type who wouldn't like her taking a harmless stroll with somebody else.

Her smile changed. Her eyes joined in on it, not just her lips. "No, I'd like that. Give me a minute and I'll change clothes."

By this point, Hanley had taken his gear and left. Miss Carol was setting the showroom back up the way it had been before the shoot. I helped, lifting bolts of cloth into their right places with tingling hands, until Justine and Louisa reappeared in their regular dresses, with light sweaters over their arms.

"Yes, a walk, Lou," Justine was saying. "It's a nice day and I'd like one."

Louisa came over to me. "Mr. True, will you make sure my sister gets home safely?"

I promised I would. Louisa and Miss Carol both stood and watched Justine and me through the display window. That might have helped explain why my suit jacket suddenly felt as warm and heavy as a full-length wool overcoat.

Justine's ordinary dress was spring green, with short sleeves and a skirt that fell just below her knees and swirled a little as she walked. Her sweater, which she'd tied around her waist, was plain white. Without the model's features and figure, she looked like any girl strolling along the sidewalk, except that to me, she looked like nobody else in the world.

My tongue had swollen into a wad in my mouth. I worked it enough to say, "Would you like to go over to the market? Maybe get some lunch?"

"That would be nice, thank you."

She looked tired now, shut in on herself. I didn't know how to start a conversation. I would have liked to ask about the modeling, why the changes in her reflection had meant so much to her, but I couldn't bring up what I knew must hurt, and in any case it wasn't my business. I wasn't a friend; I was the person who had given her something she'd always wanted, and then snatched it away again. She had probably only agreed to walk with me as a distraction.

It was a beautiful afternoon, warm and sweet with the beginning of spring. The sky was clear blue, dotted here and there with wispy clouds. A breeze came and went along the sidewalk. In spite of the mild weather, by the time Justine and I walked the handful of blocks to the market, neither of us saying a word, I felt sweat prickling under my hair and all across my back. *Look at you*, I thought. *Can't you talk? Did somebody glue your mouth shut?* They might as well have. *She probably wishes she'd never seen you.* At least there were plenty of other people out. We could eavesdrop on them, if we couldn't manage our own conversation.

The two huge market buildings filled one whole city block, with vendor stalls set up inside. On a day like today, street vendors collected outside too, sitting on stools to hawk flowers, trinkets, and two-pieces-a-penny candy. From a block away, you could hear the hubbub of people talking and laughing.

Justine and I crossed the last street before we reached the market buildings. When we got to the other side, she stopped in the middle of the sidewalk. "Mr. True." No smile. "Why did you want me to come with you?"

Why did you drag me out here, you clod? You might not be surprised that my tongue wadded itself up again. I couldn't think of a thing to say. *You're hopeless, Nicky, you know that?*

Then she said, "Because you don't need to feel sorry for me."

At the angry bite in the words, my voice came back. "I don't, Miss Justine. Not at all."

Maybe I sounded annoyed too. It threw her off balance. She took half a step back and almost bumped into a crabby-looking gray-haired man going past behind her, carrying a bunch of daisies wrapped in brown paper. "I'm sorry," she told him. He sniffed and hustled on. To me, she said, "Then why?"

Because I've been thinking about you every day since we met. Because you deserve better than a fake glamor shoot. I couldn't put the words together, but the man with the flowers had given me an idea. "Look," I said, "let's go inside and get something to eat, okay? And we can, you know, talk some."

By the closest market entrance, I stopped in front of a flower vendor and paid thirty-five cents for a spray of sweetheart roses, each stem topped with a cluster of blooms. They were the deep pink of raspberry ice cream. The vendor wrapped the wet stems in white paper and tied a string around them in a bow.

I handed them to Justine. "Oh," she said. Her smile was shy and baffled and lovely. She lifted the blooms to her face and sniffed. "They're beautiful. Thank you."

Inside, she put her hand on my arm as we picked our way through the Saturday crowd, and held the roses close to keep them safe from jostling. We got a couple of sandwiches at a deli stand, sliced ham for her and roast beef for me, and two lemonades. The market had a knot of picnic tables near the back entrance. We picked one in the corner, as quiet as you could find in that place.

Justine laid the roses in their wrapper gently down on the table. "So," she said, brisk now, as if she was determined to sort things out on the double. "You're not sorry for me?"

Any sensible words I had managed to think of had, of course, gotten lost somewhere between my brain and my mouth. I unwrapped my sandwich and tried to stall. "Why would I be?"

That was the first time I saw the look I would come to know so well: one raised eyebrow and a shadow of a dimple, scolding and trying not to laugh, both at once. She said, "Because my sister is the beautiful one. She always has been. Anybody can see that." One beat of silence that almost got sad again, in spite of the chatter and noise all around us. Then she said, "All right, Mr. True. Then why are you being so nice?"

I latched onto that. My name, in her voice. What was it going to mean?

"Because, Miss Justine, I think you're perfect."

Her face went completely still. I could have looked at it always. I said, "Miss Carol hired me for the shoot, but you don't need what I do. You're exactly right the way you are." Somehow I managed to add, "I want to be sure you know that."

My face felt so hot that if you'd held a candle up to it, the wick would have caught. Justine said, "Then you..." Her hand went to the flowers and rested lightly on the wrapper. "Is this a...a date?"

A colony of frogs might have taken up residence in my throat. I coughed. "I'd like to get to know you better." *Is that the best you can do?* "I mean, that is, if you'd like."

It wasn't Clark Gable. It was barely Lou Costello, but she was smiling. "Yes. I would." The words came out so clear, in the middle of all the market racket. "Very much."

Do you remember how I said that when I first saw Justine, it felt like running into someone I had been friends with when I was tiny? Until today's photoshoot, she and I hadn't known the first thing about each other, except that she was modeling dresses and I did impossible things with my sketchbook. Now, from the way we suddenly found so much to talk about, you would have thought we'd been born on the same day and waved hello to each other from our cribs.

The sandwiches were plain, wartime-standard. Day-old bread, decent enough meat, no cheese or mustard, just oleo and a paper-thin slice of pickle. The lemonade, too, had no real lemons or sugar in it. Justine and I didn't notice where the flavors came up short. She told me she had liked my looks from the moment we'd met. "I think your glasses had something to do with it. You look thoughtful. Smart." Goodness knew I probably didn't deserve that, but I could try to. She reached over to touch my hand, a light touch that sent a current of warmth all the way up to my shoulder, and said, "I thought I'd like to know more about you."

We got rid of the "Mr." and "Miss." She said she thought Nicky suited me better than Nick, and she told me her sister always called her Jussie and no one else was allowed to. "My full name is pretty, but I always think Jussie sounds like somebody's little dog. Fussy Jussie."

It was so easy to talk with her. So easy to laugh. She told me she felt the same way I did, as if we must have known each other sometime back when neither of us could remember. "I don't usually feel this easy with people, right away," she said. "But you know, I wish we really had been friends when we were little." She sipped thoughtfully at her lemonade. "The girls I went to school with were nice enough, but I always felt a little different."

I knew about different. Of course, she and I would have been nothing alike either, back then, at least not to look at. Four years apart in age and from two different worlds. I had no trouble picturing the pretty little girl from the affluent neighborhood, in tidy ruffled dresses with ribbons in her hair. Meanwhile, I'd always been tall for my age, gangly-looking even before my growth spurt, and during the toughest years, semi-ragged like most of the Lawrence Street kids. All of us outgrew our clothes too fast. Our desperate mothers let down pants and let out shirts until there wasn't a stitch left to let.

I asked Justine why she'd felt different from her friends at school. She smiled. "Would you like the terrible truth?"

"Let's hear it."

"I always thought dolls were boring."

I couldn't help laughing. She joined in. "Boys are lucky," she said. Her eyes were so bright and warm. "Nobody expects you to want to pretend you're a doll's mother, or brush its hair and carry it around. Or have little tea parties with little tea sets."

It did sound pretty dull, truth be told. The girls Justine had grown up with had been quite a bit more proper than the ones in my neighborhood, who'd played jacks and tag and, some of them, even stickball as well as anyone. I said, "So what did you like instead?"

"Books."

She told me one of the first things she could remember was learning her letters, when she was three years old. "I begged my mother 'til she taught me." When she'd started school, she'd always taken her favorite reading along in her satchel. "I found out about poetry when I was eight. Tennyson and Shelley. Oh, Nicky, it was incredible. Like walking into the most beautiful place, somewhere you never could've imagined, and you just want to sit and drink it all in."

I knew exactly what she meant. That was what the art museum had been to Dad and me. She told me how, at recess, the other girls would play hopscotch or have their pretend tea parties, but she would sit off in the corner of the playground by herself. "There was a little beech tree I was friends with. I'd take out my poems and forget everybody."

"I used to skip recess too," I said. "And lunch, sometimes."

"To draw?"

"That's right." I told her how, some days, it couldn't wait. "I couldn't use the magic at school, of course." None of my friends or teachers had known about it. But I told Justine how sometimes I'd see something I would have to try to catch: the slant of a roofline against the sky, or the way a chair's shadow fell across the classroom floor, and how I'd stay at my desk until I'd gotten it down on paper. "My friends thought I was pretty strange. My best friend, Jake, he used to ask what was wrong, did I sit in some paste and get stuck to my chair." The memory made me laugh. "It was worth it."

Justine put her hand over mine on the tabletop. "See? I do wish I'd known you. We could have skipped recess together."

We tossed out our sandwich wrappers and found a shaved-ice vendor, where we got a couple of paper cones, strawberry for us both. The bright pink syrup, drizzled over the chips of ice, matched Justine's roses. We made our way back through the market crowd and out onto the sidewalk.

I carried the flowers so she could hold her cone and put her other arm through mine. The ice didn't really taste much like strawberry, but it was satisfyingly tart and sweet. A little distance from the crowds, as we walked along a sunny patch of sidewalk, I got up the nerve to ask her about the modeling. "Have you always wanted to do it?"

She took small, thoughtful bites of the ice. There was something about her, then and always, a kind of magic much stronger and deeper than mine. Everything she did had innocence about it, but not the childish kind. She thought about things, the way she said I did. If she thought about you, and summed you up as solid: why, you could build a house on that.

She said, "The modeling. It's a little more complicated than that. Would you like to hear?"

"Very much."

"It was Lou's idea, really. She wanted to do it. Dad's never much liked the idea of us working, but he said he guessed modeling was all right because our mother did it too, before she got married."

The wealthy backdrop of her childhood fleshed itself out in my imagination as she talked. She'd never liked dolls, but she and Louisa had both loved playing dress-up when they were little. Their mother had let them use her clothes. "Mama had such beautiful dresses. Silk and lace and sequins, and fringe that swirled around." She told me how her mother had pretended the three of them were society ladies together. "Lou and I must have looked so funny. We'd be barefoot in those gowns, the skirts all trailing on the floor, but Mama never laughed. She told us how elegant we looked and asked us wherever we'd found those lovely clothes, who had styled our hair, all those kinds of things."

My mother couldn't have bought dresses like that if she'd wanted to, and if she had, you can bet she wouldn't have let little kids put them on and drag them around. It was hard for me to imagine taking money so easily. At the same time, something about Justine's mother made me think of Dad, how he had held my hand around a pencil when I was so small. *What should we draw? Next time, you'll do it all by yourself.*

Justine said, "We were so little then, Lou and I, but Mama was always proud of us."

By then, we'd made our way along a side street to a little park, where a couple of dogwood trees scattered white petals on the grass. We sat down on a bench in the shade. I folded up our empty paper cones and put both of them in my pocket until we could find a trash can. "Mama said she wished she could keep us little always," Justine said. She brushed dampness off her palm on her skirt. "You know, the way mothers say. But she also used to tell us it made her glad to watch us growing up, she knew she'd be so proud of the women we'd be one day."

She studied a tree across from us as if it might have been listening in. When she blinked, I saw a glint as a tear crept out of the corner of her eye.

Her mother hadn't gotten to see her grow up. Carefully – it felt like a daring thing to do – I eased my free arm, the one not holding the flowers, around her shoulders.

She turned to me then, with her chin tilted and laughter in her face. "Mr. True, isn't that a bit forward?"

Two could play that game. "Should I let go?"

She answered by putting her head on my shoulder. I could have sat that way until the sun went down and the park filled up with night.

"Lou was nine and I was six," Justine said, so quietly I had to bend my head down to hear. "So I don't remember Mama as well as I'd like. Sometimes I try to bring her voice back in my head, but I can never quite do it." She put her hand on my knee. "But I do remember how beautiful she was. When you drew me the way you did, today, and I looked in the mirror...it was her, Nicky. I looked like her."

Oh, sweetheart. I wanted to say it. I wanted to kiss her lovely brown hair. I didn't dare do either, not yet, but I set the flowers down on the bench next to me and took her hand in mine.

"When Lou was going to model for La Belle Epoque," she said, "she wanted me along too, because she said it would be good for me. It would *increase my confidence.*" I heard her smiling. "That's the way she thinks. And I thought, if I tried it, maybe I would like it. Because Lou looks like Dad, but I look like Mama." Her fingers held onto mine. "At least, I do a little. That's the part I always wanted."

That was why it mattered. I tightened my arm around her shoulders. "I bet your mother would like you to look in the mirror every day and know you're just right."

She pulled away enough to see me. "You really think that."

Of course. "If you don't believe me, why, I might have to wonder if it's really me you like, or just my sketchbook."

"Nicky True!" She let go of my hand and reached across me to snatch up the flowers as if I might make off with them. "I hope you know better than that."

"Yes. Because you don't say what you don't mean."

We were, both of us, banking a lot on not much time at all. We had only known each other for a week and spent a couple of hours together. Sometimes, that's all you need. Because she said, "Neither do you," and lifted her face to mine and kissed me on the mouth.

Who's being forward now? The joke was in there somewhere, bouncing around among the fireworks that went off in my head. When she sat back, the best I could manage was "Well."

"Should I not have done that?"

"Oh, no. I think you should have. Certainly."

"Now you have to earn it, Mr. True." She rested her head on my shoulder again. "Tell me more about you. Tell me how you ended up in California and how you came back here."

I said to myself, he's quiet, but still waters run deep. I'm going to find out about him. Another woman had said that, in another life. Sitting on this bench next to Justine, I couldn't have hidden myself away if I'd tried.

I told her about the movies, and my mother, and Charley, working my way backward until I ended up at college and Dad. The warmth of her hand in mine and her soft hair against the side of my neck kept my pulse from speeding up, even when I got to the hardest parts of the story. By the time the sun had worked its way back down toward the rooftops, we knew as much about each other as if we actually had waved at each other from our cribs.

Except for one thing. When I told her about my 4-F, I said I had failed the physical, but I didn't mention a word about the dizzy spells. Justine didn't ask more. She was more concerned with how Charley and I were managing after losing both of our parents. "I'm so sorry, Nicky. That must be so hard." She squeezed my hand. "Can I tell you, though, how glad I am you didn't go back to California?"

By now, it was getting late. Justine's father might worry, and no doubt Charley would too. We got a cab. Justine gave the driver her address, on one of Center City's grand old streets, where the houses looked as if they had been there since the days when men wore embroidered waistcoats and women had to tug their hoop skirts through doorways.

Her house was the last in a row of tall houses finished in pale stucco, each with four floors, a narrow green front yard, and a short flight of marble steps leading from the sidewalk to the front door. Several of the yards, including hers, had victory gardens, with tomatoes growing up trellises and peas swarming against wrought-iron fencing.

I went around the cab to open Justine's door for her. She stepped out, holding the flowers in the crook of her arm. "Can you come in for a minute?"

I would have liked to, but I needed to make sure Charley was all right. Justine and I traded phone numbers and agreed to see each other again the following Saturday, if not sooner. Justine stood on tiptoe to kiss me good night. She went up the steps, the flowers bright against her white sweater, and turned around to smile at me one more time before she slipped inside and the door closed behind her.

The cab dropped me off at home. Charley's cane tapped quick and loud in the hallway. "Where've you been? I was worried!"

"I'm sorry, kid. Time got away from me some. Everything okay?"

The house smelled great, a rich warm food-smell that made my stomach rumble. "Everything's fine," Charley said. "I made tuna casserole. Let's eat."

We ladled noodles and sauce onto plates. Now that Charley knew I hadn't passed out in the dress shop or gotten run over by a renegade cab, he looked so innocent you could have slapped a halo on him. "So," he said. "If it took so long, it must have been pretty good."

"Are you being nosy?"

"You bet. Tell me what happened."

I told him. All about the shoot, and Hanley and Miss Carol and Louisa, and finally about Justine. We refilled our plates and I told him about the walk and the market, and the park, how she and I had talked, and, yes, about the kiss too. There was no point in hiding anything. The boy could be a corkscrew when he wanted.

By the time I finished, Charley's grin stretched from one ear to the other. He reached over to clap my shoulder. "Can I meet her?"

"Sure." I told him he and Justine and I could do something together next weekend. He said, "But won't she mind your little brother tagging along on your date?"

No, kid, I'm not going to leave you to shift for yourself all the time. The house still felt too big and empty. The two of us together, plus Titus, might be able to fill it up all right someday, but we weren't there yet.

"She'll be glad to meet you," I said. I felt sure about that, if I knew anything at all about Justine.

That night, I lay in my old bed and spent a long time looking up at the patterns of shadow on the ceiling. I thought about the park bench, and the fall of sunlight through the dogwood blooms, and Justine's head on my shoulder. She had been right. If we'd known each other as kids, no doubt we'd have skipped recess together. I could imagine us under her beech tree, her with a book of poems and me with paper and pencil, the leaves making a green curtain around us.

Silly enough, maybe, but I couldn't help smiling. Then I thought about how she and I would see each other again in a matter of days. I meant to drift off to sleep with that idea in my head, but something else snuck in, the way a screwdriver blade can slip under the lid of a tight-shut box.

Miss Carol had told the Murray girls they'd have another photoshoot. *When you drew me the way you did, I looked like her.* Justine had looked in the mirror and seen her mother's reflection.

I wondered when that next photoshoot would be. When I would have to turn Justine, again, into a different woman.

Chapter Ten

As it happened, it wasn't another week before Justine and I saw each other again. Sunday morning after Mass, she called to say that her father "hoped I would join them" that evening for dinner. I heard what she didn't mention: that he'd spent Saturday afternoon about as worried as Charley, and had decided to find out something about the stranger who had fascinated his daughter.

At five that afternoon, ten minutes before the cab was due to arrive, Charley came into my bedroom. I was still in my undershirt and slacks, standing in front of the spread of shirts and ties on my bed.

"Cripes, Nicky." Charley glanced at my gray suit jacket and pointed to a light blue shirt and navy tie. "Wear those. Didn't you go to fancy dinners in Hollywood? What's to be scared of?"

"Just you wait, kid." See how cavalier he was when he had to meet a girl's family. "Besides, I didn't do that kind of stuff often." I fumbled with the shirt buttons. "Paragon wasn't a crystal and champagne kind of place. And they were stuck with me, no matter what."

"I bet her dad doesn't care what you look like." Charley leaned against the wall and folded his arms. "Just don't draw him on your napkin and give him an extra chin or anything."

"Very funny." My hand shook so much that I almost dropped the comb I picked up to run through my hair. "Now, listen, are you sure you're okay here for a while?"

"I think I can manage. Try not to be four hours late this time." Charley pushed away from the wall to brush some possibly-imaginary cat hair off my jacket. "You look fine. Good luck."

In the blue early-evening light, the Murrays' house looked even taller and fancier than I remembered. It might have been the turret of a castle where a princess sat at her spinning wheel. Last night, I had imagined Justine and me as children together, but now I was well aware that the kid from Elmcroft, with his beat-up shoes and fraying pants, would never have dared to put a toe on these marble steps, much less smudge the brass knocker with his fingerprints.

The person who answered my knock wasn't Justine or Louisa or even their father. It was a young colored girl, maybe sixteen years old, in a dark, plain dress with a long skirt. The white wrap on her hair looked just like what Minna wore.

"Good evening, sir."

She spoke to my shoes, her voice flat and quiet. "Good evening," I said. "I'm Nicky True. I think I'm expected."

"Yes, sir. Please come in."

The carpet in the front hallway was a swirl of color, a rich Oriental pattern with a deep nap. My loafers and the girl's work shoes made no sound on it. She showed me into the nearest room, where a chandelier dripped light onto antique furniture and burgundy wallpaper washed with gold. The scent in the air made me think of old books.

"Please have a seat, sir." Without raising her eyes, the girl motioned toward a chair with delicate curved legs and red velvet upholstery. "I'll tell Miss Justine you're here."

"Thank you."

She went noiselessly away. I edged onto the chair, hoping it was sturdier than it looked. This room, I thought, belonged in a Renoir painting. There should have been a chaise longue in a corner, where a woman in a white dress would lean back to let her dark curls spill over her shoulders and over the velvet cushions. The whole house felt as if time had left it behind some hundred years ago.

Justine and Louisa had grown up here? What a place to be a child.

For that matter, what a place to be a maid. The poor girl who'd let me in probably had to worry constantly about leaving tracks on the carpet or dropping something expensive. No wonder she'd seemed to want to disappear.

Footsteps came down the hallway. "Good evening, Mr. True."

Justine had on a rose-colored dress, a little filmier and more formal than the green one she'd had yesterday, but nothing she couldn't have worn to sit on a park bench. Her hair fell in sleek waves to her shoulders. I stood up and gave her a bow. "Good evening, Miss Murray."

"You're very handsome."

I wouldn't have gone that far, but it was easy to return the compliment. She stood on tiptoe for a kiss. "Lou has been a little difficult today," she said. "She can't believe you and I hit it off that fast."

"Why wouldn't we? We both have good taste."

She laughed and took my hand. "Come on and meet Dad."

The rest of the house, what I saw of it as Justine led me up to the second floor, was no less imposing than the front hall and parlor. Rich wood and carpeting, paint so thick and smooth that it gleamed, scroll-work in the cornices and brass sconces on the walls. We arrived at a closed door at the east end of the second-floor hallway. "Dad's library," Justine said. She knocked.

"Come in."

The voice sounded brisk and preoccupied, as if the speaker had to leave off something much more interesting to take care of tiresome business. Justine pushed the door open. "Dad? Nicky's here."

It was a library, all right. It might have been transferred, book by book and wooden panel by wooden panel, out of an Ivy League college. Floor-to-ceiling shelves, all of them crammed, lined the walls. At the far end of the room, a stone fireplace held logs ready but not lit. The air had a cigar-smoke muskiness.

Dr. Peter Murray shook hands with me. I could see where Louisa had gotten her glamor. He was strikingly tall, with silver hair, blue eyes, and a profile that would have suited an old Roman coin. It also suited his profession; he was a cardiac surgeon at Philadelphia Hospital. "Mr. True," he said. "My daughters tell me you're an artist."

It might have been the name of some exotic animal with spines and too many limbs. Probably just as well that I couldn't own the title. "Not really, sir. Just an ad consultant."

"I look forward to hearing more about your work. I understand you made a great impression on the girls yesterday."

Then, and not before, I realized I might have made a mistake in coming here, even though Justine's father had every right to want to know about me. I hadn't stopped to think that he might ask what exactly I did at the photoshoots. I had no non-disclosure agreement with him, of course, and I might not have the right to insist on it when he had ample reason to care about what his daughters were involved in. Still, I certainly couldn't tell him everything.

Justine laughed. "He made a great impression on one of us, anyway. Don't forget, Dad, Nicky's here to have a pleasant meal. He's not an intern for you to cross-examine."

Her father's smile made him much better-looking. "You'll have to pardon me, Mr. True. My girls can tell you, their father is an old stick who works a great deal and forgets how to talk to people."

"Not to worry, sir." To my relief, Louisa breezed in right then, perfect in lavender, to tell us dinner was ready. She and Dr. Murray led the way downstairs.

The size of the dining room suggested that the table normally had leaves in it and enough room to seat a dozen or more. As it was, the china and silver, arranged on a spotless cream-colored cloth, made a little island in the middle of the space. Dr. Murray and Louisa sat at the top and bottom of the table, with Justine and me facing each other across the middle. Justine told me, "I thought we could have had a family dinner in the kitchen, but Dad said no."

Her teasing softened his sternness. He said, "It seems only fair that a new guest should be treated as a guest. Properly."

I told him I appreciated the compliment. If this was the kind of treatment the Murrays' guests got, I had good reason to be glad for the few times I'd been strongarmed into Hollywood opening-night dinners and afterparties. I'd never been much for that kind of elbow-rubbing, especially in the top-end apartments with grand pianos and wall-to-wall mirrors for the guests to admire their own finery, but at least the kid from Elmcroft had learned how not to fumble a crystal water glass or clatter heavy silverware against his plate.

The young maid brought in dinner. As I'd guessed, war shortages had skimmed right past this house. Steak, boiled potatoes with butter, and asparagus in lemon sauce: I hadn't eaten anything like this since leaving California. The girl set the plates carefully down on the table and slipped away in silence.

Dr. Murray cut into his steak. Red juice welled onto the gilt-trimmed china. "Justine says you've had an interesting career," he said. "You grew up here in the city, but worked in Los Angeles?"

"Yes, sir." I maneuvered knife and fork carefully to cut into my own portion. "I was a production assistant at Paragon Films." The meat was cooked to a turn. I'd have liked to savor it, but between Justine's father's eyes on me and the strangeness of eating something so rich, the best I could do was chew and swallow carefully.

"Working in the film industry must have been quite interesting."

"Yes, sir."

To my relief, he didn't ask exactly what I had done at Paragon, maybe because an "artist's" work was so foreign to him. He did ask why I had chosen to move so far away, so I explained as little as I could.

"A 4-F? I understand your regret." He salted a bite of potato. "If I were a young man, I would likely feel the same. But as one who has now watched the progress of two great wars, I can only say I have never seen such waste of life."

"Dad!" Louisa had been eating quietly. Now she sat forward, as if she'd been waiting for a chance to get in on the talk. "As if somebody shouldn't serve if he could. He's been so silly about it, you know," she told me. "He wouldn't so much as think about letting Jussie and me go to work, when we both wanted to. And plenty of women have," she added, obviously for his benefit.

Dr. Murray kept his eyes on his knife and fork. "If it comes to going to work, it seems to me that you and your sister have done exactly that."

"Not the modeling, Dad." Louisa tossed her beautiful hair. "You know I wanted the kind of job other girls got. Real hours and real work, to make a difference."

If I'd had to guess, I would have thought she was the kind of girl who'd be happy enough to stay in her comfortable life, with the rest of the world on the other side of a solidly deadbolted door. Now I wasn't so sure. Her father said, "Forgive me for saying it, my dear, but you are not a Rosie the Riveter type."

As hard as it was to picture those manicured hands stained with grease and oil, the set of her jaw made me wonder about that too. No doubt she'd had this out with him any number of times before. Justine chipped in, in a voice that reached one hand out to her father and the other to her sister. "Dad wants to be sure we behave ourselves. It's a big job for him, bringing up two girls."

"It is," Dr. Murray said. "You might imagine, Mr. True, that I wish my daughters to be happy and respectable. I don't wish them to be troubled by anything unnecessary."

He had a pretty broad definition of "unnecessary," it seemed to me, when we were talking about a war that had gone on for four years and counting and had dragged in just about every nation that could offer up warm bodies to hold weapons. We'd been insulated enough at Paragon, wrapped in our screen magic, and Allen and Allen was, if anything, worse, but Dr. Murray seemed to have burrowed into such a thatch of cotton wool that he might never get out.

Louisa said, "Working is respectable. And don't pretend you don't feel the same way I do, Jussie."

"Of course I do. I wanted a job just as much as you did." She wasn't one to raise her voice. She didn't have to, when the flush in her cheeks told me exactly how she felt about sitting on her hands and watching the world through whatever keyholes she could find. "But we send letters to the front, at least." She smiled at me. "We can cheer the boys up a little. That's something."

It was. I was glad she had that. At the same time, a little uneasiness eddied through me at the idea of how many soldiers she might be writing to. Some of those men fell in love with girls they knew only on paper. Of course they did, when the letters arrived like the first spring bloom after a gray winter, and carried them home at least for the length of time it took to read the neat script on a front-and-back page. Some men even sent proposals of marriage to a sweet face they'd never met. Deep in an uneasy corner of my mind, I wondered, if someone sent one to Justine, what chance I would have against a real war veteran.

The young maid came in again, carrying a pitcher of ice water. She filled Dr. Murray's glass first, then mine. Dr. Murray didn't seem to notice her. When I thanked her, she kept her eyes down. "You're welcome, sir."

Dr. Murray was picking up the argument again, saying something about how women might work if they must, but he didn't intend his girls to live that kind of life. The maid filled Louisa's and Justine's glasses and moved toward the door. Dr. Murray stopped her on her way past his chair. "Sarah. One moment."

She flinched. I saw her lift her eyes to his face and lower them again. "Yes, sir?"

"Send Rebecca in."

"Yes, sir." Her quick, light footsteps headed away, as fast as they could go without running.

Justine looked uncomfortable. "Dad."

"Now, ladybug." Dr. Murray could have been humoring a child. "It's important to correct the staff when they need it. Otherwise, how will they learn?"

The swinging door creaked again to let the cook, Rebecca, in. She looked old enough to be Sarah's mother or even Minna's, her features narrow, a hint of crows'-feet at the corners of her eyes. She wore the same uniform too, dark dress and white apron, white wrap on her hair. Her face had a quietness I knew very well.

"Sir." She faced Dr. Murray as if the rest of us weren't there. "You wanted to see me?"

Dr. Murray kept eating, as if it was too much trouble to set his fork down and look at her. "Rebecca, I gave precise instructions on the cooking of the steak." His voice was cold and distant.

Rebecca stood very straight, her hands clasped behind her. Unless I was imagining things, she kept her eyes on the far wall, on a spot just above her employer's head. "Yes, sir."

"I find it dry. This is unacceptable."

Justine looked down at her plate. Louisa was watching her father. I saw her bite her lip, as if she half-wanted to say something.

Rebecca said, her voice flat, "I'm sorry, sir."

"Negligence cannot be tolerated, particularly when we have a guest. I should not have to remind you of this household's standards."

My neck felt hot. *This household's standards.* I'd thought the steak was perfectly cooked. Dr. Murray was the only one still eating now. If he would at least glance at the woman, I thought. If he'd act as if she was worth that much.

Rebecca said again, "I'm sorry, sir." Her voice and face had no emotion in them.

"Next time," Dr. Murray said, "you will follow my instructions. I will not need to reprimand you again."

As if she had been a child called up to the blackboard at school for not studying enough. "Yes, sir."

"Very well. You may go."

She did. I wanted to stand up and say, *Don't listen to him! The dinner's great!* I didn't dare. This was his house, and I was a guest.

The kitchen door swung shut behind her with a final-sounding thump. Dr. Murray turned to me. "I do apologize, Mr. True. Rebecca has been with us since the girls were small, and I would prefer not to have to let her go, but sometimes there are difficulties. Colored people are terribly unreliable."

He smiled, inviting me to share a joke. The handle of my fork, with its heavy scrollwork, dug into my palm. "I wouldn't know about that, sir." In my head, I saw Minna hoisting her heavy bucket. "My brother and I do our own cooking these days. This meal is a treat."

"I'm glad you find it so."

The talk turned. Sarah brought in dessert, lemon pie with a spongy filling so light it could have floated right out of the crust, and coffee. Dr. Murray offered his condolences about my mother. "I understand you have custody of your brother now." That brought the conversation back to my job and how good it was that I had the means to take care of Charley. "I do look forward to seeing the photographs from the shoot," Dr. Murray said. "Justine assures me I'll be impressed."

Before I could answer, Louisa struck in. "You will, Dad." She looked me straight in the eye. "What Mr. True did was nothing short of magic."

Maybe she had annoyance to burn, and I was an easy target, or maybe it was a delayed comeuppance for keeping her sister out so late yesterday. Either way, her smile told me she knew exactly how close she'd put her toe to the line we'd agreed not to cross. A shiver spiraled up my spine.

Dr. Murray, of course, didn't know what she meant. Justine did. "You're right, Lou. Nicky's drawing is wonderful. But, Dad," she said, as lightly as if she was telling a joke, "we aren't supposed to say a lot about what he did, even to you. If word gets out, all the other girls would want the same treatment."

"I quite understand," Dr. Murray said. "One has to be careful with trade secrets."

Justine set her dessert fork on the edge of her plate. Under her father's nose, she reached across the table to take my hand.

Well. Dr. Murray sized up our two hands there against the table-cloth, and you could see everything about photo shoots and mysterious "trade secrets" draining out of his memory. His daughter had serious feelings for this nondescript ad consultant she had met only a week ago. You had to give him credit: his face showed no hint of what was going on behind it.

"I will be glad to see your work, Mr. True." He took a sip of coffee. "My daughter certainly appreciates you."

That was one way to put it. Laughter swirled up my throat. I bit down on it before it could fly out of my mouth. "I'm glad, sir. I appreciate her very much too."

Sarah came in to clear the table. Dr. Murray went back to his library and Louisa swept off somewhere. Justine and I had tacit permission to take time to ourselves. We went out back, into a little garden with a wrought-iron bench in front of a rose trellis. The air smelled light and sweet.

Justine drew me down to sit next to her on the bench. "I'm sorry about all that." She sounded tired. "Dad and Lou, I mean."

I could bet it got tiring to live with the two of them, such take-charge people. "Lou likes attention," Justine said. "You probably guessed that. She's a good sister, really. She cares about me, and she looks out for me, but I think she's always trying to prove something."

"What does she have to prove?"

Justine covered my hand with hers and ran her finger thoughtfully over my knuckles. "Sometimes, I think...she's always had crowds of boys around, but she's so pretty that maybe they're scared of her, or maybe they don't see past her looks. She never seems to get to know any of them."

They probably didn't get to know her either. Maybe they thought what I had: she was a lovely sculpture, meant only to sit and be beautiful. Maybe, for all the attention she got, Louisa was lonely.

"Of course," Justine said, "I don't know who'd satisfy her. She's like Dad that way too. Nothing's good enough."

I'd certainly seen that with her father. Thinking of Rebecca, I started, "Your dad..." I had to be careful what I said. "He seems strict, for sure. I thought the cook did a wonderful job."

"Oh, she did." Justine leaned against my shoulder. "Dad wouldn't fire her, no matter what he says. Sometimes it seems like he has to remind people he's in charge."

I thought about Minna filling her bucket at the kitchen sink, and of Timothy's worn face, and how he and I had laughed so hard together for no reason. I wondered if I might ever be able to tell Justine about any of that. "When I was little," she said, "I used to help Rebecca in the kitchen. Or try to, anyway." Her laugh sounded tired too. "I wanted to learn how to cook. She taught me a couple of things, sifting flour and separating eggs, but then Dad found out and put a stop to it. His daughters don't do that sort of thing."

They didn't get regular jobs either, from the sound of it. I hoped that wasn't too sore of a subject to bring up. "When you wanted to get work, what did you want to do?"

"Oh, we weren't sure." She told me that when Pearl Harbor happened, Louisa had been out of high school, but Justine herself still had a year and half to go. "We thought she could find work first, and then maybe I could get hired at the same place once I graduated. We weren't trying to be Rosie the Riveter. Dad's right about that. I'd barely know which end of a wrench was up."

She tried to make it a joke, but she sounded so sad. "Hey," I said, "no shame in that." I thought of what she'd said about the dolls. "Girls are lucky. You're not supposed to like banging on things with hammers, or making a mess with a saw."

That made her laugh. "I thought men did like handy work."

"Drawing's better. Quieter, for one thing."

"That's fair." Her fingers closed around mine. "Well, Lou and I thought maybe we could be secretaries or something, regular women's work. Because some of those women were taking men's jobs instead."

"But your dad said no."

"That's right." Another drop of sadness in the quiet air. "Nicky, can I tell you something?"

"I should say so."

She squeezed my hand, a smile I could feel. "I hope I can explain it. Lou feels the same, I think, but we don't really talk about it, because..." In the pause, I could feel her threading words together. "The way we grew up...if Mama had been here, I think things might've been different. Dad's always taken good care of us, but what he thinks is important..." Then, "I never wanted to be just a girl playing dress-up, but, you know, I don't know how to do much of anything." She turned her face toward my shoulder, so the next words came out muffled. "Sometimes I feel useless."

Her house had seemed like a capsule that time had left behind. Now I saw the two girls growing up in it like flowers in a greenhouse, never feeling real sun or tasting real rain. And *useless*?

I pressed a kiss on her hair. "You're not useless." It came out angrier than I'd meant. "Don't you think that for a minute."

She sat up to see me. "But do you understand what I mean?"

"Of course."

"I thought you would."

After that, we talked about easier things, in the peaceful half-light. Justine told me how she and her mother had planted the roses back when Justine was little. "I remember how much fun it was, getting to dig in the dirt." I got up the nerve to ask her about the soldiers she wrote to overseas, and she laughed, warm and happy. "Don't you worry. I don't listen to flattery. Besides, I like to be able to look a man in the eye before I make up my mind about him." When it was time for me to go, she walked me around front and gave me another kiss before I got into the cab. "See you soon?"

"Yes, ma'am."

That night, long after Charley had gone to bed and the house was quiet, I lay awake thinking about Rebecca's eyes fixed on the wall above her employer's head, and the maid Sarah's tense face, and how Dr. Murray had sat there working his heavy silverware while the steak's red juice pooled on the plate. Rebecca could cook that steak, but did she ever get to taste it?

Those thoughts nudged me back out of bed and downstairs to the kitchen. Minna would be coming in tomorrow to clean. I didn't know when I'd be home for another of her shifts, so I wrote her a note, standing barefoot on the linoleum with Titus coiling around my ankles.

Good morning, Minna –

Hope you're well. When I saw you last week, Timothy mentioned he would like to visit the art museum. Charley and I have been talking about that too, so I thought sometime the four of us might go together. Please let me know what you think.

Thanks,

Nicky

Of course I had to be crazy. How did I plan to walk into that place, when just thinking about it made me too dizzy to stay on my feet? But there was Dr. Murray's voice, too, passing down judgment. *Colored people are terribly unreliable.*

Timothy had loved to draw. The museum's doors were closed to him. It was time to see about that.

Chapter Eleven

THE NEXT MORNING, I got to work to find Mark Allen waiting by my desk. He was impeccably dressed as usual, in a navy suit with the jacket buttoned up and a shirt collar so well starched you could have rolled it across the floor like a wheel. "I'd like a word." He kept his voice down so that Maurice Barclay and Gus Haskins, the agency's other two artists, couldn't listen in from their drawing boards. "Let's go to my brother's office."

Stephen was leafing through the Philadelphia *Record* with his polished two-tone Oxfords up on his desk. He had taken his suit coat off and loosened his tie. When Mark and I turned up in the doorway, he closed the paper. "What's up?"

"We're going to have a problem," Mark said. "If we don't already."

Stephen swung his feet down to the floor. "Shut the door. Have a seat, both of you."

Mark sat stiffly upright in one of the chairs in front of Stephen's desk and launched in. What he had to say didn't surprise me. Dr. Murray had gotten me thinking about the same issue last night, or rather, Louisa had, with what she'd said in front of her father.

Confidentiality.

In the movies, I'd worked on any number of film shoots, but most often with the same group of people. Any newcomers always got a quick education on why it was in everyone's best interests to keep my talent quiet. Here at Allen and Allen, things already felt different. I had built up a pretty big client roster in the few weeks since I'd joined the firm: the La Belle Epoque contract, of course, plus two florists, a high-end grocer, two hairdressers, a maker of hand-carved wooden pipes, and a Rittenhouse Square imports boutique. If Stephen had his way, plenty of other businesses would join that lineup.

Every new client I worked with had to learn my secret. Not only the clients themselves, either, but anyone and everyone involved in the photoshoots. Models like the Murray girls. Grocers' boys who hauled produce in for the shots. Photographers galore. I could spend half my worktime standing over people, feeding them legalese, watching them sign agreements. Mark sketched that out for Stephen and said he believed it was only a matter of time before somebody spilled the beans. "We're using Nicky too much already," he said. "Every time someone new finds out about him, we don't know what could happen."

He had never liked me. He had distrusted the magic from the first time he'd seen it. Dad had said it, all those years ago: *People will be scared of you.*

Stephen said, "So you think there'll be trouble."

"There's bound to be." Mark's voice stayed level and pleasant, but the fingers of his left hand worked at the crease in his pant leg. "We can't keep him a secret forever."

If Stephen had asked me what I thought, I would have said Mark wasn't wrong. He didn't ask.

"Let me point out a couple of things," he said. "First, every one of Nicky's clients signs non-disclosure, as we agreed when he started with us. We have all those letters on file, for every shoot he does. That's producible evidence in a court of law."

Mark leaned forward again, but Stephen talked over him. "Second, you know how many of our top contracts we've revised since he got here, and how much extra profit that means already. Want me to run those numbers for you again?"

"You don't need to," Mark said. "But..."

"And he's only getting started." Stephen sat back in his chair and tucked his thumbs under his suspenders, which were teal-blue today. "So I don't think we should tell him to forget that guaranteed-number-of-jobs piece of his contract and sit on his hands, do you?" He sounded half amused, half irritated. *Why do I have to explain this to you?*

A yardstick would have gone down the back of Mark's jacket without touching the fabric. "I'm not saying we shouldn't use him at all," he said. "We can hold up our end of his contract with more regular jobs to make up his quota." I did a handful of those jobs now, mostly as a way to keep my cover, so that no one at the company except Stephen and Mark would know what I'd actually been hired to do. "Ordinary artwork," Mark said, "instead of the...magic."

I don't believe he could have kept that pause out if his life had depended on it. Stephen studied him as if he had been a discrepancy in the work accounts, a possible nuisance, hard to say how big. "Ordinary artwork," he said.

"Yes." Mark crossed his right leg over his left, then put both feet back on the floor. "His drawing is very good. He could take a bigger share of the regular jobs. There's enough work to go around."

Stephen turned to me as if he'd finally remembered I was there. "Nicky, what do you think about all this?"

He kept a straight face, but I saw laughter in his eyes. *Fill up your quota with regular stuff? Mark's a great guy, but what a goofy idea.* He thought I would agree with him, as if I'd been his other little brother and the two of us were kidding about how boneheaded Mark could be.

But I wasn't another Allen brother. I had to be careful. "I know there's a lot of regular work," I said, "but I don't want to take too much away from Barclay and Haskins."

"Exactly," Stephen said. "And when it comes down to it, that stuff is a waste of your skill."

"But," I said, "Mark's right. Someone could talk, any time." Louisa had certainly thought about it. "That would make trouble for me, of course."

"And for this firm," Mark said. "If rumors got started, can you imagine how they would sound? People would think we were out of our minds."

Stephen hadn't expected me to side with his brother. He ran a hand over his dark hair, a shade less confident than he'd been. "Obviously, anyone who wants to talk can talk, but why should they risk it? We have the muscle to hold them accountable."

You never knew what people might do. I said, "The thing about a lawsuit, sir, is if it comes to that, the secret'll be out in the open as it is."

Imagination rolled out a reel of film. Suppose I had to get up in front of a judge and explain the nature of my job. *Mr. True, do you honestly expect the court to believe this nonsense? Well, your Honor, maybe you'd like me to show you...* There was also the issue of what the newspapers would do with a story like that. The whole business would be all over the city in a matter of hours.

It might not stop there, either. *You could be famous,* some of the Paragon actors had told me. Certainly. In my nightmares.

Mark said, "He's right," but Stephen wasn't listening. "Nicky," he said, "I thought you weren't going to call me sir."

I hadn't realized I had. "I'm sorry."

Stephen grinned. "All right, boys. I have to settle this, so look here, both of you." He leaned his elbows on his desk. Even with his formal shirt and stiff collar, his smile made him look as young as Charley. "I hear what you're saying. We'll be careful, I promise you that. Nicky, we won't overload you, and we'll make sure we only hand you over to clients we know we can trust. Some people do like to gossip. Those people won't get the goods, agreed?"

We had to hope none of them had gotten the goods already, but I wasn't trying to lose my job. I said it sounded fair to me. Mark wasn't so sure. "Some people might still talk."

"That's a risk we take. We'll clean up a mess if we have to, but for now, I'm going to bet that people have better sense. All right?"

He was through discussing it. "Fine," Mark said. "Let's hope they do."

"Good. Now go get back to work, both of you."

In the main office, Mark said quietly, "My brother's got his mind on the money." He turned his back to the secretary at her desk, so she wouldn't hear. "You're useful there, I don't deny it, but I still don't like it."

I wanted to say, *I don't blame you.* "If this goes wrong," he said, "he can't say I didn't warn him."

~

THAT AFTERNOON, CHARLEY HAD ONE OF HIS TWICE-WEEKLY meetings after school to work on the yearbook. I got home ahead of him. Minna had left a note on the counter on the other side of mine. I'd noticed her handwriting before: neat but fluid, the kind that showed that a person wrote often and was comfortable with it.

Good afternoon, Nicky,

I'll ask Timothy about the museum, but I don't think he'll want to go. He doesn't go out much, especially to places where other people might see him. I think you understand.

We'll see you another time when you're home. Hope all is well,
Minna

In the very back of my mind, I had started to think about what it might be like to visit the museum with someone else who loved art. I had thought, just maybe, it might push a door open a crack, enough to get Timothy talking about his drawing. Now I didn't know when I would see him and Minna next. On the other hand, it felt like a heavy winter coat dropping off my shoulders to know I wouldn't have to try to walk into those galleries after all.

By the time Charley got home, I'd changed out of my work clothes, tossed Minna's note, fed Titus, and started cobbling dinner together. I'd stopped at the A&P on the way home for some cheap ground chuck. You could make pretty decent burgers on the stove, if you heated a skillet hot enough.

Charley told me about school and the yearbook meeting. "Some of those senior photos could've used your help," he joked. We ate the burgers on bread toasted in the oven, with a dollop of yellow mustard on each. "Not bad," Charley said. "We do all right for a couple of bachelors."

"I'll say we do."

When he was still very small, before he started school, Charley had helped our mother out in the kitchen. A picture flicked up in my memory: him sitting at the table one Sunday afternoon, wrapped in an old shirt of Dad's for a smock, flour dusting his cheeks and hair. He held onto our mother's heavy wooden rolling pin, one little hand gripping each end. Our mother stood behind him with her hands covering his. Together, the two of them rolled out the soft mound of biscuit dough on the tabletop. Their laughter mixed and floated in the air.

As if I had conjured up the past for him too, Charley said, "Do you remember Mom's potato soup?"

Of course I did. We used to have it on Sundays as a special treat: thick and creamy, with soft chunks of potato and sweet-sharp cubes of onion, and bacon crumbled in when the grocery budget would stretch that far. We all used to take seconds, thirds if we could get them.

The memory was enough to make my mouth water. "Sure," I said. "Do you think her recipe is around somewhere?"

"I don't know if she had one. I think she made it up."

He never talked about missing her. Both of us moved around and through the emptiness in the house as if it had never been any other way, but sometimes, last thing at night, I saw him step into the master bedroom doorway – just inside, no farther – and rest his hand on the jamb, as gently as he had covered her hand with his.

I said, "I bet we could figure out how to make that soup."

He smiled. "You do?"

"Yeah." Maybe she did have a recipe somewhere around. If not, it would be easy enough to guess the ingredients. "We're smart," I said.

We each started on a second burger. Charley took a swallow from his milk glass and told me he'd been thinking about Saturday, when we'd see Justine, "if you still want me along. Do you have a plan yet?"

I didn't, and I didn't need to tell him how we felt about having him along. "Is there anything you feel like doing?"

"If it's nice out, what about the zoo?"

We hadn't been there since we were kids. It was a perfect place to stroll and talk. We could spend a fine afternoon there, I thought, except for one consideration: Charley's wheelchair.

He wouldn't be able to manage without it. Even when he was little, he had never liked getting wheeled around in front of strangers. It was one of the few things he'd put up a fuss about. I told him I liked the idea, and I bet Justine would too, "but are you sure you'd want to?"

He knew what I meant. "If she's serious about my brother, I want to be sure about things."

Oh, kid. Don't you worry. If Justine couldn't take us as we were, for any reason, if it came down to a choice between her and my brother... well, that wasn't a choice. Charley had to know that.

Justine thought a zoo trip sounded perfect, and Saturday morning turned out bright and clear. After breakfast, I went down to the basement to bring up the chair.

These days, wheelchairs are made light and strong, easy to use, maneuver, and collapse for transport. Not so back then. The old solid-metal chairs usually outweighed the people who used them and had all the speed and control one would expect if they had been chiseled out of cement. Charley's chair had a wicker seat, back, and leg rests, but the big metal rear wheels meant it was still more than heavy enough for one person to wrangle.

Dad and I used to carry it up the basement steps together, with me going up the stairs backward, guiding, and Dad going forward and hefting most of the weight. Now I figured out pretty fast that I wouldn't be able to hoist it up over my head, which had been my first plan, so I got behind it and dragged it up the steps one at a time. Our steps were the open kind, flat planks of wood nailed to the wall. Those back wheels snagged on each and every one. By the time I made it to the top, our mother would have had me stand over the sink and scrub my mouth out with detergent flakes as punishment for the words I'd let out.

Charley was waiting. "I'm sorry."

I couldn't imagine how he and our mother had dealt with the chair all the time I'd been gone. Neither of them had ever said a word about it. "Sorry for what?" I said. "Not your fault it has a mind of its own." I parked the chair in front of the kitchen sink and wiped my forehead on my sleeve. "But tell you what, kid. Can we keep it in the living room and call it an armchair? We'll put a blanket on it, maybe a couple of pillows. Then when somebody sits in it, if they want a coffee or anything, they don't even have to get up."

He laughed. "That sounds okay."

He let me wheel him down the sidewalk to the bus stop. He could wheel himself fine, especially on a straightaway like this, but he got comfortable with his cane across his lap and tilted his head back to see me. "I'll take it easy."

"Fine with me." It had been a long time, a very long time, since I had last given him a ride.

Mrs. O'Dell was out sweeping her porch. "Where are you boys headed?"

Charley told her about the zoo. Then, in spite of my grip on his shoulder, he added that we were meeting "a girl Nicky knows from work." His tone was so innocent it yelled for attention.

"Oh!" Mrs. O'Dell peered at me over the tops of her glasses. "I hope she's a nice young lady."

"Yes, ma'am," I said. I told her we needed to catch the bus, but we'd see her later. Once we were out of earshot, Charley apologized. "I couldn't help it."

"I see that." I navigated the chair over a cracked piece of sidewalk and let myself grin. If he was willing to tease me, we were doing all right.

The bus was a trick, the way it always had been once Charley got a full-size chair. At least he could get up and get himself to a seat. I had a hard time imagining, for instance, how President Roosevelt would have managed it, with both legs little more than dead weight. The driver helped me stow the chair as well as we could in the luggage hold, which fortunately was pretty empty this morning. The chair clanged against the metal walls like a spoon in an empty bowl.

Charley and I sat close to the front, the way Dad and I used to. As the bus swung and shuddered down the so-familiar streets, I couldn't help closing my eyes. We got off in the big parking lot by the zoo's front entrance, where Justine would meet us by the ticket booth. Charley settled himself in the chair again and I took hold of the handles. "Ready?" I said.

He wasn't smiling now. "If you are."

"It'll be fine, kid." I would have tousled his hair, but he'd combed it neatly. "You'll see."

During the toughest years after the crash, joy had been plenty thin on the ground. People had gotten used to scraping pennies when and as they could, to set by in the old jelly jar, or the sock whose mate had worn past darning. When they finally had enough, they savored every morsel of whatever treat their hoarded fund could pay for. Often it was food, of course, but sometimes – the way it had been for Dad and me – it was something else you needed just as much.

Times had gotten better now. We didn't have to scrimp and save quite so carefully, but during the war years, pleasure still had that sweetness of something fragile and quick-dissolving, like cotton candy against the tongue. We reached for it as if it might not come again and stretched it out as far as we could.

On this warm spring afternoon, the zoo was packed. The line at the ticket booth went all the way down one side of the parking lot. Little kids, boys in shorts and girls in ruffled sundresses, played tag up and down the line, weaving between the grown-ups and dashing away from the parents who reached out to collar them. College students stood in knots, pretending to be too mature and worldly-wise for all this. On the far side of the wide gray curve of Kelly Drive, the Schuylkill River hurried glinting in the sun. Scents of popcorn and hotdogs wafted out of the zoo grounds.

"Nicky! Charley!"

Justine was coming toward us down the line of people. In her white blouse and daffodil-yellow skirt, she looked like the spring morning itself. Charley pushed himself up out of the chair and steadied himself with the cane.

Most people, when they first met him, couldn't keep themselves from glancing down at his foot. Even in a shoe, it wasn't hard to make out the awkward curve of it. Today, Charley had opted for just a sock on his right foot, which was more comfortable but hid nothing.

Justine's eyes didn't so much as flick toward it. She held out her hand, and Charley took it and bowed over it as if he had been one of those men from the city's grand old days, decked out in a powdered wig and embroidered waistcoat. "Miss Justine. So glad to meet you."

Have you ever felt something click into place, like a key fitting into a lock? Justine dropped a curtsey – she was smaller than usual in flat sandals instead of the heels I'd seen her in before – and reached out to pull Charley into a hug. "I feel as if I already know you," she said. "Of course, you do look a lot like your brother here."

Yes. It was going to be all right.

We followed the line to the admission booth, where we collected our pale-blue cardboard tickets and a couple of foldout maps. Inside the gate, the crowds had room to spread out. Kids ran and shrieked. Families clustered to open their maps and debate about what to see first. An older couple, both gray-haired and stooping but dressed to the nines, made their slow way down the paved path hand in hand.

Charley said, "Sometimes this chair is pretty handy." People moved aside quickly enough to give us a clear shot down the path. In crowds like this, it was faster and easier for me to push than for Charley to maneuver it himself. One little boy in a striped shirt stared at us. Just before we got out of earshot, I heard him ask his mother, "What's wrong with that man's foot?"

Charley heard it too. He smiled up at Justine, but I saw the flush on his cheeks. "That happens sometimes."

Some people might have said "Just ignore it," or "People should mind their own business." Justine said, "That must be hard."

"A little. But, you know, the hardest thing is to make sure Nicky doesn't go after them."

"Go after them?" Justine put her hand on my arm. "Nicky, you don't get into fights, do you?" There was that look, one eyebrow raised, the dimple hovering by her mouth.

I told her I hadn't fought anybody since Charley was tiny. Charley told her I used to, though. "He taught some people a lesson."

The way Justine looked at me, my face started to feel sunburned. "Nobody messes with my brother if I can help it." I squeezed Charley's shoulder. "Of course, he's big enough now to take care of himself."

"That's right," Charley said. "Plus, I've got my cane."

We decided to see the Pachyderm House first. The massive concrete-and-glass building, still brand-new, had been the zoo's biggest attraction since its grand opening two years earlier. Inside, the elephants in their cells flicked their tails with slow patience, gliding their trunks over the concrete flooring to nudge and mouth at wisps of straw. Laughter and the shrieks of children rang off the walls, but none of the elephants reacted, apart from the occasional blink of a dark sad eye.

We saw the monkeys next, and then the bears huddling in their musty caves, and the lions and tigers who paced their enclosures and stared at the throngs on the other side of the bars. Charley said, "I wonder what Titus would think of them. If he'd know they're cats too." We went into the bird house, where wings of every color flashed and caught the light, and the sour smell of guano mingled with the noises of fluting and rustling. After a while, we decided we needed something to eat, so we made our way to the little pavilion at the far end of the zoo grounds and got hotdogs and sodas.

The pavilion had some picnic tables, but the grassy area on the other side of the path looked better to us. In the middle of a small, perfectly round pond, a fountain made the water dance. A blond-haired girl and boy, maybe four and five years old, stood at the edge of the water, tossing chunks of bread to a pair of ducks who paddled lazily past.

Charley stayed in his chair – "lucky me, I've got my own place to sit" – and Justine and I made ourselves comfortable on the grass. A little cherry tree gave us some shade. Its fallen petals looked like spatters of pink paint against the green. We ate in silence, enjoying the way the afternoon breeze stirred the tree's leaves and made sun patterns on the grass.

Justine finished her hotdog and folded her thin paper napkin into a tiny square. She smiled up at Charley. "So, what was your brother like when you were boys? Tell me the worst."

I kept a straight face. "He doesn't remember much from back then. He was too little."

"Don't listen to him." Charley sat up like a professor talking over an unruly student. "I remember plenty. For one thing, he taught me about colors."

He'd been so little then, I really hadn't thought he'd remember it. Charley told Justine about how we'd sat at my desk, and how we'd looked out the window and he'd told me all the colors he could see.

"Another thing," Charley said, "he was the one who taught me how to walk up and down the stairs."

My face was getting that sunburned feeling again. It was Justine's smile. "Not exactly taught," I pointed out. "More like, this kid wouldn't let anybody help him, so I used to follow him to make sure he didn't go cracking his head open."

None of us needed to say how tough the stairs had been for him. "That was back when I first had a crutch," Charley said. "Nicky, you're the one who showed me about keeping the crutch one step ahead of me. Don't tell me you don't remember."

Well, of course I did. The one thing I'd been able to make that stubborn three-year-old promise was that he wouldn't try the stairs without me there. So we'd gone up and down, up and down, as many times as he wanted, him working the crutch and me with my arms out, ready to catch him.

"That all sounds pretty good," Justine said. "What else, Charley?"

You can only listen to people talk about you for so long. "Kid," I said, "you'd better watch it."

He stretched out his left foot to nudge my shoulder. "Or what? You said it, I'm big enough to look out for myself."

I fished a pea-sized piece of ice out of my paper cup and flicked it past his ear. It fell into the grass behind the chair, startling a sparrow that had been hunting for crumbs. "You're probably stronger than me now too," I said. "But I do have one trick you don't."

Justine bit her lip to keep from laughing. Charley said, "I dunno, Nicky, you say stuff like that, but you wouldn't do it."

"No?" I patted my jeans pockets theatrically. "I seem to have left my pencils at home. Lucky for you."

Justine leaned forward. "So, Charley, tell me. When you were little, did Nicky cause much trouble with the..." She pantomimed drawing, holding an invisible pencil between thumb and forefinger.

My brother knew about my one and only whipping, of course. He kept it to himself. "He caused trouble, all right," he said. "Usually because I asked him to." He told her about my pranks with things like forks and water glasses, and how Dad used to pretend I was a nuisance, but how his face told a very different story. "Say he'd had a tough day at work," Charley said. "Nicky's drawing always cheered him up." His eyes met mine. "He loved it so much."

He had. Charley remembered, but he couldn't possibly remember as much as I did about how hard it had been during those first years after the crash. How tired Dad had been, every day, how his head and back ached all the time and his docked wages felt like a rubber band stretched to the snapping point. I'd been a kid in grade school, wishing all the time to be old enough and strong enough to lift that load off his shoulders. At least I'd had that one thing: I'd been able to make him smile.

Now my heart sped up at the memory. I willed it to quiet down. Justine couldn't know that piece about me, not yet.

She reached over to touch my sleeve. "I wish I could have met him."

My throat felt so clogged I had to take a sip of soda before I could answer. "You'd have liked him." He would have liked her too, I knew that.

It was time to talk about something else. I asked Justine if she knew when the La Belle Epoque ads would be out. "Miss Carol says next week," she said. For a moment, excitement lit her face. Then it vanished, the way a light bulb filament fades when the power goes out. "I've been thinking a lot about all that."

She didn't sound terribly happy about it. I asked what was on her mind. "I'm glad about the pictures, of course," she said. "Dad'll be impressed." She set her folded-up napkin in her empty cup and pressed its sides together. "But Miss Carol said Lou and I would do another shoot with her. She thought we'd probably get offers for more ads too."

Charley said, "Isn't that a good thing?"

Justine held the cup between both hands as if she were holding onto a good-luck charm. "You'd think so. It's just that, for me to do it, Nicky has to change me so much." She looked up at me. "You made me exactly what I've always wanted to be," she said, "but it wasn't me anymore."

I knew what it had meant to her to see her mother's reflection in the showroom mirror. Carefully, as if the wrong words would make the idea fly away, I said, "You're not sure you want to do it again?"

She smiled. That is, her lips curved up at the corners, and she dropped the cup on the grass. "I know I don't."

Gladness bloomed deep inside me, maybe in the soles of my feet. Charley said, "Why shouldn't you be a model just the way you are?"

Justine raised an eyebrow. "Did your brother teach you how to charm girls too?"

"Him? Nah. He doesn't know nearly enough." *Thanks, kid.* "But he knows you're beautiful," Charley said, "and he's an artist, so he knows what beautiful looks like."

You can bet I did want to thank him then. The blush came up in Justine's cheeks like the bloom on a rose. She slid over to put her hand on mine in the grass. "I know what he thinks is beautiful," she said. "Unfortunately, the people who make ads don't think quite the same way."

"Then they're wrong," Charley said. "Not to mention, pretty stupid."

That made her laugh. I turned my hand over to close it around hers. "You don't want to model anymore?" I said, to make certain.

"I don't. I'm not right for it, and it's not right for me." *I never wanted to be just a girl playing dress-up.* "But if I don't...it's the only work I ever tried." She looked as if she was telling a joke on herself and didn't think it was very funny. *Sometimes I feel useless.* "What's a girl like me going to do?"

You wouldn't believe what popped into my head just then. Or maybe you would.

You could marry me.

We'd known each other for exactly three weeks and had spent a handful of hours together. In those days, people did get married on that much or even less, but I was certain I'd be out of my head to ask her. If a man wanted a girl to share his life, he ought to make sure he had a halfway decent life to offer. I didn't. Not with my dizzy spells, living in my mother's house, working all of a month at a job where one of my bosses had disliked me from the start.

All of those were good reasons not to pop the question, but they weren't the main reason. The main reason was that if – *when* – she said no, someone would have to get a dustpan and sweep the pieces of me up off the grass.

Charley said, "Can you cook? Nicky and I want to figure out how to make potato soup."

Justine laughed. "I can't," she admitted. "Lou says our mother could. I'd like to learn, someday."

I found myself imagining my mother's kitchen, Justine and Charley sitting at the table, Titus winding himself around their legs and purring. And – why not? – me at the stove, ladling out a pretty good imitation of that Sunday-dinner soup. Nothing special, just an ordinary meal on an ordinary day. The three of us eating and talking and laughing together.

Maybe? Someday?

For now, we had more of the zoo to see. I took our empty cups and napkins and found a can to toss them in. All craziness aside, I told myself, it'd be silly to try to rush anything with Justine. I needed to do my job at Allen and Allen, make Mark trust me, and maybe find a way to manage my dizzy spells or escape them somehow, the way I had in California. In a year or so, maybe two, I might be able to offer Justine a future she would be willing to share.

That was what I thought that afternoon. Before I knew how much change was coming for us, or how soon.

Chapter Twelve

You who are reading this, picture something.

A storm cloud hangs over the world, muttering with thunder and spitting forks of lighting. At this moment, it isn't directly above you, hovering over your house, ready to unleash enough rain to pulp your roof and bring down your walls. You can still look up and see blue sky. But it's out there, waiting; you can feel it, and you know that a strong enough gust of wind could bring it over the horizon.

Every day, you hear about another city flattened when the storm breaks over it. Houses filling, basement to roof beams, with unstoppable water. People trapped inside until the last bubble of air runs out, or swept away in currents that drag them under. Every day, you know that today the news might reach you: the storm took someone whose absence will make you wish it had taken you too. Every morning, before you so much as push your covers back or swing your feet over the side of the bed, you reach for your invisible armor and put it on, one piece at a time. It will hold you up. It will let you show the world a brave face. It might not be strong enough to shield you from whatever's coming today – anything, everything, nothing – but it's all you have.

You live this way for a long time. Call it four years, although you don't count it that way. Often, you count the time in light and dark.

You walk through the days and crawl back into bed at night, offering a prayer that sounds like *we survived another one.* Sometimes, when days are too long, you count the time in hours, or minutes. Each holds a series of breaths in which you try not to imagine what that cloud is doing, over on the other side of the world.

If, one day, the cloud disappeared, it if turned into harmless steam and blew away on a puff of wind…you try not to think about how you would feel if such a miracle came to be. You cannot let yourself picture it. Otherwise, the reality of what is will step on your heart and drive it into the ground.

But then, one day, it happens.

~

MAY 8, 1945. THE DAY WHEN GERMANY GAVE UP THE FIGHT.

Have you ever seen a busy city that just got such news? Better yet, have you ever been in the middle of it? I don't imagine you have. In all the years I have lived through since then, I've never seen anything quite like what happened on the day we celebrated victory in Europe.

It didn't mean everything was over. Emperor Hirohito was still out there. His soldiers were trained to choose death over surrender. The battle for the Pacific would struggle on, men blasting each other to pieces for those flyspeck rock outcroppings in the ocean, the Allies working their way foot by painful foot to the heart of the Japanese homeland, until the United States unleashed a weapon that would change the course of history. Most of us had no idea that weapon existed, or that such power was possible. Once it did its work, the world would feel its aftershocks forever.

That was all still months away. The *Enola Gay,* the bomb they called "Little Boy," and what we would do to Hiroshima and, three days later, to Nagasaki. For now, the storm cloud hadn't vanished yet, but it had shrunk down to a tropical storm instead of a hurricane. Hitler was done.

In Philadelphia, if you had been dropped in the middle of Center City, you would have thought the very squares of pavement would get up and shout with joy. Whole neighborhoods piled out into the streets, neighbors and total strangers laughing and crying and hugging each other. Block parties sprouted up everywhere; dancing, music, and cacophony went on all through the night. To this day, I believe that if you stand on any sidewalk in Center City and close your eyes, letting the traffic and foot noise swirl around you, and plant your feet on the pavement and listen for the city's own breath and pulse, you can still hear echoes of that spring day back in 1945.

Now, all these years later, I'm sitting at my kitchen table in the almost-quiet of an ordinary city dawn, with nothing more than traffic noise outside. It takes no trouble at all to conjure up the explosion that was that day. I've promised not to pull any punches in this telling, but I'm afraid that what you need to hear about my own experience of V-E Day will make me sound more than a little tiresome.

Jo stopped by yesterday afternoon to see how the project's coming. I told her that maybe, after all, she's the only one who should see these pages. "Who else'll be interested in this old cuss?"

"You're not just any old cuss, Dad." She knows I think about the magic and how it's not in the world anymore. She knows I think about how the world might look after I'm not here to see it. "This story's important," she told me. "Think of it as your way to keep doing something, from wherever you are."

She's certain it could be that useful. I'd like to believe she's right. "Still," I said, "I'd rather leave out some things. That young fool didn't always have his head screwed on."

She gave me the look I know so well. Her mother's look. "You promised it'd be a true story."

Using my joke against me. That daughter of mine.

MAY 8 WAS A TUESDAY. I HAD BEEN AT WORK AS USUAL, BUT when the news came over the radio, every pencil went down, every typewriter stopped mid-tap. From upstairs in the Allen and Allen offices, you could already hear the cheering and shouting out on the street. All of us at the agency crammed ourselves into Stephen's office to hear the words coming out of the radio speaker: "...all forces under German control to cease active operations..."

That ended the workday. Everyone who had someone in the city tore off as fast as they could to get hold of the people they loved. The streets were jammed, cars and buses blowing their horns, people boiling in all directions.

As for me, I thought I might as well start walking. Charley was still at school, unless the teachers there had given up on the day too. It would take me a while to walk all the way home, but he'd be there by the time I made it, and I didn't much feel like seeing anybody else. I could have walked to Justine's house in a lot less time, but I didn't even feel like seeing her.

Strange, right? The whole city going crazy with happiness, and I only wanted to slip into the crowds and disappear. *Nicky,* you're probably thinking, *what on earth was wrong with you?*

Pretty soon, I was thinking something along those lines myself. For a start, and believe me when I tell you I should have known this, the walk home would take quite a bit more than "a while." I might have managed it if I'd had the whole afternoon and a canteen or two of water, and if I'd been wearing jeans and sneakers instead of the three-piece and the oxblood loafers so stiff they might have been carved from teak.

Still, I was determined. I didn't want to get into a cab, or a bus, or any other place where somebody might want to know why I wasn't one of the men over there who would now be lining up to come home.

That was it, you see. The 4-F.

I walked as hard and fast as I could, head down, sidestepping knots of people, looking nobody in the eye even while strangers stopped one another on the sidewalk to shake hands and clap each other on the back. Storefronts and office buildings went past in blurs of gray and brown, with quick dashes of gleam from windows. My coat got hotter by the second, my briefcase handle dug into my palm, and my shoes gripped my feet like cast iron pincers, but I hustled on, not paying much attention to where I was going except to know I was getting closer to the river. I wanted to walk holes in the bottoms of those shiny shoes and let all the shame drain out.

Boneheaded determination doesn't stand up too well against tough leather. Before long, I found myself actually limping. I wasn't going to make it home on foot. When I had to accept that, can you guess where I was?

It sounds like a bad joke. Sure enough, I limped to a stop at the foot of the hill that led up to the big stone bulk of the art museum.

Fine. Why not.

At least catching a bus here would be easy. I sat down on the curb to wait. My feet throbbed, pushing against the shoe uppers with every heartbeat. All the while, I felt the museum looming behind me, as if it had eyes fixed on my back.

The bus got me to my stop in Elmcroft not much later than I'd normally have gotten home. Charley was right in the hallway and threw his arms around me, briefcase and all. "Can you believe it?"

I hugged him back, wishing I could be as glad as I should. "I know."

He told me Mrs. O'Dell had called to ask us over for dinner. "She's getting a bunch of neighbors together. She says we can't eat by ourselves on a day like this." He drew back to look into my face. "What's the matter?"

In our own neighborhood, boys I had known at school hadn't come home whole, and some still might not make it back at all. It was one thing to slip back into the Lawrence Street life and learn to wear it again after the years away. It helped, too, that people figured I was doing all right by Charley. But it was another thing entirely to face everyone and try to share in relief and celebration I hadn't earned.

I was so shut in on myself, in a tiny cubicle with walls ten feet high, that I couldn't begin to tell Charley what I was thinking. He didn't need me to. "Nicky." He gripped my shoulder. "It wasn't your fault you couldn't go. Nobody's blaming you for anything. Except, if we don't go to Mrs. O'Dell's, she'll probably never forgive us."

I think he would have planted me in his chair, if he'd had to, and somehow dragged both of us down to her house. As it was, after I changed into comfortable clothes, we walked down together.

Her place was jammed. Four or five families, little kids and all, packed her kitchen to overflowing. Houses in our neighborhood didn't have fancy things like dedicated dining rooms. Mrs. O'Dell set all the food out on her kitchen table and everybody served themselves, scooping up meatloaf and mashed potatoes, succotash and macaroni salad, pie and cake. Mrs. O'Dell hadn't made the whole spread, of course. Mrs. Franklin and Mrs. Parker from down the street had chipped in their ration cards and helped too.

With our full plates, we shoehorned ourselves into the living room. Every chair in the house had gotten pressed into service there, joining the horsehair sofa and the matching velour-upholstered armchairs with handmade crochet antimacassars. Charley and I ended up on the sofa, with him in the middle and Mrs. O'Dell on his other side.

The food was good, especially the red velvet cake someone had said Mrs. Parker made. "You wouldn't even guess, would you, it's got powdered eggs and saccharine!" Even so, I had a hard time swallowing. The living room wallpaper had columns of daisies alternating with sunshine-yellow border lines. Mrs. O'Dell had had the same pattern forever. I chewed mechanically and counted the flower heads, the way I used to do when I was a kid and my mother, visiting Mrs. O'Dell for coffee, had told me to sit still and behave.

During a lull, after some of the little kids had left their plates and raced outside, Mrs. O'Dell said, "Nicky, I know I've said this before, but I'm so glad you're home now and you boys are doing all right. Seems like life is finally getting back to the way it should be." She reached behind Charley to pat my shoulder. "Home's better than California any day."

I hung a smile on my face. "Sure. No place like home."

Somebody took that up and turned the talk to the soldiers who would come back soon. Someone else mentioned how today was President Harry Truman's birthday – nobody doubted Truman anymore, you can bet – and could we imagine a better birthday present? Charley said, "We listened to his speech on the radio at school. He said the only thing he wishes is that President Roosevelt could've seen this." Everything quieted then. We all wished that.

Mrs. Franklin spoke up into the silence. "I'm hearing about this GI Bill that's going to help boys who served go to college. Nicky, it's a shame you couldn't join up. You always wanted to go to college, didn't you?"

She wasn't a bad person, Mrs. Franklin. She was built on the same model as Mrs. O'Dell, except that her hair was still dark more than silver. She was a widow now too, with a son in Chicago and a married daughter living in Connecticut.

Now I kept my eyes on my plate. The war hadn't affected my chances at college; I could have gone without help from the GI Bill. Mrs. Franklin had known that at one time, but she could easily have lost track of it. My glasses, that fake excuse for the 4-F, felt as if somebody had run an electric current through them so the frames burned against my nose and ears.

Next to me, Charley straightened up. "Mrs. Franklin," he said, "now that it's safer to travel, I bet your son will come visit soon, won't he?"

Charley would never be rude to a neighbor, especially not one who had helped us so much when our mother was sick. Everybody knew, though, the way everybody always knew things, how Mrs. Franklin's son, too old for the draft and with a family to support, had used the war as a reason not to visit, even though no one had ever said it wasn't safe to get on the train if you couldn't round up enough gasoline for a trip. Everybody knew, too, that even before the war, Mrs. Franklin hadn't seen her grandchildren any too often.

"Well, yes," she said. "I'm sure he will."

Charley said, "That'll be good. Families should stick together." I heard what he didn't add: *My brother did that for me. Who's doing that for you?*

Mrs. O'Dell stepped in. "I'm sure those boys who want to go to college more than deserve it. But now, let's talk about something else. When do you all think we'll get real eggs again?"

Everyone chimed in with what they wanted as soon as life went back to normal. Fresh eggs, fresh milk, more cuts of meat, everything cheaper once the wartime prices went down. Not having to count up ration cards for every grocery trip. The market as full and busy as it used to be. Someone pointed out that we shouldn't forget how lucky we were, we didn't have to rebuild whole cities the way they would have to over in England. We all agreed that Winston Churchill must be one of the smartest and bravest people who had ever lived, to keep his country alive and fighting while the Nazis tried to bomb it to the bottom of the Atlantic. "Not quite as good as our Chief, of course," somebody said, "but not half bad." And speaking of bombing, wouldn't the Allies just whip Japan now? "We'll give 'em what the Jerries gave England," Mrs. Parker said, "only worse. See how they like it when that island of theirs is in pieces." None of us knew, that night, how right she was.

Charley and I got going soon after that. Charley told Mrs. O'Dell he was pretty tired, thanked her for the great dinner, waved at everybody else and said we'd see them soon. He took my arm as if he needed it for support and wasn't towing me along at all.

Once we were alone on the sidewalk, with the dark around us and only faint noise coming from a few houses along the street, he stopped and leaned on his cane to face me. "You okay?"

I was supposed to take care of him, not the other way around. "I'm fine."

"Your 4-F is no one's business. You know that."

I did. In truth, I couldn't make much sense out of the tangle in my head, except to know it had gotten worse the longer we'd sat on Mrs. O'Dell's stiff scratchy couch. Did I wish I really had failed the eye exam and hadn't been able to serve because of something I had no control over? I couldn't control the dizzy spells either, but failing a vision test would have felt less shameful. Or did I wish I'd been healthy, and could have gone overseas with the rest of the boys those four long years ago?

Maybe. But on the other hand, knowing what would happen to our mother, and how Charley would need me back – *and,* a corner of my mind whispered, *how you'd meet a girl you never could have dreamed up* – could I wish I had gone?

Charley and I went the rest of the short distance down the sidewalk arm in arm. We got to our front stoop to hear the phone jangling in the kitchen.

Justine. I should have called her before we left. I was so certain it was her that, at first, I couldn't recognize the voice on the other end, and thought it had to be a wrong number even though they were calling me by name. "I'm sorry," I said, "who is this?"

"It's Minna."

The voice fell into place. "I'm sorry to bother you," she said. "I know you didn't give me this number, but there aren't many Trues in the phone book."

I could've thought to give her the number myself. "It's fine." Now that I was listening right, I could hear how her voice sounded tight and thin, like stretched fabric. "Are you okay?"

"It's Timothy." She hesitated. "He's not doing so well. Today's been hard."

Of course it had been. I'd been so caught up with myself and my shame that I hadn't thought of that. "I'm sorry," I said. "Can I help?"

"He went to bed a little while ago, or I'd try to put him on the phone." From the way she kept her voice down, I suspected she thought he was still awake, and might not like this phone call if he knew about it. "I didn't know the next time you'd be home when I'm working, so I wanted to ask if you might..."

She paused for so long that I said, "What is it? Please tell me."

"It seems like a lot to ask, but if you might come and see him. Sometime." Then, with an openness that threw her caution away, "He won't talk to anybody else. Not me, not anyone, but I thought he might talk to you."

"Of course I'll come." I didn't know what the Allens planned for tomorrow, a regular workday or what, but I didn't care. Surely no one would mind if I asked for at least part of the day off. "In the morning, first thing?"

"Please. If you can."

She gave me the address, in north Philly. I told her I'd be there as early as I could, as soon as I got hold of someone at Allen and Allen. "And listen, Minna, you don't need to come over here for your shift tomorrow, if Timothy needs you at home."

"I don't know if he'd want that." I heard the faintest catch in the words. "I have other Wednesday jobs anyway. But if you can get him to talk...he's stubborn, that man." One heartbeat of silence that held a world of ache. "Please try."

I told her I knew about stubborn. "We'll see who's worse, him or me." She laughed, a sound halfway to a sob, and I wanted to promise her that I'd get Timothy to talk if it involved propping his mouth open and holding a cup to catch the words when they fell out.

The phone rang again almost as soon as I hung up. This time, it was the call I'd expected. "Can I see you tomorrow?" Justine asked. "That is,

I'd rather see you right now, but Dad would keel over if I left the house this late."

It turned out I could still laugh too. "Would you like to have dinner tomorrow?"

"Very much. And I was thinking, you saw the house I grew up in. May I see yours?"

The idea sent a trickle of ice down my back. She wanted to come to this house? "It's anything but fancy." It sounded like an apology. "I mean, it's a different neighborhood, and all." Cramped, plain, poor. Nothing like her own.

"I'm not worried about fancy." I heard her smiling. "I'd like to see those stairs Charley talked about."

She wanted to be able to picture us as boys. Once she did, I had to hope she'd still want to see me again. "We'll be glad to have you."

By the time I got to bed, I was so tired that even the sheet felt heavy when I dragged it up over myself. I knew I should sort out what to cook for tomorrow's dinner, but as I drifted off, I only saw one thing.

Timothy, as clear as if he was standing in front of me. His arms folded, his eyes full of sadness and distance, his mouth clamped stubbornly shut on all the pain he carried.

We'll see about that.

Chapter Thirteen

In the morning, I called Allen and Allen as soon as the office opened. The secretary, Barbara, answered. "I'm sorry, Mr. True, the Mr. Allens aren't in yet." No doubt they were sleeping off the celebrations, along with at least half the city. I asked her to tell them that I probably wouldn't make it in today. They could go ahead and think I was hungover too.

Charley's school had declared a holiday, so he offered to go to the A&P and get the groceries for tonight. I'd decided on hamburgers again; that was safe enough. After breakfast, I took a cab across Center City and out to a part of town I had never spent time in.

Center City showed its money in every pillared façade and wrought-iron lamp, but on its northern edge, the streets began to change. Smooth pavement gave way to cracked and bumpy asphalt. A row of squat brick boxes, each patched in places with uneven mortar, announced "Mens and Ladies Footwear," "Haberdashery," and "Finest Hair Styling" on carefully-stenciled but faded signs. Farther along, a rusty chain-link fence boxed in a baseball diamond, bare dirt with a few rough bleachers. The cab turned down a residential street, where narrow rowhouses flaunted carved woodwork and what had once been brightly painted shutters and molding. Now the woodwork was cracking and falling away in pieces, the paint peeling and so weather-stained that I couldn't tell what its original colors had been. Here and there, a house stood empty, its windows covered with raw plywood.

The folks in these neighborhoods didn't have much money. Elmcroft was different only in that our single-family brick houses were a little newer, and we'd never had the pretty paintwork or gingerbread carving; a good thing too, because we couldn't have spent the money or time to keep them in repair. The run-down feel of the area didn't make me uneasy, but I did notice one thing. Every face I saw – a line of men waiting at a bus stop, two women walking arm in arm down the side-walk, a cluster of little boys in front of a corner drugstore – every face was dark-skinned.

The apartment building where Minna and Timothy lived made up one side of a square that had a tiny park in the middle. Two determined trees reached up for the blue sky above. A little girl in a ruffly cherry-red sundress chased an older boy around the nearest tree. "Can't catch me!" he called, but he slowed down enough for her to snag the loose tail of his shirt and she shrieked in delight. Another boy, maybe twelve or thirteen, threw a rubber ball for a wiry brown terrier to fetch. All three kids were colored.

The cab driver let me off in front of the apartment building. It was newer than the houses I had seen, blocky and plain, built out of dark red brick. "You want me to wait?"

"No, thanks." I tipped him extra for bringing me to a place off his usual routes. He took off so fast he should have left skid marks behind.

Two young men, maybe eighteen or nineteen, stood under the building's dark green awning, passing a cigarette back and forth and talking quietly. They stopped talking as I came up. Both wore plain shirts and worn-looking jeans and sneakers, and I was glad I didn't look much different at least when it came to clothes. The Center City ad man had no place here. Neither of the men said anything to me, but I felt their eyes follow me inside.

I took the stairs up to the third floor. The building was very clean and plain, beige linoleum, white paint. The air carried scents of soap, coffee, and cigarette smoke. The Davises had apartment 301, down at the far end of the third-floor hall, on the left side. The white door had a steel-gray metal knocker in the middle. I knocked, wondering if Timothy might refuse to let me in.

The door swung open. He looked almost exactly the way I had pictured him last night: face closed off, mouth tight, jeans and white cotton T-shirt rumpled as if he'd slept in them, whatever snatches of sleep he'd had. Pain hovered around him.

"So you came," he said. The words could have been gray stones tossed down on a gray sidewalk. "Minna said you might."

"May I come in?"

He shrugged and moved aside to let me by. I took one step in and stopped. The small, neat front room had the most beautiful rug I'd ever seen. It was round, big enough to cover most of the floor space. Strips of cloth in shades of green and blue, from mint and frost to emerald and midnight and everything in between, coiled and swirled together, with tiny accents here and there of yellow and gold. Precise white stitches held it all in place.

"That's gorgeous," I said.

"Minna's aunt made it. Wedding present. There's coffee if you want."

I pushed my sneakers off and left them by the door. A half-wall divided the front room from a narrow kitchen that looked spic and span, all white paint and white tile, with a square table in one corner. Another doorway led into what must be the bedroom. Timothy poured coffee from a saucepan into two matching ceramic cups, plain white with thick sides and thick handles. He gave me one and dropped into a chair at the table with his back to me.

"I don't know why Minna asked you to come. You can't do a damn thing."

I was as welcome as a cockroach in the icebox. It felt like walking into a headwind to move around the table and sit down across from him. On the other hand, he hadn't actually thrown me out. "Would you rather I go?"

Timothy shrugged, eyes down. Heat climbed up my neck. I hoped he knew he didn't have to put up with me, that he could challenge this white man, at least, and I would respect what he wanted. I felt how stupid I'd been to barge in here where I didn't belong, to think I could help a man who had been through a hell I had been unable to face.

I would have stood up then and apologized for bothering him, except for two things. One was that I had promised Minna I would try. The other was that an idea waved a tiny flag in my head.

Timothy was in a pit. Its steep, smooth walls rose high above his head, with no handholds to let him pull himself up or crevices to give him a footing. Minna tried, every day, to throw him a rope. I wanted to try now, but he was shut away from me. Unless something shook him out of his silence, he would never start climbing.

Words and questions wouldn't do it. But – the flag in my head waved harder – I had one surefire way to make him say *something*.

I said, "Do you have a pencil and paper I could use?"

He didn't ask why I wanted them. "Yeah." Out of a drawer by the icebox, he got a lined notepad and a stub of pencil. He pushed them across the table and picked up his cup again.

What I was about to do went against everything the Allens and I had agreed on, and right after Mark had gotten into a knot about confidentiality too. If for any reason he or Stephen found out, I stood to lose my job.

Hell with that.

I chose the cup because Timothy couldn't miss it. As the pencil skimmed over the paper, I felt something I hadn't felt in a very long time. Charley had told Justine how I'd made Dad laugh even after his toughest days at work. This, I knew all through my body, *this* was what the magic was for: to strike a match in the dark.

One line, then another. The cup on the page was taller, thinner, with no handle, and a lip that curved up and down like the pinched edge of a pie crust. One final line, and the cup in Timothy's hand changed.

His eyes went wide. He started as if he'd found himself holding something else entirely: a sharp-spined cactus, a huge insect. For an instant I thought he might let the cup fall, but he held on and set it gently down.

"Nicky. What is this?"

The shock had woken him up the way a jet of icy water would wake a sleeper. I passed him the drawing.

He studied it, line for line, comparing it against the cup in front of him. With one steady fingertip, he traced the curvy ceramic lip. "I'm not dreaming," he said, "or seeing things. You did this."

"Yes."

"How?"

I explained all of it to him, how I'd stumbled on the magic when I was a kid, how it worked, why it meant I'd been able to land a job so easily with an ad firm. I even told him about the non-disclosure rules. "It's useful, I guess. But I always thought the best thing about it is making somebody laugh."

The smile that dawned on Timothy's face was, and is to this day, one of the best things I've ever seen. "Damn, man. This is crazy." He picked up the real cup again and turned it around, examining its curves, feeling its sides for any trace of the missing handle. "Damn." His face brightened like a sunrise. "So you could change something else?"

"Sure."

"Right now?"

"Yeah. What should I change?" I picked up the pencil and pretended to roll up the long sleeves I wasn't wearing. "Give me a challenge."

"You know, for a guy who worries about knowing what's real, you sure do mess with it."

I couldn't help laughing. "This is real. Just temporary."

It could have backfired. Timothy could have decided he was hallucinating; the magic could have sent him into a darker place that he might never have escaped at all. We were both more than lucky that he could take it for what it was.

He rapped on the table with his knuckles. It was good solid maple, about an inch thick. "What could you do with this?"

"What would you like?"

"Surprise me."

I could do that. I got down to work. Timothy sat with his hands in his lap, watching.

First, because nothing was easier than changing one simple shape to another, I made the square tabletop into a circle. Then I put cutouts in it. An oval, a rectangle, a diamond, a triangle: as I drew, the wood reformed so quickly that it might always have been that way. Except, of course, nobody in their right mind would've designed a table like that. It could have been a match-the-shape toy, where kids have to put the right-shaped blocks into the right-shaped holes. A kid with a set of big enough blocks would've had a fine old time.

Timothy didn't say a word. Each time I raised my eyes, I saw his at the edge of vision, studying either my pencil or the tabletop as it changed with each new addition to the drawing. His face stayed perfectly quiet.

I finished the last cutout. "There. How about that?"

He shook his head, slowly, with a dazed look I knew. I remembered Dad's face the first time he had seen the magic.

Timothy reached out to touch the wood, sliding one hand all the way through the triangle cutout first, then the diamond. I sat quiet, watching him prove to himself that the new shape was real. He felt the insides of the cutouts, running his hand over what he might have thought should be a raw, unsanded edge; but the magic didn't work that way, and the surface was as smooth as if the carpenter had intended to make exactly this design.

"I wish Minna could see this." His wonder made me think of a little boy pulling the wrapping paper off the birthday gift he'd begged for. He ran his hand again over the inside of the triangle cutout. "Boy, would she give us hell."

"I wouldn't blame her. This is one ugly table."

Timothy started to laugh. He laughed helplessly, his whole body shaking, the laughter spilling out of him like water from a punctured hose, and then he put his elbows on the table and hid his face in his hands.

In those days, grown men weren't supposed to know how to cry. Sometimes things don't seem all that different, all these years later, although I like to think we're learning.

I set the notepad down and edged my chair around the table's curved side. Timothy didn't move when I put my hand on his shoulder. The sobs came on and on as if they had been dammed up for months, tearing at him as they pushed their way out.

We sat that way for a long while. The flood slowed to a trickle, interrupted each time Timothy caught his breath. I didn't sit back until he lifted his head and wiped his eyes on his sleeve.

"Ah, hell." He dug a handkerchief out of his jeans pocket and blew his nose. "Hell with it."

"Yeah."

He mopped at his face. "Minna keeps asking me, can't I tell her about France. What it was like. She says maybe if I can talk about it, the dreams'll stop." He was so tired. The lines at the corners of his eyes stood out, dark and deep. "But how can I do that? How can I take that... all that..." His free hand, the one not holding the handkerchief, gestured helplessly. "All that filth, that shit, how can I dump it all out in front of her?" His mouth twisted painfully. "How can I tell her that life's ugly and death's worse, and most days I don't see any point to anything?"

Anything I might have said felt empty. Men in trenches, fighting and falling and bleeding out in mud and rain. Killing each other over a few feet of ground. Even if you crawled out of that darkness, you could never scrub out the stains it left on you. No doubt it made hopes and wishes weigh less than a grain of sand.

"Then you get back here," he said, "and everyone says you're one of the lucky ones. You made it home." His voice was flat now, drained of all feeling. "You're supposed to go back to work and pretend nothing happened. That's how you show you're glad you survived. But how about if your job's gone and nobody wants to hire some wore-out colored boy?" He was looking straight at me, but I wasn't sure he saw me at all. "So you have to let your wife wash people's clothes and haul out their garbage, and you sit around and wonder why some bullet didn't finish you off."

"I'm so sorry."

It fell out before I could stop it. It was sure as hell nothing to say, and I'd have deserved it if he'd laughed or chewed me out. He blinked. His lips twitched in a smile, as if he had just remembered I was there. "I like you, man. You're all right, but damn you, you got all the luck."

"I know. It's not right."

That was pretty stupid too. At least I managed not to say *I'm sorry* again. If anybody deserved better luck, it was him, and I wished I knew how to take some of mine and pass it over the way you would pass the salt. I wanted to come up with something, anything, that would tether him to solid ground a few minutes longer.

One thing had made him happy, before the war. I knew about that, because it was the same thing I had always leaned on. "Hey," I said. "Show me your drawing."

He pulled back as if I had flicked him in the face. "What?"

"I drew for you. Now it's your turn."

"Come on, man. You know I don't do that anymore."

Now he was angry. Anger was all right. It would keep him from slipping back down into the dark. "I get a feeling you can," I said. "It's like riding a bike, right?"

"Nicky, you're a pain in the ass. Anybody ever tell you that?"

I heard a tiny ripple of laughter. He was willing to challenge me, all right. "Not in those exact words."

"Then somebody should."

He didn't take the pad and pencil back, but the way he looked at them, I could feel him reaching for them in his head. "I'll fix what I changed," I said. "Then it's your turn."

When I finished drawing, the mug and the table looked exactly as they had when I'd first come in. Timothy rapped on the table where one of the cutouts had been. "That is some trick."

I held the pad out to him. "Go ahead."

"You won't quit, will you." I didn't see any need to answer that. "Fine," he said. "But I told you, I'm no artist."

From across the table, I watched him settle the pencil between his fingers. If I had gone to school the way Dad and I had planned, I would undoubtedly have watched plenty of other artists draw by then. I would have examined different techniques and styles and traced how physical motion translated into line and color. As it was, I didn't have much to compare Timothy's approach with, but I can tell you one thing. If you had seen how his lines took shape on the paper and flowed together until, in a moment you couldn't capture, they became much more than lines; if you had seen how the face that emerged on the page had a living soul behind it, then you would have known as well as I did that Timothy was an artist.

He drew Minna. She had told me how, when he used to draw, his hand had moved so fast she could barely see it. Maybe it wasn't quite that fast now, or maybe it was easier for me to follow because the process was familiar, but even though I could see the motions, I couldn't understand how he did what he did. One moment it was a pencil sketch. The next moment it was Minna herself, so real it could have breathed. Somehow, on that flat paper, he caught the spark that made her only and exactly who she was.

I imagined him drawing her this way in France, again and again, while he waited for whatever horror the next day would bring. He'd had her photo with him, he'd told me, but this would have brought her as close to him as she could come.

He finished and set the pencil down. I had told myself that if he didn't want to give me the drawing for a closer look, I wouldn't ask him to, as much as I wanted to snatch it up to stare at it. He shrugged and held the pad out. I took it, trying not to grab, and studied the sketch. Did Minna know how he saw her? Surely, if she had seen anything like this drawing, she did. Maybe that gave her hope, even when she couldn't reach across his silence.

I said exactly what I thought. "I wish I could draw like this."

"It felt all right," he said. "Doing that. I guess some things stay with you."

Why had he ever stopped doing it? Could it help keep him going now? I didn't know how to ask those questions. "It's funny," he said, "sometimes the sketches don't turn out the way you thought. There was a guy in my unit. Roger Ellis."

I was almost afraid to breathe, in case any tiny interruption stopped him. "Nothing ever seemed to get him down," Timothy said. He traced a line on the tabletop, where the edge of one of the cutouts had been. "We'd be sitting in the rain, waiting for the next round of shelling to blast us to kingdom come. Roger'd be cracking jokes like we were off at a carnival." A smile washed over his face and vanished. "One night I wanted to draw him. I thought I'd make him laughing."

I had passed him the pad back. He'd been flipping idly back and forth between Minna's picture and the next page, which was blank. Now he stopped on the blank page, picked up the pencil and turned it around in his fingers.

"Instead, Nicky, you'd have thought that pencil drawing would start to cry, right there on the paper." He raised his eyes to mine. "I didn't mean for that to happen. I was scared to show it to him, because I figured he'd laugh at me, or tear it up, but he just sat there and looked at it for a long time. Didn't say a word. Just looked at it, like he'd never seen his own face before."

Timothy's drawing had reached past what anyone could see and laid out what was really there. I had never known that kind of magic. "Roger died at Nancy last September," he said. "He had a wife and kid at home, a girl, about two years old. He never said much about them, but he must have missed them all right."

Again, I wanted to say, *I'm so sorry.* For this unknown man who had never made it home to his family. For Timothy, bent under the load he had to carry. I wondered if he'd kept his drawings of the men in his unit, stashed them in a box somewhere, or if he had torn them up and thrown them out, trying to forget. I wondered if Roger Ellis had a quick, clean death, if he'd had time to know it was coming or that it hurt, or if the lights had simply gone out.

"I know Minna told you I had a bad day yesterday," Timothy said. "I did. Because I keep thinking how some of those guys, they had kids, they had people who needed them. They're not here and I am."

You wonder why some bullet didn't finish you off. "Minna needs you," I said.

"Did you know she went to college?" He set the pad down and laid the pencil neatly across it. "She went to Lincoln, here in the city. Did two years before we got married. Then when I left, she quit school to keep things going here. She did some secretary work for one of her professors. But then I got back, wounded and all, so we needed more money."

Burden. Drag. Waste. The words he didn't say hung loud in the air. "Look, Timothy," I started, "she..."

He cut me off. "English, that's what she studied. You never saw anybody who loved to read like she did. She wanted to be a teacher someday. She shouldn't be cleaning houses, and I can't do a damn thing about it."

The very kitchen walls felt like a trap shutting him in. He couldn't protect Minna, couldn't set her free to do what she loved, couldn't fight a world that scorned him because of his color and the sickness that hung on him. My magic might have lightened his load for a little while. Just like always, though, just like with Charley's foot so long ago, it couldn't make changes that would last.

Damn it. Anger welled up and opened my mouth for me. "Listen, Timothy, one of these days let's go to the art museum. You tell me when."

"Where the hell did that come from?"

I was in it now. Even if we could manage it, I had no idea what good it would do, but I said, "We're artists, you and me. You said they don't want you there, and I'm scared of the damn place. So let's go sometime and prove we don't give a shit."

His face made me think of that tree again, planted deep, weathering storm after storm that tried to tear it down. "They might not let me in," he reminded me. "Besides, Minna probably told you, I don't like people looking at me. Especially in a place like that."

I knew what he meant. On the other hand, he had as much right to be there as anyone. More than plenty, if you thought about it. I saw Dad again, in his worn corduroy jacket, studying a still-life of a goblet so real you could feel it in your hand. *My son is an artist.*

I said, "The people there won't look at you." The bare thought of walking between those columns made me feel as sick as I'd gotten in front of Charley. "They'll all be watching me when I pass out and hit the floor like a sack of potatoes."

Laughter woke up in his eyes. "Brother, I like the way you think."

"Then let's do it."

I held my hand out. He gripped it hard. "Okay," he said. "When?"

We decided to make it the coming Saturday at noon. No point in waiting longer. "My brother might want to come along," I said. "Charley. He's all right."

"Minna too," he said. "Sounds like we'll be an invasion."

"They won't know what hit them," I said. Timothy smiled.

～

By the time I got home, Minna had finished her shift and left. Charley had just gotten back from the A&P. We put away the few groceries and I told him about the plan for Saturday.

"The museum? Are you sure?"

He was right to worry. I would have liked to pretend I wasn't worried too. "Timothy should see it," I said. "He and Minna probably can't get in on their own."

Charley understood why not. He scrubbed a potato at the sink, his hands tight, the motions quick and sharp. "I dunno if you can get in a fight with the guards."

"Shouldn't come to that," I said. "I can argue all right."

Charley set the potato on the counter. "So can I." As far as I knew, he had never thrown a punch, but it was hard to believe in that moment. "Okay," he said. "We'll do it."

Justine was coming over at five that afternoon. I had offered to go and meet her at her place and ride back with her, if she didn't like coming to a strange part of town alone, but she'd laughed. "Nicky, it's your home. Why would I be nervous?" Four-thirty found me pacing the downstairs, checking and re-checking that everything was as neat as possible. It was, after Minna had swept and dusted that morning, but nothing was going to hide the scuffs on the old floorboards, or those faded patches on the wallpaper where the sun had hit it day after day. I told myself Justine wouldn't mind any of that, she wasn't that kind of girl...but it was too easy to picture her in the cab on the way over, watching the scenery change. Wondering, after all, what she'd gotten herself into.

I was in the middle of my third pass through the living room when the knock came. Five on the dot.

"Evening, handsome." Justine's cornflower-blue dress looked like a piece of sky. Behind her, the cab pulled away from the curb. Our patch of yard looked dingy and mottled, with the new spring green finally taking over the winter brown. The late-afternoon sun slanted across the stoop, bringing out the crack across one corner.

Justine held up a white cardboard box. "This is for dessert. I didn't make it, so it's safe to eat."

We caught a kiss in the front hall before Charley came down to say hello, with Titus on his heels. Justine bent down to pet the cat. "There was a lady, a couple of houses down," she said, "out in her yard. An older lady with glasses? I think she was watching me."

Charley grinned at me. "That'd be Mrs. O'Dell."

"Ah." Justine stood up. "And let me guess. She's known you both since you were little, and she wants to know if I'm good enough for Nicky."

My face felt warm. Charley said, "That sounds about right."

Justine slipped her arm through mine. "We'll have to find out what she decides. For now, would you show me around?"

There wasn't much to show. I couldn't help thinking the house felt smaller and shabbier than ever, even though Justine made no sign that she thought it was any less comfortable or gracious than her own. We went up to my room last. Justine walked over to my desk. "This is where you used to draw?"

"All the time."

She touched the back of the chair gently, the way she might have touched the shoulder of a person sitting there. "What did you like to draw when you were little?"

"Anything I could, really." I went over to stand next to her. It felt odd to be so tall, to see out the window down into the street so easily. "Dad taught me shapes, one line at a time. I'd copy them for him, and then I'd practice them, over and over."

"I bet you did. Let me see...you were a little boy, sitting right here at this desk. Your bangs were probably a little bit messy, just like they are now." They always were. I started to reach up and smooth them back, but she laughed and caught my hand. "You look fine. And I bet, when you were drawing, you'd be so caught up in it that you wouldn't notice anything else."

She knew, all right. "That's right. The same way you were with your poetry."

"Yes." With her free hand, she reached up to touch my face. "I'm so glad you didn't mind me coming over. I love seeing your house."

I wanted to trust her. With all my heart, I did, but at the same time, I couldn't quite relax. Something felt ever so slightly wrong, like an out-of-focus photo.

The dinner turned out pretty well. Justine and Charley and I sat at the table together, talking and eating the way I'd hoped we might. Justine seemed as comfortable in my mother's kitchen as she had been in her father's dining room. She talked and laughed with Charley and me more freely than she had in front of Dr. Murray and Louisa, but every time I looked at her, at the smooth fall of her hair and her crisp lovely dress, I wondered if it was just possible that she had learned to be polite no matter what. She'd have been taught perfect manners, so she would know how not to show what she really felt about cheap glasses and tin dinnerware, and a kitchen that hadn't had steak in it since I didn't remember when.

We cleared away the plates and opened the dessert box. Justine had brought a strawberry tart, just the right size for three, as bright as paint and heaped with mounds of whipped cream. "It's my favorite," she said. "I asked Rebecca to make it so I could bring you something."

It was delicious, of course. The berries were perfect. The cream was real cream, incredibly rare. I wanted to close my eyes and savor the way it melted and eased down my throat. At the same time, I couldn't forget how much it must all have cost: the fruit, the cream, the butter in the crust, all the sugar to sweeten it. I couldn't forget, either, how the woman who had made this tart was the same one Dr. Murray had called into the dining room to scold as if she were a clumsy child. When I thought of that, the berries seemed to turn watery and sour.

Charley said – *nudge, wink* – he had to go through some proofs for the yearbook, so he would go upstairs and leave us to ourselves for a while. Justine and I cleaned up the dessert dishes and went to sit in the living room. Charley's chair was in here now, the way he and I had agreed on, with a wool blanket and an extra pillow on it as if it had been an armchair. We'd decided it didn't look half bad.

Justine sat down on the couch. "Nicky, what's wrong?"

She was too quick. I sat down beside her, wishing I could answer "nothing" and mean it. She said, "Have you been thinking about the 4-F again?"

It would have been an easy out. "I was," I said. "Yesterday, a lot."

"But there's something else."

I didn't know where to start. Part of me wanted to tell her what I was thinking about her, how it scared me to know that, after all, the world I came from had so few of the things she'd always had and always counted on. I wanted to tell her about Minna and Timothy, too, and how as far as I could tell, the world wasn't set up right when some people had too much luck and others had none. Mostly, though, I knew perfectly well that I had no business spilling all that to her. We had known each other such a little while.

She was watching me. "What are you thinking?"

"Right now, I'm thinking that this sofa is about a thousand years old, and it sure looks like it."

Its upholstery was at least as old as I was. The pattern was worn and faded, the fabric fraying at the corners. I'd meant to make a joke, but I'd bet her father would set fire to a sofa like this before he let it into his house.

"Nicky True. Are you thinking I don't belong here with you?"

"Not that you're not welcome. It's just that you..." A bead of sweat started down my back. "You deserve much better."

It sounded awkward enough. She didn't laugh. More than that: I had never seen her angry.

"I don't know whether to kiss you or slap you." It didn't take her long to decide. She drew my head down and planted such a hard kiss on my mouth that it hurt. "Don't you go thinking I'm some silly girl who has to have silk and lace and three forks at dinner. You know better."

You do have those things. You've never had to do without them. I could have said so, though it might have earned me the slap too. Instead, I thought of Timothy's drawing hand, and the way Minna's face had come to life on the paper.

"Justine," I said, "can I tell you about something?"

"Please do."

It wasn't easy at first. I started with bald facts, Minna's and Timothy's names, the fact that they were colored, how I had met them. The words came more readily as I explained that I'd hired Minna to help us while our mother was sick, and how she had started to tell me about her life. "Timothy lost his job. He hasn't been able to find something else, so she's keeping them going." I told her a little, as much as I thought I had the right, about what Timothy had done in France and how he was treated here at home, and what it was doing to him. "He's an artist too. You should see what he does with his drawing." Finally, I told her about the museum trip on Saturday. "Timothy's always wanted to go, but he and Minna can't get in on their own because they're colored. Charley and I are going to try to help."

Justine listened without interrupting. I couldn't tell what she thought: whether she could imagine what Minna and Timothy went through every day, whether she could understand being friends with a colored maid and her husband. When I finished, she was quiet for a moment. Then: "This Saturday?"

"Yes."

"Could I come with you?"

I hadn't considered she might want to. I wanted to say yes, but it wasn't my decision to make. "I'll have to ask Timothy. Minna will be here Friday, so I can leave her a note for him."

"Good." She reached over for one of my hands, lifted it to her lips, and kissed it. I didn't know what to make of that. "Ask him, and then call me and tell me what he thinks."

Her father expected her home soon, so she said good night to Charley and Titus. I called a cab and rode with her back to Center City. It was late evening by then, the sky dark, the streets busy with headlights. The gleam and excitement of yesterday had quieted but not faded.

On her front porch, I put my arms around her and she drew my head down again. If any neighbors had been watching us, they would have had plenty of time during that kiss to size me up and decide whether or not I was good enough for her. "Good night, my love," she said. "Call me about Saturday."

"I will."

My love. The door closed behind her. The marble porch steps could have been cloud, for all I felt them under my feet.

Chapter Fourteen

Jo has been looking over what I've written so far. Yesterday, when she came by for supper, she sat down at the laptop and read through the last few chapters. It's quite a thing to feel like a schoolboy again, waiting for the teacher to hand back an essay.

"You and Mom were something. Falling for each other that fast."

"We both had good taste."

"You said that." She scrolled back through the last five or so pages. "I can't believe you've written so much already, Dad. It's only been a few weeks."

"My calendar is pretty open these days, sweetheart." In truth, it's been pretty open ever since I finally retired from teaching, although for the first ten of those years, while Justine and I still had each other, we helped with the grandkids and kept ourselves busy.

Jo said, "You must type faster than I do." She sized me up over the top of the laptop screen. "Are you sure you're as old as you say?"

"My birth certificate is around someplace. You want me to find it?"

She laughed. "That's okay. But if you're still in this good shape, maybe there's hope for me."

"I should think so."

She reached over. Her hands are still strong and steady, and I hope they'll stay that way for a long time yet. She gripped mine good and tight.

"You told me once, you think you and Mom will find each other again sometime."

I used to think death was the end of the line, no matter what the church always said. These days...well, I told you how I can imagine shedding this old body like a coat. Justine and I were such a part of each other in life that, yes, when it's time for me to call it a day, I think we'll find each other again. Wherever and whatever we are.

Jo said, "I have a feeling you will." She gave her head that little toss that's always meant she is keeping her game face on. "Just don't be in too big a hurry to head out of here, okay?"

"I can't be in a hurry, darling. Not when I've been around this long already."

That made her smile. "Fair. But listen, whatever you do, you've got to finish this story first."

She doesn't need to worry about that. This old cuss still has some steam.

~

ON THE DAY BEFORE TIMOTHY AND I PLANNED TO "INVADE" the museum, I went to do a photoshoot with a florist named Dexter Marshall. Dexter and his photographer both knew me and had already signed the non-disclosure paperwork, so I didn't expect any trouble.

The bell on the shop door jangled me inside. "Mr. True!" Dexter hustled out of the chilly storage room in the back. "Right on time. Better days are on their way now, wouldn't you say, sir?"

Someone else was waiting near the front counter, by the array of vases and stems laid out for the shoot. Dexter was small, with blond hair carefully pomaded into place. The second man was closer to my height, with dark straight hair and high cheekbones. He considered me as if he was going to write an "Observers" column for the newspaper.

"This is Abel Swift," Dexter told me. "He's a florist too, a friend of mine from outside the city. His shop is in Haverford." I knew Haverford, a quiet, well-heeled college town. "I gave him a hint or two about what you do," Dexter said. "He's most interested in seeing it. Your firm wouldn't mind business in the suburbs, I'm sure?"

Of course not. We'd be delighted. That's what he expected me to say, and it certainly would have been natural, but I couldn't have been farther from it. In fact, I had frozen as thoroughly as if I had gone into that chilly storeroom too. This went against every rule I had.

Now, you might wonder why. Abel Swift was one person. How much could it matter if he found out what I did, or if he'd already heard something from Dexter? I had shown Timothy the magic myself, with no legalese in sight.

It mattered because Timothy had been my choice, but Dexter had broken the trust Allen and Allen and I had put in him. A hairline crack in a dam can matter too.

If I'd had an extra copy of the non-disclosure letter, I might have pulled it out for Abel Swift to sign. I hadn't brought one because I hadn't expected to need it. "Mr. Marshall," I said, "I'm afraid I can't do the job if Mr. Swift is here. He isn't authorized to see it."

Dexter's face fell. "Oh, but you're here now. Everything's ready."

The photographer didn't look any too happy either. He had set up all his gear and didn't want to pack it up again without a single shot to show for the trouble. Abel Swift stepped in. "Mr. True, Dexter tells me that your trick is worth seeing. I took time away from my own business to drive into the city today, so I would appreciate the opportunity to see the demonstration."

If I'd been thinking more clearly, I could have gotten out my sketchbook and written a quick non-disclosure letter myself. Or I could have told Dexter to call my boss and let Stephen read him the rules, which he had apparently forgotten. Instead, I drew myself up and faced off against Abel Swift as if he had been Matt Jeffries, the Lawrence Street bully, grown up.

"Sir, if you decided to take time off today and come down here, that was your call. I didn't ask you to do it and nobody warned me you'd be here. And Mr. Marshall, as for you." I'd never taken such a tone with Dexter before. Under other circumstances, his wide, stunned eyes would have given me a twinge of guilt. "You violated the conditions you agreed to with my employer," I said. "I can't do this job, and I won't."

It was all dramatic enough, down to the way I about-faced and walked straight back out of the shop. I hadn't set my briefcase down, so I didn't have to stop to pick it up. The bell jangled me back out onto the sidewalk.

Dexter might have come outside and called after me. If he did, I didn't hear it. I didn't bother hailing a cab. A cloud of steam carried me back to Allen and Allen, straight up the stairs to the fourth floor.

By the time I got there, Dexter had obviously phoned over, because Mark and Stephen were waiting by Barbara's desk. Stephen looked calm, amused even. Mark was a different story.

"What do you think you're doing?" Mark hardly bothered to keep his voice down. "How dare you abandon a client in the middle of a job?"

Stephen put a hand on his brother's arm. "Not here. Nicky, come on in my office. Let's sort this out."

Over at the desks in the main area, I saw the other two artists, Maurice Barclay and Gus Haskins, looking toward us. They probably wouldn't mind if the upstart new hire was in bad trouble. Stephen ushered Mark and me inside his office and shut the door. "Now. Let's talk this over."

Mark didn't think there was much to talk about. "You, Nicky, you had no right to behave that way." He was about a head shorter than me, but he squared up as if he wanted to back me into the wall. "You violated your professional commitment, and you showed the utmost disrespect to a long-standing client of this firm."

"*I* showed disrespect? I did?" If he wanted a fight, he'd have one. "If he called here, then you know he told someone else what I do and invited that person along to see it. He might as well have ripped up his contract with us right there." I knew I couldn't start shouting, not with people within earshot on the other side of the door, but my palms tingled and the pulse beat in my temples. "What kind of respect does that show me, or this firm for that matter?"

Stephen put one hand on his brother's shoulder and the other hand on mine and drew us back from each other. "Boys. Pipe down and sit down."

It might have been funny, a playground fight waiting to start, but I sure didn't see any humor in it. Neither did Mark. We dropped into the chairs in front of Stephen's desk.

"Now." Unhurried, Stephen moved around to his own chair, sat down, and propped his elbows on the desk. "Nicky, you're right. Dexter violated the terms of his agreement with you and with us." *Damn right he did.* I bit my tongue. "That said, you did have a commitment to do this job today, and quite frankly, I'm surprised at you."

"Really, *sir?*"

He smiled. That hadn't been what I was after. "None of that. We'll fix this, but yes, I'm surprised. I know you're a professional. Professionals don't storm out of a job."

Next to me, Mark was simmering. It was anybody's guess which of us would hit boiling point first, him or me. Stephen said, "I explained to Dexter where he went wrong, and he fully understands and apologized most sincerely. I told him, Nicky, that you and I would discuss the situation, and I was sure that once we did, you would go back there – yes," he said, seeing that I was about to interrupt, "I was sure you would go back right away, with a letter for his friend to sign, and complete the job as agreed. Now, was I right?"

I wanted to tell him no. I wanted it so badly that the word filled up my mouth. *Say it, say it and be done with it.* Not just today's shoot: the whole mess of the job, selling the magic for this.

The saner part of me cut in like a jet of cold air. *What about Charley? How else will you take care of him?*

"Okay." It was so hard to spit that out that my jaw seemed to creak. "I'll do it." Stephen's smile, as if he would have liked to pat me on the head, did not make it any easier to add, "I'm sorry."

"No harm done." Stephen took another copy of the letter out of his filing cabinet and passed it across the desk. "Go on back and give them your best."

I went. By the end of the shoot, Abel Swift told me that he wanted to "retain my services" and would be more than happy to compensate extra, on top of the commission, for my commute to the suburbs. I told him to give Stephen a call to arrange a contract. Adding him to my roster felt like strapping a sack of bricks to my back, but Stephen would be thrilled and Mark might unbend a little. I told myself it was worth it.

That afternoon seemed to stretch out long enough to cover most of a workweek. When I finally made it home, I found an answer to the note I'd left in the kitchen for Minna that morning. Not in her handwriting this time; Timothy's scratch looked a lot more like mine.

Nicky – you didn't tell me there's a girl in your life. That's serious business, so you be careful.

If you say she's all right, I guess I don't mind her coming along tomorrow.

See you then,
Timothy

〜

I DIDN'T SLEEP A WHOLE LOT THAT NIGHT. THE NEXT DAY, the bus let Charley and me off at the museum stop at noon. He settled in his chair for the ride up the hill. "I bet you know more than the docents do," he said. "We'll get a better tour than anybody."

His "this'll be a fun day out" tone was as brittle as a skim of ice on a puddle. "I'll try," I said. "We'll see how much I remember." If only, I thought, I didn't remember anything; if I could go into the place as if I'd never set foot in it before.

Minna and Timothy were waiting for us in front of the column at the far end of the building. Both, I couldn't help noticing, had dressed as if they were going to church, when Charley and I had worn jeans and sneakers. I pushed the chair down the row of columns. They looked enormous, even bigger than I remembered.

It was a warm day, cloudy but with a taste of summer around the corner. Back in March, when I'd arrived in Philly, the wind had wanted to push me away. Now the columns seemed to do the same. They scrutinized me with invisible eyes, daring me to get closer.

Charley pulled himself up from the chair to shake hands with Timothy. "Good to meet you finally," he said. "Nicky says your drawings are incredible."

Timothy looked about as tense as I felt. "He only saw one of them," he said, "but thanks. Good to meet you too."

Footsteps came up behind us. Justine looked so pretty, in a white blouse and the daffodil-yellow skirt she'd worn for the zoo trip. She smiled at me, but went straight to Minna and held out her hand. "Mrs. Davis? So glad to meet you."

The two of them stood about eye to eye. They both looked like the spring itself, Justine in the daffodil and Minna in warm peach. Minna returned the handshake. "Miss Murray," she said. "I'm pleased to meet you too."

"Please, call me Justine."

Minna introduced her to "my husband, Timothy." Justine shook hands with him too. "I'm so glad you didn't mind me coming along today," she said. "I know this matters a lot to you and Nicky both. Thank you."

You who are reading this, so many years after it happened: I wonder if you can understand why this ordinary-sounding talk mattered so much.

The invisible wall that separated Minna and Timothy from Justine, the white daughter of a rich city doctor, was high enough to nudge at the clouds. Justine had chosen to ignore it. That's why Timothy looked directly into her face and considered her, the way you would size up anyone who'd said something unexpected.

He knew much better than I did that in some places, for instance anywhere south of the Mason-Dixon line, he could never have dared to do such a thing. If he had looked her in the eye, especially with a couple of white men there to see it – as my brother and I were – a trap would have closed around him that he wouldn't walk out of.

As it was, he smiled. "I'm glad to meet you, Justine. If you'll excuse me saying it, you and Nicky make a good couple."

She put her hand over mine, where I held the back of Charley's chair. "I think we do."

Timothy had said we'd be an invasion. I certainly felt as if we were, or at least, as I forced myself to march between those columns and through the glass doors, I wondered if I might be getting the faintest sense of how soldiers felt as they started across no man's land. The great, cool, echoing space opened up around us. My chest felt so tight I wondered if my lungs would flatten into pancakes.

Even though it was a Saturday, the lobby was mostly empty. People wanted to be outside to savor the warm weather. Charley rolled his chair up to the ticket counter, with me just behind. The attendant, a brunette who looked like a high-school freshman, smiled at the two of us.

"Good afternoon," I said. My mouth felt as if someone had coated it on the inside with glue. "Five entrance passes, please."

"Five, sir?" Her eyes moved to Minna and Timothy, just behind me. "For you and..."

"For me and my brother here, and these two ladies and the gentleman with us."

Trouble could start right now. I needed to brace for a fight, but already, the light seemed strange, the counter in front of me distorted as if I was looking at it through the bottom of a glass. I had stood in this exact spot with Dad, my head just at his shoulder, watching him count out the coins he had put by for our trip this week.

You see, Nicky, some people'd think it's a treat to come here. Really, we need it just the same as food.

"I'm sorry, sir." The girl's voice tugged me back to this day. "Do you mean that this...the..." She motioned toward Minna and Timothy with a thin white hand. "Do you mean they're with you?"

Charley cleared his throat, ready to wade in. "That's right," I said. "That lady and gentleman are my guests."

She hesitated, glancing from me to Timothy and back again. Her fingers edged toward the stack of pasteboard tickets on the counter. No doubt she was afraid of hearing about it if she let the wrong kind of patrons in, but I was standing in front of her, and her boss wasn't. To cement things, I took out my billfold and counted the money out. "Two dollars and fifty cents?"

She gave in. "Yes, sir." My chest eased a little when she passed the tickets and two museum maps over. One hurdle down.

We moved over to a corner of the lobby to look at the maps. Timothy said quietly to me, "You got *this* in. Thanks."

"It's such shit." If I could get angry, maybe that would help with the rest of it. "They have no right to..."

"I've been called worse," Timothy said. "We're here now. Let's just see as much as we can."

In the corner, the group of us unfolded the two maps to decide where to start. So little had changed since the last time I'd been here. The layout of the galleries was the same, though some of the exhibits had changed...but the ones Dad and I had known best, the Impressionists, the Flemish gallery, Modern Art, were exactly what they'd been.

The last time I'd been here. It had been close to the same time of year, the weather warm enough that stepping into this cool space came as a relief. I had come here then with my dreams and plans still whole. In a few hours, they would all be in pieces.

Charley said, "Nicky, you're the expert. What should we see first?"

More than anything, I wanted to turn around and go back outside and forget all this. We were here now, and the point was for Timothy to see what he wanted. "You pick," I said to him.

His glance told me he guessed how I was feeling. "I don't know art, man."

Minna said, "Well, somebody choose. What's Modern Art like?"

I had to do better than this. Not least because Justine couldn't know how hard it was for me to be here. "Modern Art's good," I said. "They have Georgia O'Keeffe and Frida Kahlo, and Thomas Hart Benton, or at least they used to."

"Georgia O'Keeffe?" Charley said. "You have some of her stuff, don't you?"

The prints that still sat in their box in the basement. "Yeah. I've always liked her."

Timothy said, "Then let's do that."

Inside the first gallery, the paintings stood out as splashes of brilliance against the drab walls. Three college-age boys with sketchbooks, art students, stood in front of one of the canvases on the far wall. A family of four, mother and father and two little girls, wandered from one painting to another. I saw the father glance sidelong at Timothy and me, but, wisely, he left us alone.

Charley wheeled straight to an O'Keeffe near the gallery entrance. The chair's tires squeaked against the gleaming floorboards. "Nicky, this is her, right?"

The painting was *Black Mesa Landscape*, a study of the textures and colors in a New Mexico view. Charley recognized O'Keeffe's style from the prints, but I had seen the canvas before, sure enough. Dad and I had studied it together.

Timothy said, "Can you tell us something about it?"

My hands and face tingled as if I'd been walking in a hard wind. Dad and I had admired the landscape's textures and shapes, as complex as a sheet that had been crumpled and smoothed out again. We had studied the contrast of the melon-orange hills in the foreground with the mountains behind, blue shading to black, and we'd agreed that even though the painting was nothing like a photograph, O'Keeffe had captured something in it that a camera couldn't touch. It was alive and breathing, not just what a place looked like, but what it *was.*

Timothy did the same thing with his drawings. I pulled in a breath. "I don't know a whole lot," I said, "but I'll tell you what I remember."

That was more than I'd thought. Dad and I had learned about O'Keeffe's technique and how she'd used color and line to guide the viewer's eye. Those details had stayed filed away in my head from the time when I'd thought I might need them. When I finished describing what I could, Timothy raised an eyebrow. "You don't know a lot?"

We moved along to the next O'Keeffe canvas. *Petunia* was a single purple-black bloom with a lavender heart like the sky just after sunset. Justine edged up as close to it as the red-velvet guarding ropes allowed.

"I wish I could touch it," she said. The lush petals looked like the swirl of a girl's dress. "It should feel like satin."

I had felt the same, the first time I'd seen it. I'd had to lock my hands together behind my back so I wouldn't give in to temptation. Minna said, "There's another flower over here, come look." She and Charley went to the next painting, but Justine and Timothy and I stayed behind.

"Timothy," I said, "your drawing reminds me of O'Keeffe. The way you show what's really there."

He turned around to see me. "You're kidding, right?"

Justine said, "He doesn't say what he doesn't mean."

Timothy's smile lit his face up and disappeared. He stepped closer to look at the shading in the heart of the flower. "I've never used paints at all. This kind of makes me want to try. Don't know why I should bother, but...these colors. It seems like you could taste them."

We made our gradual way through the galleries. In the last one, we found a Kahlo painting I hadn't seen before: *Still Life: Pitahayas.*

Its textures caught me right away. At that time, I had never seen a dragon fruit and had no idea what I was looking at, but it fascinated me just the same. Those smooth red oblongs, gleaming softly where light caught them, cool to the touch, leathery maybe, with small patches of roughness. The interiors, laid open no doubt by a neat knife slice: they looked feathery-soft, dotted with black points like grains of sand. If I could reach through the canvas and touch them, they might feel silky like milkweed floss, or like cream.

Dad would have loved this. Knowing it, I felt for a moment as if I could share it with him if I tried hard enough. The painting itself reached out for me, like an old friend I hadn't seen in too long. I even forgot to be afraid of where I was. *Do you see this? Isn't it something!*

Charley and Minna and Timothy started back toward the main lobby. Justine waited for me. When I finally remembered to look around, she was smiling.

"I'm sorry," I said.

"Don't be."

We headed after the others, hand in hand. "When you looked at that canvas just now," she said, "what were you thinking?"

I tried to explain about the textures, how I'd always wanted to know how artists made them so real using only flat layers of paint. "I'd love to try that," I said. "But if I got hold of some oils, I'd probably just make a mess."

We were outside the gallery now, still a little distance behind the others. Justine stopped in the hallway. "Nicky." She looked up into my face. "When you look at the art, when I watch you..."

She was so intent and serious that I thought something had made her sad. "What is it?"

Her smile came back, but the searching look was still there. "I love seeing what it means to you." She reached up to touch my cheek. "That's all."

Charley's voice reached us. "Are you two coming, or what?"

In the lobby, we got the maps back out. Timothy unfolded his. "You know," he said, "being here, it almost makes me think about drawing again."

Minna caught my eye. Her face told me she wanted to shout *Yes! Do it!* as much as I did. We couldn't, not right there and then, so I said, "If you want to draw, you should."

This time, his smile didn't flash away. "You remember what I called you the other day?"

You're a pain in the ass. "Sure do."

"Good." He glanced over the map. "What's your favorite gallery? That's the one I'd like to see."

He knew what he was asking. After everything we'd talked about, he could figure that my favorite place, from the times when Dad and I had come here, would probably be the one I'd want to avoid now. I did have the sense to hesitate. On the other hand, I didn't want to refuse, and the idea of seeing those canvases again had caught me. It had been such a long time.

"My favorite?" I said. "That's the Flemish gallery."

We all went. I had hoped the place might have changed a little during my years away, but one glance told me it hadn't. The dark walls, the heavy gilt frames catching the light, the rich layers of oils, the soft, cool air and the hush: all of it was exactly what I remembered.

This was dangerous. My throat tightened and my chest felt as if someone had filled it with snow. But *I* wasn't the same, I told myself. I wasn't that kid anymore.

The nearest canvas was the Rubens still-life of the glass and basket. I said, "That was my favorite painting." My hand held steady when I pointed it out, but my voice seemed to come from a long way away. I told Timothy how Dad and I had loved these canvases partly because they were some of the oldest art we saw, how fascinated we'd been at the idea that we could follow brushstrokes the artists made hundreds of years ago. I said, "See how Rubens uses the light here? It's just white paint at the edges of where the glass would be. It's what you *don't* see that makes the glass look real."

"You're right." Timothy moved closer to the canvas. "I do see that."

Then it happened. With no warning or shift at all, I was sitting on the bus again with Dad.

It's what the artist didn't *paint.*

His face, as he turned around from the window to listen to me. His eyes.

Nicky, what would you think about college?

The floor felt solid under my feet. The air was cool against my face and hands. Justine and Charley were right nearby, and Minna and Timothy had stepped over to another still-life a few feet away. I knew all of those things...and yet I didn't.

This was it. My nightmare.

What happened to you, Nicky?

I clenched my hands, driving my nails into my palms. *Not now. Please.* I knew where I was, and when. The gallery was real, I hadn't stepped back in time, I wasn't dreaming or someplace else...

...and yet I was back there on the bus, too, heading home, and now I was alone because Dad hadn't come with me that day. He had said he felt too tired. I had left him at home, and my mother and Charley were out too, and he was by himself.

Footsteps came into the gallery. Out of the corner of my eye, I saw a guard in a dark uniform walking toward Minna and Timothy.

Justine and Charley were still looking at the first canvas. Charley was saying he wondered how artists had learned to use light that way. He sounded fuzzy, muffled. Then, loud and clear, I heard another voice.

"Do you have tickets, boy? Show me."

I had been underwater, fighting to breathe. I'm not even sure how I heard what the guard said, but his handful of words went through my head like a live wire.

Show me.

Boy.

The next thing I heard was my own voice. "Hey. You."

The words had enough edge on them to split wood. I was moving by then, toward Minna and Timothy, on feet that felt as if they had turned into concrete blocks. The guard was a blur, red face above dark collar, thatch of gray hair. "Sir," he said, "please don't be concerned. I'll make sure that these people..."

There Minna and Timothy stood in their church-going clothes. I wore jeans and a plain cotton button-down, and my white skin.

"These people?" My voice again. I don't think I actually towered over the guard, but it felt as if I did, or rather as if I was floating up near the ceiling, watching all of this happen. "This lady and gentleman are here with me. They have tickets like anyone else. Why are you harassing patrons who are here to enjoy the art?"

My mouth said it with no help from my brain. The guard backed away as if he thought I might scoop him up and wing him out of the gallery. "I apologize, sir. I didn't realize."

I wanted to say, *I think you owe them an apology too, don't you?* Or maybe, *Next time, think before you stick your nose in.* But he was walking away, leaving the room, and now it started to spin, and the past closed in and squeezed my breath out.

He said he was too tired. He told me to go to the museum. He was home by himself.

If I had been there...

The floor seemed to drift up to meet me. It felt cold and hard under my palms. Somebody was saying something, a bunch of voices, quick and sharp, but my heart felt like a jackhammer in my chest and my head was full of blood.

Couldn't you have said goodbye?

Dad.

I wrapped my arms around my knees and pressed my forehead against them. They felt hard and bumpy through the rough fabric of my jeans. The dark closed in.

THE NEXT TIME YOU WANT TO EMBARRASS YOURSELF SO much you think you might as well shrivel up and blow away on the next breeze, you could try that on for size. Passing out in a public place, in front of a bunch of people, including the girl you'd hoped would never see your biggest weakness.

I didn't actually hit the floor like a sack of potatoes, and it didn't last long. I came around knowing exactly where I was and what had happened. The shame felt as if someone had opened a boiling faucet over my head.

Timothy crouched beside me. Justine knelt on my other side, holding onto my arm. Timothy said, as calmly as if taking note of the weather, "You're okay, aren't you."

"Yeah." I was covered in cold sweat. Justine had to let go when I took off my glasses and mopped my face on my sleeve. "I'm fine."

Timothy got to his feet and held out a hand. "Come on."

He pulled me up. My legs wanted to give way and I still felt plenty sick. *That's enough of that,* I told myself. *You can walk.*

"Nicky." The fear in Justine's voice made my head throb again. "What…"

Timothy said, "Let's get outside before anybody comes along. We can talk out there."

I counted "at leasts" as we made our way out. At least nobody else had been in the gallery. At least I had come around before anybody thought they should call for an ambulance. At least Justine hadn't thrown me over yet.

The warm air outside thawed my icy skin. We got away from the doors and I sat down in front of one of the columns. Justine sat with me. The solid stone against my back felt good.

"I'm so sorry," I said.

Timothy, of course, knew what had happened, better than anybody else. Minna and Charley had an idea too. Justine didn't.

"Nicky." She took my hand between both of hers. "Tell me what's wrong."

I had to try. I didn't have the words, of course; at that time, I had never heard of *panic attack, anxiety disorder,* or *trauma.* Neither had Timothy. Between the two of us, we did the best we could.

I told Justine about the dizzy spells and how they had kept me out of the war. "It wasn't my eyes. I didn't get to take the vision test." Saying it felt like dredging some dark, slimy thing out of the deepest place inside me, letting it splat down on the concrete in front of her. Timothy explained that he had the same trouble. I knew how big a favor he was doing me, talking so openly about his sickness to someone he had only met a couple of hours ago. "It feels bad," he said, "and it looks bad, but as far as I can tell, it's not really dangerous."

"But what is it?" Justine said. "Why does it happen?"

"I don't know," Timothy said. "The only thing I'm sure of is I was all right before the war."

Minna had been sitting on Justine's other side, listening quietly. She said, "He's right. Something about his time overseas, it made him sick."

Justine said, "But, Nicky, you didn't serve."

"No." I didn't want to imagine what she must think of me now. "With me, I think it's because of Dad." I decided I might as well say all of it. "I was thinking about him right then. How I wasn't with him when he died."

Charley leaned forward in his chair as if he wanted to say something, but Minna got there first. "Then it wasn't the guard that did it?"

Timothy laughed, a tight, harsh sound. "No, you saw his face." Meaning mine. "Man, if you'd turned any whiter, we'd have seen clear through you. It'd started by then, right?"

"Yes."

"I could've handled that fool," Timothy said. "Could've shown him our tickets and no harm done."

"You shouldn't have had to." It felt good to get mad, to know I could still do that.

"I told you how it is."

I wished he had sounded angry too. I wished there was a way to force the world to stop treating him like a scrap of trash stuck to the sole of a shoe. I wished I could do anything but slump against the column as if my bones had turned into sand.

As it was, I knew getting up again right away would be a mistake, so we all stayed there a while longer. I closed my eyes as if that would make me invisible. Minna said to Justine, "I think the flowers were my favorites. What about you?" Somehow, she got the others talking about canvases as if nothing had gone wrong, although Justine never let go of my hand.

When the time came for Minna and Timothy to get to the bus station, I pushed myself to my feet. The ground underfoot stayed steady. "Us too," I said. "Justine, we need to get you a cab."

"No, you don't," she said. "I'm going with you and Charley."

"I'm all right. I promise."

"I'm still going with you."

She probably had plenty to say to me and wanted us to be alone when she did. Minna and Timothy caught their bus first. Timothy shook hands with me. "You take care of yourself. Let's talk drawing again sometime."

Justine and Charley and I didn't say much to each other until we got back to the house. With the front door closed behind us, Justine told Charley, "I'd like to talk to your brother, if you don't mind."

Charley didn't mind at all. "I've got a couple of things to say too, but they can wait."

I was in hot water, all right. *I didn't want any of this,* I wanted to tell them. *I said I was sorry.* Justine and I went into the living room and sat on the couch, the same way we had the other night, except now we kept a little space between us.

I was afraid to try to read her face, so I talked to the floor, to give her the apology she deserved. "Look, I'm sorry I didn't tell you the real story about the 4-F. I don't like people knowing about it, but I should have been honest with you."

"I wish you had been."

Her voice was gentle, but she sounded disappointed. I was sure she was wishing she'd known the truth before we got serious. Before she'd told me she loved me.

She said, "I wish you'd thought you could trust me."

That forced me to lift my head. "I did. I do." If nothing else, she had to know how I felt about her. "I didn't know how to talk about it. It went away for a while, when I was in California, and I thought I was better, and then I got back here and it started again." I had to turn my face away; it was that or close my eyes again. "I hate being that weak."

She touched my cheek. "Nicky." At least she still cared. Her voice told me that. "You don't think it's dangerous, whatever it is?"

"No." After the failed army physical, Dr. Sanders had given me a once-over, but he couldn't undo the classification when he couldn't explain the dizzy spells either. "I've been checked out. Looks like I'm okay, except I get sick for no reason."

"Can I tell you what I'm thinking?"

If it's what I'm afraid of, please don't. I couldn't fall apart in front of her twice in one day. "Of course."

"I was thinking it before this happened, too, in case you start getting any strange ideas." Before I could decide what to make of that, she smiled, and something in her smile reached inside me and put a hand around my heart. She said, "I would like to marry you."

Marry you. It hung in the air. I hadn't really heard it, had I? I didn't want to breathe in case it disappeared.

"I love you, Nicky. Whatever happens, tomorrow and next year and whenever, I'd like us to go through it together." She took my hands in hers. "But I need to know you'll tell me about things, no matter what. That is, if you'll have me."

If? Somehow my mouth opened. "That day at the zoo, I wanted to ask you to marry me then."

She raised an eyebrow, that wonderful scolding look. "Why didn't you?"

"Because how could I do that, when..." I had been about to laugh, but out of nowhere, it felt as if I was about to cry instead. "When I know what a mess I am?" She wanted me to be honest with her. Well, I would, and see how she liked it. "You saw what happened today. Then there's this house, and my job. I don't want to draw for those damn ads, I'm sick of selling the magic, but I don't have anything else." I hadn't admitted that out loud before, even to myself. My throat ached. "I don't have much to give you, Justine. I wish I did."

I thought she might get angry, the way she had the other night. *Don't go thinking I'm some silly girl who needs three forks at dinner.* Had she thought, had she really thought, what she would give up for me?

She said, "You're right about the ads. Art means so much to you. There has to be something better you could do."

It sounded so simple. It wasn't, though, when I had walked away from my chance to do anything with art at all. She let go of my hands so I could take off my glasses and rub my eyes on my sleeve. "I'm not sure what I could do instead," I said. "I never got any training, you know that."

She shifted closer so that our knees touched. "I think we can figure it out. Maybe it's funny, when we've only known each other this little while, but I'm sure about you. That's what I need."

You who are reading this: I wonder if you know how it feels to have somebody say that to you. I hope you do.

I put my arms around her. She rested her head on my shoulder. "Justine." With my lips against her hair, I asked the question. "Will you marry me?"

Her laugh was the gentlest sound. "Yes, my love. I will."

~

AFTER SHE WENT HOME, CHARLEY COLLARED ME STRAIGHT off. "I need to talk to you."

"That's fair. I need to talk to you too." Justine and I had agreed I would tell him our news tonight. The next time she and I were together at her place, we would tell her father and Louisa.

Charley said, "Me first." He'd been rummaging in the cabinets for something to make for dinner, but he stopped and braced himself against the counter. "Nicky, listen. That stuff you said at the museum about Dad. You have to quit blaming yourself. It wasn't your fault."

"I know."

"Because if that's why you get sick, you shouldn't. I wasn't here either, and neither was Mom. Even if we were, you remember the doctor said it was so sudden. Probably nobody could've helped him."

I knew all of that. Dr. Sanders had said that even if we'd been home, we might not have realized what was happening until it was too late. Probably Dad wouldn't have had time to call out. I ask you, though: wouldn't you have wondered too?

Charley was too upset for me to try arguing. "I'm okay, kid," I said. "Really."

"You passed out."

"Tell me about it." He didn't smile. "I'm okay," I said again. "It feels bad – all right, it feels horrible – but it goes away. I'm fine."

"You'd better be. You're all I've got."

I should haave realized how much it would scare him, having to watch me get sick, not knowing what was happening. I leaned against the counter next to him. "You think I'm going anywhere? Nobody'll get rid of me that easy."

His left hand, the one I could see, was closed tight around his right bicep. "Promise?"

"You bet I do." And, I told myself, if he was worried about being left to shift for himself, there couldn't be a better time to tell him the other news. "Plus, listen," I said. "One of these days, not right away but pretty soon, you'll have more than just me."

Charley's brow furrowed as if he had run into an unexpected question on a test. "What's that mean?"

He would be glad to hear this, I was sure of it. It was just that everything was happening so fast. "It turns out, Justine likes me all right." I willed my voice to hold steady. "She thinks we should make a more permanent arrangement."

His eyes looked so round, he could have been a little boy again, seeing a jack-in-the-box for the first time. "You're going to marry her?"

"That's what we figure." My heart turned a cartwheel. A smile wrote itself across my face; I couldn't have stopped it for anything. "Like I said, not right away. We have plenty of things to figure out. But when we do get married, you know, you'll have a sister, and it'll be the three of us."

The three of us. A family.

We did have plenty to figure out. Where we would live, what my line of work would be if not ads, and for that matter, when Justine and I would tie the knot in the first place. More than anything else, I had to know for certain that I could do right by both of them. My brother and – what a word it was – my wife.

"Oh, Nicky." Charley reached out and pulled me into a rib-bruising hug. "I'm glad."

He was trembling the same way he had that night in March before our mother died. I held him tight and put my hand on his hair, the way Dad used to do with us.

"We'll be okay, kid. I promise."

Dad would have made the same promise. For a moment, I let myself imagine that he was there too, standing in the room with us. *I'll make sure we're okay,* I told him in my head. *I will.*

Chapter Fifteen

HERE I'LL STEP BACK AGAIN for a minute. Ask you to bear with an old man.

If I hadn't fainted in the Flemish gallery, most likely I would still have told Justine the truth about myself, sooner rather than later. Judging from what happened afterward, she probably would have taken me anyway, but since I'd dragged my feet up until then, you could say it was convenient that I embarrassed myself three-quarters to death.

These days, of course, we know quite a bit more than we did back then about people's minds and how they work. I didn't find out exactly what was wrong with me until a long time after that day in the gallery. By the time I learned the words I mentioned, *anxiety disorder*, *panic attack* and so on, my daughter was pretty much grown up. Later still, I learned about the worst thing that happened to me: *derealization*. If you've never had it, all I can say is, what doesn't kill you sometimes makes you stronger.

Back then, we didn't know that when a brain ran off the rails the way mine did, it was trying to get away from a grief it couldn't tolerate. It's too bad our minds can't just hop out of our heads and take a quick stroll in the cool until they calm down. After the Vietnam War, when soldiers came home trapped in all kinds of noise and darkness, people finally started to understand conditions like trauma and PTSD. Many of the veterans of the Second World War had the same troubles, but in those days, we didn't talk about them. Men were supposed to be tougher than that. Besides, we didn't have the words.

Timothy had his trouble, exactly as he said, because of what he had lived through in France. I had mine because of the way I'd lost Dad. It was that complicated and that simple.

Now I'll go back to where I left off earlier. Justine had seen the worst in me, but she wanted to marry me anyway. Who'd have thought?

~

ON SUNDAY, THE DAY AFTER OUR MUSEUM TRIP, THE Philadelphia *Record* was waiting on the front porch when Charley and I got back from Mass. The whole front page shouted about Germany's unconditional surrender.

Charley and I didn't bother to go inside. We sat right down on the porch, split the "A" section of the paper between us, and scanned for the continuations of the headlines. Charley found a column a couple of pages in. "Says here, the Allies want to cut Germany up. England and France and Russia and the States all get a piece."

We didn't know, of course, how that would turn out: how East and West Germany would become two different worlds, the blockade would split Berlin down the middle, and four decades later, Ronald Reagan would stand in front of the Brandenburg Gate and say the words that became legend. *Mr. Gorbachev, tear down this wall!* Justine and I watched that broadcast together. I still remember the goosebumps.

On that Sunday morning after V-E Day, all the rest of it was long in the future. Charley and I read about the Allies' plan to rebuild Germany and squeeze out payment for damages at the same time. "We bombed them all to pieces," Charley said. "If they have to give us whatever they've got left, what will they live on?"

I didn't know, but it was hard to argue with reparations when you looked at what the Luftwaffe had done to England. We all knew about the Blitz. We also knew about the old cathedral town, Coventry, with its church that had gone back a thousand years. Hitler had flattened the place until you could barely find one stone to stack on top of another. Generations' worth of prayers and memories, celebrations and tears, were cut loose and scattered in the dust or blown away on the wind. Germany wouldn't be able to pay enough for that, I thought, if they tried for the rest of time.

Charley opened his section of the paper to a new page. "Nicky. Look." He held up the La Belle Epoque spread featuring Justine and Louisa.

So much had happened since the photoshoot that I'd lost track of it. I took the page from Charley and scanned it. Miss Carol had chosen three of the pictures from the shoot, each featuring the two girls in different dresses. In every one of them, sundress and tea dress and evening gown, Justine had the flawless face and figure of a born model.

Damn, boy. You did all right. That thought bloomed and faded. Charley said, "It looks great. But..."

"Yeah."

Inside the house, the phone rang. I scrambled to my feet and made it to the kitchen before the caller could give up. Sure enough, Justine said, "Am I speaking with the artist?"

"At your service, ma'am."

We both laughed. "You did an incredible job," she said. "You should have heard Dad. *Ladybug, you look simply perfect. I am so proud of you.*"

She wasn't laughing now. She didn't sound happy at all. "And," she said, "he wants to thank you too, in person. He'd like you to have dinner with us again soon."

She was too far away, just over there in Center City. If I imagined putting my arms around her, if I pictured it clearly enough, maybe she would feel it. "I'll be glad to," I said. "But listen, you don't need my magic. You never have and you never will. You know that, right?"

"I know you're a sweet man."

I imagined pressing a kiss on her hair, sending that touch down the phone line. "So that's why you want to marry me? I figured there had to be some reason."

"Yes, that's the reason. Among others."

She told me that Louisa was ready for another photoshoot, for Miss

Carol or anyone. "When she gets one, I'll tell her to go ahead without me. I should've known better in the first place."

"Never mind what you should've. Don't you be hard on my wife."

"Nicky, I..."

She hesitated for so long that I wondered if she wasn't sure about the marriage after all. "What's wrong?"

I heard her breath catch. "You were worried about what you could give me, but look at me. I won't even know how to iron your shirts. Good wives do that, right? And you know I can't cook. I don't want to be a burden."

"You'll never be that." It sounded angrier than I'd meant. "Listen, Justine, you wanting to be with me, you should know how lucky that makes me. Besides," I added, calmer, "you don't have to iron anything. I can handle it."

"The ironing's covered?"

She was smiling. I could hear it. "That's right."

Sometimes, when you talk with someone, even if you can't see them, you can feel your thoughts and theirs reaching out and taking hold of each other like outstretched hands. That's how it felt right then, as the idea of marriage grew and bloomed into life between Justine and me.

I said, "Remember what you told me last night? Whatever's coming, you want us to go into it together. That's how I feel."

You don't say what you don't mean. "All right," she said. For a little while, we were both quiet, leaning into each other's thoughts. Then she said, "Nicky, I want you to promise me something."

"What's that?"

"The ads. I need you to promise you won't keep doing that so you can take care of me. You're too good for that. I won't just be something you have to pay for."

I still didn't know how else I could take care of her. "It's not just you," I said. "There's Charley too." I had promised him college.

"I have a feeling he doesn't like it either."

She was right, of course. He had been suspicious of my job since the day I'd brought home my contract. "I have to take care of you both," I said. "I want to."

"I know that, but you won't do it with Allen and Allen. Promise me."

I stalled a little longer. As much as I wanted to believe there was another way, the only other work I'd ever done was in the Phillips dye house. Factory pay wouldn't be enough, even if I, soft and out of shape as the past three years had made me, could wrangle a job from somebody. "Then you'll have to help me figure out how," I said. "You're smarter than me."

"I'll help, but don't you say my husband isn't smart."

My husband. In the face of that dazzle, I couldn't hold out anymore. "All right," I said. "I promise."

"Good."

We settled that I would have dinner at her house in two days, on Tuesday. I hung up thinking about what her father might say to the news we were going to spring on him.

Later in the afternoon, I'd brought a load of shirts up from the washer when the phone rang again. The caller was a girl who addressed me as Mr. True, in a polite, brisk voice that didn't quite hide a thread of nervousness. "I go to school with your brother," she said. "I wonder if I could speak with him about our Latin homework."

"Certainly." I was tempted to mention that I wasn't Charley's father and didn't need a rundown of their business, but I let it go. "I'll get him for you." I called upstairs to Charley that he was wanted on the phone and carried the pile of damp shirts outside to the clothesline.

Mrs. O'Dell came over to say hello. She took a couple of shirts off the pile and got to work next to me, clipping them on the line. The warm breeze would dry them in no time. We chatted about the news from Europe and agreed that splitting Germany up and shaking the pieces until reparations fell out sounded like the thing to do. "Serves them right," Mrs. O'Dell said. "They've caused more than their share of trouble. Of course, the Great War was before you were born, but I can tell you, we ought to have fixed them for good back then." Hitler had used the Treaty of Versailles as a step to power, but Mrs. O'Dell was certain the country had no steam left now. "They'll learn their lesson this time," she said, clamping Charley's T-shirt on the line as firmly as if the clothespins could keep Germany in its place. "This'll set them straight."

I got back inside to find Charley sitting at the kitchen table. The phone was back on its hook, and he was grinning at the floor as if the linoleum had told him a joke. "What's up?" I said.

His head jerked around as if I'd been a teacher who caught him passing notes in class. "Nothing. I mean, nothing much." He sure didn't blush often.

"Homework, huh?"

"Yeah." His eyes met mine, then slid away. "That is, you know, some."

"It's okay," I said. "I won't be nosy unless you want me to."

He laughed. "You can be nosy. That's fair."

We got started on supper and he told me about the girl. Her name was Denise, she was in Charley's English and Latin classes, and she worked on the yearbook too. "She's smart," he said. "She likes to laugh. And her eyes, they're this sort of gray with blue mixed in, like the sky when it's cloudy." That sounded pretty serious. Charley finished, "I think she kind of likes me."

We were making tuna melts, thick with chopped onion. I slid the bread under the broiler. "She ought to like you," I said. "You said she's smart."

"Yeah. The only thing is..."

His voice trailed off. I straightened up from the oven, wiping the heat-steam off my glasses. "What?"

He was leaning against the counter. His bad foot, in its sock, slid back and forth across a linoleum square. "It's just, you know I could never take her to a dance, or anything like that."

When he was first born, his foot had looked as if an angry hand had closed around it, curling it out of shape like a piece of clay. It had been so small and fragile. You could almost have believed that the right touch would have uncurled it back the way it should be. Now, even with the sock covering it, I knew how the bones had grown, how the muscles had settled into hard twisted lines.

He had never been serious about a girl before, at least that I knew of, but he had good friends, he was just like any other kid except a little slower getting around, and he made up for it by being a good slice smarter than most people. For now, I told myself, he was still my little brother. It was too early to worry about the romance side of things. "If she likes you," I said, "she won't care about a dance."

"Maybe not. I still do."

He had never been a complainer. Dad had wanted him to have surgery when he was a baby, but our mother had refused. I cleared my throat. "Any girl who wants to date my brother had better like him the way he is. Otherwise, she'll be in for a mess of trouble."

That brought his smile back. "You wouldn't fight a girl."

"Fighting isn't the only possibility."

The melts only needed to broil for a couple of minutes. I dished them up and we sat down to eat. It seemed impossible that only two months ago, I had still believed I was rooted in Los Angeles, and I'd planned to pull up my last ties in the east and take Charley back to California with me. Now those years on the west coast seemed like a slice out of someone else's life. In a way, I couldn't help thinking, they were.

Someone knocked at the door while we were cleaning up. Charley guessed it was Mrs. O'Dell, needing to check that we really could feed ourselves, but when I went to answer it, Minna and Timothy were waiting on the stoop.

It was getting toward evening, the light fading to dusk. Lamplit windows stood out yellow in the house across from ours. "Hey," Timothy said. "Sorry to barge over here like this. Can we come in?"

I had never seen him like this. He was restless, full of energy, shifting from foot to foot as if standing still was a chore. "Sure," I said. "Is everything okay?"

"I think so." Now I noticed the manila envelope he held. It was laced shut, stuffed so full that it could have split at the creases. He said, "I need to talk to you for a minute."

Minna caught my eye and shook her head. *I don't know what his trouble is.* "I told him we ought to call first," she said. "In case you were busy, but he didn't want to wait."

"It's a nice evening for a bus ride," he said. "Besides, you're always telling me I can't sit home all the time."

"I won't argue with you."

In the kitchen, Charley joked about how long it'd been since we'd last seen them, and Minna laughed and said they kept turning up like a bad penny. "Nicky," Timothy said, "I'd better talk to you alone."

Minna sat down at the table with Charley. "Don't you mind my husband," she told me. "But if you find out what's going on, I'd like to know."

Timothy and I went down to the living room. The moment we were out of earshot, he said, "I couldn't tell her. You said it was a secret."

His face was alive with excitement. I could almost, almost have believed that someone had put a hand on the great clock that kept the world's time, and turned it back far enough that the bullet had never found Timothy's leg, and the friends he had lost were still alive, and that in fact, he had never gone to France at all.

Neither of us sat down. He paced back and forth in front of Charley's chair, a couple of steps in each direction, as if only that would keep the energy in him tamped down enough. "What you showed me the other day," he said. "I didn't quite get it then, but I've been thinking about it ever since. Damn, man. You did *magic*."

I couldn't help smiling. "You knew it was magic."

"You know how I was feeling that day. It's like being under water, you can't hear or see right." I knew, sure enough. "But yesterday, Minna and I got back from the museum, and we sat down and had dinner at that table."

"The one I wrecked?"

"Yeah." I'd never seen him so pleased. "I thought about those holes you made, how I put my hand right through them, and what Minna'd have said if she'd seen it."

"You said she'd give us hell."

"She would have!" He stopped pacing and turned the manila envelope over and over between his hands. "Nicky, look. What you did, can you see why it matters?"

To tell you the truth, I couldn't see much at all. "It's not that useful," I said. "I told you, it goes away. The changes don't last."

If he hadn't been holding the envelope, he might have grabbed me by the collar and given me a shake. "That's not the point. You did something *impossible*."

I tried to tell him it wasn't impossible, he'd seen that for himself, but he cut me off. "Just shut up, will you?"

I shut up. He held the envelope tight in both hands, looking into my face as if he wanted to send what he was thinking straight into my head. "The way the world is," he said. "There's a hell of a lot of shit, right? A hell of a lot. You look at it, and you figure it's never going to be different. You can't fix anything. Yeah?"

"Okay, but..."

"Then one day, you meet this guy. White-bread guy, probably an asshole like the rest of them." He laughed at my expression. "Come on. If I hadn't learned different, we wouldn't be talking right now."

Fair enough. "And?" I said.

"The point is, this guy looks like anybody else, and then he sits down and does this thing. It's not how the world works. He still did it."

I was starting to get a glimmer. "The world doesn't work the way you thought?"

"Maybe." His eyes gave me that searchlight feeling again, except this time it wasn't because of Dad, my memory of Dad. It was a real person here in front of me. Timothy said, "Or maybe there's more to the world than I thought. Maybe, if magic can happen, other things can happen. Now do you see?"

He was talking about hope. I understood that much. He had to know, though, that what I did couldn't fix the world. "Look, Timothy, the drawing's good for a paycheck, but..."

"But nothing, man."

"No, listen." My pencil couldn't even fix my brother's foot. "I can make things look right, or wrong, but I can't make real changes. Not the kind that last."

He brushed that away like a spiderweb. "You can do something that shouldn't happen. I saw it with my own eyes. I don't know, anymore, what can and can't be, and believe me, that makes things better than they were."

I tried to wrap my head around that. He said, "I want Minna to see it too. Would you show her?"

I couldn't turn him down. We went back to the kitchen. Timothy didn't want me to give Minna any hint about what was going to happen, so he told her only that he'd asked me to show her my drawing. Charley, of course, knew what that was about. "Are you going to?" he asked me.

"Sure."

He had read my contract and knew as much about the non-disclosure rules as I did. "Good." He pulled himself up from his chair. "Let me pick something."

Minna thought this must be a demonstration of what I did at work. I could see she didn't know why it would be so interesting, but she paid polite attention. Charley handed me one of the heavy stoneware dinner plates. I set it in the middle of the table, where we could all see it, and got to work.

One line after another, the pencil moved across the paper. It didn't take long at all. When the plate had a wavy edge and two missing cutouts from the middle, like a pair of round eyes, I set my pencil down.

Timothy brought his hand down on the table. "There it is."

He and Charley were both grinning, but Minna's face looked as closed off as it had the first time I'd met her. She didn't say a word. Slowly, she reached one hand out toward the plate, as if it had been an animal that might snap.

"You can touch it," Charley said. "It's safe. Nicky does this stuff all the time."

She didn't answer, but she lifted the plate carefully by the edge and moved it back and forth, looking at the room through the two holes. "He showed me this the other day," Timothy told her, "when he came by. That's part of why we had to come here tonight. You had to see it."

Lately, I had seen a lot of reactions to the magic. Everyone else I had shown it to, the ad men and the clients, had thought about how they could use it. Even Justine, at first, had thought how it could change her.

Minna and Timothy were different. The point wasn't what I did. It was the fact that I could.

Minna peered through the plate again, and then, the same way Timothy had done with their kitchen table, reached her finger through one of the holes and ran it around the place where the stoneware had vanished. She didn't question that it was real. She also didn't look at me, for so long that I started to think she was going to get up from the table and say she wouldn't spend another minute in this freak-show's house, much less work for him anymore.

She balanced the plate carefully on its edge and ran her finger over the wavy border. "Nicky." Her voice sounded distant, as if she wanted to imagine she was standing in another room, or maybe safely outside the house altogether. "When you first did this, who saw it?"

"My dad."

"Your dad." She set the plate down. Finally, her eyes found mine. "He must have been scared to death."

She didn't jump up and run. That was something. "Not really," I said. "He was pretty surprised, sure." I remembered his voice: *Child, what did you do?* "I think he'd always figured magic was real, even if he'd never seen it before."

"I've always hoped it was real," Minna said. "But this...this is..." She turned to her husband. "You saw this, and you didn't say a word to me about it?"

"He isn't supposed to tell people." Timothy explained my agreement with Allen and Allen. "Besides, you might've thought I'd lost my mind for good."

"I might have," she admitted.

"I wished you'd been there. You should've seen it." Swallowing laughter, he told her what I had done to their table. Her eyes went wide. "He took *pieces* out?"

"Not exactly," I said quickly. "The magic doesn't take anything away. It just moves it around."

She gave me a long look. "If I'd been there..."

"You'd have put us both in the doghouse," Timothy said. "We'd probably be there yet."

"Too right you would." Try as she did, she couldn't hide her smile.

Charley said, in an uncanny imitation of our mother, "Nicholas, you put that plate right." That made all of us laugh. I obeyed, a few quick lines on a clean sheet of paper, and the intact plate sat before us as if nothing had happened.

Minna picked it up to examine it again. Timothy said, "Nicky, remember I told you I felt like doing some drawing?" Of course I did. "I did a little," he said, "last night. After Minna was asleep."

Minna put the plate down. "What's this?" She pretended to scold him, as if the very apples and pears on the wallpaper couldn't see how glad she was. "Aren't you going to tell me anything anymore?"

"I'm telling you now, aren't I?" He passed the bulging manila envelope over to me. "I didn't do all that last night. Just the couple of things on top. But, Nicky, you said you'd like to see other stuff, so I brought some over."

I undid the envelope's string and pulled the thick sheaf out. The papers inside were all different sizes, some regular letter-size, some small sheets from notepads, a few envelopes, and a handful of scraps that looked as if they had been torn off of something else, maybe the corners of a flyer or poster. As hard as it must have been for Timothy to keep all those memories from overseas, a wave of relief washed over me. His art hadn't ended up in a trash burner or landfill. I could sit and study it for as long as he would let me.

The drawing on top had been done on the same lined notepad I'd seen at his apartment. It was a self-portrait.

"I never used to do that," he said. "Draw myself." It sounded offhanded enough, but I saw how his right hand, the drawing hand, fidgeted on the tabletop. "Not sure what got into me."

I had wondered how he'd looked before the war. Now my throat tightened as I saw it. The face on the paper was young, open, with a suggestion of a smile around the mouth and in the dark eyes. This was who he had been before he'd shouldered the pain he had to lift and carry every day. He'd believed the world had some good in it. Every day, he had gone out ready to find it.

Minna leaned over to see the drawing too. "Oh yes," she said. "I know him."

I wanted to know whether this version of him was more than just a memory. Whether here, too, his drawing got at what was really there, no matter how deeply life had buried it. "Come on," he said to me, "look at some of the others."

I handed the self-portrait to Minna. If he wanted me to hurry up with the pile, he should have put a different sketch under the first one, because now I found myself looking at my own face.

Sometimes you can catch your reflection unexpectedly, in a shop window, for instance, or a car's side mirror. Out of context, seeing it only out of the corner of your eye, you might not recognize yourself. *Who was that?* It's disorienting, but this was much, much stranger. Timothy hadn't just drawn the way I looked. He'd drawn what he saw.

The man in the sketch carried his own weight of sadness. You could see it around his eyes and in the set of his mouth, but something else stood out more. He was someone who would listen to anything you had to say, keep a secret if you wanted him to, or cheer you up if you needed it. You could lean on his kindness.

Timothy knew nothing about Dad. Otherwise, I might have thought that's who I was looking at, and I'd have said he was a little different – younger, for a start – than I remembered, but that Timothy got the essential stuff right. But if it was me?

"Come on," Timothy said. "It's not that bad."

Charley plucked the paper out of my hand. "Yeah," he said. "That's Nicky, all right."

"Give me that." I snagged the drawing and went to slip it on the bottom of the pile, but Timothy said, "You hold onto it. It's yours."

Charley took it back. I started on the rest of the pile and tried not to notice him still looking at that sketch. He saw the same things Timothy did. Well, that ought to be worth something.

I leafed through the rest of the drawings, trying, with each one, to understand exactly how the simple lines and shadings revealed so much about their subjects. Timothy told me about each face. They were men from his barracks, soldiers he had crouched with in trenches, patients he had met at the hospital. He told me about two of his buddies who hadn't made it home, and another one who had. "He's in Michigan now," Timothy said. "Back with his family. He always talked about the quiet on the farm."

By the time I set the last sketch down, I felt as if I had met them all, the ones who were still out there and the ones lying under a stone on the other side of the world. I wondered whether they had been real people to the politicians and generals who sent them into combat. Did those leaders know about the men's faces? Did they imagine the lives left behind, the dreams wrapped up and put away? Or, at the end of the day, were the soldiers just so many playing pieces? The ones in decent shape would go back in the box for another day, while the beat-up ones got tossed in the trash.

President Roosevelt hadn't seen them that way. He had cared. But, I thought, if you were sending men out to fight knowing that plenty of them wouldn't make it back, you couldn't think too hard about who they were. Then I thought how disposable Timothy might have been. Even before he became a soldier, he had been someone the world tried not to see.

"Nicky," he said, "you awake?"

I was still staring down at the last sketch, but I wasn't studying it anymore. Something was hanging around on the edge of my brain. Something about Timothy's drawing and what it did, and something about my own magic, what it might be good for.

I couldn't see it. Not even the start of an outline. I shook myself. "You impress the hell out of me, but you knew that."

"You're no slouch yourself."

It was getting late. Charley had school in the morning, Minna would be back here first thing, and I would have to go to work. We gathered up the drawings, except the one Charley still held onto, and put them back in the envelope. I walked down to the bus stop with Minna and Timothy. Nobody was out and about, but you never knew who might try to stir up trouble if they saw "colored" people in our neighborhood at night.

When I got back, Charley told me he would keep Timothy's sketch in his own room. "I know what you'll do. You'll shove it underneath something and lose it." I told him I appreciated the vote of confidence. Meanwhile, the big question, the real question, nudged at me.

Timothy's drawings and my magic. Something about the two of them, together.

Chapter Sixteen

Two evenings later, on Tuesday, Charley went to the yearbook editor's place for a staff get-together to celebrate wrapping up the issue. I went to the Murrays' house for dinner.

I didn't ask Charley if Denise was going to be at the yearbook party. In fact, I was so worried about facing Justine's father as his intended son-in-law that I didn't manage to tease my brother at all. Charley promised I would do fine and approved the jacket-and-tie combination I finally settled on. "You already know her dad likes you," he reminded me. He gave me Timothy's sketch back. "Show it to Justine," he said. "She'll like it. But don't lose it."

The cab seemed to crawl toward Center City. I was sure about Justine, and she was sure about me, but even so, how did I think I had the right to crash into this white-tower world and drag her out of it? The small, silent maid, Sarah, answered my knock again and showed me into the same parlor. This time, I didn't sit down. I straightened my tie for the eighth or ninth time and locked my hands together behind my back.

"Thank you, Sarah." Justine's voice, not far away. Then her footsteps, and then her face, and warmth washed over me as if I had stepped into a shaft of sunlight.

She wore a simple skirt and blouse, the kind she might have put on to run errands, and she looked more beautiful than the staged ads in the paper ever could. "Hello, my love." We put our arms around each other. "Dad said we could eat in the kitchen tonight, like family."

I swallowed. "Wait'll he finds out he's right."

Justine smiled. "I wish Mama could have met you. She'd have been so glad."

"Would she?"

"Absolutely." She took my hand. "Dad's waiting to talk to you."

Dr. Murray was in the library, finishing up a case report. "Mr. True," he said, "so good to see you."

His eyes had real welcome in them. No chips of ice tonight. I thanked him for having me over, and he told me it was a pleasure. "I must congratulate you on your artwork in those photographs," he said. "Justine told you, of course, how delighted we all were with the results."

He might have been delighted, but I had reason to know that his daughters, or one of them at least, felt quite differently. He told me he was proud of both of his girls, "but when I saw Justine in those pictures, I must say, the effect was extraordinary."

Justine had caught a glimpse of her mother again. For Dr. Murray, the photos had no doubt brought back the image of his wife. His eyes moved away from me to the far corner of the room, and for the first time, I saw the surgeon's patrician veneer slip, baring the loneliness and wistfulness underneath. He had lost his wife long before his daughters grew up, but he had never stopped missing her.

He recollected himself. "In any case, Mr. True, thank you for your work."

"I was glad to help, sir."

Louisa met us in the kitchen. She had dressed for the "family meal" in a cobalt-blue dress with a flared chiffon skirt and white trim, and pearls at her throat and in her ears. "Mr. True," she said, with no particular warmth. "Good to see you again."

The kitchen itself wasn't much less imposing than the dining room. A glass-fronted cabinet held an impressive display of silver and crystal, along with a pewter tankard that looked so old that Ben Franklin might have drunk out of it. For all I knew, he had. The round table, with its deep grain, could have been something out of colonial days too. It was set with a brown cloth and heavy white dinnerware.

Rebecca and Sarah were both working on the "business" side of the room, on the far side of a low half-wall. Sarah chopped vegetables on the ceramic-tiled counter while Rebecca stirred a pot on the stove. Neither woman looked up as the four of us settled ourselves around the table.

Dr. Murray filled his water tumbler from the glass pitcher on the table and passed the pitcher to me. Now that he'd seen my work, he said, he would venture to guess that I must be sought after in the ad business, and he trusted the firm I worked for was compensating me well. It wasn't a bad conversation opener, especially once we got around to my qualifications as a son-in-law, but he didn't know that I wouldn't hang onto my success if Justine had her way. "Yes, sir." I tried to ignore the nudge of guilt. "When I was hired, they let me write my own contract." Might as well use it while I could.

Dr. Murray said he could see why. Louisa said, "I must say, Jussie, you have all the luck, meeting a successful young man and hitting it off with him so quickly. Of course, the two of you hardly know each other at all."

She wore a polite-as-pie smile, but every word had prickles in it. Justine lifted her chin. "We know each other well enough, Lou."

"You might think so, Jussie, but the fact is, you've barely spent any time together." She turned the battery of her smile on me. "Not to say anything against you, Mr. True, but we girls have to be careful about the men we meet. We have to be sure of what we're doing. After all, everyone has secrets."

That word was no accident, of course. "You're absolutely right, Miss Louisa," I said. "You want what's best for your sister, as anyone who cares about her would."

That set her back a fraction. "Well, yes. Naturally." She did care about Justine. On that first day in Miss Carol's office, when I'd met the two girls, Louisa had played an essential part in getting her sister to trust me. Whatever resentments she had now, I would rather have her as an ally again if I could.

I said, "I'm lucky that the shoot with you and Miss Justine was one of my first assignments. If you'll forgive me saying, with the two of you as models, my job was almost too easy."

She almost smiled. Sarah and Rebecca brought dishes to the table, interrupting the talk for the moment. Rebecca set a platter of sliced roast chicken by Dr. Murray's elbow and a loaf of fresh bread, on a wooden carving board, next to Justine's place. Sarah put a tureen of baked squash and another dish of green beans down at Louisa's end. She stepped back from the table with her head down, as if that might let her fade out of sight.

Rebecca stood by Dr. Murray. "Will there be anything else, sir?"

He didn't look at her, the same way he hadn't the first time I'd had dinner here. As if she wasn't worth his notice. "Not at the moment." She and Sarah moved quietly away from the table.

Dr. Murray picked up a serving fork. "Kindly pass me your plate, Mr. True. I'll help you to some chicken."

We passed the dishes around. Sweat pricked under my collar and I wasn't sure how I would manage to chew and swallow the food being dished onto my plate. The sooner we got to the real business of the evening, the better.

Justine seemed to feel the same. She handed the bread across to me and touched my wrist. *Let's do it now.*

I nodded back, stomach tight. Justine set her full plate down. "As far as I'm concerned," she said, "the best thing about modeling was who I met at the photoshoot." Her smile reached me through the fog of nerves closing in. "Now I've thought it over, and I don't plan to model anymore."

Dr. Murray looked startled. "Ladybug," he said, "it's entirely up to you, of course, but I thought you enjoyed it."

"I did, at first." Justine sounded so calm, as if she made momentous announcements at the dinner table every night. "But Nicky and I talked about it, and he thinks I don't need to pretend to be something I'm not. I think he's right. Without his help, I'm not a model."

It's the only work I ever tried. I don't want to be a burden. In my head, I promised her and myself that whenever she found the thing she wanted to do, the real thing that was hers, we would make sure she got hold of it with both hands. Meanwhile, Dr. Murray opened his mouth again, but Justine went on, "Besides, Nicky and I have more important news we'd like to tell you."

Here it came. I held out my hand and she took it, nudging one of the tall white candlesticks to the side to make room. Her fingers felt warm. Her eyes met mine, full of confidence. *Tell him, my love.*

I took a breath and looked Dr. Murray in the eye. "Sir, I would like to ask your permission to marry your daughter."

His knife and fork stopped moving. His hands hovered in the air, holding onto the utensils as if they were all part of a sculpture together. His face looked so blank that I wouldn't have sworn he could see me at all.

Louisa could. You could bet on that. "What?" She tried to cover it up with laughter, but her anger could have sliced the meat by itself. "That's absurd, you two. It's crazy!"

Warmth rushed into my hands and face. "Really?" I said. "What's crazy about it?"

She tossed her head. "Exactly what I already said. You and my sister only just met." She turned away from me. "Jussie, this is your life we're talking about. For goodness' sake, you don't know this man, except for..."

Justine's hand tightened around mine, and I knew we were thinking the same thing. What would happen if Louisa came out with the single most important fact she knew about me? If she threw my "secret" down on the table in front of her father, what would he say, or do?

She didn't do it. Maybe, in spite of everything, she remembered that Miss Carol wouldn't hire her to model again if she ratted me out. "Except for," she started again, "the fact that he can draw. That's nothing to bank on. Tell her, Dad." Dr. Murray had lowered his knife and fork. "Tell her it's too soon."

This is your sister's decision, Miss Louisa, not yours. Justine squeezed my hand again and spoke up before I could. "Lou, I appreciate your concern." She could have been the secretary at Allen and Allen taking a message about an order of drafting paper. "I'm quite sure of what I'm doing. Nicky and I have talked about all this." She smiled again, straight at me. "After a few weeks, you can know someone a lot better than you might think."

Louisa's cheeks flushed through the heavy layer of powder she wore. Dr. Murray held up a hand. "Girls. That will do."

Quiet settled over the table. Dr. Murray ignored me for the moment, as if I had been an intern hanging around on the sidelines while he performed a coronary bypass. "This is rather sudden, Justine."

Justine didn't hesitate. "I know it seems that way, but I'm sure about this. Nicky and I both are."

Now Dr. Murray turned to me. The friendliness of a few minutes ago had disappeared. "Are you in a hurry to marry?"

"No, sir." I would be honest, even if I wasn't quite telling him everything. "I need to know I can take care of your daughter as she deserves. We aren't in a rush that way, but I do want to marry her, when I'm sure I can provide for her." I added the full truth. "I love her very much, sir."

"Love?" Louisa blurted out. "I don't see how you can talk that way. You don't know her well enough to..."

Dr. Murray didn't take his eyes off me. "Louisa," he said. She stopped talking.

Justine stepped into the new silence. "If it comes to providing, Nicky, you know I don't intend to sit back and let you drag all the weight." She was saying it to me, but for her father and sister to hear too. "I'm not good for much, yet, but I can learn how to do things."

Her fingers were warm and strong around mine. We could have been by ourselves. "I know that," I said. "Like you said, we'll figure it all out together."

I don't know, for certain, what Dr. Murray saw in the two of us. Without a doubt, this turned all of his expectations for Justine upside down. He had imagined her marrying a man from her own world, someone who had always had the security of money and family behind him, someone who had never scraped for the next dollar or stretched it from one week to the next. Now she wanted to give up that hazy but rosy future in favor of a factory worker's son from blue-collar Elmcroft, a nobody who drew pictures for a living.

I don't know what he saw as he looked at Justine and me, sitting there with our hands joined across his table. I only know what he said.

"I was some years older than you, Mr. True, when I met my wife. I was fortunate to find her." I knew he must have been, if she had been as much like Justine as I guessed. "You are fortunate to find my daughter."

A pause, long enough for me to wonder if I should try to tell him how lucky I knew I was. "Very well," he said. "You have my consent."

Warmth ran all through me, relief and a happiness so sharp my eyes stung. Justine let go of my hand. She went to her father and put her arms around him, pressing her lips to his gray hair. "Thank you, Dad."

He patted her arm and closed his eyes. In that moment I saw, again, the loneliness of a man who had lost the woman he loved, and now imagined living without the girl who kept her memory alive. It only lasted an instant. "Now," he said, picking his knife and fork back up. "Let's eat this meal before it's cold."

At first, everything stayed civil, if not exactly comfortable. Justine teased her father about how she wanted to learn to cook. "Mama knew how, didn't she? She cooked for you sometimes."

That got a reluctant smile from him. "When we were first married, yes. I didn't want her to feel obliged to do chores."

I didn't want Justine to feel obliged that way either, but she said, "I think cooking would be fun. I'll be proud to have dinner ready for my husband when he gets home from work, as long as he can eat it, of course."

My hands and face still tingled with nerves, but I could operate my knife and fork, and even string a sentence or so together. "Don't forget, I survived on my own cooking for a while. I can probably eat just about anything."

Justine raised her eyebrow at me. "That doesn't mean you should. I'll learn how to do it right."

Louisa said, "If the two of you wait until Jussie can make a dinner, the wedding won't happen any time soon."

I hadn't wanted to dislike her, but it was getting easier by the minute. Just then, Rebecca came in to take the serving dishes away. "Rebecca," Louisa said, "Miss Justine is getting married. She wants to learn to cook, so I guess you'll have to teach her."

"Married, Miss Justine?" Rebecca said it with no expression at all, though she did glance at me. "To this gentleman?"

Justine said yes. Rebecca congratulated her, and Justine thanked her as naturally as she would have thanked a friend. "Please don't worry," she added. "I won't pester you for cooking lessons. I'd only like to learn a few things, if you can teach me."

"Certainly, miss. I'll be glad to."

I wondered if Rebecca meant it at all. Teaching Justine to cook might be better than endless rounds of cooking and scrubbing dishes without respect or thanks of any kind. Timothy'd told me that Minna had hoped to teach English one day. Had Rebecca had dreams once? I wondered if she took her pay home to a family. I wondered if taking care of them made up for other things.

Dr. Murray said, "Bring the dessert in, Rebecca." Without the courtesy of "please," as if she had been no more than a pair of hands.

Timothy's sketch of me, which Charley had given me earlier, was folded in my jacket pocket. Justine hadn't told her father or Louisa anything about Minna and Timothy, only that she had visited the museum with Charley and me and friends of ours. Dr. Murray would never want to know that those friends were colored. As Rebecca and Sarah brought in the dessert, frosted slices of cake served on little glass plates, the sketch started to feel warm through the fabric of my shirt.

I could have waited until after dessert, when Justine and I would be alone. Instead, after a couple of bites of the cake, which was lemon with some kind of nuts in it, I set my fork down and reached into my pocket. "Justine," I said, "I almost forgot. Charley had me bring this over. He thought you'd like to see it."

She unfolded the sketch. "Oh."

Cake forgotten, she took the drawing in as if her father and sister and the table and I had all vanished into the air. Louisa leaned forward. "Jussie, what's that?"

Justine looked up at me, her face alight. "Timothy?"

"Yes." I told her how he'd let me look through some of his drawings. "He said I could keep that one."

"It's perfect." She hugged it to herself. "Maybe I want to keep it now."

That made me laugh. "You'll have to ask Charley."

Dr. Murray had gotten curious too. "What is it?"

Now Justine and I both knew we had a choice. How much were we going to say about the drawing and the artist who'd done it? Justine lifted her chin and gave me the smallest nod. *Tell the truth.*

"It's a sketch, sir," I said, "that my friend Timothy Davis did. He and his wife Minna came to the museum the other day with Justine and my brother and me."

"Ah," Dr. Murray said. "Your friends. Justine mentioned them."

Justine unfolded the sketch and handed it to her father. "Nicky told me how good Timothy's drawings are. I'd never seen one before."

Dr. Murray's eyes went from the paper to me. "A fine likeness," he said. "A rather rough drawing, of course, but it captures a certain quality."

Part of me was afraid, all right, of what Dr. Murray would say when he knew everything. The rest of me decided to push things a little farther. "Timothy's pretty incredible, sir. I wish I could draw the way he does."

He handed the paper back to Justine and took the last bite of his piece of cake. "This Mr. – Davis, you said?"

"Yes." *Mister, indeed.*

"Is he a coworker of yours?"

Justine was showing the sketch to Louisa, who was trying not to look too interested. Justine glanced up and caught my eye. *Here we go.*

"No, sir," I said. My voice stayed even. "He's not a coworker. I met his wife first, actually. She's been helping Charley and me out since I got back from California." Here I had to take a breath. "She's a maid."

Well. Dr. Murray had already had one shock tonight. You could see the words *a what?* getting ready to barrel out of his mouth. I was friends with a maid and her husband. Justine had visited the museum in that kind of company.

Justine put the seal on it. "They're colored, Dad. The Davises are. They're Nicky's and Charley's friends, and mine."

Until that exact moment, I hadn't known what a backbone of steel she had. Louisa reacted first. "*Colored?*" Her fork clanged against her plate. She turned on me. "Are you out of your mind? My sister does not socialize with those people. In this house, we have standards. If you aren't going to adhere to them, you have no business marrying her!"

Justine's jaw set. This time, I got in first.

"Your sister has agreed to marry me, Miss Louisa. Your father has given us permission." I had to hope he wasn't about to yank it away, but any fear I'd felt was long gone. "Justine chooses her friends for herself, and you can safely trust her judgment. The Davises are good people." When I thought of Timothy sitting at his kitchen table with his head in his hands, his grief pouring up out of him, I could have reached across the table and caught Louisa's shoulders and shaken her until her teeth rattled. "Timothy served in France and came back with worse damage than you can imagine. His wife is working hard to take care of them both. They deserve your respect."

I don't know how I managed to keep from shouting. I do remember that Sarah and Rebecca were on the other side of the kitchen, behind the half-wall, waiting to collect the dessert plates. They could hear every word. Justine's face had flushed dark. Her eyes glittered with an anger I had only seen once before, when she'd told me off for thinking she was too refined for my poor house. Louisa stared at me as if I had slapped her. I couldn't have picked up my fork and swallowed another crumb of cake if it would have kept me from dropping dead on the spot.

And Dr. Murray? He didn't say a thing. He picked up his coffee cup and sipped at it as if the last sixty seconds or so had gotten scrubbed out of time. The other three of us could have been an installation at the museum: *Study in Hostile Statuary*.

The spell broke when he cleared his throat and set his cup down. "I expect there will be much to arrange, regarding wedding matters. I have no expertise in this." The words were distant, but perfectly polite. "I'm afraid, Mr. True, that you and Justine will need to settle details between yourselves, unless you have someone else to consult with?"

The "colored friends" didn't fit with the world as he saw it, so he had erased it. Louisa hadn't. I thought she might actually start boiling over like a kettle, but her father's authority seemed to have silenced her. As for me, the blood that had been pounding in my head a few minutes ago had all drained into my feet. You could have wrung me out like a dishtowel.

"I don't know anything about it either, sir," I said. "I'm sure Justine and I can sort things out."

Justine said, "We certainly will." She stood up. Before anyone else could say a word, she came around the table, took my arm, and got us both outside into the back garden.

The door shut behind us. She pushed the sketch into my hand. "Oh, Nicky." She wrapped her arms around me and pressed her face against my chest.

It was blessedly cool out there. The roses on the trellis stood out pale in the dark and the noise of the city seemed a long way away. I slipped the drawing back into my pocket and held my sweet girl. Her hair felt soft and silky against my cheek. If I had worried in the smallest way about us getting through things together, finding out about life together one day at a time, that worry was gone.

"I love you," I said.

"I love you too. Oh, I'm so glad I found you. Or you found me. I don't know what I'd have done."

What *she'd* have done? "Sweetheart, is it going to be okay, with your dad and Louisa?" I didn't like the idea of going home, when I'd have to, and leaving her there. "Will they be decent to you?"

"They will." She raised her head. "Don't worry. I can manage Dad, and Lou will have to sort herself out." She stood on tiptoe to kiss my cheek. "But let's not wait too long to get married. Let's do it soon."

"I promised you something," I reminded her.

"Then let's work on that too."

We sat down on the wrought-iron bench in front of the rose trellis. A couple of hours ago, I had thought we might need to wait months to get married, or even longer. Now I asked Justine if she would be willing to marry me now, as soon as we could. We could figure out the rest later. "Would you mind living in my parents' old place for a while?"

"Of course not. But Nicky, your job's the main thing. I won't let you keep settling for the ads."

I told her I would do something else as soon as I knew what that was. "I'll only keep the job while I have to, but I don't know how long that'll be."

"We'll sort it out." She smiled. "Because once we're married, I can nag you all the time."

"Then let's do it."

We talked it all through. In those days, plenty of couples went to the local courthouse and got the whole business done in a matter of minutes. "The ceremony doesn't matter," Justine said. "The marriage is the important part." Dr. Murray and Louisa wouldn't like it. Justine said they both would have expected a big fancy wedding, but then, they hadn't liked much of anything else either, and here we were.

We could have a civil ceremony at the courthouse by City Hall. I could get the license and rings any time. Justine said it wouldn't take long to sort out her packing. "So," she said, "a week or so to get organized, and then...shall we say a week from Saturday, Mr. True?"

Eleven days. It was so soon, to change our lives for good, but what else did we have to wait for? "A week from Saturday," I agreed.

"First, you'd better make sure Charley doesn't mind having a new roommate right away. Especially one who still won't know how to cook."

"I have a feeling he won't mind."

We sat there for a while longer, holding hands in the quiet dark. Soon enough, we would be together for better or for worse. You might not believe me when I tell you that the idea didn't scare me a bit. We did agree that we wouldn't break this latest update to Dr. Murray and Louisa until we had the official okay from Charley.

When I had to leave for home, Justine walked out to the cab with me and gave me a kiss at the curb. "Good night, my love."

"Good night." Thinking, as I said it, *Mrs. True.*

Chapter Seventeen

CHARLEY WAS ALREADY BACK by the time I got home from the Murrays'. He had fed Titus and spread his physics book and notes out on the kitchen table. "How'd it go?"

That was a story, all right. "You first." I draped my jacket over my chair and sat across from him. "How was the party?"

The yearbook editor's mom had made a spread, from the sound of it. Fried chicken, macaroni salad, chocolate cake. People were ready to splurge all they could for a taste of pre-war cooking, now that we had hope it was on its way back. Denise had been at the party. Toward the end of the evening, the kids had put the radio on and moved the living room furniture out of the way so they could dance. Charley had sat and watched. Denise had sat with him.

"A couple of the other guys asked her to dance," Charley said. "She said she didn't want to." She had wanted to, and he knew it. He couldn't hide how it had knotted him up not to ask her, but he couldn't hide his grin, either, when he told me how she'd stayed on the couch beside him, never mind how her feet tapped in time with the music. I hadn't so much as caught a glimpse of this girl, but I liked her already.

"Your turn," he said. "What happened at Justine's?"

I started in. When I repeated the talk about *colored friends*, he gripped his pencil so hard I thought it might snap in half. I told him how I'd answered Louisa, and he nodded once, his jaw tight. "Good." If he'd been there, I knew, he'd have had a few things to say too.

"Afterwards," I said, "Justine and I talked things over." This was harder to tell him than I'd expected. Charley had dealt with so much, all his life, really, and more than ever in the past few months. He shouldn't always have to brace himself for the next explosion. I said, "She and I both thought that maybe, you know, we could get married sooner than we figured."

He started to smile. "When were you figuring?"

"Well, I thought we might have to wait a while." I hadn't even told him, yet, how Justine wanted me to find a better use for my drawing. "But we decided we don't have to do anything fancy for the actual wedding. That'll make it easier."

Now he was grinning. "And...?"

"And." I decided to make a clean sweep of it. "We thought, maybe next Saturday, we'll go up to the courthouse. That is, like she said, if you don't mind having a new roommate so soon."

His grin disappeared. "Next Saturday."

It was only a hitch, only for an instant. He propped a smile back in place, but I had seen it. I'd seen how his eyes looked, too, like a scared little boy's.

"Charley," I said. "What's wrong?"

"Nothing. It's great. You two should do it."

That was Charley. He never would ask people to slow down for him. "Kid," I said, "tell me what you're thinking."

"Are you eyeballing me?"

I was. "Whatever it takes."

He knew I meant it. He talked to his physics book, where it lay open in front of him, instead of to me. "I like her," he said. "You know that. I'm glad you're marrying her. It's just, this is our place." He fiddled with a corner of a page. "We lived here with Mom and Dad, and you haven't been home that long. You know?"

Yes. I knew. I had told Justine that Charley wouldn't mind this, but here he was, minding it, and he had every reason in the world.

When we were growing up, we had known Dad loved us the same

way we had known the sun would come up in the morning. Our mother had been more complicated, sometimes, but we'd tasted her love in the meals she put together, and the way she stretched grocery money as much as she could, to buy things we liked. We'd seen it, too, in the stitches that mended our clothes, and felt it in the rough cloth that scrubbed our faces and the backs of our necks for Sunday Mass.

As for me, from the first moment I'd laid eyes on Charley, I had known he was the best thing that ever existed. I had mostly shown it by whaling the stuffing out of anyone who said he wasn't.

"Charley," I said now, "you know I love you, right?"

Startled, he raised his head. "Yeah. 'Course I do."

Justine and I wanted to be together, but we had also been willing to wait. "Look," I said, "there's been a hell of a lot going on. We don't have to shake everything up more just yet."

"I don't want to..."

"If you say 'get in your way,' kid, you will wish you hadn't."

He straightened up in his chair. "That's a nice way to talk. Besides, you don't know what I was going to say."

"Come on. You think I can't see into your head?"

His mouth worked, fighting against a smile. "You know something, Nicky, maybe I just don't need you and Justine both bossing me around."

I had to laugh. "Maybe you don't. Just think about it, okay? And if you don't like it, I want you to tell me straight."

He didn't want to tell me any such thing. It was written all over his stubborn face, but he bit his lip. "Okay."

THE NEXT DAY AT WORK, I SPENT A GOOD SLICE OF TIME trucking out of Philly for a photoshoot in Haverford, the suburb where Allen and Allen now had a new client. The client was Abel Swift, the florist who had come awfully close to killing the shoot at Dexter Marshall's shop. To get to his place, I had to take the commuter train from Philly into Bryn Mawr, the upper-crust suburb just up the road from Haverford, and then catch a cab the rest of the way.

The art was easy. The flowers only needed small touchups, smoothing out tiny flaws in petals, putting precisely the right curve in a stem, brightening colors here and there. Abel was thrilled with the results. You might not be too surprised to hear that I felt differently, or that the job nagged at me all through the clattering train ride back to Philadelphia. I had no reason to care what Abel did with his money. No doubt he could afford the expense, but he had shelled out a lot today for a service he didn't really need. My magic had become an expensive luxury for the already-rich. Nobody needed to tell me how Dad would have felt about that.

Back at the office, Stephen was as buoyant as ever. "Out in the suburbs now, son! Next thing you know, we'll be clear across the state!" I tried to hang the right kind of expression on my face. It was early for me to clock out for the day, but Stephen wasn't about to argue.

I got home to hear Charley talking on the phone. "Thanks," he said. "Yeah, see you soon." A pause, and a laugh. "Don't worry about that. See you."

I went down to the kitchen to say hello, wondering if he was making progress on the romance front. Not that I would pry, of course. "Hey, kid," I said. "How's tricks?"

"Hey!" It was something, to see him so glad I was home. That welcome would make up for a lot of uselessly expensive photoshoots. "You're early," he said.

I got a glass of water at the sink and drank it down. It had been a warm train ride, under the heavy blanket of the city's summer humidity, and my shirt stuck to my back when I peeled off my suit jacket. "That Haverford job was pretty quick," I said.

"If I'd heard you come in, I'd have asked if she wanted me to put you on."

"She?" I was still thinking about Denise. "Why would she want to talk to me?" They couldn't be that serious yet, could they, that she wanted my okay?

He laughed. "I guess your fiancée might want to talk to you."

The penny dropped. "Justine? Why did she call?" Instantly I wondered what her father and sister had been saying to her since the night before. "Is she all right?"

"She's fine," Charley said. "And she didn't call, I called her. So now I can tell you, if you want to go ahead and get married next week, it's good with me."

"Hang on a second." I loosened my tie, to concentrate better, and refilled my water glass. "Back up and tell me what happened, will you?"

We sat together at the table and he told me how he'd spent the school day half-listening to the teachers talking about finals, all the while mulling over the idea of having a sister-in-law. "I paid attention enough," he said, before I could pretend to scold. "I figured, before I could tell you anything for certain, I needed to talk to her myself."

He had called her as soon as he got home. I wondered who'd answered, and whether it had thrown them for a loop. *May I speak to Miss Justine? This is Charley True, her almost-brother-in-law.* Justine herself had been surprised to hear from him, but she'd understood fast enough.

"I said, so you and Nicky want to get married next Saturday. She said yes, if I was all right with it. And I told her I like her and all, and I'm glad she's marrying you, but like you said, there's been a lot going on."

It sounded as if he'd had an easier time talking with her than with me. He'd told her how much he missed our mother and how he thought about her every day. He'd said it was hard to think about making changes here at the house, to get ready for the new "roommate," especially when it came to the idea of sorting through our parents' things. "You'll need the master bedroom," he said. I hadn't yet thought about myself, but he was right; and all of our parents' personal things were in that room. Charley said he'd told Justine how it felt to think about someone else living here, someone who hadn't known our mother and dad. "I said, I guessed maybe that was the tough part, how she never met them." He scanned the cabinet doors above my head. "To me, you know, sometimes it's like they're still here."

He hadn't told me half of that. "I didn't plan to say so much," he said. "But, Nicky, the way she listens, it makes you want to talk."

I listen too. But he was right. It wasn't the same, was it, with your older brother, who'd been gone for such a while. "She's a good listener," I said.

"She said she wishes she could've met Mom and Dad. And she told me she misses her mom too, and she still thinks about her a lot. We talked about that some. What it's like remembering somebody, trying not to lose them." I wished Justine had been with us in the kitchen right then, so I could've thanked her the way I wanted to. "And then," Charley said, "you know what?"

What's that look? "What?"

"She told me a bunch of stuff about why she loves you."

Nothing could have kept my face from firing up, especially when he grinned like that. "She did?"

"Yeah." He propped his elbows on the table. "She said you see things most people don't, and you care about things most people never notice, and being with you feels like being home." He ticked off each piece on his fingers. "And she said now that she knows you, things would seem awfully empty without you. She wouldn't want to spend her life with anybody else."

Well. I was surprised the linoleum tile didn't melt into a puddle under my sockfeet. "She said all that?"

"Sure did. She said that's why she wants to marry you as soon as you can, but she also wants to know for a fact that I'm okay with it. Because, she said, I mean the world to you. You'd never want to see me hurt, and she wouldn't either."

That about summed it up. I said, "She's got that last part right."

"She's got the rest of it right too. So I told her, if that's how she feels about things, it sounds like the three of us will get along fine, and she should marry you as soon as you want."

Part of me wanted to laugh. He had signed my permission slip. Part of me, I don't mind admitting, was pretty well choked up. He went on, "She told me, if we wouldn't mind showing her some of our parents' things, she'd like to come over and see them. Before we pack anything up." I didn't much want to think about that, going through Dad's closet and replacing his belongings with mine. Charley said he'd asked if she'd like to come over on the weekend. "She said sure, and you should call her and make a plan."

That brought me back to what I'd overheard. "And you told her not to worry about something."

"Yeah. She said she'd try not to boss me around as much as you do."

"Good." That didn't really cover it. Not even close, if you want the truth.

~

WHEN DR. MURRAY AND LOUISA LEARNED ABOUT THE NEW plan for the wedding, they washed their hands of Justine and me. Louisa couldn't have made it clearer that she thought her sister was throwing her life away, but if Justine wouldn't listen to reason, what could anybody do? Dr. Murray was a little kinder about it, but he didn't hesitate to tell Justine and me both that he didn't approve of this haste and could only hope we wouldn't repent at leisure.

On Saturday morning, exactly a week before we planned to tie the knot, Justine came out to the house right after breakfast. Today we would go through the master bedroom and try to set it up as the room she and I would share. "You're sure you don't mind me being here?" she asked.

"It's good you're here," Charley said. "We'll need the moral support."

He and I had decided to start with Dad's things. They had sat around in the bedroom longer, packed away since his death. I tugged on the flimsy handle of his closet door, feeling as if I might set a swarm of hornets loose.

Inside, there wasn't much to see at all. Old wooden hangers held a navy-blue suit, a long winter coat, a jacket, and two pairs each of slacks and dungarees. On the floor, a pair of brown loafers sat next to a pair of brogues. Two heavy wooden crates, stacked one on top of the other, took up the rest of the space.

Not much, for sure. But the dye stains on the dungarees, the scuff marks on the brogues, made it seem as if Dad had gone to work yesterday. A flash of a long-forgotten afternoon: I'd been so little that I could just about scramble down from a kitchen chair without help, and I'd heard the front door creak open and done exactly that, running down the hall as fast as my short legs would carry me. There was Daddy, home from work, the tiredness of the long day dragging at him, but his eyes lighting up when he saw me. He hadn't bothered to take his jacket off before he bent down and scooped me up in his arms. "Here's my boy!" In the background, my mother said something about how he was filthy, "at least change your clothes first, Des," but he hadn't set me down. I wrapped my arms around his neck, smelling the dye and sweat and cigarette smoke on him, feeling his chin stubble rough against my cheek.

Now I made myself reach in and pull out the corduroy jacket on its hanger. Dad had worn it through every spring and fall, and as deep into the winters as he could, to save wear on his best coat. He'd worn it the first time we had gone to the art museum. That day, when we rode the bus home, I had rested my head on his shoulder and drifted into a doze, with the nap of the corduroy pressing against my cheek.

After all this time, I told myself, the jacket couldn't smell like anything but old dusty cloth. I lifted it to my face. When the fabric touched my skin, I could have sworn I caught a whiff of the smoky scent that had meant *love* since my earliest memories.

Oh, hell.

Dad.

The bed was right behind me, his side, where the mattress had the depression he had worn into it all the nights he'd slept here. I sat down and hid my face against the cloth. My glasses dug into the bridge of my nose.

The mattress shifted next to me. Justine's hand cupped the back of my neck. "I'm sorry," I said, through the fabric.

"Don't be."

She and Charley waited. The room was quiet. I tried, oh, I tried, to understand once and for all that he was gone, that he wouldn't walk into this room again, that losing him hadn't been my fault.

Couldn't you have said goodbye?

I miss you, Dad. All the time.

After a minute or two, I could breathe again. "Okay." I lowered the jacket. "Let's get this done."

We took everything out of the closet. Dad hadn't had many things of his own. There were his clothes and Bible, his reading glasses and pills, his billfold and the old ivory comb he had brought over from Ireland. The work shirts and dungarees were too faded and stained to wear anymore, so we would have to toss them out now, or cut them up for rags. I set them in a pile at the foot of the bed.

"Nicky," Justine said, "you worked in the factory too, didn't you?"

"For a little while."

"What was it like?"

To someone like her, it would have been a foreign place. I told her about the deep-down pleasure Dad had gotten from his work, and how he'd taught me the rhythms of it during those last months when we'd worked together. The long hours and hard labor, coming home dirty and sweaty, not making much money: all of that had been real, yes, but as I dug down, I remembered the satisfaction of earning those paychecks, bringing in real and steady wages for the first time in my life. Dad had insisted I put most of the money by for myself – that was the reason I'd been able to go to California – but some of it went into the family pot too. I told Justine how Dad and I had walked to Phillips together in the early-morning light, and walked back home together every afternoon, and how we'd shared that time and talked about what was coming next.

Justine smiled. "He must have been proud of you."

Charley was sitting on the floor, going through the crate we hadn't finished emptying yet. "Nicky," he said. "Look." He pulled out a pair of plain white button-down shirts. "These are practically new. I bet you could wear them."

They would have fit him too. Both of us had about the same height and build as Dad, but I knew why he was giving them to me. I tried not to clutch at them. "Thanks, kid."

We kept what clothes seemed useful, along with the ivory comb and Dad's pocket Bible. I held onto the old reading glasses too, not that we needed them, but I put them back on the bedside table where Dad had always kept them. The rest of his things would be given away or tossed. When we finished, the closet stood mostly empty, ready for me to put my own clothes in it.

We took a break then. "You both could use some tea," Justine said. "I'll make it, if you tell me where everything is."

Our mother had kept a stash of dark loose-leaf Irish tea, one of her and Dad's few indulgences. Justine brewed it up strong, the way we'd always liked it. "I've been practicing," she said, setting mugs in front of us. "I can boil water pretty well, don't you think?"

The good, sweet tea felt like a friendly hand on my shoulder. "Nicky," Charley said, "you know what else we should do today? We should get your California boxes out of the basement."

I started to say we had enough to do without that, but Justine said, "California boxes?"

"The stuff he had in his place out there," Charley said. "Artwork and stuff. I think you two should hang the pictures up in the bedroom."

"Kid," I said.

Justine said, "Pictures? Your own drawings?"

"They're prints." I gave Charley a look over the tops of my glasses. "There's a Rubens and an O'Keeffe and a couple of others, but like I said, we've got plenty to do."

They didn't pay any attention. "So we'll get them out," Charley told Justine. "They'll look good in there."

I was outnumbered, because Justine thought it was a great idea, and I couldn't have scolded Charley anyway for bringing it up. Not when the next part of the bedroom project was the hardest for him.

We went through the same process again with our mother's things, emptying the bureau drawers and her closet. Along with the everyday housedresses, and the few nicer skirts and blouses she had worn to church, she had a small stash of pretty things I couldn't remember seeing before. She hadn't wanted to risk them getting spoiled, no doubt, so she'd kept them tucked away safe.

There was a little pile of handkerchiefs with hand-embroidered lace. Our mother wouldn't have made them herself, but a great-aunt or grandmother might have, either back in Ireland or here in the States. There was a cream-colored blouse with blue forget-me-nots stitched around the scalloped collar and cuffs. In the closet, we found a dress our mother would have worn as a girl. It was tea-rose pink, with elbow-length sleeves and an empire waist. A placket of snowflake-delicate lace ornamented the neckline.

Charley leaned against the closet door to hold it up. "I sure don't remember this. Do you, Nicky?"

I didn't. Justine said, "It's so pretty. Maybe it was her wedding dress."

If she had kept it for so long, well after she had stopped wearing it, it must have been special for sure. I realized how pretty the girl who had worn it must have been, and how the soft warm color would have set off her dark hair and eyes. That girl had fallen for a tall young factory worker fresh off the boat from the home country. I could picture how she must have smiled up at him when the two of them walked home from Mass together, that first Sunday they met, her arm close in his and her hand resting on the sleeve of his coat.

Justine said, "Do you think there's a wedding picture? We'd be able to see if that's what she wore."

I had never seen any wedding pictures. Charley said, "Any photos around, they'll be in this room, I bet." They, too, would have been tucked away safe. We had never had money for a camera, so pictures were rare gifts.

We found them, a little pile of black and white shots, in a shoe box in our mother's closet, pushed back in the corner behind the black heels she had worn to church. There were only a few, none from the wedding. The three of us sat on the floor, with our backs against my mother's side of the bed, to leaf through them.

The first one showed our parents standing on the tiny lawn out in front of our house. The little boy between them was about two years old. He looked as if something wonderful had just surprised him: his whole face was lit up so that you couldn't help smiling back.

Charley said, "That's you, Nicky."

I had forgotten my hair was so close to blond back then. Dad and my mother each had hold of one of my hands. We were dressed for Mass, Dad in a dark suit, my mother in a light-colored dress with a belt, and me in the kind of short pants and loose-fitting blouse young boys wore in the twenties. All of us looked happy.

I couldn't take my eyes off my parents' faces. They were so young. Justine put her head on my shoulder to get a closer look. "You look like your dad," she said. "Both of you do. And you, Nicky, you were awfully sweet."

Charley said, "*Were* sounds about right."

"Watch it, kid."

Next was a picture of Dad at the dye house, looking older. It might have been taken around the time Charley was born. He and a couple of his factory buddies stood in front of one of the vats, their arms draped around each other's shoulders. They looked pretty tired, their work clothes rough and stained, but they were all smiling. I wondered who had taken the photo, and why. Then there was a picture taken at church: Easter Sunday, when Charley was about a year old. The church doors stood wide open, draped with garlands of lilies. My parents and Charley and I were grouped in the entrance. You could see past us down the aisle to the altar, which had more flowers piled up in front of it. In the photo, Dad was holding Charley, with our mother standing next to him, and me in front of her. I remembered that day. Mrs. Franklin had taken the photo and promised my mother a copy.

"Charley," Justine said, "you were pretty sweet yourself."

"He was cute, all right," I said. "Noisy, too."

"What was that you said before?" he asked. "Watch it?"

The last photo was taken on my high school graduation day. This time it had been Mrs. O'Dell with the camera, the Kodak she'd scrimped for and bought a couple of months earlier. I remembered her coming over to the house before the ceremony at the school. *Of course we've got to have a picture. Come on, all of you.* She had herded us out into the yard to pose.

In the photo, Dad and my mother and I stood side by side, with me in the middle. I wore my cap and gown. Dad had on his good suit, and my mother wore a dark skirt and one of her Sunday blouses, with a touch of ruffle at the neck and wrists. Charley stood in front of me, wearing a suit that I remembered had been dark brown, a hand-me-down of mine. He still looked like a little kid, but anyone would have recognized his grin. While Mrs. O'Dell took the photo, he'd leaned against me for support so he wouldn't have to hold his cane. I remembered his weight against my legs and how thin and slight his shoulder had felt under my hand. Between him and Dad, you'd have been hard pressed to say who looked prouder. My mother was smiling too, in spite of her misgivings about me and my future. I had tried for the kind of serious face I thought suited a guy who was planning to go to college and be an artist, but I remembered how hard it had been not to beam as wide as Charley.

Within a couple of years after that photo was taken, we had lost Dad, and I had fled for the west coast. Now, while we sat on the floor by our parents' bed, Charley rubbed his eyes with the back of his wrist.

I put my hand on his shoulder, which was broad and solid now. His eyes looked bruised. "That looks like all we've got," he said. Not just all the photos, but everything that had belonged especially to each of our parents. It wasn't much to sum up two lives.

We kept our mother's pink dress and the embroidered blouse and handkerchiefs. The rest would be given away or go into the scrap bag with Dad's work clothes. We took down her crucifix, from where it had hung over the bed, and packed it away too. By the time we finished, I felt so hollow that a breeze could have pushed me across the room.

Justine took charge of things. "How about if we keep the photos out?" she said. "We could put them up somewhere where we can see them."

Charley had been sitting on the floor with his head down, his hands resting on top of the crate that now held both of our parents' belongings. He turned to see her. "I'd like that."

"Good. And, Nicky, we need to get one other thing before next Saturday."

Next Saturday. Our wedding day. "What's that?"

"A camera. My dad has one, but I'd like us to have our own and take our own pictures."

Charley pushed himself up onto the bed. "Can I take your wedding pictures?"

Justine told him she'd hoped he would. She was right about the camera, too; we needed one, not just for the wedding. "Because, kid," I said, "when you graduate next year, we'll need plenty of photos then."

We'd get his senior yearbook too. We hadn't gotten mine, because it had cost too much along with the cap and gown everyone had to have, but Charley should have memories he could keep. "Of course we will," Justine said. "The older sibling doesn't get to have everything."

Charley rubbed his eyes again, but now he smiled. "Sounds fair."

Justine and I went down to the basement and brought up my boxes from California. Charley helped us decide where to hang the prints in the bedroom. It was surprising what a difference those few new patches of color made, over the bed and dresser and by the window.

Our parents had slept in this bed. Our mother had taken her last breaths here. Now I began to wonder if the room didn't have to belong to ghosts after all; if Justine and I could make it ours. Charley said, "Mom and Dad would have wanted that."

I hoped he was right. I hoped that, somehow, they knew what we were doing. That night, after I took Justine back to her place, I stood for a while in front of the photos we had set up on the fireplace mantel. My eyes kept resting on the earliest one, where I was so small.

I remembered when the Easter photo had been taken, and the graduation one, but I couldn't bring back that long-ago Sunday morning in the front yard. I wished I could feel the warmth of the sunshine and Dad's and my mother's hands around mine. I wished I could remember what had made me light up the way I had, what wonderful thing had made me so happy.

And my parents looked so young. *You look like your dad,* Justine had said. If I'd glanced at the photo without knowing who was in it, I might have mistaken Dad's face for my own. I was no older now than he'd been then.

A week from now, I'll be married. I said it in my head, to him and my mother, wishing I could know they heard.

Chapter Eighteen

Justine came over again early the next morning, in time for Mass. Saints Peter and Paul was a few blocks north of our house, pretty much in the middle of the neighborhood, but quite a bit older than everything else. It dated back over a hundred years, to a time when our part of the city had still been countryside, and the parishioners would have driven out here in their wagons and carriages.

The three of us walked up there together. The church still looked proud, with its tall stone walls, high spire, and arched stained-glass windows. It looked a little dingy and run-down too, like most everything else in our part of town, with grates over the windows to stop kids from pitching stones through. Justine said, "You've been coming here since you were little?" She'd told me her family had never been churchgoers.

"Since we were born," I said. Charley and I had both been baptized here. The church also had one of the biggest patches of green in Elmcroft: the cemetery. After Mass, Charley and I usually took a quiet few minutes to visit its eastern corner, where the headstone "True" stood in the shadow-tracery of a tall holly bush.

We stepped into the nave. Incense floated in the cool air and light through the stained glass splashed the floor with color. Justine stopped and looked up at the vaulted ceiling, where the beams joined together like hands lifted in prayer. She drew a long breath.

"It's beautiful." The whisper rang against the floor and walls.

Pretty much everyone in the neighborhood came to Peter and Paul. Most families had their own pews that they'd occupied for so long that the wood had shaped itself to particular backs and thighs. Charley and I surely knew the view from our own pew, off to the left side about halfway up to the altar. We took our seats there, with Justine on the inside and Charley on the aisle.

It never took long for the sight of a new face to cue glances and murmurs around the church. I could feel them starting as Father Hagerty stepped up to the lectern. Justine had introduced herself to the Parkers, who were sitting on her left, as "Nicky's fiancée," and the news spread up and down every row in less time than it took to pass the collection plate.

Mrs. O'Dell pounced on us the moment the service ended, before the echoes of *Ite, Missa est* had faded. She hugged Justine tight. "Saturday? You're marrying this boy on Saturday?"

Justine said yes, ma'am, she was. Mrs. O'Dell folded her arms. "Nicky, child, if you get any quieter, your mouth will plain disappear. Now you listen to me. You and your brother and this young lady here are coming over for dinner Saturday, after your wedding. I won't hear a word of argument."

I didn't forget how some people had eyed Minna, or what others might have thought of me for not going overseas. At the same time, when I saw how the neighborhood held its arms out to Justine, and when I knew how they would turn out to welcome the new bride, forgiveness wasn't hard to find.

The wedding day was overcast and muggy. If you've ever been to Philly in late spring or summer, you know how the air can get so thick you'd think you could take a shovel and tunnel right through it. Charley and I arrived at the courthouse early. I had offered to pick Justine up, but she'd said she would come with her father and Louisa. "Don't worry, my love," she said, answering my unspoken fears about the last-minute fights they might put up. "It'll be all right."

Inside the courthouse, the thick stone walls helped keep the heat out, and the ceiling fans swirled just enough to stir up a breeze. Charley and I needed it. We both wore our best suits, full three-piece, with our shoes polished mirror-bright. Charley had the camera, a sleek Mercury, slung on its strap around his neck.

The evening before, Justine and I had brought the last of her things over from her father's house. She had saved her books for the final load: the collections of Tennyson and Keats she'd snuck to grade school in her bookbag, the volumes of Millay and Frost her father had given her as gifts, the W. H. Auden and William Carlos Williams she'd bought on the sly during high school. "Dad never liked modernists," she told me. We organized her books on the new shelf I'd put up in the master bedroom. "I want to read Langston Hughes next," she said. I didn't recognize his name, but I had a lot to learn about poetry. "He's colored," she said. "One of the most famous colored poets." I wondered if Minna knew about him too. "Of course," Justine said, "I couldn't talk about him in front of Dad, but you won't mind your wife reading his work, will you?"

"As long as you read it to me too."

I hadn't felt nervous at all on my last night of bachelorhood, but now, as Charley and I waited in the courthouse lobby, a knot tightened in my stomach. I couldn't help worrying, never mind what Justine had told me. This was her father's and Louisa's last chance to say whatever they wanted. Nothing would make Justine change her mind about me, but I didn't want her facing one more fight alone, lifting her chin to hide her hurt, bracing herself one more time against *How can you do this?*

Louisa, too, hovered in the back of my mind. She cared about Justine and wanted her to be happy, and she knew Justine was happy with me. Was there any chance, though, that her jealousy at her sister's marriage, or her loneliness, or, when you got right down to it, the fact that I wasn't the kind of man who should have won Justine at all, finally push her to spill my secret to her father? *Dad, you can't let Jussie marry him, he's a freak!*

Just as I decided I couldn't sit still for one more second, the court-house's heavy front door swung open. I was on my feet in an instant.

Right away, I wished I could sit back down, because the room started to spin, and how would it look if I fell over?

Then I saw her. My beautiful girl.

In her simple, high-waisted white dress, with her dark hair coiled at the back of her head and her veil draped over it like mist, she could have been a nymph in a pre-Rafaelite landscape. She carried a cluster of raspberry-pink sweetheart roses that stood out like jewels in her hands.

My bride. How could I be so lucky?

People were saying things. Dr. Murray, dressed in a salt-and-pepper three-piece and holding a box wrapped in white paper, offered a chilly greeting to me, then to Charley, whom he had never met. Louisa, frilly in goldenrod-yellow, cast her eyes around the lobby and the portraits of judges past and present that glared down at us from the walls. She made some comment about them, but the only thing I heard clearly was Justine's voice when she came up to me.

"Good afternoon, Mr. True."

"Good afternoon, Miss Murray."

The guard at the lobby desk directed us upstairs to the right courtroom. We went up, Justine and me first with her arm through mine, Charley behind us, Dr. Murray and Louisa bringing up the rear. The clerk of court was a blurry face with a halo of white hair and a dark suit. He stood in front of a desk, and Justine and I stood in front of him, and Charley backed me up, and Louisa flanked her sister. As far as I knew for certain, Justine and Charley were right there near me. Everything else came and went.

Such a small handful of time, to link two people for life. Out of the blur of it, I remember Justine's hands warm in mine, and her steady eyes on my face, and my own voice saying *I will.* I remember her answering, the two words as clear and sweet as a chime. The light from the ceiling lamp caught our two gold wedding bands and I could have stood there and stared at them while the world went on without me.

I remember the clerk pronouncing us man and wife. I remember Justine stepping into my arms, and her eyes, always her eyes, as she reached up and took my face between her hands. I remember hearing the camera's shutter clicking as her lips found mine and time seemed to stop.

Then I remember Justine laughing, holding my hand tight in hers, rounding on Charley to pretend to scold him for taking a picture of us kissing. Charley was all wide-eyed innocence: "But you *wanted* pictures!" The clerk slid the register across the desk. *Nicholas Joseph True. Justine Elizabeth Murray True.* My hand only shook a little as I signed it. Justine signed and whispered to me, "I've been practicing my new last name."

We might have floated downstairs; I don't remember anything as ordinary as walking. Somehow, we were outside on the sidewalk in the muggy warmth. The sky looked no less gray than before, but to me, there wasn't a cloud in it. Charley grouped us in front of the courthouse door for another handful of pictures. Justine slipped her arm around me and leaned her head against my shoulder. The scent and softness of her hair woke me out of one dream into a new one. *My wife.*

Louisa hugged her sister. "I hope you'll be happy, Jussie." Her mouth was set so tight that the words had to squeeze out. When she blinked, something glittered on her perfect eyelashes. She shook my hand. "I suppose we're brother and sister now."

"Don't worry, Miss Louisa. I'll take good care of her."

The *miss* almost made her smile. "You'd better."

Dr. Murray had drawn Justine a little distance away. I heard her say, "Dad, you'd be more than welcome," and saw him shake his head. "No, ladybug. You settle in. When things quiet down, we'll have a family dinner."

"If you're sure." Justine's voice had an edge of tears in it. I stepped up beside her.

Dr. Murray's face looked so remote that he and I might have been facing each other through a six-inch pane of glass. "I was saying to Justine," he said, "that while I appreciate the invitation to the dinner at your neighbor's house this evening, I think it will be better to host you another evening at my own." He handed Justine the white-wrapped box he had held all through the ceremony. "You may like to have this," he told her. "Open it later."

Justine swallowed. "Thank you."

He wouldn't make my wife cry, not if I could help it. At the same time, the deep lines at the corners of his eyes told me that he had already started imagining her absence. He knew how much he would miss her. He didn't know how to tell her that, or how to live with it.

"Sir," I said, "I promise you, I'll take good care of her." My second promise in as many minutes. "We aren't far away, you know. We can all visit each other any time."

Elmcroft was a different world to him. The wall between us flickered for an instant before his reserve it locked back into place. "To be sure." He shook my hand, his fingers strong and chilly. "I congratulate you, Nicky." The first time he had used my name.

Then he was hailing a cab, and Charley was hailing another, and we were heading home: Dr. Murray and Louisa in one direction, Justine and Charley and I in the opposite one. Charley sat in the cab's passenger seat, holding the camera and the bouquet of roses. In the back, Justine hid her face against my shoulder.

"I'm not sad about being married." She hadn't cried after the ceremony or after any of the arguments with her father and sister, but now the tears came, in the safe shell of the car. "Please don't think I am. I just wish that Dad..."

She couldn't finish. I held her, wishing I could make myself a shield against anything that ever tried to hurt her. Charley turned around. "People are supposed to cry at weddings," he said. "Nobody cried yet today, so it'd probably be bad luck if you didn't."

That made Justine laugh, sunshine through rain. She lifted her head and mopped at her eyes. "You'd better not take any pictures of me like this, you hear?"

"I have to save some film for Mrs. O'Dell's. Otherwise..."

He pointed the camera at us. Justine reached out to cover the lens with her hand. The wedding band glinted on her finger. "Don't you dare," she said.

"Put that thing down," I told Charley. "By the way, kid, I notice you finagled it so you weren't in any pictures yet." He hadn't let anyone else take so much as a single shot. "We'll fix that when we get home."

Charley tucked the Mercury into its leather case. "I'm the camera expert. I don't have to trust either one of you with it."

"This kid," I told Justine. "What are we going to do with him?"

"Am I allowed to call him 'kid' too?"

"No," Charley said. "Nicky isn't allowed either. Not really."

"Kid, that's news to me."

The way we all laughed, the cab driver probably thought we were crazy. No doubt wedding parties need a lot of slack. At the house, Mrs. O'Dell came hustling up the sidewalk to meet us. "Don't worry," she said. "I won't get in your way, we'll have plenty of time to talk tonight. I just have to give this beautiful young lady a hug."

She wrapped her arms around Justine. "Congratulations, Mrs. True." I swallowed pretty hard at that, especially when she added, "Dear, I've known Nicky all his life. This is a fine man you've got," and Justine answered, "I know."

Mrs. O'Dell took the camera from Charley and got a few pictures of the three of us together in the yard. "Now," she said, "you'll need time to yourselves. We'll see you for dinner."

In the front hallway, Justine held the roses between her hands and looked up at me as if we were back in front of the clerk of court. "Mrs. True," she said.

I wanted to ask if she was sure she was glad, now that it was real. If I was worth it. If this house, so different from the one she had left, would really do for a home. She reached one hand up to cup the back of my neck, and stood on tiptoe, and the kiss went on long enough that Charley cleared his throat and pretended to have important business in the kitchen. All the answer I needed.

JUSTINE WAS SORRY TO CHANGE OUT OF THE BRIDAL DRESS, but for dinner at Mrs. O'Dell's, she looked no less beautiful in the rose-colored one she had worn the first time I'd gone to her father's place. She asked me to help her pin a couple of the sweetheart roses in her hair. "Have you ever helped a woman with her hair before?"

"Only with my drawing," I said. "I'm afraid you can't have that, Mrs. True."

"Good."

A big slice of the neighborhood filled Mrs. O'Dell's little house. Welcoming a new bride was a serious business. Justine stood out, the girl from a different world, and normally, she told me, she'd have felt shy around so many new people, but tonight she found herself talking and laughing with everyone as easily as if she had grown up on Lawrence Street too and run in and out of this house every day of her life. The neighborhood drew her in as if she had always belonged to it. I returned handshakes and thanked people for their congratulations, wondering all over again that this was real. That Justine had decided to link her life to mine.

Everyone had brought a dish of some kind. A fancy expensive wedding with a full reception couldn't have afforded a better meal. We crowded into the living room to eat chicken and casserole and salads and went back to the kitchen to refill our plates from the array of cakes and pies. Justine told Mrs. O'Dell that she didn't know the first thing about putting a dinner together, but she wanted to learn. Mrs. O'Dell went straight to a drawer and dug a notepad out. The neighborhood women passed it around, filling pages with recipes and tips.

Afterward, Justine and Charley and I walked slowly home up the dark street, Charley ahead and Justine and me following arm in arm. I felt as transparent as a lamp, as if a candle inside me had lit and the brightness of it should fill the night.

Justine said, "Mrs. O'Dell and Mrs. Parker both want me to visit them this week for cooking lessons."

"You'll be an expert in no time."

"It'll keep me busy while you're at work." Her face was like a night-blooming flower. "Which, by the way, is another thing we need to sort out."

"Is this when you start nagging me?"

"Every chance I get."

The master bedroom almost felt like ours now. The books and artwork, Justine's clothes and mine in the closets, her brush and comb on the bureau, my glasses case on the bedside table where Dad used to keep his. I had never slept in this bed, but tonight I thought it might be all right. I was lightheaded enough to drift off on a breeze.

Before we turned in, Justine opened the gift from her father. Charley and Titus sat with us on the bed to see. The white box Dr. Murray had given her held a photo album about the size of Dad's pocket Bible. It was brand-new, its front and end plates covered in pale blue damask.

Justine opened the cover. "Oh."

The black-and-white frontispiece showed a woman and two little girls sitting together on a high-backed couch. All three looked as if they were about to go to a party: the woman in a long, slim-fitting gown with a fringe of beads at each shoulder, the girls in frilly dresses and slippers tied with ribbon. The woman wore her dark hair in marcelled waves that framed her cheeks.

She looked as perfect as a fashion plate, but that wasn't what drew me most. She had turned her face slightly away from the camera, as if the photo mattered less to her than the person taking it. She was looking directly at him. Everything about that look, everything in her dark beautiful eyes and her smile, said that he was her heart.

Dr. Murray had called himself lucky. He surely had been.

The older of the two girls, the blonde one, might have been about eight years old. She lifted her chin and posed with an already-glamorous, conscious beauty. The smaller girl was about five. She had her mother's dark hair, and the same smile too, full of sweetness.

Justine swallowed and handed me the album. I passed it to Charley, on my other side, and put my arm around her. "She was beautiful."

"She was."

"You're like her, you know." I didn't mean in looks. Justine's own face and body weren't, couldn't be, the perfect reflection of the woman in the photo, but she had inherited something much better. "Her smile..." As best I could, I tried to put words to it. "Maybe I should say I think she's like you."

It was clumsy enough. Justine said, "You do?"

"Absolutely."

"You're a sweet man. I've told you that, haven't I?"

Together, she and Charley and I leafed through the album, sitting shoulder to shoulder on the bed. Justine said her father must have gone through other albums and stashed-away files to put this collection together. Every picture showed her mother. In one of them, Justine was a baby in a white wrap, cuddled in her mother's arms while a toddler Louisa stood alongside. In another, Dr. Murray stood behind his wife's chair with his hand on her shoulder. They both looked so young that they might have been newly married. In his expression, though he looked as patrician as ever, I saw the same awe I had felt today at the sight of my own bride.

Toward the end of the album, there was a picture of Justine and her mother together, just the two of them, standing next to the trellis I'd seen in their back yard. Justine's mother wore a blouse and a long light-colored skirt and floppy straw hat. Justine had a short dress on, and a hat that was a miniature of her mother's. "That must have been the day Mama and I planted the roses," Justine said. Sure enough, two little bushes stood in front of the trellis, in what looked like freshly-dug soil. "I'd forgotten Dad took pictures of us."

The last sleeve in the album held a piece of folded white paper. Justine eased it out. It had the date written at the top and a few lines in precise, fluid handwriting.

Ladybug –

Your mother would have wanted to be with you on this day. May these memories bring her closer.

With love,

Dad

Justine pressed her face against my shoulder. The words made such a small scattering on the page, but I could feel how heavy each of them had been to Dr. Murray as he lifted them and pieced them together. The most intricate surgery he had ever done was nothing, compared with telling his daughter goodbye.

I kissed my wife's hair. She raised her head. "I'll have to call him." She dabbed at her eyes. "I'll do it first thing tomorrow. He went to so much trouble, finding all these pictures."

We put the new album on the fireplace mantel with the True family photos. That night, for the first time, our new family was together under one roof.

Chapter Nineteen

ONE OF THESE DAYS, I will finish this story. I don't know whether you'll be glad or sorry when I do. To tell you the truth, I don't know which I'll be, either.

This morning I'm following my usual routine. As we get deeper into summer, the wet heat outside will get so breathless that it'll seep through this old house's walls, and I'll start getting up earlier yet, to spend time with my wits about me before the rest of the day turns into a drowse until evening. For now, the sun is fully up, at just the right angle to slant through this window and across the tabletop and the laptop's keyboard. I have the mug of chamomile tea that I traded coffee for a long time ago, and two triangles of toast with the ruby beach-plum jam that Matthew and Kathryn and Hallie brought back from their trip to the shore. Justine used to say that beach-plum jam felt like such a treat: preserves made from roses. It was one of her favorite flavors.

Last night, I got out a little stack of pencil sketches to keep by me while I work. They usually stay in a plastic sheath in my desk drawer, because the paper they were drawn on is now yellow and crumbling at the edges. I don't take them out often in case they crumble away for good. They bring Justine, and those days when we were first married, back to me as nothing else can.

If you live as long as I have, you get used to loss. Everything lets you down eventually: muscles, eyesight, plumbing, hearing, and memory too, although I can tell you that no matter what else you might forget, you will always remember how you used to hop out of bed in the morning and stand up to put your pants on, instead of hauling them over your old legs while you lean back against the pillows. You also remember that you didn't used to have to take a rest afterward. The biggest loss, though, might be hard to imagine if you haven't made it to this absurd age: what it's like when the people who sit at the heart of your world leave it one by one. Leaving you behind.

Of course, you still have plenty of people to care about. I know how lucky I am to have so much time with my daughter and grandchildren and even my great-granddaughter. How many of us get to count three generations? Sometimes, though, it's been hard to tell this story not because I don't remember, but because I do. Dad was the first person I lost. In these pages, I've brought back others who have been gone too long now. Justine, my life. And Charley: my brother had a good long innings, but I don't think it's fair for the younger one to leave first. You can bet I'll tell him about that when we find each other again.

For now, I'd better get myself moving on these pages, or Jo will have something to say about it when she stops by this afternoon. I told you that I started writing about this long-ago time because she thinks people need to know what my magic did back then. I need to tell you how we realized what the magic should do, and what happened because of it. Once I do that, we'll be about ready to wrap this up – and I think I'll be both glad and sorry.

~

MINNA AND TIMOTHY INVITED JUSTINE AND CHARLEY AND me to dinner at their place on Sunday evening, the day after the wedding. Justine and I had both wished we could ask them to witness the ceremony. If we had, though, Dr. Murray and Louisa would undoubtedly have sat it out, and Justine loved them too much to let go of her old life without that goodbye.

"This newlywed business is wonderful," Justine said, during the cab ride up to north Philly. "I don't have to worry about cooking at all." We talked about where we ought to take a trip once Charley's school year ended. "Just make sure you want me along," Charley said. "Most people probably wouldn't want their kid brother tagging after them on their honeymoon."

"We're not most people," I said. "Matter of fact, neither are you."

He was sitting in the passenger's seat again and turned around to grin at us. "Okay. But when you want me to leave you alone, you just say so...and I'll think about it."

Justine didn't miss it when the neighborhood changed. She didn't say anything, but I saw how she glanced out the window more often, no doubt noticing, the same way I had, that nobody around here looked much like us anymore. She moved a little closer to me on the seat.

When we arrived at the apartment, a delicious smell of meat and spices wrapped around us. Justine exclaimed over the gorgeous hand-made rug in the front room and Minna hugged each of us in turn. Timothy clapped me on the back. "So, married life," he said. "Good luck. You'll need it."

Minna swatted his arm. "You quit that." She looked happier than I had ever seen her. Justine went into the kitchen with her to see if she could lend a hand with anything. Timothy told me he'd been doing more sketches. "It feels better every time."

I noticed he didn't say, this time, that he didn't know why he was bothering with it. "Can I see them?"

"After dinner. Minna said she has to feed us before we talk art, or we'll never eat."

Dinner was a rich ham-and-dumplings stew that Minna said had been her mother's favorite. She brought it to the table in thick ceramic bowls. "Good and cheap and sticks to your ribs," she said, but it was better than good. It was outstanding. None of us was bashful about second helpings.

During the meal, Justine brought up something I knew she'd been thinking about. "Minna, it doesn't seem fair to ask you to keep coming over and cleaning for us. You're our friend. I should be able to do the housework myself."

Minna cut into a dumpling. "Can you?"

She knew as well as we did that Justine had a lot to learn. "Not really." Justine blushed. "At least, I still can't do much, but I'm working on it."

"Here's how I see it," Minna said. "The job with you is good money, and that helps Timothy and me. I think it makes sense for me to keep taking care of your house, but if you want, I'll teach you what to do."

"I'd like that." Justine added shyly, "I just don't want you to think I'm hopeless."

Minna laughed. "I have a feeling you can do as good a job as anybody. You just have to start somewhere."

After we finished eating and cleared away the dishes, Timothy brought out his new sketches. He had drawn a couple of his neighbors from down the hall, and a young husband and wife he'd met out in the square with their little girl. Every one of the sketches had the precision and energy I had admired before. More than that: the strength and fluidity of the lines told me how the pencil had become an extension of Timothy's hand, as connected to him as the fingers that held it.

We passed the sketches around the table. Justine looked for a long time at the one of the little girl. Timothy said her name was Olivia. She was about four years old, her hair in curly puffs at either side of her head. Timothy had sketched her in mid-laugh. The simple lines on the paper showed how free and happy her laugh would sound, like a butterfly winging from one flower to another. They showed how she would twirl around in her sundress and run to find dandelions and violets in the grass.

"She's beautiful," Justine said.

"I did a couple more sketches of her for her parents to keep. Not as good as a photo, but not too bad."

Justine said, "I think it's much better. A photo wouldn't catch all of this."

Timothy wanted to get down to more drawing. "Nicky, I'd like your permission to sketch your brother and your wife tonight."

Your wife. Those words might have been painted in my head in gold. "You don't need my permission," I said. Justine and Charley were both more than ready to be sketch subjects, so Timothy said he'd get out his paper and pencils. "But first, Nicky, if I'm going to draw, so are you."

"Did this turn into some kind of contest?"

Timothy kept a straight face, but his eyes were bright with mischief. I could imagine the boy who had gotten detention for drawing in class. "I don't plan to be the only entertainment this evening."

"Everybody here's seen my trick before," I pointed out. Not that I minded drawing for them, but my magic seemed pretty thin and pale next to his.

Timothy said yes, he'd seen it, and he wanted to see it again. Charley said he and Justine wanted their portraits done, "so, Nicky, you don't have a lot of choice."

I pretended to sigh. "Fine."

Timothy got out the drawing implements. And then, all I can say is, I wish you had been there.

Timothy sketched Justine first. I couldn't decide whether to follow his hand or look for the details he captured from her face, but it wouldn't have mattered. I wasn't fast enough to catch anything. His lines were so quick and confident that it seemed to take no more than a handful of seconds before he passed the first drawing across the table. Without a pause, he started another one, asking her to turn her head and let him draw a profile. Then a third, a three-quarter turn as if she was looking over her shoulder. Finally, he asked her to look straight at me, and then I couldn't take my eyes from her long enough to watch his hand at all.

That last sketch. In it, Justine's face looked more like her mother's than ever, though it was still her own real face in every detail. I had known she loved me. Somehow, until I saw it there on the paper, the same way her mother's face had shown what the person behind the camera meant to her, I hadn't understood how much.

"You can keep those, of course," Timothy said. We did, too. I have had them ever since. Today, I took them out of their sheath to see her again.

Timothy told me it was my turn to draw. "Change something."

Minna said I had to use something small. "I'm not ready for a big mess." She reached into the drawer behind her chair and passed me a teaspoon. "You can't go too crazy with that, can you?"

On paper, I put a hole in the spoon's bowl and looped the handle through it. When the real spoon changed, Charley burst out laughing. Timothy and Justine joined in, and even Minna, who still had her doubts about the magic, let herself smile. Charley told them how when he and I were kids, I'd transformed the silverware at the dinner table, sometimes even when it was carrying food from a plate to a mouth. "Your poor mother," Minna said. "What a handful you must have been."

I fixed the spoon and Timothy drew Charley next. As he had with Justine, he asked for one facial angle after another. Those sketches showed my brother's face, exactly as it was, except that he no longer looked much like a kid at all. A man's wisdom and patience overlaid the features I knew so well.

"Change something else," Timothy told me. Minna let me use a dishtowel, but she held her breath until I undid the new patterns I put into the weave. She asked Timothy to draw someone we would all recognize. He thought for a moment before he put pencil to paper, and then, so quickly it was impossible to point to the moment when the lines and shadings came together, President Roosevelt's face took shape on the sketchpad.

We had all seen his face in newspaper photos, of course. Now we saw him as if he was still with us, his strength and tiredness and compassion alive on the paper. The drawing captured everything that had made him our Chief.

Timothy set the pencil down. "That's not bad."

It was quite a bit more than that. Charley cleared his throat and Minna touched a napkin to the corners of her eyes. That might be why Timothy said, "Minna, let Nicky draw the table."

Minna crumpled the napkin in her lap. "Oh, no, you don't! You're not putting holes in my furniture."

"You see how easy he changes it back," Timothy said. "Trust me." He leaned toward her with exactly the grin a kid uses to wheedle a parent. "You want to know there's magic, for a fact? You've got to see this."

"I know there's magic," Minna said. "I'm not doubting that. I just don't know *why*."

I said, "If it helps any, I don't know 'why' either."

Minna looked at me as if I were a cab driver who had just announced that he didn't know how to use a steering wheel. "No," she said. "That doesn't help."

Charley struck in. "He means he doesn't know why it happens, but it's completely safe. Please let him draw the table." Timothy was good, but nobody could wheedle like Charley when he put his mind to it. "Please."

Minna was outnumbered, and she knew it. "Fine." She sat back and folded her arms. "But if you ruin this table, Nicky True, you'd better believe you'll buy us a new one."

"Of course."

I got to work. The first step was to put a rolled edge on the square tabletop, all the way around, so that it had a lip on it. Then I started the cutouts, all circles this time. First, in the center of the wood, I made one the width of a palm. Minna gasped.

"It's okay," Charley said. Timothy seconded, "Keep going, man."

I added a few tennis-ball-sized cutouts around the first, and finally, closest to the edge of the table, a perimeter of rounds no bigger than golf balls. "Look at it this way," I said, putting in the finishing touches on what now looked like an extraordinarily large and well-organized block of Swiss cheese. "Nothing can roll off it anymore."

"No," Timothy said. "It can fall through instead."

Minna was horrified, but fascinated too. "I don't believe this." She ran her hand along the edge, measuring the depth of the lip with her forefinger, and then spread her palm across two of the smallest holes. "This is the ugliest table there ever was." She wasn't wrong. "Nicky, I don't understand this at all, but it's incredible."

"What Timothy does is better. Should I fix it now?"

She stroked the tabletop as if it had been an animal's back, feeling each of the empty places slide past under her skin. "Yes," she said. "Please. I don't think I'll relax until you do."

After I did, she did relax. In fact, we had quite a time. Timothy drew Gregory Peck and Lena Horne, and then Edward Murrow and Walter Winchell, whose faces we all knew from the papers. I made a temporary mess out of two of the cabinet doors, and turned the sink into a fountain that sent water up toward the ceiling instead of down into the basin. No doubt the neighbors could hear us laughing clear down the hall.

In the middle of it, I saw Minna and Justine catch each other's eye more than once, as if they were sharing a thought. We kept at the drawing game until all of us had to start thinking about Monday morning on the way. Minna hugged Justine at the door. "I'll see you tomorrow," she said. "We'll put our heads together."

"Yes." Justine glanced at me. "We'll make a plan."

Timothy walked downstairs with us to hail a cab. On the ride home, gliding through the fans of light from streetlamps, I asked Justine, "What was that about? A plan about what?"

Her smile teased me. "You'll have to find out."

I didn't find out anything else until the end of that week. Justine set about claiming the house and the neighborhood as her new home. She visited Mrs. O'Dell and Mrs. Parker for coffee and cooking pointers, and took housekeeping lessons, as she called them, from Minna. The two of them talked about books while they worked. It turned out that Minna had read many of the same collections Justine had, so they compared notes and favorites. Justine didn't try any solo cooking ventures that first week, but with her and Charley and me together in the kitchen, making dinner was more fun than it had ever been.

On Friday, I got home from work in a lousier mood than I'd have liked. Stephen had thought it was a good joke to tease me all week about my "fast-worker" marriage, although he was decent about it too, agreeing at once to the time off I wanted for a trip in the summer. Mark still disliked me as much as ever and gave me side-eye whenever we met, undoubtedly waiting for me to cause another round of trouble. I was too used to that for it to bother me much. What did bother me was the fact that every day, I heard more noise about building up a "suburban clientele" for Allen and Allen.

Abel Swift, the Haverford florist, had lined up a group of businessman friends who wanted to know about the special service our firm offered. That Friday afternoon, Stephen called me into his office to talk through which places I would visit over the next couple of weeks. "Let's get you set up with these new clients, son. Get their contracts signed before you head off on your honeymoon."

"Sure," I said. The word felt like sand between my teeth.

He put together a list of the businesses that sounded like the "best tickets," while I used every scrap of self-control I could find to sound pleased about the whole thing. Better for him not to know how I felt about those train rides back and forth to Haverford and Bryn Mawr and Gladwyne, to help people with too much money burn through it faster.

By the time I got through the door at home, I couldn't wait to shake the office out of my clothes and try to forget about it until Monday. Justine met me in the hall. "How was your day?"

We had been married all of six days. She shouldn't have to worry about me already. "It was okay."

She folded her arms as if I'd been a teenager trying to sneak in after curfew. "Really?"

"No, but I shouldn't whine about it."

"I don't hear you whining. Give me your jacket." She hung it up on the old wooden rack by the door. "Now go on and get changed. Charley and I will start supper."

"I can help."

"Not in the mood you're in, you can't. You'd curdle the milk just looking at it."

That made me smile, whether I wanted to or not. "That's better," she said. "Go get comfortable. We have some things to talk about tonight, and from the look of you, it's not a minute too soon."

"What things?"

"You'll find out." She waved me toward the stairs. "Go."

I scrubbed the day off in the shower and climbed into a fresh T-shirt and jeans. Back in the kitchen, Justine and Charley had gotten a fair way along with dinner. "You have to guess what it is," Charley said, "or you can't have any."

That smell was wired into my brain from childhood. It took no effort at all to guess, even though I hadn't eaten that meal in more years than I wanted to think about. Charley and Justine both looked pleased with themselves. "Mrs. O'Dell gave me a recipe," Justine said. "Charley helped me figure out how to make it more like your mother's."

I cooked up some bacon to crumble into the potato soup once it had finished simmering. Tasting the finished product, if I closed my eyes, I could see the four of us around the table the way we used to be: our mother and dad, Charley and me as boys. The view when I opened my eyes was just as good. The best part was how glad it made Charley.

I asked Justine again what we needed to talk about. "Never mind," she said. "Finish your dinner first." I might have wondered if I was in trouble for something, except that Charley had the same look on his face he used to get on Christmas morning when he was waiting to open presents. I asked him, "What do you know about this?"

"All of it, pretty much. Like your wife says, you have to wait." To Justine, he said, "He's in a better mood now, don't you think?"

"I think so."

"He might even listen."

While we cleaned up the dishes, Charley told me that he did know what Justine wanted to talk about, and he figured it would surprise me. "But it's a good idea," he said, reaching the last bowl up into the cabinet. "You should think about it."

It was clear I was in for something, though nothing could have prepared me for what it was. I draped the dishcloth over the edge of the sink and sat back down at the table. "Then let's hear it."

Justine and Charley sat down too. Justine told me that she and Minna had been talking a lot during the week, about Timothy and me. "Both of you deserve better than what you have."

I didn't understand at first. Timothy deserved better, beyond question. He deserved a world that respected him for the person and artist he was. I was already luckier than I had any right to be, but Justine reminded me how she felt about the ads. "Your art deserves more. Minna and I think that between you and Timothy, what both of you do, so much is possible."

Once – it felt like a long time ago now – I'd started to wonder if Timothy's art and mine could work together. I had almost forgotten that. Justine said, "The trick, we think, is to have more people see it." She explained that she and Minna had thought of a special demonstration. "A drawing demonstration, a public one, at a good venue. People would pay admission to see how you and Timothy work."

I could see right away how an audience would want to watch Timothy draw. It was captivating, pure and simple, and whether you had the least skill with pencil and paper or not: to see how those smooth lines and rapid shadings became so alive. But my work? I could draw things the way they looked, sure, but I couldn't bring the spark to it that Timothy did. Because of course Justine meant my ordinary work. She knew I couldn't do anything else at the kind of event she was talking about.

"Timothy, for sure," I said. "But I don't think anyone would want to watch me. My regular drawing is..."

Justine interrupted, gently. "I don't mean your regular drawing, my love. I mean your magic."

The room went still. The only sound was the faint tap of water falling drop by slow drop from the faucet. My magic, for a public audience?

Can you think what kind of trouble you might get into? I heard Dad asking the question, saw his eyes full of worry for me. *Can you think what people might say, or do?* I remembered, too, the day I'd met the Allen brothers, how I'd forced myself to stay in that boardroom until I landed the job, so I wouldn't have to try selling the magic to any other strangers.

I didn't realize I was shaking my head until Charley said, "Don't say no yet. Keep listening."

"Minna and I talked more about what you do," Justine said. "Especially what it meant to Timothy. It made such a difference, Nicky. You changed things for him."

I knew that, and I was glad, but that wasn't the point, was it? "I can't do a demonstration, even if I wanted to." The idea scared me so much that the words came out in fits and starts. "My contract with Allen and Allen. The non-disclosure." In my head, Mark Allen said, *You won't do this unless we tell you to.*

"I know," Justine said. "That's part of the point, love. You have to get rid of the ads."

My head felt as if someone had stuffed it with wool. "Sweetheart, my bosses would fire me. If I don't have another job, what'll we do?"

Charley leaned forward. "Nicky, think about it. Do you think you'd have a hard time getting paid for a demonstration?"

"He's right," Justine said. "Minna and I thought you could take a proposal to the museum. Show them the magic first." She made it sound as straightforward as getting measured for a new suit of clothes. "Then you could suggest the demonstration by you and Timothy both. Maybe they could also display some of Timothy's work."

This was all going much too fast. "The museum," I said. "You mean the art museum?"

"Yes." Justine's smile was like a hand reaching out for mine. "The museum we went to together. That one."

I couldn't think straight. I could barely think at all, but I did know that at that place – the one where I had fainted, let's not forget – they hadn't even liked having Timothy in the building. Exhibit his drawings? Let him do a demonstration?

Justine put her hand on my arm. "That's another piece of this," she said, as if I had spoken out loud. "Suppose you went to the museum and showed them what you can do. Suppose you offered to do it to bring people in. Whatever other conditions you put on that offer, do you think they would want to say no?"

Then, at last, the whole size of the thing sank in. Would they say no to an exhibit of a kind they had never imagined, that stood to bring in ticket sales they might never have dreamed of? Would they turn me away? Not likely. No more than Jonah Eberly had, or Stephen Allen.

If that was true, I could unlock that door for Timothy. I could push it open good and wide.

The idea still scared me down to my bones. If I took out my sketchbook and pencil in front of a public audience, with no paperwork or legalese to protect me, if I showed them the gift that Dad had always wanted me to keep secret, would anyone believe what they saw? I could make sure they didn't have a choice. I could do things they would have to believe if they ever wanted to trust their senses again.

And if I did, what would happen then?

Charley said, "Nicky, I can't help but think Dad would've liked this."

Liked it? I almost swung around to snap at him. *How dare you!* Charley had been too small to know about my only whipping, but I'd had to tell him about it, once he got old enough to want to brag about "what my brother can do." He'd had to understand why he shouldn't. *Dad hurt me himself to keep me from doing anything like this.* I wanted to say it out loud, remind him how much shame I carried because I had broken my promise.

I didn't, because memory cut in first.

Dad and me in our shabby clothes, arriving at the museum for the first time. We had ducked inside, heads down, sure someone would scold us and shoo us right back out again. Even after we'd gotten our tickets, we'd crept around the galleries bracing ourselves for the moment when someone would come and tell us we didn't belong there, we had to leave that astonishing feast of color for the rich people in their sleek coats and polished shoes to enjoy.

No one had done that. They had welcomed us.

All these years later, suppose Dad could have seen Timothy's art. Suppose he'd been with us at the museum, heard the guard demand to see tickets and call Timothy *boy*. I didn't know what Dad had thought of colored people – so far as I knew, he'd never had much to do with them at all – but I knew, as deeply and clearly as I had ever known anything, that he wouldn't have stood by and let that wrong happen. Not my father.

Justine and Charley were waiting for me to say something. My thoughts reached out into the dark. *Dad, what would you think now? Is Charley right?*

You ache for an answering echo or the touch of an invisible hand on your shoulder. It's never that easy. "Let me think about it," I managed. "And see what Timothy says." He might not want to try it. It might sit wrong with him to need my help again.

"That's fair," Charley said. Justine agreed, "You can tell him the whole thing. Minna hasn't said anything to him yet because we knew your part had to come first." Without "my part," the rest of it didn't stand a chance.

That night, long after Justine had gone to sleep beside me, I lay awake and stared up at the dark ceiling. No doubt Dad had stared up at the same spot, plenty of nights, when he was worried about a grocery bill, or the new clothes one of us needed, or some repair to the house. He had listened, the same way I was listening now, to the faint tapping of the old floorboards as they settled for the night, and he had kept still and breathed quietly, not to rustle the sheet too much or bother his sleeping wife.

The museum had been another home for him and me. I had never seen my magic as useful, except for a joke or a paycheck, but what if I'd been wrong? What if it could reshape that place, that one corner of the world, for just long enough?

I could do that for Timothy, Dad. I could open the door for him.

What would you think if I did?

Chapter Twenty

The next evening, Saturday, Minna and Timothy came over for dinner. I'd called in the morning and told Timothy I knew he couldn't get rid of me these days, but I wanted to talk to him about something important. In between that call and the meal, I spent a lot of time thinking about how to explain our wives' plan to him.

It didn't help that I still wasn't any too sure about it myself. I hadn't had any trouble convincing bigshots that I could make them money, but this was a different kind of task entirely. This time, I would have to reel people in with my magic. If they were going to see Timothy and his art, and understand real magic in action, they would have to look at the world differently. My magic would have to make that happen, if only for a little while.

It had seemed possible last night, but it looked a lot bigger and scarier in daylight. And that was without even looking at the question of what anyone might say or do, what might happen to me, if I succeeded. I couldn't admit to Charley, or Justine, or even myself, that I might be too scared to try.

We had enough potato soup left for a meal for the five of us. I told Timothy I'd like him to hear me out and not make up his mind about anything before he had time to think, and then I laid out Minna and Justine's plan as straightforwardly as I could.

The idea of a demonstration surprised him. At first he did seem to be thinking about it, but by the time I got to the part about showing the museum's directors my magic, he was shaking his head. I had already put my spoon down so he wouldn't see my hands trembling. "The point wouldn't be the magic itself," I said. "It would be for people to see our work, yours and mine. To see what art can do."

He barely waited for me to finish the sentence. "It won't work, man. They'll never let me show my drawing in that place."

Minna said, "Timothy, you've said it yourself. Nicky's magic changes things. If people have to accept that it's real, who knows what else they can swallow?"

Timothy was already thinking about a different problem. "Nicky," he said, "you're not supposed to do the magic in front of just anybody. If you tried this, you could lose your job, right?"

I couldn't deny it. "Probably. If the Allens found out."

"You're saying you'd risk that to give me a chance at something. I appreciate it, I have to, but the fact is you'll still be wasting your time. Nobody there is going to hear a word you say about my work."

Do you have tickets, boy? Show me. That afternoon unspooled in my head, backward, like a tape rewinding. The moment when Timothy had told me that being in the museum made him think about drawing again. The modern art galleries, where we'd stood in front of the brilliant O'Keeffe canvases, and I had said that what he did with portraits was like what she did with landscapes. *You're kidding, right?* Justine assuring him I wasn't: *He doesn't say what he doesn't mean.*

Timothy was right. They wouldn't want him or his art in that place that should have been home to him, the same way it had been to me. Knowing that, how right he was, sent a tendril of heat up my spine.

"I can make them listen," I said. "I'll show them something they can't have unless they give me what I want."

"You could get fired," he insisted. "I'm telling you it's not worth the risk."

"Yes, it is." I'd have liked a swallow from my water glass, but I wouldn't risk reaching for it in case my hand shook enough to see. "If you want this, I will go in there and show them actual damn magic and see if they're stupid enough to turn me away. I'd bet my last dollar they're not. I don't care what happens afterward."

Until I heard myself say it, I hadn't realized I'd made up my mind. Charley ducked his head to hide his smile. Justine didn't bother hiding hers. The look she gave me melted the last of my doubts.

Timothy sized me up, very much the same way he had the first time we'd met. "You'd show off your magic to whoever walks in the door, as long as they look at my stuff too."

"As long as they look good and hard." My spoon was an inch or so away from my fingers. I pulled it into my hand and gripped it tight, willing the pressure of the handle against my palm to hold off the dizziness that lapped at me.

"You know something?" Timothy said.

"What's that?"

"You're still a pain in the ass."

Minna and Justine burst out laughing. Charley said, "He's bossy too, don't you think?" My chest relaxed enough to let some air in. "So," I said, "do you want to try it or not?"

"Let me sleep on it. We'll talk again tomorrow." The idea was starting to put roots in his head, the same way it had in mine.

The next afternoon, I was later than usual getting home, thanks to a trip out to Haverford to meet a shopkeeper who sold high-end cigars. He thought my "unusual skill" would be useful for pictures not of the cigars themselves, but of the businessman-types he wanted to show smoking them in his ads. Justine met me in the hall at the same time that Charley called down from the kitchen, "Nicky! Phone for you!"

The three of us clustered around the receiver as if we were waiting for the bottom-of-the-ninth score in the final game of the World Series. Timothy said, "You sure about this?"

No time to back out now. "I'm sure."

"Then let's do it."

With that, we were on our way.

THE NEXT MORNING, TUESDAY, I MADE A CALL TO THE museum before I left for work. It took a bit of doing to get shunted to the right secretary, but I left a message to the effect that I was a "local businessman with a strong interest in art," and I wanted to meet with the appropriate person about a possible exhibit. Hanging around Jonah Eberly and his kind for three years had taught me a few things. I managed a decent impression of a person with money to spend, who would throw some around for the right kind of deal.

Not many arts organizations turn up their noses at an idea like that. Coming on the heels of the Depression and the war years, I knew they wouldn't likely resist the hook, but I couldn't help imagining the wash of relief if they did. That possibility didn't last long. On Wednesday, I got home to Justine triumphantly waving a piece of notepaper. She had taken a message from one Randolph Jefferson, who'd introduced himself over the phone to her as a member of the museum's board and said he "would be glad to speak with Mr. True" about the exhibit of interest. The money side of things had snagged him, right enough.

He was quick off the mark, too, when I returned his call on Thursday morning. "A pleasure to hear from you, sir. Would you have time to come in on Monday?" It was all moving faster than that brakeless freight train you hear so much about, but I knew this was no time to try to slow it down. My courage would fizzle at the first excuse.

I agreed to meet with Jefferson at nine on Monday morning. When I told Stephen I'd be late to work that day, using Justine's invented excuse of a doctor's visit to see if she needed glasses, I kept my face as still and quiet as I could. Until we got through this, if we did, nothing could give him any hint of the fact that I was about to violate my contract so badly that I might as well set fire to it under his nose.

Monday morning, I walked up the museum's steps and between the columns, calculating the odds that I might pass out again before the meeting was over, or even before I'd put pencil to paper. I wished Timothy could have come with me, but we'd all agreed that I had to do this first part alone. My suit felt so stiff that it might have been made of sheet metal instead of linen. My briefcase, which held clean copies of Timothy's favorite drawings along with my sketchbook and pencils, hung off the end of my arm like a lump of concrete.

Randolph Jefferson met me in the lobby. I'd imagined someone along the lines of Dr. Murray, but Jefferson was short and round, with a shock of curly black hair and a necktie that hung down a decent distance farther than it needed to. "Mr. True?" He had a small hand with stubby fingers, but an impressively strong handshake. "A pleasure to meet you." He couldn't hide his surprise either. He hadn't expected someone so young.

He'd reserved a meeting room on the fourth floor. I didn't notice much about what we saw on the way up, or much about what the room itself looked like, apart from the fact that it was small and dim and had a table that just barely fit between the walls. The only thing that seemed real to me was what I was about to do.

Dad. What would you think of this?

"So," Jefferson said, once we'd settled ourselves across from each other at one end of the table. "I understand you'd like to propose an exhibit."

No doubt he'd taken advantage of our walk upstairs to size up my clothes and decide whether I might actually have the goods to back up my request. Just as well that I'd gone full Paragon-style, with three-piece suit, fedora, and polished oxbloods. If I looked like a trust-fund kid, so much the better.

"Yes, sir." Last night, Justine and Charley'd helped me practice my lines. That kept the nervous rasp out of my voice. "Before I give particulars, I'd like to show you something, if I may."

"Certainly."

I opened my briefcase and took out my sketchbook and pencil. *This is it.*

My hand was trembling, only a little. Justine and Charley and I had practiced this too. I looked across the table and imagined my brother's face, ready to break into delighted laughter.

Jefferson waited, resting one hand on the tabletop as if he would start tapping his fingers any moment. No doubt he'd expected me to show him a sample of artwork first, or a profile of the artist I wanted to feature, and he was wondering when I planned to get to the point of this meeting. No sense going small with my demonstration. I started on the table itself.

My drawing hand moved across the paper, quick and steady. The same way I had at Timothy and Minna's apartment, I gave the table a new shape first, changing it from a rectangle to an oval. One line, then another. Then, to make my point as quickly as I could, I delivered the punch.

Jefferson had noticed the table's corners disappear. He was staring at the closest one, or rather, at the place where the closest one had been, when I drew a square cutout exactly where his hand rested on the wood.

His hand dropped through the hole, dangling slack from his wrist, his fingertips touching empty air. "Jesus!" He yanked it out. His knuckles knocked against the edge that hadn't been there a moment before.

I thought I'd gone too far. For all I knew, he would jump up, fling open the door, and yell for security. My breath roared in my ears.

His eyes were so wide that someone might have pinned them open. He looked at his hand, at the cutout, and again at me. Then, to my astonishment, he started to laugh.

"Jesus!" He leaned back in his chair, laughing as if he'd just heard the finest joke ever told. "How did you do that? No, no, I shouldn't ask." Still chuckling, he reached into his breast pocket and pulled out a navy-blue handkerchief. "That's a hell of an illusion, I don't mind telling you." He wiped his eyes and tucked the handkerchief away again. "I'm a sucker for stage magic. The misdirection and all that, it's fascinating, what you can get away with! But I know you never ask a magician to tell you the trick."

Misdirection? Stage magic? I almost started laughing myself. Did he think I'd somehow snuck in another table while he sat here?

"It's very impressive, Mr. True, but I'm afraid my fellow board members won't agree to it as an exhibit. We don't go in for that sort of thing." Another chuckle got the better of him. "Although it's certainly the best I've ever seen. That's a nice touch, too, how you make it look as though you're doing it with your drawing."

Some people will believe anything except the evidence in front of their faces. Just my luck, I couldn't help thinking, that he was one of them. "It's not an illusion, sir," I said. "I did change the table by drawing it."

"Oh, now, you can't ask me to believe that. I understand you have to say so."

My nervousness had gone. I'd do whatever it took to make my point. "It's no trick, sir. You can see that cutout for yourself. You can see that the table is a different shape."

He couldn't help reaching for the cutout again. "I have to admit, it does look real." He touched the inside edges of it, exactly the way Minna had done on her own table. "It feels real." Uncertainty flickered in his face. "But it can't be. That's impossible."

"I assure you it's not, sir. I can prove it, if you'd like."

He hesitated. "How would you do that?"

The idea of *real magic* had snagged at him like a cat's claw, but I still had to be careful. It was a tiny step from fascination to out-and-out fear. "First," I said, "if you'll permit me, I'll change the table back to the way it was."

"Will you really." He tried to sound skeptical, but his eyes stayed on my drawing hand as I redrew the table in its original shape. He kept his own hand over the cutout. When the hole disappeared, he knocked on the wood, proving to himself that it was solid again.

I said, "You mentioned misdirection, sir. You're right, but in this case, you were watching the table while I drew it."

He conceded that. "I still don't see how you could've changed it. You're telling me that you actually made that square of wood...what? Dematerialize?"

"No, sir. All I did was move it around." I told him how the magic worked. All of it. This time, I had no non-disclosure letter, no gentle-man's-handshake confidentiality agreement, nothing to protect me from whatever might happen afterward. I ignored that as best I could, the same way a tightrope walker doesn't look down. "If you'd like real proof," I finished, "I could change something about you."

He chewed on that. "Change the way I look?"

"Yes."

Everything depended on how he decided to take it. Jonah Eberly and Stephen Allen had jumped on the magic and ridden it straight to their businesses' bottom lines. Timothy, and of course Dad, had cleared the disbelief hurdle and caught onto delight and wonder. Mark Allen, on the other hand, had seen it as nothing but danger waiting to happen.

Nerves coiled in my stomach again. I thought about that door I wanted to open for Timothy, how I would shove my shoulder against it, prop it with my foot on the hinge. Randolph Jefferson eyed my sketchbook and pencil as if he thought they might start wandering around the room on their own. "What would you change?" he said.

"That's up to you."

He drummed his fingers on the tabletop. The noise rattled off the wood-paneled walls and seemed to give him an idea. "Could you change my hand somehow? Make my fingers longer?"

People reveal a lot when they tell you what they'd change if they could. "Of course," I said. "Keep in mind it'll make your hand thinner overall."

"That wouldn't be a bad thing."

"Remember also, please, it'll change back as soon as I tear up the drawing."

"Yes, yes." He waved his left hand, brushing the words away, but rested the right one on the tabletop as if I was about to do surgery on it. "Show me what you can do."

I did. It didn't take much longer than it had to change Mark Allen's nose, that day I'd met the same demand for proof of the impossible. When I finished drawing, Jefferson's left hand looked exactly the way it had before, but his right could have belonged to a surgeon, or a pianist.

He held both hands up, palms down, thumbs touching. Long seconds ticked past while he studied them as if they were features on a statue. Then, with the index finger of his left hand, he ran down the length of each finger on his right.

Yes. It's real. Touching them, feeling not just the shape of the "new" fingers, but the sensation in them too, he couldn't have any doubts left. I braced myself. Anything might happen now.

He lowered both hands. "Tear up the drawing, please." No expression in his face or voice.

I did as he asked. The changed hand went back to its normal shape. Jefferson lifted both again and this time laid them together, palm to palm, measuring how the fingertips met. I held my breath.

"Mr. True. This is incredible."

Long after Dad and I had lost our uneasiness about visiting the museum, long after we came to feel we belonged there, we still spoke in whispers in the galleries. The canvases demanded our wonder and hush. In this moment, Randolph Jefferson sounded just as we had, as if his very words were walking on tiptoe.

Relief surged up my spine. I had him where I wanted him. He lowered his hands and leaned forward, eager now. "This isn't stage magic. It's the real thing."

"Yes, sir."

"But I've never heard of you before. Doesn't anyone know about this? Surely..." He revolved one hand in the air as if trying to conjure up something too big for words. "Surely, you should be famous."

He didn't need to know how I'd always felt about fame. He probably wouldn't have believed it anyway. "To be honest," I said, "I've never gone public with it, but lately I've thought I'd like to try. I hoped you and the museum might help."

"Actual magic through art. You'd like to offer an exhibition of this?"

"Yes, sir. That's part of what I'm hoping for."

He didn't ask what the rest was. "Yes, I certainly do think we could generate interest. I think there's solid potential." That sounded like any jargon-jawing executive, but then the business-mask crumbled. "What on earth am I saying?" He laughed. "Mr. True, I can only imagine what ticket sales would look like once the word got out. If you want to exhibit your work here, I don't think my colleagues on the board will have the least difficulty with that."

Before he promised anything, he might want to make sure his colleagues really were as enthusiastic for the magic as he was. Any of them might be another Mark Allen. I would ask about that, but first, it was time to get to the real purpose of the exhibit.

"There's also another part of this," I said. "I'd like to show you something else, if I may." Now I was back on the script that Justine and Charley and I had worked out. We had crossed all of our fingers that I would get this far.

Jefferson was hoping for more party tricks, as eager and round-eyed as a kid waiting for Santa Claus. I got the drawings out of my briefcase.

"These were done by a colleague of mine, Timothy Davis." I passed them over to Jefferson. "He's a veteran, and a Philadelphia resident like me. I think you'll agree, sir, that his art represents another kind of magic."

Give him credit, Jefferson leafed through the pages carefully, although he was unmistakably disappointed that the "exciting" part of the show was over. Timothy had given me four sketches of men he had served with, one sketch of Minna, and one of the little girl Olivia. Jefferson stopped on Minna's, looking at it closely.

"Yes," he said. "I see what you mean." I couldn't tell how much he did see, compared to how much he wanted to agree with what I thought, but past a certain point, I didn't care. He said, "These do have quite a spark."

"I've watched Mr. Davis work," I said. "It's extraordinary to see. I wish I had that kind of technique."

"I don't see anything to argue with in your technique, Mr. True." Jefferson examined the sketch of Olivia. "Yes, though, as a portrait, I do see what you mean. You would want his work to be part of your exhibit?"

I explained the idea of both of us demonstrating our drawing, and how Timothy's work lent itself to display in a way that mine didn't. I'd called Timothy a colleague to make sure that Jefferson made certain assumptions about him, but I wasn't trying to trick anyone. Timothy wouldn't sneak into this place under false pretenses. He would walk in as an honored guest.

Jefferson mulled it over. "That does sound interesting," he said. "Both of you are local, which always has appeal, and with your magic, there again, Mr. True, it's very difficult to argue with what you do. I'm confident we can organize the exhibit you propose." He glanced back at the drawing of Minna. Something seemed to strike him. "I can't help noticing..." The pages rustled as he flicked through them. "Does Mr. Davis prefer to draw colored subjects? A bit unusual in an artist, isn't it?"

He had made exactly the assumption I'd banked on, and handed me what I needed to say next. Now we were at the last and most important hurdle.

"Mr. Davis is colored," I said. "The men in those drawings are soldiers he served with in France. The lady is his wife, and the little girl is a neighbor's daughter."

Jefferson set the drawing of Minna down. "Colored?"

"That's right."

Jefferson laced his fingers together as if to keep them from touching the sketches anymore. "Mr. True. As much as I appreciate your work – which really is extraordinary," he couldn't seem to help adding, "you must recognize that this museum cannot..." He ran an uneasy hand through his thatch of hair. "That is to say, it would not be consistent with our regular policy to..."

I'd been ready for this, or something like it. "It would not be consistent with your policy to showcase work by a colored artist?"

Jefferson ran his hand through his hair again. It didn't improve his looks. "Well, a *recognized* artist, certainly, there would be grounds. Someone with the proper record and reputation. After careful evaluation, of course. But you must understand, we cannot simply allow a person off the street to..."

I cut him off. Politely. "Pardon me, sir, but I'm not a recognized artist either."

"Well, but your work, now. The value of your work goes without saying." He flexed the fingers of his right hand, as if remembering what he'd just seen.

"You agreed with me about the value of Mr. Davis's work too." I didn't wait for him to try to make a case for why Timothy's work was worth less than mine. He only had one reason, and I'd make no promises about how I'd respond if I heard it. "I'm afraid my terms for the exhibit are non-negotiable. Mr. Davis and I will both have the opportunity to show our work, or we will not pursue this idea further."

His mouth pursed as if he'd swallowed a spoonful of vinegar. In memory, I heard Stephen Allen telling his brother, *If he walks out of here now, we won't get another chance. Is that what you want?* Jefferson fiddled with his too-long tie, glancing around the room as if someone in a corner might hold up a cue card telling him what to do next. I waited.

"Both of you," he said, "or neither."

"Yes, sir."

"But, Mr. True." He put on a let's-all-be-reasonable smile. "I'm afraid I can't make that decision without input from the board. That is to say, we have to consider how our patrons will respond to such an exhibit."

"Sir, you mentioned the likely ticket sales for my magic. Do you really think Mr. Davis's involvement would undo those sales?" I knew he didn't. And he knew, perfectly well, that there would be no sales at all if I packed up and left right now. "I would be more than happy," I said, "to demonstrate what I do for the rest of your board, if that would help their decision. I must also tell you, if this is not the appropriate venue for our demonstration, we'll do our best to find another." What I'd told Jonah Eberly echoed in my head: *You do what you have to, and I'll do what I have to.*

That spoonful of vinegar might have become a whole bottle. The wheels were turning in Jefferson's head. If I left here now, and if Timothy and I showcased our work somewhere else, with the ticket sales and notoriety and everything else that might happen as a result, and if anyone here at the museum had reason to know that Jefferson had held the opportunity in his hand and let it go... in essence, I'd backed him into the same corner my former boss had found himself in. How much did Jefferson's post on the board mean to him?

The *damn it* he didn't say rang in the room. I waited, keeping my face empty of expression. He cleared his throat and uncoiled his tie, which he'd wrapped around his hand like a bandage.

"I'll repeat your proposal to my fellow board members. I do think you should prepare a demonstration for them."

"Gladly."

"If, in the meantime, you would keep this conversation between us, I would take it as a favor. Likewise, if you don't enter negotiations yet with any other venue."

It was hard not to smile. "Certainly. Would you like to keep Mr. Davis's drawings, to show your colleagues?"

He looked down at them on the table as if they might snap at his fingers. "I think it would be best if you presented them yourself."

He was ready to see the back of me for today. "I'll be happy to." I gathered up the drawings, along with my sketchbook and pencil, and slid them into my briefcase. "I can find my way back to the lobby, sir." I reached out to shake hands with him. "Thank you very much for meeting with me."

I arrived back downstairs with my shirt glued to my back and my scalp as damp as if I had stuck my head under a faucet. More than anything, I wished I could go home and dive into the shower, and maybe huddle safely in a closed room for the rest of the day, but the Allens expected me at work. Best not to start raising eyebrows before I had to.

～

That was Monday. On Wednesday afternoon, I got home to another message from Randolph Jefferson. Justine told me that the board wanted to meet with me on Friday morning. However much Jefferson didn't like the idea of showing Timothy's art, he hadn't wasted any time pulling his colleagues together.

I had to come up with another reason to be late for work, so I told Stephen that Justine did in fact need glasses and was having a follow-up appointment for a fitting. Justine joked about how lucky we were that my boss believed I'd married a woman who couldn't manage her own doctors' appointments. I also called Timothy and talked him into coming to the meeting with me. "Let them meet the artist," I said.

"Are you sure? It might foul things up, having me there."

"They have to meet you sometime. Besides, I'm not doing this one alone."

On Friday, we met up at the museum and presented ourselves. The board members, all of them white men, hadn't expected to see Timothy, but they didn't quite dare snub him. Randolph Jefferson couldn't hide his excitement about the magic, no matter how he felt about the way I'd boxed him in.

I did the same kind of demonstration for the whole board that I'd done for him. We met in an actual boardroom this time, around a long oval table. I sat at one end of it with Timothy in the chair to my right. Jefferson had given his colleagues an idea of what to expect from me, so they weren't caught as entirely by surprise as he had been, but there was still plenty of confusion and questioning and up-close examination of the cutouts I made in the table's surface. I answered the questions as best I could. Jefferson added his vote: "You have to admit, gentlemen, this kind of thing doesn't come through the door every day."

The chairman, David Halliday, did look the way I thought a chairman should. He was tall and narrow-faced, dressed in an impeccable navy suit, his silver hair neatly combed and parted. "This is certainly extraordinary, Mr. True." Out of all of the board members, he had done the best job of hiding his shock. "Please tell us more about this exhibit you have in mind."

I launched in. Timothy's drawings went around the table. Halliday asked about them, particularly the soldiers in the sketches, so Timothy joined the conversation. Between the two of us, he and I laid out our plan: my part of the exhibit first, to get the attendees warmed up, and then Timothy's part. He would provide a live demonstration too, drawing one or two volunteers, but his main role would be to show his work, to talk about the subjects of his drawings and what he had captured in them.

I gave the board the summing-up that I'd been thinking about over the past few days, through the cloud of nerves that never quite left me alone anymore. "The way we see it, this exhibit isn't only about my magic, or Mr. Davis's art. It's about what art itself can do." I made myself look from one face to another, meeting each man's eyes. "Art can make change and show truth. We think, too, that art can push against the limits people believe in. Show them that there's more possibility in the world than they knew."

To be honest, I felt more than a little silly, as if I'd dressed up as a professor to lecture to a pretend class. The board listened, though. Most of them undoubtedly had the same shiny dollar signs in their heads that Jefferson did. A couple of them nodded at what I said, as if they thought there might be something in it.

Halliday thanked Timothy and me for coming. "We will discuss this and contact you soon." The room had started its slow spin during my "closing argument," as attorneys would call it, so once Timothy and I were out in the hall with the boardroom door safely shut behind us, I leaned against the wall and closed my eyes.

Timothy leaned next to me. "Man, the way you talked in there, you could've been a tent preacher calling the sinners home. *Find the truth! Come to the water and get saved!*"

"Damn it, don't make me laugh." Too late. I let go of my briefcase and bent over, hands on my knees. "Catholics can't be tent preachers," I pointed out, as soon as I managed to resurface.

"You did all right." Timothy put a hand on my shoulder. "You okay now?"

"Yeah."

We both knew, and found out for certain the next day, that we'd done it. We'd caught them. The sketch of Minna and Justine's idea had turned real and solid, ready to push our lives into a new shape.

Chapter Twenty-One

Now I have to tell you about that day.

In the great scheme of things, it was small enough. Jo has gotten me to think that this story might do something good in the telling, but in fact, what Timothy and I did at the museum weighed as much as one raindrop in a gale. The real work got done in the months and years and decades that followed, when legions of brave and determined people put their shoulders to the wheel to make the changes our country needed. More changes still need making, if you'll bear with an old man's tendency to moralize.

I'd like to be sure I could help out some before I'm done, and it wouldn't hurt, either, to know that my great-granddaughter Hallie could take up the magic where I left it off. For now, here's what I have. That one raindrop.

~

The museum's board decided not to let the grass grow after they met with Timothy and me. They had a potential moneymaker on their hands, but they also knew what a radical idea the exhibit was, for more than one reason, so they were eager to light that fuse and stand back for the boom. They scheduled our event for the afternoon of the last Saturday in June.

It's important to remember that the war wasn't over yet. Soldiers who had served in Europe were coming home, but any number of people still had loved ones in the Pacific. Hirohito wasn't backing down. After the jubilation of VE Day, everyone was exhausted and worn tissue-thin. The end of the years-long trial seemed so close, so real that we should be able to reach out and touch it with our fingertips, but we couldn't. Not yet.

The people who came to see Timothy and me make art: that is what they carried with them.

~

DURING THE FEW WEEKS BETWEEN THE BOARD MEETING AND the event, life ran along. I went to work, and Charley went to school, and in the evenings he and Justine and I made dinner and ate and talked. Justine carried on with her cooking practice. During Minna's shifts, the two women talked about poetry and literature while Justine wrestled with the old washing machine and took on more and more of the house-keeping.

Mid-June, we celebrated the end of Charley's schoolyear. He invited some of the yearbook staff and a couple of other buddies over for a get-together, where Justine and I got to meet Denise. She was as smart and pretty as Charley had said. It was also clear how much she liked him. Justine and I introduced ourselves and faded into the background, but we couldn't help keeping our ears open. That night in bed, Justine told me, "She might be about as lucky as I am."

Her hair was silky under my fingers. "Maybe so, but neither of you is as lucky as me."

Those quiet times, with the rest of the world on the other side of a closed door, felt few and far between. The days to the exhibit ticked away one after the other, too slowly and yet much too fast. Every day, I braced myself for a showdown at work, ready to lose my job on the spot if the Allens got wind of anything early, knowing at the same time that every hour at my desk counted because I still didn't have another plan.

At my request, the museum's publicity didn't mention my name or Timothy's. Brief writeups in the papers said only that the Philadelphia Museum of Art was "proud to showcase an extraordinary demonstration of work by local artists" which would "offer our audience an entirely new view of the possibilities inherent in drawing." They would have loved to mention the magic outright, whether or not anyone would've believed it, but I had put my foot down about that too. If the Allens did find out what was going on, they would have grounds not only to fire me, but to try to stop the whole thing.

By the Friday night before the exhibit, everything was still in order. Minna and Timothy came over that evening for dinner and Timothy and I had another draw-off. All of us were laughing, having fun, but the laughter had an edge on it and those hands around my chest never let go.

Timothy knew it. "Nicky, you know I appreciate this. You've got more to lose here than I do."

He meant not only my job, but whatever else might happen when my magic went public. It was worth it, I never doubted that, but at the same time, that was the real fear. Showing my secret to the world, or at least that part of it who showed up at the museum the next day. That was why I felt as if I was about to step out on thin ice over water deep enough to flatten a submarine.

Minna asked if my bosses really would fire me. "I know what your contract says, but couldn't this bring in a lot more business for them?"

Technically, yes. The exhibit could hand the Allens more potential clients than even Stephen had had time to dream up, but it wasn't a given. "You never know how people'll take it," I said. "Besides, one of my bosses never did like the magic. This show is pretty much his worst nightmare."

Justine put her hand on mine. "It doesn't matter. Whatever happens, you won't keep that job any longer than you have to."

I did wish I had something else lined up and ready. We had money in the bank, but it wouldn't last forever. For all I knew, if someone got upset enough tomorrow, we'd need some of those savings for bail. Or the Allens might decide to try a little courtroom drama, the way Mark had thought someone else would. They could easily have me in front of a judge for breach of contract. We couldn't be sure what would happen, but chances were, the actual exhibit tomorrow would be just the start.

To cap the rest, Dr. Murray and Louisa would be there too. Justine and I had finally had dinner with them the week before. We'd agreed ahead of time that they might as well see the show in person, because there was no point trying to hide something that could well pop up in the newspapers the next day, so we told them about it over the rather frosty meal. Dr. Murray still didn't know exactly what "my work" involved, only that he would see it in action. Louisa knew more, of course, but apart from a sidelong look at me, she stayed surprisingly quiet. Justine's marriage seemed to have taken wind out of her sails.

On Saturday morning, Justine forced me to swallow some toast and scrambled eggs at breakfast. We took the bus to the museum well ahead of start time, earlier than we needed to, but as Charley said, my pacing was liable to wear a hole in the floorboards. The cool air in the great lobby seemed to wrap around me like a net. For one insane instant, I wanted to turn around and bolt.

Justine slipped her arm around me. "It's all right."

The attendant at the front desk waved the three of us past. "Of course, Mr. True. Mr. and Mrs. Davis are already here."

From his chair, Charley caught my eye. *Mr. and Mrs. Davis.* If nothing else, maybe we'd made one tiny change already.

The ground floor had a small gallery dedicated to special events like ours. Today, a white pasteboard sign hung on the gallery's closed doors. Its crisp black lettering announced, "Drawing Exhibition." A table, not manned yet, stood ready for ticket collection.

Inside, we found rows of wooden chairs set up and ready for the audience. There was no actual stage, but a space at the front had upholstered chairs for Timothy and me, a big easel with a stool in front of it, and an array of eight smaller easels. The big easel held a poster-sized drawing pad, which Timothy and I would both use during the demonstration.

Timothy and Minna were setting up his drawings on the smaller easels. Minna saw Charley and Justine and me first and set the sketch she held down on the nearest chair. "You're early!"

She and Justine hugged. In their bright floral dresses, they could have been a Monet canvas. Justine said, "We couldn't wait around any longer."

"Neither could we." Minna shook my hand. "Goodness, Nicky! Your fingers are frozen!"

"They'll warm up," I said.

Timothy joined us. "They'd better. We need them working."

I had never seen him dressed to the nines before. His well-tailored steel-blue suit, with a white pinstripe running through it, would have fit right in at Paragon. I'd gone as far as I could in that direction myself, except that instead of one of my Los Angeles oxford shirts, I'd worn one of the almost-new white ones of Dad's we had found in the master bedroom.

"You look decent, at least," Timothy told me.

"You too."

"You going to manage this all right?"

"If I pass out, just haul me off to the side and get on with your part of the show."

"I'll do that."

He had withdrawn into himself, bracing against whatever was coming. I thought of the first time I'd met him, but now, no exhaustion shadowed his face, and I could see a glimmer of laughter far back in his eyes.

Minna and Justine and Charley claimed their places in the front row. Timothy and I double-checked the easel setup and evaluated the upholstered chairs, which were considerably less comfortable than they looked. I took my sketchbook out and tried to warm up my drawing hand with a few sketches of one of the chairs. At first, the lines wavered so much that the magic would have failed if I'd tried it. I did what I'd done as a kid, sitting in my room at my desk: I pinned my attention on the shapes and drew the same lines, over and over, until they smoothed out and the piece of paper showed me a reflection of the real shapes in front of me.

I was so caught up in it that the noise of the door opening again brought me back to the gallery with a jolt. One of the guards, a teenager with a spray of freckles across both cheeks, stepped inside. "Is everything in order?"

Timothy glanced at me for confirmation. "Yes. Thank you."

"Good." The kid said our audience was arriving. "We'll open the gallery shortly."

The not-so-comfortable chair I sat in seemed to shiver, as if a train had gone past underneath the floorboards. Justine came over to me. "Stand up." When I did, she put her arms around me. "You can do this."

I closed my eyes, shutting out everything except the scent of her hair and her warmth in my arms. I knew I shouldn't admit out loud how scared I was, I'd sound like a little boy, but I couldn't help it. "What if I can't?" What if my hand shook too much? What if I did get sick and faint again? And even if I managed it, what would happen afterward?

"Nicky," she said.

I made myself open my eyes. "Of course you'll do it," she said. "And whatever happens next, you and I will get through it together." She reached up to smooth my hair. "I have a feeling your dad is proud of you today," she said. "So am I."

A mist came down on the room, blurring the chairs and walls into a vague haze of brown and cream. Justine stepped back. I slipped my glasses off and clipped them over my shirt pocket to press the heels of my hands against my eyes, hard enough to shut out every trace of light.

The gallery doors swung open. I lowered my hands to see the audience filing in, well-heeled city people dressed in sleek going-out clothes. They filled up the chairs and filled up the air with their chatter. When they noticed Timothy and Minna, the talk abruptly died down, as if someone had flicked the light switch to announce the beginning of the show. Then a new murmur started up. *What are* they *doing here?*

I didn't hear the words themselves, but the question hovered around us in the air and I realized I didn't feel cold anymore. Warmth radiated down my arms and through my hands. My fingers itched to pick up my pencil.

Justine took her seat between Charley, on the end of the first row in his chair, and Minna. Timothy sat down in one of the upholstered chairs and caught my eye. *Ready?*

I squared my shoulders. *Let's do this.*

David Halliday from the board had offered to do introductions, but

Timothy and I had agreed we preferred to handle it ourselves. I slipped my glasses back on and stepped in front of the big easel. The noise quieted down.

Looking out into the room, I recognized the faces of board members. No one from Allen and Allen had talked about the exhibit at work or connected it with me, and no one from the firm was here now; that was a small relief. In the middle row of chairs, I saw the Murrays. Dr. Murray sat rigidly straight, his face expressionless. Next to him, Louisa looked tense. Her eyes narrowed as she caught my glance. She didn't know what I was about to do, but she didn't expect to like it, especially because her sister would be caught up in it too.

I cleared my throat. "Ladies and gentlemen, good afternoon. My name is Nicky True." Nicholas would have sounded more dignified, but in this place, I couldn't be anyone else. "My colleague Timothy Davis and I would like to thank you for joining us today."

That word *colleague* caught them. I talked over the surprised whispers. "This afternoon, Mr. Davis and I intend to demonstrate possibilities that exist in art, particularly in line drawing, which you may not have experienced before." *May not*, indeed. "Some of what we show you might surprise you. We hope you'll keep an open mind about what you see here, which we offer for your enjoyment."

Now to get things rolling. The room held steady; my drawing hand was ready to go. "Mr. Davis and I agreed that I would lead off the demonstration part of this event." I explained that the sketches on the small easels were Timothy's and he would talk about them shortly. "My own work doesn't lend itself to that kind of display. It's more useful for something else."

I didn't look out at the middle row now, where the Murrays sat, or at any of the board members, or even at Timothy. The only eyes I met were Justine's. Her smile carried me forward.

"When I was a kid, I found out one day that I could do something most people couldn't." In my mind, I saw Dad at the kitchen table, cradling newborn Charley against his chest. I saw my brother's curled foot and felt that shift inside me. *A car getting into gear.* "I already knew I was pretty good at drawing," I said. "Matter of fact, I knew I was *very* good at drawing, and I would have told you so if you'd asked."

Laughter rippled around me. On the edge of hearing, Timothy said, "I bet you would."

"When I was eight years old," I went on, "I realized I wasn't just talented, or like teachers sometimes say, precocious. It went a little farther than that."

At the end of the front row, Charley was sitting at attention. "I won't tell you the full story now," I said. "My brother here will vouch for me, if you want to ask him later. He knows about the first time I realized what else I could do." Charley gave me a thumbs-up. Now it was time. "What I discovered then is what I'm going to show you now."

The stool for the big easel was directly behind me. I sat down, facing the two comfortable chairs. Timothy caught my eye and winked. *Show them what you've got.*

At first, in spite of everything, my drawing hand did shake: only a little, but more than enough. With the pencil between my fingers, I closed my eyes and took a long breath. I heard a faint squeak as someone shifted in their chair, and a cough somewhere at the back of the room, but those sounds seemed far away. Much nearer, I felt the bottom rung of the stool under the soles of my shoes, and the weight and texture of my suit pants, and under my coat and vest, the fabric of Dad's shirt against my skin.

You see, Nicky, some people would think it's a treat to come here. Really, we need it just the same as food.

I opened my eyes. My hand held steady. I raised the pencil to the easel and began to draw.

The easel faced outward, so that the audience could see what I was doing. I drew the empty upholstered chair. The chair had a high back, a low-set seat with stiff padding, and four squat legs. First I stretched out the legs, bringing the seat up higher. Next I pulled the arms of the chair toward each other, narrowing the back and lengthening it even more. Now the chair looked thin and spindly, impossibly tall, as if designed for a giant: except that if anyone tried to sit in it, it would likely snap in pieces.

The audience saw what was happening. At first the silence seemed thicker than before, as if the air had turned into invisible jelly. Then I heard a gasp from one side of the room, and another from the back, like the first patter of raindrops at the beginning of a storm. I didn't stop drawing. The pencil moved fast, inverting the top line of the chair's back as if someone had taken a scoop out of it. I added two diamond-shaped cutouts to the back too, one directly above the other. Through them, the audience could see the small easels and the wall behind.

When I finished and set my pencil down in the easel's tray, the noise in the room was like a rush of wind. Mutters and whispers ran together, no distinct words, only one long buzz of disbelief and astonishment. My cheeks smarted and my fingers stung as if I had touched a hot stove. In the other chair, Timothy had his head down. His shoulders shook with laughter. *Will you look at that. That is one ugly piece of furniture.*

I pushed myself up off the stool and found Justine's eyes again. She didn't need words, this time, to tell me how proud she was.

"Ladies and gentlemen." My voice shook a little. No one likely noticed: they were too busy putting their heads together, questioning and arguing. As soon as I spoke, the noise stopped and every face turned toward me.

I caught as much of a breath as I could. "You may think this looks like a trick of some kind. Misdirection or stage magic." I didn't look at Randolph Jefferson, in his seat near the front, but I could imagine how he must be grinning. "I realize it's quite a stretch to ask you to believe there is no trick, but that is exactly the truth. I've made changes in that chair by drawing it. What you've just seen, if I may say so, is real magic in action."

If the noise before had been like a gust of wind, this was the storm, full-blown. Snatches of exclamations reached me. "That's crazy!" "Ridiculous!" "Nobody would believe such a…"

I held up a hand. By all rights, I should have been doubled over with dizziness. The room seemed so hot that someone might've cranked a furnace up to the limit, but standing there with the noise swirling around me, I felt like a tree that had sunk its roots deep, deep into the ground.

Silence fell again. "I won't ask you to take my word for it," I said. "Allow me a few minutes for another short demonstration, and then you'll be able to inspect what I've done for yourselves."

Now I risked a glance at the Murrays. Louisa's face had a deep flush on it, as if someone had slapped her, but I had trouble reading her expression. If I hadn't known what she thought of me, I would almost have called it awe. Dr. Murray looked as if something heavy had dropped on his head. For now, I could guess, he didn't believe what he'd seen. That shock might turn into anything when he realized what his daughter had married.

I sat down at the easel again and flipped the top page on the pad over to the back. The room was so full of tension that if someone had flicked a finger in the air, we all might have heard a noise like a rubber band twanging. When I picked up the pencil, my drawing hand still held steady.

Timothy and I had talked through this next part. I had to do something that would prove, as much as you could prove such a thing, that the magic was real, the same way I'd proven it to Randolph Jefferson. I couldn't risk changing people, though. Not here.

I said, "I assure you that I can undo the changes I've made as easily as I made them, and I'll do it after you've had a chance to examine them. For now, let me show you this."

It had to be something they could all see or feel, or preferably both. Only one thing in the room fit that bill. This time, nobody said a word as I started to draw. I'm not sure anyone remembered to breathe.

The floor was made of polished strips of hardwood. I got to work on its texture. Thinner here, thicker there, bumps and waves, nothing too drastic...but everyone could see it, and before long, they could feel it too. Chairs tipped gently as one leg settled into a dip that hadn't been there a moment before. A handbag slid an inch or two sideways when the level surface it sat on rose into a curve. Charley's chair rolled forward, ever so slightly, when I put a low ridge under its back wheels.

The whispering and muttering started again. People were peering around, running the soles of their shoes over the changed wood underneath them, even lifting their feet clear as if they thought the boards might catch hold of their ankles. Now I heard not just wonder in the steadily rising noise of talk, but an undercurrent of something that hadn't been there minutes before.

When people are scared, they can be very dangerous.

If this was working, they knew it was no illusion or misdirection. If they thought it was real magic, it might be too much to take in. If they didn't believe it, they might think I was somehow making them halluci-nate. Either way, the uncertainty in the room would solidify, very soon, into something else.

This was the part I had dreaded. I was standing out on that ice, knowing that any moment, it might shatter and catapult me fathoms down to the ocean floor. None of my preparation helped now. My vest felt like a straitjacket and my jaw was so stiff I couldn't open my mouth to speak.

From the middle of the room, someone else did. "It's not a trick." One voice, clear and strong. "Mr. True's magic is quite real."

I blinked. Louisa Murray had gotten to her feet. Yes, it really was her; no one could mistake that cornsilk hair, or that perfectly-sculpted face.

Every head turned toward her. "Mr. True works in ad design," she said, "at the firm Allen and Allen, here in the city." She sounded like a newscaster on the radio, delivering the weather report for the weekend. "Some weeks ago, my sister and I did a photoshoot for La Belle Epoque. You might have seen us in the *Record*," she added, as if anyone ought to remember seeing the ads, which wasn't as far-fetched as it might sound. "Mr. True used his magic to help us both look our best."

I realized I was breathing again. Louisa went on, in the same matter-of-fact way, "It's a strange ability, I will admit, but I can vouch that it's not at all dangerous. In fact, I find it intriguing." Up until now, she had been talking to the room. Now her eyes stopped on me. "Mr. True is also my brother-in-law," she said. "My sister seems happy enough with him, so I feel confident in saying that he is, himself, no more dangerous than his magic."

It was too much. I almost burst out laughing. *Happy enough? And not dangerous. Thank you, Miss Louisa.* I wanted to ask her straight out, the two of us facing each other across a roomful of baffled people, what had made her decide to speak up for me.

She turned her attention back to the room. "What interests me today," she said, "is not so much the magic itself, although this is of course a remarkable demonstration. Rather, I would like to know why he has chosen to display it for all of us." She told all the listening ears how I'd always kept my "talent" as secret as I could. "I would like to hear what's changed."

Finished, she took her seat. She was so stately and striking, the image of a lady of society, that the audience couldn't disbelieve or dismiss what she'd said. In the front row, I saw Justine shaking her head, smiling. *That's Lou for you. Taking charge.*

I stepped into the new silence. "Thank you, Miss Murray." I had no idea how I sounded so calm, but she'd given me what I needed to say next. "My sister-in-law has raised an excellent point. As she says, I've always kept my magic as quiet as I could. It can certainly make talk, as you see."

That got a scatter of nervous chuckles. At least they weren't too afraid of me to laugh. I told them that I'd wanted, for a while, to do more with my magic than make beautiful ads. "Ads are all right, but mostly, their job is to make money for someone."

Someone called out from the far-right corner. "Young man, there's nothing wrong with making money."

That snapped the tension. Everyone let their held breath out, all at once. The room filled up with laughter.

I made out the person who'd spoken, a middle-aged man with salt-and-pepper hair and the kind of suit that announced *banker.* "You're right, sir," I told him, when the noise died down enough. "Money's a useful thing. To tell you the truth, I've made a decent share of it with my drawing."

"I believe you," he said. "I don't know about anybody else here, but I'd pay to see more of this."

That got more laughs. Even better, I could see people relaxing. The ones who'd been sitting frozen, with their feet either barely touching the floor or crammed as far under their chairs as they could get, leaned back in their seats. Shoes edged out over the changed floorboards, testing them. At the ends of rows, some of the people who had enough room leaned over to touch the textures with their fingertips. Best of all, I saw heads nodding in answer to what the banker had said. *Yes, I'd like to see more of this too.*

Relief washed from the crown of my head all the way down through my feet. The balance had tipped. Now we could get to the most important part of all of this.

"If I can have your attention a little longer," I said, "I'd like to tell you why I'm here today. Then we'll get to the next part of the exhibit."

I told them how my father had been the first person to see my magic. "He couldn't believe his eyes, as you might imagine." They could. "But," I said, "it wasn't long before he came to love it." My chest tightened, but the words came out clear and strong. "Drawing, art itself, was magic to him."

Now I kept my eyes on the back wall. It was so easy to picture him standing there, listening. If he could have come with us today, no doubt he'd have worn his best suit, but I saw him in a work shirt and dungarees and the corduroy jacket he'd had on for so many of the visits we'd made to these galleries. His eyes were as warm and kind as they had always been. *Nicky, son, you're doing fine. Keep going.*

I told the audience how Dad and I had come to the museum as often as we could, whenever he could save up the money, and how we'd studied the paintings together. "He always thought I would do something good with my art." The audience might be wondering where this was going. I talked straight to the back wall, telling Dad what I hoped he could hear. "My colleague and friend Mr. Davis, who'll speak to you soon, helped me understand what that *something* should be."

The attention was so strong that it felt like a vacuum, pulling the words out of my mouth. "When Mr. Davis saw the magic, he said that if it was real, then the world must have more possibilities in it than we think. The rules we live by aren't as hard and fast as we've believed. I'm sharing my secret today because I want to change the rules."

If that puzzled them, they would put it together soon enough. "I've always liked to surprise people," I said, "and make them smile." *Am I raising boys or monkeys?* "As you'll see shortly, Mr. Davis's brand of magic can do much more than mine. He will show you another side of what's possible in art."

I went back to the easel and pulled up another clean page. My hand wouldn't hold steady much longer; I was so tired that my fingers barely wanted to close around the pencil, but I managed to draw the floor again, as it should be. As the bumps and dips smoothed out, I heard more whispering and muttering. There was a good measure of relief in the sound, but also a little disappointment. The chair I'd changed would stay the way it was, so that people could examine it later if they wanted.

I put the final touches on the repaired floor and set the pencil back in the tray. "Please welcome Mr. Davis."

Applause started, quick and eager. The audience hadn't thought he belonged here, but now they were ready to hear what my colleague and friend had to say. Timothy got to his feet. As he and I traded places, he whispered, "Shit, man. No pressure."

"You can handle it."

I thought I might fall asleep right there in the less-than-comfortable chair. We'd survived so far. I wasn't sure I cared, anymore, about Allen and Allen, or what would happen tomorrow, or anything else.

Then Timothy started talking. If I could have been so rude as to drift off, his words would have snapped me awake.

He told the audience how he had loved to draw since he was a boy, and how he had always wanted to see the museum but had known he wouldn't be welcome. "My wife and I finally visited here a few weeks ago with Mr. True and his family. They made sure we could get in." By now, I'd forgotten my tiredness. Timothy said, "Is it hard to owe them that? Yes." He tossed that word down like a challenge. I wanted to applaud. "Do I appreciate it? Yes. But I would like to be able to provide things like this myself, for my wife and me."

They were curious about him, this all-white audience. We had pushed the door open enough to make them willing to listen to him, at least for now. I wondered if anyone of his color had told them those kinds of truths before.

"I served in France," he said. "I was like most everybody else who stood in line to get our names on those lists. We were full of mustard, had no idea at all what we were getting ourselves into. If it hadn't been for my drawing, I don't know if I would've made it home."

He went to the first of the small easels. "This is my wife," he said. "I drew her every day, while I was over there. It kept her with me."

For so long, he hadn't been able to talk to Minna about France. Now, as the audience took in his drawing of her, he told them what it had been like overseas. "Some of you are probably veterans too, or know someone who is, so you don't need to hear this from me. This is if you're lucky enough not to know."

He talked about the fear that ground soldiers down until they wanted to crawl into the smallest hole they could find and curl up tight. It was worst not in battle, he said, but while you waited for battle, during the endless nights while the silence pressed down until you thought it would flatten you into the earth. You knew you couldn't admit you were scared, you could never say it out loud, because if you did, you would break. He talked about coming to understand what it meant to kill another man because you knew he would kill you if he could. He described how, as day after endless day went past, you felt as if your home wasn't yours anymore. It had belonged to some other person who didn't exist now, and if by some miracle you ever got back there, it wouldn't have room in it for you.

"I wasn't going to forget Minna," Timothy said. "I wouldn't let myself lose her."

In the front row, Minna sat with her head lifted, her eyes fixed on her husband. Her hand and Justine's were interlaced in the lap of her skirt.

Timothy talked about the wound that had sent him home, and how he'd come back to find what he had feared most: the place he had known, the apartment he had lived in with his new wife before shipping out, wasn't his home anymore. He wasn't the man who had left it. That man might as well have died in France, for all that he could take up his life again where it had broken off.

Drawing, he said, didn't seem to mean much either. It brought back too much of his time with the army, and besides, what difference had it made? The men who had died were gone. Lines on a paper would never change that.

"My wife was working then, cleaning houses," Timothy said. "She had to support us because I couldn't. I couldn't find work, no matter what I did. I'd have given one of my hands to change that, but then she'd have been dealing with a cripple too."

He told them how he had been back for a couple of months when Minna started working for a new client, a white man who lived in a part of town she didn't usually go to. "This man," he said, "turned out to be pretty strange."

Out of the corner of my eye, I saw Charley grin. Warmth climbed into my face. I focused on the floorboards under my shoes. "He was decent, this man," Timothy said, "but he was different. One day, he came over to my apartment. I hadn't asked him to, you understand, and truth be told, I didn't much want him there." He was smiling now. I could hear it. "But he sat down and drew my kitchen table. Except, the way he drew it, he made it a circle instead of a square, and put holes in it you could reach your hand through. When he was finished, it was the ugliest table you ever saw."

The audience understood it and laughed, a release of delight. I risked looking up at Timothy. Energy seemed to light him up from the inside, the same energy he had brought over to the house the first time he let me see his artwork. *Real magic. Don't you see?*

"This man knew about my drawing," he said. "I'd made the mistake of mentioning it to him." He caught my eye. The glance between us felt like a handshake. "He wanted to see me draw, wanted to see the work I'd done in France. He was pretty stubborn about it." That got another ripple of laughter. "I held out awhile, but in the end, it's hard to argue with magic. So I got out some of the sketches I'd kept."

He moved to the next drawing on display. "This is my friend Roger Ellis. We served together. He died at Nancy last September."

He told the audience about Roger, who had always been able to find laughter in the darkest moments of the war. "When I drew him, this is what the pencil wanted to do. Roger never let us see this side of him."

Timothy had re-drawn the original sketch, scaling it up to make the details clearer. No one could have missed the truth of what Roger Ellis had lost, the depth of his longing for the home and wife and child he would never see again. Timothy let quiet settle over the room. I counted a handful of heartbeats before he went on, "This is what Mr. True referred to as my magic. If I'd taken a photo of my friend, he would have smiled the way he always did. The drawing let me see what was under the surface."

A new murmur started up as people digested this. Timothy said, "As you can tell, my magic isn't as showy as Mr. True's. I'd never thought of it as magic myself, but I've started to see why he does."

One by one, he told them about the other drawings. Olivia and her family. The soldiers who had come home, and those who hadn't. What it meant to him now, to have the memories of the friends he had lost. "When I first got back," he said, "I almost got rid of all the sketches. Now I'm glad to have them."

The country was still holding its breath, waiting for the end of the interminable war years. Everyone in the gallery that afternoon knew about loss, grief, and the pendulum-swings between hope and despair that had worn so many of us raw. Some of our listeners, I had no doubt, thought of a loved face that had left a blank behind, and wished Timothy could have captured that face with his magic.

He said, "It's been a pleasure to share my work with you. Now I'd like to offer a brief demonstration." He sat down at the big easel and invited anyone who wanted to come forward for a portrait.

We hadn't been sure whether people might hurry to take him up on his offer, or whether that might feel too much like being put on display for everyone to see. For a long minute or so, no one volunteered. Charley had told us he would if nobody else did, and I was starting to think he'd have to, when someone in the middle of the room stood up.

"I would like a portrait."

Dr. Murray. Timothy had never met him, didn't know who he was, but Justine and Charley looked as startled as I felt. "Certainly, sir," Timothy said. "Please come forward."

My father-in-law's footsteps were loud in the quiet. I couldn't guess why he had spoken up. His expression told me nothing, but when I stood up to give him my seat, his hand closed briefly around my shoulder.

Timothy settled in to draw with the fluid skill I had admired so much before. From where I stood, I couldn't see the easel, only the motions of his arm. The room was so quiet that you could hear every line as the pencil glided across the paper. Dr. Murray sat perfectly still, with the same look of concentration I thought he must have in his surgery.

It didn't take long at all. When Timothy finished and set the pencil down with a click, applause started up. Timothy let the audience get a look at the easel, and then turned it carefully, the wooden legs scraping on the floor, to face Dr. Murray and me.

The face on the paper was unmistakable. Anyone who knew Justine's father would recognize it. Timothy had drawn him with the same silver hair, the same glasses, and the lines around the eyes and mouth, but somehow, the man in the drawing looked much younger. His face had a brightness in it I had never seen, an eager curiosity that said he knew the world was full of marvels. Something wonderful waited around the very next corner.

Dr. Murray looked at his portrait in silence. He took his glasses off, methodically closed them, and took a handkerchief out of his jacket pocket. No one in the room made a sound. He wiped his eyes, re-folded the handkerchief neatly, and put it away again. "I knew someone who saw me that way," he said. He slipped his glasses back on with a steady hand. "That was some time ago."

I thought of the beautiful mother of two little girls, the way she had smiled for the man who took her photograph. Timothy had drawn the man she loved. If he'd drawn it, then that man was still there, under whatever shield the years had put up.

Timothy promised to give him the sketch, if he liked, once the demonstration was over. Dr. Murray said he would be glad to have it. Then he stepped forward and held out his hand.

The audience might have held its breath. I certainly did. Timothy shook hands with him. Dr. Murray said, "Thank you, sir," and I knew, and would wager everyone else in the room did too, that he had never called a colored man "sir" before.

After that, a few other people stepped up for portraits. Each sketch got another round of applause. When Timothy finished his demonstration, I got to my feet again and thanked the audience for coming. "Mr. Davis and I hope you've enjoyed the afternoon." With the board members, I had talked about the possibilities of art and the change it could create. Now I gave the audience something different to think about, something Timothy and I had worked out together. "We hope, too, after what you've seen here, that you'll think of magic as more present than you may have believed. We hope you'll consider where your own magic might be, and how you might use it."

Before our exhibit, I could bet not one of them had considered magic as real, much less as something they might have themselves. I wondered if the question made sense to them and if they would take it away to mull over. For now, the applause started up again, louder and louder until it seemed to slosh against the walls.

My face felt as if I'd been out baking in the sun. Timothy and I stood side by side for a bow. Given the way he stared at the floor as if the boards might get up and do a dance, he felt at least as embarrassed as I did.

We weren't through with the day yet. The audience surged up out of their seats and made a steadily widening lake around us. People examined the chair I had changed, sizing it up from every angle, touching the cushions and the wood and putting their hands through the cutouts. Timothy's portrait subjects all came back up for their sketches. Everyone wanted to talk to us both.

David Halliday made his way through the tangle and neatly co-opted us. "Gentlemen, this was outstanding. I have no hesitation in saying we will want you back for another exhibit." He said he knew I had reservations about bringing the press in, but he hoped I would consider it for another show. "You both have extraordinary gifts to offer," he said. "The city should know it."

Even with no press here today, it probably wouldn't take long for rumors to spread, but an offer like this was exactly what Timothy and I hoped for. We agreed to discuss dates with the board during the coming week. Finally, the crowd started to thin out, just in time. I was ready to look for a nice soft patch of floor and flop down with my sketchbook for a pillow.

As the last stragglers left, I fixed the 'remodeled' chair and Timothy collected his displayed sketches. Then the room was empty except for us, Charley and Minna and Justine, and the Murrays.

Justine had been talking with her father and sister. The moment the gallery doors shut behind the last visitor, she came to me and took my sketchbook out of my hand so she could put her arms around me. "Come here, my love."

We held each other. Minna was hugging Timothy, laughing and crying together. Charley grinned up at all of us. "Save the sappy stuff 'til we get home, can't you?"

Never you mind, kid. Timothy held Minna tight and looked at me over the top of her head. "Brother, I'd say we did it."

Dr. Murray answered before I could. "So would I."

He sounded almost – almost – like the man I had known, these past few months, but his face wasn't quite the same. "I can only tell you both what you've already heard," he said. "This afternoon was incredible. I would think I'd dreamed it, but that doesn't seem to be the case."

Justine laughed. "I promise it's not a dream, Dad. Besides, you've got Timothy's sketch to prove it."

He did, neatly folded and tucked into his jacket pocket. "Nicky," he said, "I suppose it's best, for the sake of your marriage, that I didn't know of your unusual skill before you asked for my daughter's hand." I had no doubt of that. "I'm amazed that Justine kept such a secret." He wasn't scolding. "But I must say that today, I am particularly glad to call you family."

He didn't use the word *son*, not out loud, and he couldn't have been much more different from Dad, but something made my throat tighten. "Thank you, sir."

Louisa said, "You know your magic won't be a secret anymore. Everybody who was here today will blab to anyone who'll listen."

"I'm pretty much counting on that, Miss Louisa."

"I think you can quit the *miss* business." To her sister, she added, "Jussie, let me give my brother-in-law a hug."

How about that. It was a pretty big step from chilly handshakes. I thanked Louisa for saying what she had, during the show. "You got us out of a tough spot."

"You looked like you needed a hand." She let go to look up at me. "Besides, I meant it. You do seem to make Jussie happy."

Justine said, "I should say so, Lou." She gave her sister's hand a squeeze. "I'm so glad you were here today. Thank you."

Justine and Charley and the Davises and I were headed home for dinner together. Charley had promised to cook, because "we'll probably have to scrape Nicky off the floor, he won't be good for anything." Now

Justine said, "Dad, why don't you and Lou come and eat with us? You haven't even seen my house yet."

Her house. I swallowed a smile. Any other day, I would've been sure that the Murrays wouldn't want to see it, that they would never be comfortable sitting down to a meal with Timothy and Minna. This day wasn't like any other.

They did come with us. That, more than all these other words I have put down here, might tell you something about what Timothy and I did in the gallery that afternoon. We all went back to my parents' old place, on our shabby old street, and it was one of the best evenings I can remember.

Chapter Twenty-Two

We're nearly to the end of this story. Before I close out these pages, I do need to tell you what happened after that day in the gallery. I had looked forward to getting through the show as if it meant touching the ground again at the end of a cross-country flight. But, as we'd all suspected, that afternoon turned out to be only a beginning.

Louisa had been right. It made no difference that no actual reporters had come to the show. We found out very soon that plenty of our audience went out and gossiped as far and wide as they could. The exhibit struck them that way: they needed to share what they'd seen, needed someone else to hear about it, as if that would cement its truth. Between Saturday afternoon and Sunday evening, the news spread like spilled paint, trailing color through the city.

Justine and Charley and I went to Sunday Mass as usual. We hadn't told the neighborhood about the show, so we didn't have to field questions. Everything seemed quiet, but we all felt the energy building up in the wings and knew it would break over us soon enough.

On Monday morning, the phone rang while I was getting dressed for work. Justine was fixing breakfast in the kitchen. I heard her pick up the receiver and tried not to listen in, but I couldn't help stepping closer to the bedroom door, which was shut. My fingers had gone so stiff and chilly that I fumbled with my shirt buttons.

"I'm sorry," I heard her say, "he can't come to the phone at the moment. Would you like me to take your number?" A pause. Then, "I'm afraid I can't comment on that." Another pause. "Yes, I am Mrs. True, so far as that is your business." Now I heard her trying not to laugh. "No, I will not speak to that. It's for my husband to decide how much he wishes to tell you. As I said, I'll let him know you called."

The receiver landed in the cradle with a decisive click. By then I'd dealt with the shirt, but the tie was hopeless. I went into the kitchen for help.

Justine's face was bright with mischief. "That was someone named Ted McKay, from the *Record*. He wasn't very happy with me."

The *Record*. It was starting. She sat me down at the table to sort out the tie. I managed, "Did he say how much he knew?"

"He didn't know much, I think, but he wants to find out." With a few deft twists, the tie was perfectly fixed. Justine had told Charley and me she'd learned to help her father with his. "He wanted to 'inquire' about the show," she said, "and ask you for a comment."

My lips felt numb. "He didn't exactly know about the magic, then."

"He never used the word." She dished out a bowl of oatmeal and set it down in front of me. "When I said you couldn't speak with him, he asked if I could tell him what you did at the show, and I said no."

I'd overheard most of that. I tried to eat, but my spoon clanged against the stoneware and my stomach had curled into a fist.

Justine sat down and cupped the back of my neck. Her fingers were warm. "Nicky, whatever happens, we'll manage it."

I should've been ready for this, we had all figured something like it might happen, but it was one thing to think so and another thing to stand under the wave when it broke over your head. Justine kissed my cheek. "Eat your breakfast, my love. You'll need it."

While we ate, two more calls came in. The first was Timothy, telling us that he'd just gotten off the phone with this same Ted McKay, who hadn't wasted any time after hanging up with Justine. "I told him about my part of the show," Timothy told me. "All I said about you was you'd talk to him yourself if you wanted. He didn't much care for that."

I leaned against the counter, gripping its edge so tightly that my hand ached. "I bet he didn't."

""I think you'll have to talk to him."

He knew how I felt about that, but he was right. "I'll call him back later." This morning would bring bigger problems, I had no doubt at all.

We didn't answer the second call. It rang for quite a while before whoever was on the other end gave up. Charley, who'd come downstairs by then, offered to pick up and hang up right away, but Justine nixed that idea. We were sure that the caller was either McKay again, or – my guess – someone from Allen and Allen. If reporters knew how to get hold of me at home, they surely knew where I worked. Louisa had mentioned it at the show, after all.

I didn't dare stall in leaving for the office. I would have begged Justine or Charley, or both, to come along with me, but who drags his wife and kid brother in as a bodyguard against his bosses? At the door, Justine kissed me again and promised we would see this through together. Charley said, "Give 'em hell. You never stand for any crap."

Normally, he'd have been right. This time I was in the wrong, and I knew it. By the time the cab dropped me off in front of the building, my chest felt as if my suit jacket had shrunk down at least three sizes. I didn't turn tail and go home, but it was a close call.

The ride up in the elevator felt endless. My briefcase seemed to be filled with bricks. When I stepped into the main office at Allen and Allen, Stephen and Mark were both waiting by the front desk.

Trouble. No question.

The last time they had confronted me about anything, the day I walked out of Dexter Marshall's photoshoot, Mark had been steaming, but Stephen had been trying not to smile. Now there was no hint of friendliness on either brother's face. Stephen said, "Nicky. My office. Now."

The whole place had gone very still, much quieter than usual. Pencils scratched on paper, but I felt glances prickling against the back of my neck and knew that if I looked around, I would see heads bending quickly over work. McKay, or someone like him, had no doubt gotten hold of someone here at the office and fed them as much about Saturday as he could. Enough for everyone to know that I had crossed some line with the bosses, and maybe enough to know that I was different: that in coming to this firm, I had brought something with me that they'd never imagined.

I followed the brothers into Stephen's office. Stephen shut the door. "Sit."

I did. Mark did too, his face a cold mask. His unspoken *I told you so* shouted in the air.

Stephen sat down in his own chair. He folded his hands on his desktop as if gripping his temper between them. "Nicky, explain yourself."

I could have stalled, or tried to prepare a defense, by asking him what he already knew or guessed, who he'd spoken with and what they'd said. By now, though, warmth was trickling back into my hands, and the fog in my head had thinned.

I was in the wrong. All three of us in the room knew it. I had violated my contract and had done my best to hide it so that the Allens wouldn't get a chance to interfere before it was too late. That hadn't been honest. Here and now, though, I knew one thing for certain: I was not ashamed of what Timothy and I had done.

Your father is proud of you today. So am I.

"I apologize, sir," I said. "I went against the terms of my contract, as I think you know. You would be entirely justified in firing me. But you've asked me to explain, and I will, if you're willing to listen."

This time, Stephen didn't tell me not to call him sir. He nodded, the faintest motion. Mark didn't move or speak.

I laid the facts out baldly. "Two days ago, I exhibited my magic for a public audience at the Museum of Art. There was no paperwork. No one signed any non-disclosure."

Mark shifted in his chair, but still, neither brother said anything. I went on to describe the exhibit and everything Timothy and I had done. I told them how I'd used the magic to change the chair and the floor, and how the audience had reacted, and how I'd wanted to open the audience's minds so they could see and hear what Timothy had to show them. "The point of the exhibit wasn't my magic," I said. "It was his. I can't explain it well enough without showing you his work, but I assure you, what I did was both necessary and entirely worth it."

Neither interrupted as I went on to tell them about Timothy's drawings and what he had shown everyone in that room. "We didn't know what people might think of our work," I said, "or what they would do when they saw it, but I can tell you that it was an entire success." Finally, I told them that the museum's board wanted us back for another program, and that Timothy and I had agreed to do it. "No press came to this first show," I added, "but as of this morning, I see the papers found out about it anyway. Next time, the board wants reporters there to see us."

By the time I finished, my fear had washed away. I didn't know what the Allens would say or do now, but I realized I didn't care. Timothy and I had done, and would keep doing, what we had to.

Mark turned to his brother as if I hadn't been there. "You heard him." His voice was hard and flat. "He's admitted all of it. Now we have to decide how to contain the damage."

Stephen didn't look away from me. "Nicky, I have trouble understanding why you would do this, and in such an underhanded way." He sounded more disappointed than angry. "Especially after everything we've done to protect you and make this a good position for you."

I didn't forget that I had done plenty for Allen and Allen too. They had made a good slice of money off me, more than they'd dreamed about before I had walked into their building with my sketchbook. Stephen's words might have gotten my dander up, but clearer than anything else, I kept hearing what Dad had told me long ago.

You're doing it, Nicky. I can't wait to see what you're going to make of yourself.

I said, "I believe I've explained my reasons, sir. I understand your position, but this was necessary."

"Obviously, we'll let him go," Mark said. "Immediately if possible. We can also make a case for more disciplinary action."

I didn't intend to stand for that. "I have no quarrel with you firing me," I said. "But I could also make a case that the publicity you've gotten from this past Saturday, and the publicity you'll likely get in future, would more than compensate for any trouble this firm has to deal with because of what I did."

Stephen's eyes moved from me to his brother. Mark said, "That's irrelevant." Now heat cut through his ice. "He broke the rules he promised to follow when he signed with us. This *exhibit* is bound to cause some kind of trouble for us, not least because prospective customers might think we're lunatics, employing someone who says he can do magic." His fist clenched on the knee of his impeccably tailored slacks. "And it might be worse yet that he actually can, and people saw him do it. Do you know how dangerous it sounds?" Now he was pleading with Stephen. "If the whole city knows Allen and Allen employs something like that, what will people think of us?"

Something like that, was it? Stephen said, "None of our clients so far have had any complaints about Nicky's ability." He sounded as if he was explaining a mistake in a sum. "Quite the opposite. Everyone who's seen it has been more than impressed."

"Everyone who's seen it!" Mark snapped. "*We* decided who saw it. Who we could trust. Who wouldn't panic or start spreading nonsense all over town. He wanted that himself!" He jabbed a finger toward me. "Now we have no control over who knows what, or how much, or what they say to anyone. He just said he'll do it again, in front of the press this time! If that happens, he *cannot* be affiliated with this company, under any circumstances. We cannot take that risk."

Dad had been right. Mark had never stopped being afraid of me. The good part was, he didn't scare me at all.

Stephen had barely moved a muscle since he'd first sat down at his desk. Now he picked up a pen and turned it between his thumb and forefinger, examining the nib as if it held some kind of secret. I could hear Mark breathing. "Nicky," Stephen said, still studying the pen, "you and this fellow, this Davis, you plan to do the exhibit again?"

"Yes, sir."

"Here's the difficulty." He raised his eyes to mine. "My brother is exactly right. You might as well have torn up your contract and thrown it out, as I seem to remember you saying about somebody else, not too long ago." I saw the barest glimmer of a smile. "But I also understand

your point. The publicity our firm could get from an event like this…
well, from where I'm standing, we couldn't pay for better."

"Stephen." Mark looked as if his brother had struck him. "You can't
want to keep him on."

Stephen set the pen back down, neatly aligned with the edge of the
desk. "I think it's worth considering this a little more. Yes, Nicky might
have opened the door for some kind of trouble for us. On the other
hand, those people who saw him, you've got to figure some of them will
think, I could use some of that magic myself, and I'd pay top dollar
for it."

Mark brought his fist down on his knee, so hard that I winced. "No.
If he stays with this company, I don't."

Stephen seemed to think it was a bad joke. "Mark, come on, now.
You don't mean that."

"You choose," Mark said. "Him or me."

He meant it, sure enough. I might have felt pretty smug. I might
have thought that I could have my cake and eat it too, use my magic
however I wanted and still keep my job, and if I played my cards right,
maybe see the back of the one person at Allen and Allen who had always
had the biggest problem with me. Which would weigh more with
Stephen: his loyalty to his brother, or the big contracts and big payouts I
might land him? Maybe it was worth pushing a little to find out.

I might have thought all that, but I didn't. Not least because I'd
made Justine a promise.

"There's no need for a fight, sir," I said. "I've already thought that I
shouldn't stay with this company. Since I do plan to keep using my
magic publicly, it'll be best if I do it on my own."

Mark sat back in his chair so hard that the wood creaked. Stephen
looked baffled. Between me and his brother, he had more than both
hands full. "What'll you do instead?" he asked me. "You just got
married. Before you know it, there'll be kids on the way. Believe me, I
know how it goes."

Mark or no Mark, and somewhere in between the bank balances in
his head, he had real concern for me. "I'm not sure yet," I said. "My wife
says she's sure something good will come out of all this." I let myself
smile; I'm not sure I could have helped it. "I trust her."

Long and short, we did our best to sort things out. It took some doing, between Mark, who didn't want me wasting any more of the air in the building, and Stephen, who still didn't want to lose what I had brought his firm, but we managed to hammer out an arrangement we could more or less live with. I wouldn't have minded emptying my desk and going home that morning. On the other hand, I had projects in the works, and even Mark saw it wouldn't look good for anyone if I didn't fulfill those contracts. Stephen said, "You'll stay on until they're done. Then we'll see."

I got home that afternoon to find out that more reporters had gotten hold of our phone number. Justine had been fielding calls off and on all day. "I told them you'd talk to them if and as you wanted to," she said. "Charley said if you'd rather, he'd call them back and tell them off."

"That's all right. I'll take care of it."

I hung up my coat and we sat together on the couch, away from the phone. With the house quiet around us, her head resting on my shoulder and her fingers laced through mine, I felt the way a sailor might after a long ocean crossing, when he first steps ashore and feels solid ground under his feet.

"I still have my job," I said. "Just until I finish a few projects." I told her Stephen wanted to think I'd change my mind about leaving, but I wouldn't. "I'll be out of there in a couple weeks."

"Good. Then we'll see what comes next." She wasn't worried. For that moment, I forgot to worry too.

On Tuesday and Wednesday after work, I went down Justine's list of phone numbers and returned each reporter's call. I told them all exactly what had happened at the museum. Every one of them wanted to come to the house with a camera crew, to see the magic in action and have proof for themselves that I wasn't feeding them one of the wildest lines they'd ever heard.

I held them off politely. "You're welcome to contact the museum's board of directors. They can corroborate what I've told you." I added that Timothy and I would offer another event soon, and this time, the press would be invited.

Features came out in the papers that Sunday. The newsboys I'd spoken with didn't have as much to go on as they wanted, but it was enough to put out columns that lit up our neighborhood like fireworks. *Philadelphia residents Nicky True and Timothy Davis...extraordinary exhibit at the Philadelphia Museum of Art...this reporter is given to understand, by respectable and reliable witnesses, that neither illusion nor sleight-of-hand was performed, but rather, verifiable magic...an interview with Mr. True confirms his extraordinary gift...* In proper newspaper fashion, there was plenty of extra scrollwork and jargon, but no one reading it could have missed the meat.

The *Record* arrived on everyone's doorstep first thing on Sunday morning. Justine and Charley and I had debated staying home from Mass – or rather, I'd debated it, but they had both overruled me, pointing out that no one on our street would be bashful about marching over and banging on the door.

We got to the church just in time to slip into our seats. I'd won out that far, sneaking in at the last second, but it didn't do anything to hold off the web of stares and whispers that closed around us. Heads leaned toward each other in the pews. The same question bounced again and again off the old stone walls: *D'you think it's real?*

I don't know whether anyone heard a word Father Hagerty said during the service, or how many forgetful people left their dimes in their pockets when the collection plate came around. I do know that Mrs. O'Dell, of course, was the one who took things in hand.

She came over to our pew the moment Mass ended. "Nicky True." She'd brought her copy of the *Record* with her so she could put it under my nose and point to Ted McKay's column. "Child, what on earth is all this, and why didn't we know?"

It turned into quite a conference. Justine and Charley and I stood out in the sunny churchyard, surrounded by everyone who had been at Mass, including the priest. "Ted McKay got it right," I said, watching a car tooling down the street so I could avoid all the stares. The museum had been worse, but only by a hair. It wasn't much easier to tell people who'd known me all my life that they had missed quite a sizeable piece of the story. I said, "My drawing does let me do magic."

Everyone seemed to talk at once. *How?* and *What do you mean?* and *Don't be stupid, there's no such thing as magic* buzzed around me like cicadas, but Mrs. O'Dell made herself heard. "Nicky, child. We all know what a fine artist you are, but you can't ask us to believe this."

Charley spoke up. "She's right, Nicky. You'll have to show them."

I hadn't planned on that, but he had a point. If nothing else, it was the quickest way to end the debate. Someone produced a pencil. Someone else handed me their grocery list, which was blank on the back. I propped the paper against the nearest headstone. It wasn't the best drawing surface, but in a minute or two, I managed to turn Charley's cane into a spiral and back again.

When I finished, no one said a word. Silence, as thick as the muggy air, lay over the churchyard. I heard a sparrow chirping and a car's horn off in the distance.

Mrs. O'Dell found her voice first. "But..." She was standing close enough to touch my drawing hand, and she brushed her fingertips across my knuckles as lightly as you would smooth a sleeping child's hair. "That can't be real." I had never seen her at such a total loss. "Can it?"

Charley was still grinning about what I'd done to his cane. "It's real, all right," he said. "Nicky's done that stuff as long as I can remember."

Mrs. O'Dell focused on him. "Did Desmond and Mary Anna know?"

"Of course."

That brought down the storm. Everyone wanted answers. *You've been doing this all along? Sure, he was always good with a pencil, but this is crazy! People don't do things like this. His mother and father saw it? Why didn't they say?* And, loudest, as if all the questions rolled together into one, the same one Mrs. O'Dell had asked first: *Why didn't we know?*

I started to think Justine and Charley and I would have to make plans to move to a different part of town, as soon as we could, if we could find any part that would be safe after this. Somehow, I raised my voice over the hubbub. "Please, I'll tell you about it, if you want to hear."

They did. All those eyes: it was harder to talk than ever, especially when I made myself look at them, Mrs. Franklin and the Parkers and Mrs. O'Dell and everyone else who had known our family for so long. I told them about the first time I'd used the magic, and what happened, and how I couldn't fix Charley's foot, and what Dad had said. I told them why I'd always kept the magic secret. I explained about the movies and what I'd done there, and what I did now for Allen and Allen. Finally, I told them about the show at the museum, and why it had seemed right to bring the magic out in the open at last. "You should see Timothy's drawings," I said. "And you'll have a chance, too. We're doing another show soon."

"You are?" That was Mrs. Franklin. "At the museum?"

"Yes, ma'am. Probably in a week or so." We hadn't set the date yet, but the board wanted it to be soon.

Mrs. O'Dell said, "Anyone can come see you?"

"Yes."

Sometimes people surprise you. The neighborhood took a deep breath and swallowed my crazy story. Mrs. O'Dell summed it up: "You're one of ours, Nicky. If this magic is real, you'd best believe we'll be proud of it."

The following week, when Timothy and I did our next show, the museum staff had to move us into a bigger gallery. Even then, it was standing room only. The neighborhood turned out in force, including plenty of folks who had never set foot in such a place before or imagined they would. The press was there. Every paper that had a kid who could hold a pencil stub had sent at least one reporter. Most of them had photographers. The line of curious people hoping for tickets stretched out the front doors and threaded between the columns.

Timothy and I presented the same program again. In spite of the packed house, and the flashbulbs going off every which way, it was easier the second time. At the end, after I had given the audience the "what's your magic?" question to think about, the room erupted in applause. Timothy and I took our bows and I hoped with all my heart that my mother and father did know something about this, somehow.

This was what the magic was for. It always had been, all along.

~

A LONG WHILE BACK, NOW, I ASKED YOU TO IMAGINE WHAT it might have been like for a boy to discover that he could make magic when he drew. You know that the boy is now very old and hasn't been able to use his gift in a long time. As I type these final pages, I have to pull myself out of the past. I hope Jo is right and that these many words are worth something. If nothing else, revisiting these old times – and especially the people who were part of them – has been a great joy.

I will be sorry to leave them. But maybe I've handed them on: to you, whoever you are, and certainly to Jo, who will take all these pages from me when they're finished. Maybe, in a small way, I've put my magic back into the world for a while. More importantly, this has made me remember that whether I can use my gift or not, the world still has magic in it. As many kinds of magic as there are people.

For now, what else should I tell you?

After our first two museum shows, Timothy and I decided to see how much farther we could open the door we'd unlocked. Our first two audiences had been white-only, but Timothy's and Minna's friends and neighbors wanted to see our art too. Timothy and I used the leverage we had with the museum's board to open its galleries for an integrated audience. I have never forgotten, and never will, the first time I looked out at a room full of faces, black and white side by side. All people together.

Meanwhile, too, the world kept moving. Timothy and I did the exhibit several more times that summer and eventually took it to other venues, in both the city and the suburbs. My projects at Allen and Allen wrapped up. Over Stephen's objections but with Mark's enthusiastic approval, my contract with them ended. Justine and Charley and I took a trip to upstate New York, to the Finger Lakes. When we came home, we watched another huge change and celebration in the city: Victory in Japan Day, the day Hirohito surrendered and the war ended at last.

Timothy and I found that this time, the outflow of joy and relief didn't leave us stranded. We could celebrate too. We had our wives, our anchors, who brought out the best in us. We were doing work we were proud of. The museum, wanting to hold onto us as long as possible, brought us on as regular employees, to teach drawing classes in a new program they more or less created on the spot. We used our magic and our more ordinary skills to share the things we loved with as many people as we could. That's the job I did up until I retired.

It's fair to say that I was famous for a while, or at least, more famous than I had ever planned on. A few years after the war ended, television came along to knit the country even closer together. Some people wondered why I didn't use that new medium to take my magic into every home I could reach. From the start, though, I wanted my gift to belong to my home city. Justine and I did all we could to keep it there.

For Timothy, one of the great rewards of his work at the museum was the freedom it gave Minna. She went back to college to finish her English degree. Before much longer, she was working in the Philadelphia school system, where Timothy joined her a few years later as an art teacher. Every boy and girl who went through their classrooms – generations of them – was lucky.

In the autumn of 1945, Justine and Charley and I moved to Center City, which was a better commute for me. It was better for Justine, too, when a couple of years later, she started work at the poetry publisher Doncaster Books. Jo was born in our new house, where I still live.

And Charley? He and Denise stayed together through the rest of high school and through college, and it was Denise who convinced Charley that it would be worth it to see what a surgeon could do for his foot. Not because she wouldn't have him otherwise – she made that clear enough to satisfy even his over-protective older brother – but because she wanted him to have the freedom he'd never known. You might be able to guess how it felt to watch the two of them have the first dance at their wedding.

And now I believe I've told you everything that mattered most about those long-ago days: enough, even, to satisfy my daughter, who can put this slice of history together with all the years she does remember. It really is time for me to finish these many words. So I'll leave you – *and about time, Nicky,* I hear you thinking, *long-winded old cuss that you are* – I'll leave you with the same questions Timothy and I asked our first audiences, seventy-some years ago.

Where is your magic? And what will you do with it?

END

Line Magic

KRIS FAATZ

READER'S GUIDE

Discussion Questions

1. Nicky's gift lets him use magic to physically change anything. If you could tap into a magical ability, what would it be? What would it do?

2. For many years, Nicky keeps his gift as hidden as possible. If you had a similar gift, would you hide it? Why or why not?

3. Nicky's father Desmond is striking for his appreciation of art and support for Nicky's ambitions, especially given his own background. What do you think makes him this kind of parent?

4. Given the pervasiveness of racial prejudice in his time, what do you think lets Nicky see Minna and Timothy so immediately as people, in a way others (for instance, Dr. Murray) can't?

5. By the end of the book, we know that Nicky is no longer able to do the drawing magic. Do you think such magic could make a difference in the world as it is now? If yes, how?

6. Are you left wanting to know more about anything in the story? If so, what are you curious about, and why?

7. Leaving "real magic" off the table, how would you answer Nicky's last questions to the reader: *Where is your magic? And what will you do with it?*

About the Author

Photo credit: Laura Walker

Kris Faatz (rhymes with skates) is a musician and award-winning writer. Her short stories have appeared in many journals and have received honors from *Tiferet Journal*, *Black Fox Magazine*, and DISQUIET International, among others. Her second novel, *Fourteen Stones* (Highlander Press, 2024), marked the start of her immersion in fantasy and magic. Her third novel, *Line Magic* (Highlander Press, 2025), blends magical realism with a fascination with history, and pays tribute to her home city, Philadelphia. *Line Magic* was shortlisted in the Santa Fe Writers Project's highly competitive 2023 literary awards.

Kris lives in Baltimore with her husband and feline contingent. She and her husband are enthusiastic hikers who love to explore all green spaces. When not escaping into the world of story, Kris teaches creative writing, provides editing services, and is a performing pianist. Visit her at krisfaatz.com.

facebook.com/kristinfaatz

instagram.com/krisfaatz

tiktok.com/@krisfaatz

About the Publisher

Founded in 2019, Highlander Press is a vibrant, mid-sized publishing house dedicated to transforming the world through the power of words. We are deeply committed to diversity and bringing big ideas to the forefront. At Highlander Press, we help authors navigate the journey from initial concept through writing, editing, and publishing, culminating in the release of a book that not only fulfills a lifelong dream but also solidifies their expertise and boosts their confidence.

Our unique approach centers on forging strong, collaborative relationships with women-owned businesses across the publishing spectrum, including graphic design, marketing, launching, copyright management, and publicity. We believe in the power of community and operate by the mantra, "a rising tide lifts all boats." This philosophy not only enhances our business model but also ensures that our authors receive unparalleled support and opportunities to succeed.

Join us in making a mark in the literary world, where your voice is heard, and your message has the power to change lives.

facebook.com/highlanderpress

instagram.com/highlanderpress

tiktok.com/highlanderpress

linkedin.com/company/highlander-press